Barely aware of the murderous humans sweeping down on him, Handil the Drum stood and swung his vibrar under his arm. An arrow buried itself in his thigh, but he hardly felt it.

The humans were only yards away now, rushing at him, but when he turned to them, they slowed, stunned at what they saw in his eyes. In that instant, a few of them may have realized that they were looking at their own deaths. Handil raised his mallets and brought them down, and the Thunderer began to sing.

No Call to Balladine was this, no glad song of the high peaks. The rhythm of the big vibrar was a dirge, and it filled the great hall of Grand Gather with sound so intense that the humans reeled back from it.

Another arrow struck Handil, and then another, but the mallets increased their tempo, and the vibrar thundered. All around, hewn stone took up the vibrations and began to disintegrate. The cavern roared and bellowed, and huge chunks of broken stone showered down from above, crushing everyone and everything beneath them.

And above it all the sun of Krynn approached the zenith of its solstice day.

The DRAGONLANCE® Saga

**Dwarven Nations Trilogy
Volume One**

the Covenant of
the forge

Dan Parkinson

DRAGONLANCE® Saga
Dwarven Nations

Volume One

The Covenant of the Forge

© 1993 TSR, Inc.
All Rights Reserved.

Cover art by Tim Hildebrandt. Interior art by Valerie Valusek.

DRAGONLANCE and GEN CON are registered trademarks owned by TSR, Inc. The TSR logo is a trademark owned by TSR, Inc.

First Printing: February 1993
Printed in the United States of America.
Library of Congress Catalog Card Number: 92-61078

9 8 7 6 5 4 3 2 1

ISBN: 1-56076-558-5

TSR, Inc.
P.O. Box 756
Lake Geneva, WI
53147 U.S.A.

TSR, Ltd.
120 Church End, Cherry Hinton
Cambridge CB1 3LB
United Kingdom

To Randy and Jenny Scott

With special thanks to Pat McGilligan for his patience,
to Harold Johnson for sharing his knowledge
of the dwarves of Krynn,
and to Sue Weinlein for a touch of sunshine.

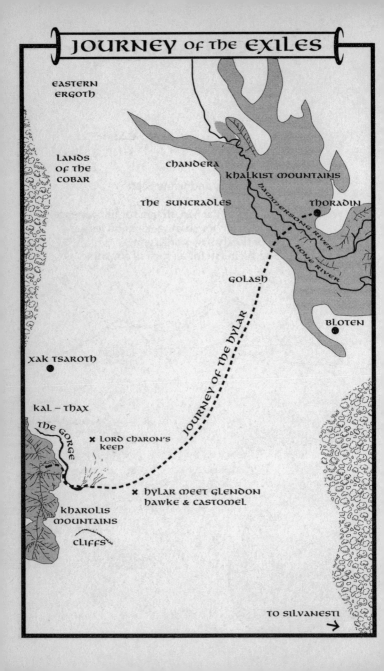

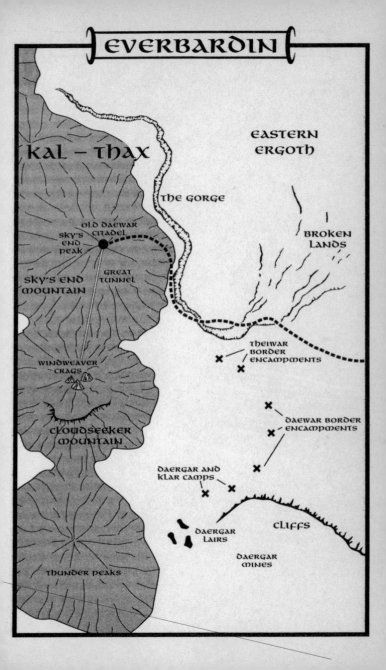

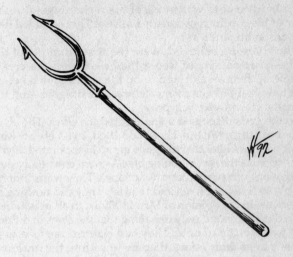

Prologue
A Glimpse of Prophecy

Except for the dragons, who sprang from the world itself, the first people of Krynn were the elves. This was a conclusion reached by Mistral Thrax early in his search for certainties among the complexities of an uncertain world.

Few would recall his early pronouncements regarding the sequence of origins, because in those days Mistral Thrax was considered to be full of strong ale and vagaries, and because few among the people of the high mountains really cared about such things as who came first and why. Such thoughts were for the very old, who had nothing better to do than think them. Even then, when he began his studies of lore after being maimed in a rockfall, Mistral Thrax was more than two hundred years of age.

Thus little note was made of his reckonings. But the logic of his conclusions satisfied Mistral Thrax and led him onward in his studies.

The elves, he believed, were the first attempts of the gods—particularly of Reorx the Life-Giver—to create people of their own design upon the world which before that time had only its own creatures, the dragons, and the animals which were their prey.

So the gods discussed it and created the elves. The elves were beautiful, Mistral Thrax admitted, in an elvish way, but it was his belief that the gods grew disappointed after a time because the elves—being elves—were essentially decorative but not particularly functional. They were content simply to live long lives and to exist. They did nothing of real value, in the opinion of Mistral Thrax. In all his studies, the old dwarf found only one thing that the elves had done that was worthy of note. They had claimed the forests of Silvanesti as their home, thereby upsetting the dragons, many of whom considered Silvanesti as their own.

This, according to Mistral Thrax, was why so much of history was punctuated by periodic skirmishes and at least one full-scale war, starting with dragon attacks against the elves.

In their concern for proper balance, the gods tried again. This time, they created the ogres. And again, as time passed, they grew disappointed. The ogres had been a promising race—though unimaginative and boring—but with time they began to deteriorate in their culture and eventually they became the ogres of the present—great sullen, surly brutes who were at best a nuisance and could be a real threat.

Various gods, Mistral Thrax decided, had then tried their hands at designing a better kind of people. Which gods might have originated such monstrosities as goblins and minotaurs and the like was a question Mistral Thrax ignored, on the assumption that those particular gods were probably ashamed of what they had done, and it was not his business to lay blame.

But Reorx the Life-Giver seemed to have recognized the problems besetting his world and turned his full attention to designing the perfect race of people. As Mistral Thrax viewed it, Reorx must have created humans next, using the basic model of the elves but instilling within the new creatures great energies, driven by the realization of short life spans. Again, in Mistral's opinion, it was a good try but not yet perfect. Humans proved to be far too chaotic a race for Reorx's taste, he was sure, and somehow even managed to so distort their basic strengths that some of them turned into gnomes and, possibly, even kender (though there was some evidence, Mistral conceded, that kender might have originated from some unexpected deviation among the elves).

His intention and his vow—in his two hundredth year—had been to devote the rest of his life to the study of lore. Thus, a hundred years later, being still alive, he was still at it. Copious armloads of scrolls did Mistral Thrax produce through those years, dwelling on the mysteries of the world and dealing with them one by one, using good, dwarven logic. But the thread through all of his theories was that Reorx, once determined to create the proper race of people, did not stop trying until he had done so.

The true race—the masterpiece of the life-giver—was all that any god could have wanted in a chosen people. Not as tall and awkward as humans, and neither as short-lived as humans nor as indecently long-lived as elves, the new race was equipped with all the skills people needed. They made fine tools and excelled in using them. Sturdy and strong of limb, they could hew stone as other races might hew soft wood. They had the imagination and inventiveness that ogres lacked, the sense of progress and stubborn determination that elves lacked, and the continuity of purpose that humans lacked.

Through trial and error, Reorx in his wisdom had finally created the proper people for the world of Krynn—the race of dwarves. Legends held that Reorx was so pleased with his best people that, originally, he named them all Smith, though that proved so confusing that they gave themselves other personal names as needed, and eventually none of them—so far as Mistral Thrax knew—were named Smith.

Thus did Mistral Thrax clarify the origin of the dwarven race, for any who cared to consider it.

From there, being now more than three hundred years old and still alive, he went on to summarize the history of the world to date.

The dwarves in the early times had scattered over the face of the land, seeking the highest places, and tribes had become separated. There were legends of a place called Kal-Thax, where many had settled, and maybe other such places as well, but the dwarves of Mistral Thrax's acquaintance—the Calnar—had all wound up in the realm of Thorin and had been there for a very long time.

Fact and legend became very confused on many points, but some things were clear:

—The race of humans had spread and multiplied until no one knew who or where they all were.

—The race of elves had clung to the forests of Silvanesti through a dozen dragon sieges and one full-scale war, though some elves had migrated to the west and now lived somewhere else.

—There were still ogres here and there, including a large colony to the south of Thorin, at a place called Bloten. The original architecture of Thorin was of ogre design, but had been abandoned long ago, and after a few skirmishes with the Calnar, the ogres tended nowadays to leave the dwarves alone.

—And somewhere in the now-distant past—at least four hundred years ago, by the reckoning of Mistral Thrax—magic had been introduced upon Krynn. Some said that Reorx himself had done it, led astray by other gods. Some said magic came in the form of a gray gemstone that descended upon the world and was captured for a time by humans, then released by gnomes. There was even a legend of a brave and tragic dwarven fisherman who had stood in the path of the source of magic and had tried to stop it by knocking it down with his spear.

But wherever it came from, magic had come upon Krynn, and for the dwarves it was the ultimate abomination—a power without logic, a force without the rational, comfortable rules of stone and metal, light and dark, moons and mountains, and the rhythm of hammers and drums.

The dwarves wanted no part of magic, and they ignored it. But its effects were felt.

This latest dragon war in distant Silvanesti, for example, was far worse than the any of the previous disputes there. This time, the dragons had attacked using magic, and the results were widespread. Little was known in Thorin about the war itself, except that as the elves clung to their forest and fought back, the war spread to other realms. Everywhere now, throughout the known lands, great migrations were under way, and the dwarves and their neighbors were much concerned. Evil was afoot, and everyone knew it.

On a spring evening, when the light from the sun tunnels began to dim, Mistral Thrax pondered over his scrolls and what they all might mean. Within the threads of fact and legend which he attempted to weave—as one might weave a tapestry of many colors in order to see the pictures it would reveal—were puzzling, disturbing hints of more to come. Mistral Thrax had attempted to capture history, and in grasping it realized that it went both ways— back through time to what had been and forward somehow to hint at what might yet be. And not all of what he saw there pleased him.

He sensed that change was at hand—a change that would be painful for all of his people. He sensed that, somehow, magic might touch the lives of the Calnar, and that nothing would ever again be the same.

High-dwellers, their human neighbors called the Calnar. People of the high peaks. In the dwarven manner of speech, the word for that was Hylar, and somehow that word held special meaning in the threads leading toward the future.

That, and a tiny piece of legend he had found, which seemed to fit nothing in the past and therefore tasted prophetic—a legend that somewhere, some time, someone very important was to be named Damon. That, the legend said, would be the name of the Father of Kings.

As he had so many times in the past when pondering such things, Mistral Thrax sighed and rubbed hard old hands against his aching skull. Then he put away his scrolls, picked up his crutch, and turned down the wick of his lamp. It was a long walk from his cubicle to Lobard's establishment on the main concourse, but at the end of the walk little comforts awaited him, as they did each evening—a mug of good ale, pot meat, and a half loaf of rich Calnar bread.

Never in all the years he had been searching had Mistral Thrax found real answers to his questions in the ale at Lobard's, but it eased his aches and did no harm.

Part 1:
The Drums Of Thorin

The Dwarven Realm of Thorin
Khalkist Mountains

Century of Wind
Decade of Oak
Year of Iron

1
First Blood

Sledge Two-Fires eased back on the reins as the patrol entered Crevice Pass, and Piquin responded. The big horse slowed his mile-eating trot to a fast walk, then slowed again as the silver bit on his tongue retained its slight pressure. The oiled saddle on his back creaked softly, and the fine steel mesh of his skirt whispered with the shift.

Behind Sledge Two-Fires, the others also slowed, turning bright-helmed heads as they studied the rising slopes on either side of the trail. Just ahead, the slopes closed in and became the steep, brushy cliffs that gave the pass its name. Sledge Two-Fires glanced back the way they had come. Late sunlight slanted into the pass, and shadows were climbing the backtrail as the sun lowered toward the jagged peaks of the Suncradles in the distance.

Two hours of daylight remained, time enough to make it through Crevice Pass and make night camp on the far side, where the sugar fields began. From there, in evening, the lights of Thorin would be visible across the Hammersong Valley. Enough daylight remained, providing the ride through the narrow pass was uneventful. But Sledge Two-Fires felt the hackles rising beneath his helmet and raised himself high in his tall saddle to peer around, squinting and frowning. Something seemed out of place—something that for a long moment he could not identify, then did. It was too quiet. On a bright midsummer evening like this, with the sun above the Suncradles by the width of a fist, there should be sounds in the mountain wilds. There should be eve-hawks wheeling and whistling above and cliff pigeons homing from the fields. There should be squirrels a-chatter and rabbits scurrying through the brush—a whole chorus of muted wilderness sounds.

But there was nothing. It was as though the world had gone silent, and the silence gave the closing cliffs ahead an ominous feeling.

Sledge had never cared for Crevice Pass. The place was perfect for ambush, a narrow defile where enemies could lurk unseen above the trail and attack at will. Once, long ago, the Calnar themselves had used it so. Still, not since those long-ago times had such a thing as ambush ever happened to a Thorin border patrol.

After all, Sledge thought, who was there now to make an ambush? Ogres? One or two of the brutes might conceive of such a thing, but despite their size and ferocity, no one or two ogres would be a match for a mounted, armored dwarven patrol, and even the most vicious-tempered ogre would realize that. Humans, then? There were humans everywhere these days, more all the time, it seemed. Thorin was flanked by human realms north and south, but not in the memory of anyone had there been serious conflict with Golash and Chandera. The people of those regions depended upon the dwarves of Thorin for many of their commodities, just as the dwarves depended upon the humans for trade.

Wild humans? There were those, too, of course—traveling bands of nomads, occasional clots of fugitives from some distant conflict or another. Sledge and his patrol had seen bands of humans in the distance during the weeks of their patrol—more, it seemed, than ever before. But the wanderers had kept their distance, and none seemed to pose any real threat. It was following and observing one such group that had caused the patrol to be here now, miles north of the usual route. Normally, returning patrols crossed the ridge at Chandera Road, not Crevice Pass.

Elves, then? All the elves that Sledge knew about were far away to the southeast, beyond the Khalkists. In times past, a few of them had visited Thorin for Balladine, but not in recent years. The elves had their hands full, it was said, fighting dragons for control of their beloved forests. Besides, there had never been conflict between the elves and the Calnar. They were both intelligent races and had no reason to fight.

Still, a sense of foreboding hung about Sledge, seeming to come from the cleft ahead. It made his beard twitch.

Agate Coalglow and Pierce Shard had eased their mounts forward to flank their leader. Now Agate noticed the same thing that Sledge had noted a moment before. "It's quiet," the split-bearded dwarf said. "No birds."

"None," Sledge agreed. "There may be someone in the Crevice."

"No sign of anyone," Pierce said, studying the rising banks.

"Probably nothing," the leader admitted. "I'm just feeling hunchy. If there were trouble, our scout would have seen it and reported back."

"Not much that quick-eyed Dalin's likely to miss," Agate nodded. "He's probably waiting for us right now at the sugar fields. You have travel nerves, Sledge. It'll do us all good to get back home. Let somebody else do border patrol next shift."

Sledge took one more hard look at the crevice ahead and shrugged. "You're right. Travel nerves." He raised his hand and swept it forward. "By twos!" he called. "Tomorrow we'll be in Thorin Keep!"

Piquin needed only the lightest heel-tap to pick up his long-legged gate, and the patrol trotted up the incline as the crevice walls grew around them. The sun now was directly behind, and their long shadows stretched out ahead, into the silent pass.

A mile went by, silently except for the echoes of their horses' shod hooves and the occasional rattle of swords in their bucklers. Another mile, and the crest of the trail was in sight—the narrowest part of the defile, where stepped stone walls stood above the strewn floor like ramparts, and clear sky shone between them. From there, the pass would widen again, and the trail would be downhill all the way to the outer ford, just above the roaring canyon where the Bone River joined the Hammersong.

Tomorrow they would cross the two rivers, with Thorin in sight. Tomorrow night they would sleep in their own secure beds.

Nearing the crest, the dwarves felt a surge of relief. Sledge's mood had touched them all, and there had been tension in the climb. But now the crest was just ahead, and beyond was the open sky where crevice walls slanted away. The sky of Thorin. They were past the worst of the defile, and nothing had happened.

"I'll pay for a keg of Lobard's best ale tomorrow evening," Agate Coalglow offered, turning to glance at those behind him. "As soon as Sledge has given our report to Willen Ironmaul, I promise it. One full keg. After that it's up to someone else to ease our patrol aches."

"I'll buy the second keg," Pierce Shard offered, "if that's the sort of ease you have in mind."

"I doubt if that's it," someone in the ranks chuckled. "Agate finds more comfort in the bright eyes of Lona Anvil's-Cap these days than any of Lobard's ale can match."

"Mind your own bright eyes, and keep them sharp," Agate snapped. "We're not out of this crack yet."

At the very top of the trail's crest, Sledge Two-Fires scanned the towering banks above, then glanced down as Piquin snorted. The dwarf's eyes went wide, and he hauled on the reins. "Arms!" he bellowed. "Shields up! It's a trap!"

Just ahead, where the trail began its downward slope, lay two still forms. Dalin Ironbar would scout for no more patrols. He was dead. A few feet away lay the body of his horse, a broken javelin protruding from its ribs.

"Eyes high!" Sledge shouted. "Defend!"

But it was too late. Even as the word "defend" left his lips, an arrow flew from above to thud into his exposed throat and downward into his chest.

In an instant, the air sang with the whines of arrows and bolts, the luffing whisper of thrown spears, and the clatter of flung stones.

Agate Coalglow saw his leader fall and raised his own oval shield just in time to deflect a deadly arrow. He dodged another, and a third buried its ripping head in his thigh just below his buckler. Two arrows protruded from his horse's neck, and Agate flung himself from the saddle as the big animal began to pitch and dance, blind with pain. He lit hard on the stony trail, rolled, and slid behind a fallen boulder as other arrows sought him, whining down from the steep slopes above.

There were men up there. Where moments ago there had been nothing, now the slopes were alive with humans springing from hiding. A human voice, harsh and commanding, shouted, "Block that trail! Don't let any of them escape! Kill the dwarves! Kill them all!"

Near at hand, Agate heard a familiar whirring sound and glanced around. Pierce Shard was still in his saddle, his shield dancing here and there as his horse spun and pivoted. Pierce was blocking bolts frantically, spinning his mesh sling while desperate eyes roved the slopes above. He found a target, let the sling fly, and a fist-sized stone whistled upward. Above, someone screamed, and a rough-bearded human pitched outward from the brushy face of the cliff to land in a sprawl not a dozen feet from where Agate huddled.

The pain in his thigh was excruciating, but Agate gritted his teeth, cleared his misted eyes, and drew his steel sword. He broke off the shaft standing from his thigh and got to his feet. Deflecting an arrow with his gauntlet, he staggered slightly and roared a war cry. Then, crouching, his sturdy legs pumping, he headed up the nearest slope, directly into the face of the attack.

His charge caught some of the humans off guard. Arrows whisked past him, and then he was on a narrow ledge in the midst of a gang of them, and his sword flew and danced in silver arcs that abruptly turned bright red. A human fell from the ledge, then another and another as the raging dwarf continued his charge, right into the thick of them.

Six ambushers fell from that ledge, their blood spraying in the light of the setting sun, before one of them got behind Agate Coalglow and put a spear through his heart. Even then, with the spearhead thrusting from his chest, Agate managed one more cut with his dripping sword, and a severed human hand dropped into the shadows below.

He staggered then, dropping his sword and sinking to his knees. Dimly, he heard the sounds of combat echoing back and back in the narrow crevice. Some of the Calnar, somewhere, were still fighting, making the ambush as costly as they could for the humans who had sprung it. But there was no chance, and Agate knew that as his world went dark. Too many humans! Fifty or more of them, at least. Maybe a hundred, and only fourteen dwarves—or whatever number remained now.

"Thorin!" he tried to whisper as blood rushed from his mouth. "Thorin-Dwarfhome! Thorin-Everbardin . . . hope and comfort, welcome this one home. . . ."

Below, in the bottom of Crevice Pass, shadows crept

across a tumble of carnage. Here a dwarf crouched behind his dead horse, still fending off attackers. There, another—blood dripping from many cuts—used his shield as a weapon of attack in a last effort to regain his fallen sword.

But it was over now, as howling humans boiled into the narrow pass to complete the work of slaughter. The last of the Calnar to die was a fierce young defender named Tap Bronzeplate. As the final arrow pierced him, he tried to say the words that Agate Coalglow had whispered. But only some of them got past his lips.

"Thorin," he gasped. "Thorin-Everbardin!"

2
Song of the Drums

Here on the outer shelves of Thorin, lush meadows crowned the gigantic, stair-step terraces carved into the slopes of soaring mountainsides. Vast fields of grain formed curved mosaics, vivid patterns of color in the late morning sunlight cresting saberlike peaks to the east. On the lower terraces, the fields were hues of gold and deep red where early crops ripened. Above these were patterns of rich pastels, and higher still—where the rising terraces flanked floral gardens—were greens as deep and rich as emeralds.

Here, more than anywhere else in the realm of Thorin, the landscape and the creature-works had the look of ogre about them. Not like the brutish, dark lairs of the ogres who yet lurked among the wild mountain passes, far beyond the neighboring lands of Thorin, Golash, and Chandera, but the solid, regimented design of ancient times when the ogres—some said—had ruled all the lands of the Khalkists.

It was in the scope and breadth of the terracing, in the precise spacing of the rising ways between terraces. Not in memory or certain lore had ogres dwelled here, and while ogres still were seen from time to time—lurking on the distant slopes—they and their kind were not the original builders of Thorin.

The ogres now were primitive, often savage creatures, wild in their ways and in their surroundings. But once there had been ogres of another kind. Ancient ancestors of the huge, brutish creatures of today, those ogres of the distant past had hewn mountainsides to their liking and had delved their cold, monotonous lairs into the very hearts of the peaks.

So said the wisest among the short, sturdy, energetic race that now occupied Thorin. This had once been the home of ogres. But the ogres fell from power and lost their skills. Over time, what might once have been a great civilization had deteriorated into savagery. What they left behind was theirs no more, the ballads said. Delvings belong to those who live within them, who hold and improve them. Thorin belonged now to the Calnar, by right of habitation and tradition.

Thorin now was Thorin-Everbardin, home of the Calnar.

On the outer shelves, the look of ancient ogre craft remained because the Calnar had found no need to improve it. The vast, rich meadows ranking the slopes of the highest peaks of the Khalkists served the purposes of the dwarves very nicely. Crops, flocks, and herds were rotated from level to level with the seasons, an enterprise as bustling and busy as the foundries and crafters' halls within Thorin itself, deep in the stone heart of the mountain. Not in memory had the Calnar—the people known to their neighbors of other races simply as "the dwarves"—known famine.

Now midsummer's harvest was proceeding in the lower fields and among the orchards and vineyards that flanked them. Now the drums had begun to speak on the sentinel crags above.

Colin Stonetooth, riding out from Thorin Keep to inspect the harvest, heard the talk of the drums and drew rein to look upward, knowing the distances would show him nothing of the drummers. Thorin was vast, and they were far above and far away. Yet their drums floated the muted thunder of the Call to Balladine on the bright air of morning, and the sound was good to hear.

Handil would be up there with them, of course. It was always Handil's great vibrar that spoke first, setting the deep rhythm of the call. Colin Stonetooth squinted against the high sun, and his eyes sought the monolith of the First Sentinel. There, at the top of that mighty spire, was where Handil would be. Though he could not see him there, Colin Stonetooth envisioned his first son—strong and sturdy, his kilt rippling around his knees, his dark hair and trimmed beard giving him a feral look as he slung the great, iron-bound drum that was of his own crafting. The vibrar, designed and built by Handil, was like no other drum when it struck the first thunders of the Call to Balladine.

Thinking of his eldest son, Colin Stonetooth felt the play of emotions that Handil always aroused in him. Though still young, Handil had the breadth of chest of a seasoned delver, shoulders like the knotted boles of mountain pines, and powerful hands on the arms that rippled with strength.

At three inches over five feet, Handil was not as tall as Willen Ironmaul, Thorin's captain of guards, but nearly so, and his bearing was as imposing as his father's had ever been—erect and sturdy, powerfully muscled, with the natural grace of a born rock-climber. His features were strong, chiseled planes in a wide face framed by a mane of dark hair and back-swept whiskers, trimmed short in the Calnar fashion. Solemn, thoughtful gray eyes set wide apart above high cheekbones seemed always to see the world and all within it as objects of curiosity.

Handil resembled his father, they said, and Colin Stone-tooth was pleased at the comparison, though he could not see it himself.

Of all his sons, Colin Stonetooth thought, Handil was the one best equipped to become chief among the Calnar. A natural leader—even in his early youth, Handil had always chosen his own course and others had always followed—the young dwarf had an inborn skill with tools of any kind and a cool, thoughtful manner in all that he did.

Yet Handil had never displayed the slightest interest in chiefdom. He seemed devoid of leadership ambition, preferring instead his crafts, his tinkering and inventing, and—above all—the music of the drums.

Since his early youth, Handil had been called Handil the Drum by all who knew him, and he seemed perfectly content with the name.

Colin Stonetooth gazed upward, hearing the drum-talk grow in volume and complexity as more and more drums joined in—the harvest song of the Calnar, rumbling and rippling among the peaks. Its rising echoes drifted back to add texture to the call. The Call to Balladine it was, reaching out beyond the peaks and the slopes, out toward the human realms of Golash and Chandera. The people there would hear the song, and they would pack their goods and come. Within a week they would be arriving, and their encampments would fill the valleys below Thorin. It was the custom of the Calnar, the midsummer Balladine. And it had become the custom of their human neighbors, as well.

It would be a time of trading, of exchanging news and views, of wrangling over borders and trading prisoners, of settling disputes and renewing pacts; a time of feasts and contests, or bargaining and barter; the time when humans of two nations came to Thorin to trade for the wares of dwarven foundries and forges and to listen in awe to the deep, haunting rhythms of dwarven mountain music. It was the Balladine, and the drums were the call.

Colin looked forward to it, as he always did. It was diverting, once a year, to see the valleys below Thorin thronging with the frantic, always impatient crowds of human visitors. It was interesting to visit their pavilions, to see what works the strange, tall creatures had produced since the summer before. Colin would not bargain with their weavers and grain traders, their spice merchants and wood builders. He would leave business to Cullom Hammerstand and his barterers. But there would be occasions to trade tales with Garr Lanfel and Bram Talien, and maybe to set out good dwarven ale for that old scoundrel Riffin Two-Tree, and see who could drink whom under the table.

Regular association with humans, Colin felt, could drive a reasonable person to insanity. But once a year, it was pleasant to visit with those who had become friends.

Colin Stonetooth nodded to himself, then looked again toward the First Sentinel as the drums increased their volume. Handil might have no interest in governing, but the lad could make the mountains sing when he decided to.

Handil the Drum! Colin Stonetooth shook his head, frowning. Among the Calnar, no person could tell another person what he must become, but there were times when the old chief wished that he might yet take Handil by the shoulders—as he had when the youth was younger—and shake some higher ambition into that mysterious mind of his.

Still, there was plenty of time. Though his mane and beard were streaked with frost, Colin Stonetooth was yet a mighty dwarf, his mind clear, and his sturdy body as strong as any ox. There was no hurry about succession.

Handil would be married soon, to Jinna Rockreave, and marriage might change his ways.

"It comes of associating with humans," he muttered to himself. "Sometimes I feel as impatient as those short-lived creatures." In his own good time, Handil would decide what he would be. And if not Handil, then there were others of the chief's blood who might yet prove themselves. There was Tolon, who might yet outgrow his dark moods. And Cale, if ever he could clip the wings of that elfish spirit of his and plant his feet on the mountain stone where they belonged.

Cale Greeneye, Colin thought, and frowned. *Cale Cloud-walker!* What names my sons acquire!

Future chieftains? The thought troubled him. A chieftain must be rooted in the clan, for the chieftain *is* the clan. But Cale Greeneye had roots only in his dreams of far places.

Tolon troubled Colin even more. Brooding and intuitive, Tolon kept his own counsel, living always within himself so that it was hard to tell what course he was likely to take. But it was clear that Tolon had no liking for outsiders. In particular, he deeply distrusted all humans, though many of their human neighbors had become valued friends to Colin.

Thorin relied upon trade, and therefore upon friendly dealings with neighboring realms. But how friendly would those relationships someday be if Tolon Farsight were chieftain of the Calnar? A chieftain might make small mistakes, but he must never make big ones—the kind of mistakes that would bring disaster upon his people. To Tolon, his father's willingness to accept outsiders was a dangerous thing. But to Colin, Tolon's distrust of humans was ominous. Such distrust could result in a cessation of trade, and trade was essential.

No, the successor ought to be Handil. Handil the Drum.

Irritated with himself for daydreaming, Colin Stonetooth straightened in his saddle, flicked the reins of his great horse, and headed downslope at a trot to inspect the lower fields, miles away. Behind him, the Ten wheeled in perfect formation to follow. In their bright steel and rich-hued leathers, they fairly glistened in the high sunlight, and bore their bannered lances proudly. Each was mounted on his own tall, gold-and-white horse, each animal a perfect match for their chieftain's own mount.

* * * * *

High above, on the outward wall of Thorin Keep, Tolon Farsight—who was often called Tolon the Muse—stood on a shadowed balcony and watched his father and the ten selectmen of his honor guard as they pranced their big horses down the long incline toward the second ring of fields. Beyond and below, the realm of Thorin spread in majestic beauty, stepping away to the shadowed valleys of the Hammersong and Bone rivers, then rising beyond toward the spike-crested Suncradles, westernmost peaks of the Khalkist range.

From the Sentinels above, but seeming now to come from everywhere, the drumcall rhythms grew and intertwined until it seemed that the very mountains throbbed to the deep, haunting music. Forty-one times—forty-one summers—Tolon had heard the Call to Balladine. Like the seasons and the landscapes of Thorin, like the comfortable delvings within the mountain's heart, the drumcall was part of his life and had always been so. Never twice the same, yet as unchanging as the mountain crags themselves, the Call to Balladine was as familiar to him as the sun over the peaks. Yet now he sensed a new tone—not in the rhythms themselves, but somehow in their echoes or the way they carried on the air. Something more sensed than heard, it had a dark, prophetic undertone to Tolon's ears. A deep frown creased his dark brow.

All his life, at each midsummer, Tolon Farsight had listened to the Call and observed the gathering of realms which followed it. At Balladine, the humans came—humans from Golash and Chandera, and often others, as well. Nomadic tribes from the plains beyond the Suncradles came sometimes, drawn by the drums and by legends of the glory of Thorin . . . and often, Tolon knew, drawn by their envy of the wealth of the dwarves. But for whatever reasons, each summer they came, and sometimes others came as well. Ogres from the high passes would lurk beyond the Sentinels, listening to the drums. Even elves had come, on occasion, though not in recent years because of the dragon wars. It was the nature of the Balladine. No two times were exactly alike, but never did it really change. Often at the height of Balladine the visitors in their encampments would outnumber the dwarves of Thorin by ten to one. Often, at the contests and the trading stalls, there was strenuous argument. Sometimes there were incidents—a minor riot, a fight over some trinket or over how a contest was won. There was the inevitable thievery, the usual squabbles, the occasional knifing or angry duel.

But these were just part of Balladine. They were the predictable results of too many people, of different persuasions and different races, intermingling freely. Seldom were the consequences serious, and the human chiefs of Golash and Chandera seemed as determined as was Colin Stonetooth himself that nothing irreparable harm the tradition of the summer fair. They were human, of course, and hardly to be trusted, but they *seemed* to be in concert with the dwarves.

Yet, now . . . Tolon shivered slightly and pulled his woven suede robe—human-made, by some weaver in Golash—tighter around his broad shoulders. He turned, strode to the alcove behind the balcony, and pushed open the iron-framed door set in the stone arch. He hesitated for an instant while his eyes adjusted from daylight to fireglow, then called, "Tera! Are you here?"

Soft, padding footsteps sounded, somewhere beyond the outer room, and an intricate tapestry parted on the far wall. The person who stepped through, a young dwarf woman, had the same dark, swept-back mane and wide-set eyes as all of her brothers, but was otherwise as unlike any of them as they were unlike one another. As with most females of her race, she was shorter by several inches than the males in her family, standing barely over four feet in height. But where her father and brothers had wide, strong-boned faces with high cheekbones and level eyes, Tera Sharn's features were like their mother's—softly tapering cheeks, a small, slightly buck-toothed mouth above a stubborn chin, and wide, almost-slanted eyes beneath arching brows . . . eyes that missed very little and that could look very wise when glimpsed unaware.

By any standard, Tera Sharn—only daughter of Colin

23

Stonetooth, chieftain of the Calnar of Thorin—was a strikingly beautiful dwarven maiden, and in recent seasons
there had been no shortage of highborn young dwarves
coming to call. Of late, it was unusual to find her without
Willen Ironmaul or Jerem Longslate or some other strapping suitor lurking nearby.

She was alone now, though, and she paused, gazing at
Tolon. Something in his tone had sounded worried . . .
almost ominous.

Tolon Farsight nodded at his sister and gestured. "Tera,
come to the balcony. Come and listen."

Curious, she followed him through the open door,
which closed behind them on weighted hinges. Sunlight
had found the stone parapet of the balcony and reflected
on the glittering pattern of metallic particles in its polished
surface. Tera shaded her eyes, looking around.

"Listen," Tolon said. "Tell me what you hear."

She listened, then shrugged. "I hear the drums," she told
him. "The drums of Balladine." She looked around. "Is
there something more?"

"Do the drums sound strange to you?" He frowned,
gazing past her, concentrating on the muted, complex
thunders of the dwarven music.

Again she listened. "They sound strong. Strong and
sure. I recognize the voice of Handil's drum among them
. . . and others, too. They speak well this year." Again she
glanced at her brother. "What is it, Tolon? Do you hear
something that I don't?"

"Maybe not," he conceded. "I may have imagined it."

"What did you imagine, then?"

"It sounded as though . . . I don't know, maybe it was
just odd echoes. But for a moment it sounded . . . well, as
though the drums were saying good-bye."

* * * * *

Haunting and powerful, seeming to build upon itself
minute by minute, the call of the drums echoed outward

across Thorin, reaching for the realms beyond. A drum . . . a dozen drums . . . a hundred drums, one by one, by twos and fives, joined the mighty voice of the Call to Balladine. As the high sun reached its zenith, it seemed the very mountains absorbed the intricate, commanding rhythms and throbbed with them. Today was the first call. They would call again tomorrow, and the day after that, and each day until the harvest reached the middle ledges. Then would begin the great fair of the Calnar, the time of Balladine.

High above Thorin Keep, on the platformed cap of the First Sentinel, Handil the Drum leaned into his music, corded shoulders rippling in the sunlight as his mallet beat a steady rhythm for all the rest to weave their beats around. Slung from his shoulder, cradled under his left arm, the mighty vibrar boomed and throbbed its invitation. Its voice at each stroke of the mallet rolled like thunder and seemed to make the very mountains dance.

Beyond him, where trumpeters and lookouts manned the parapets, Cale Greeneye—youngest of the brothers—leaned casually on a narrow railing above dizzy heights and gazed off into the mountain distances, letting the music of the drums pulse in his blood while he dreamed of faraway places.

In misted distance, beyond the valleys of the Bone and Hammersong rivers, beyond the far, rising slopes, clouds drifted among the peaks of the Suncradles. As he often did, Cale Greeneye—called by many Cale Cloudwalker—fantasized that he might harness such a cloud and stand upon it, feel it rise and flow beneath his feet, carrying him off across strange, distant lands to places he had never seen and could not even imagine.

Nearby, a trumpeter glanced around, gazed at the chieftain's youngest son for a moment, then nudged a lookout. "The Cloudwalker is off again," he whispered. "Strangest thing I ever heard of. Why in Krynn would a person ever want to travel?"

"Not the only strange thing today." The lookout frowned. He pointed westward, into the hazed distance.

"What do you see out there, Misal?"

The trumpeter squinted, shading his eyes, then spread his hands. "Nothing. Why?"

"That's just it," the lookout said. "The patrol from Farfield was due this morning with the border reports. I've never known them to be late, but as far as I can see—and on a day like this that's at least twenty miles—there isn't a sign of them."

Cale Greeneye glanced around, overhearing the words. It *was* odd. Sledge Two-Fires was a seasoned scout and not one to be late finishing a patrol circuit. And Cale had friends among the perimeter guards. His eyes lighted. Maybe it would be a good idea, he thought, if someone went to look for them.

3

Grayfen Ember-Eye

In a deep, steep-walled canyon where a narrow trail cut through the crest of a ridge, rays of the midday sun smote the canyon floor and glinted on the burnished armor, rich leathers, and spattered blood of those who lay there, tumbled and silent in death. Fourteen in all, they lay where they had fallen. Some had been dead for hours, their pooled blood darkening as it dried. But here and there among them were splashes of bright red—fresh blood still steaming in the cold air.

Men walked among them, crouching and stooping as they picked up weapons, pausing to loot the bodies that had not yet been robbed. Nearby, just beyond the trail's crest, a fire had been built, and other men gathered around it to warm themselves.

"Should have been over in minutes," a man grumbled, tying fabric around a bleeding gash in his arm. "There were only fourteen of them, and our arrows took down nine before they knew we were here. Five left, and it took us all night to finish them!"

"Stubborn as dwarves, like they say," another muttered, stuffing steel coins into his pouch. "The little vermin fight like demons." He glanced around. "Anybody count our losses yet?"

"Seventeen dead," someone told him. "Few more won't last the day. Don't know how many wounded. Twenty or thirty, maybe. It was a mistake, letting the dinks get to the slopes. For that matter, it was a mistake charging down on them after the first volleys. We should have stayed in cover, held a defense, and finished them from a distance."

"Sure," the first man growled. "And maybe have one or two of them get clear? Maybe slip away to warn the whole kingdom about us? Lot of good our ambush would have done, then. Use your head, Calik! In this world you use it or lose it."

"One of the horses did get away, Grak," a man said. "The one out in front when we attacked. I put an arrow into its saddle but missed the next shot. It was gone before anybody could catch it."

"As long as its rider didn't go with it." Grak shrugged, scowling. "I wouldn't want to have to tell Grayfen that we let a dwarf slip through."

"No dwarves," Calik assured him. "I counted them myself. Counting the first one—the scout—we killed fifteen stinking dwarves and fourteen of those big horses. Wouldn't have minded keeping one of those beasts, though. Wouldn't I like to have a horse like that!"

Grak gazed at him, leering. "The day you can ride a dwarf's horse, Calik, will be the day snails learn to fly." He turned, looking around. "Do you hear that?"

Several of them raised their heads, scowling. "I hear *something*," one said. "Like thunder, a long way off. What is that?"

As they listened, the sound seemed to grow, not so much in volume as in clarity. It was a continuous, rolling throb that seemed to have a texture of its own. It thrummed in the high sunlight and echoed weirdly off the chasm walls.

"It's the drums," Grak decided. "The dinks and their drums, like Grayfen told us. That fair of theirs, it's beginning."

Calik stood with his face upturned, his eyes wide. "I never in my life heard anything like that," he muttered. "It almost sounds like they're singing. How can drums sing?"

Grak shook his head, as though to rid himself of the haunting, distant sounds. "It doesn't matter," he growled. "Except it means we have to hurry. Grayfen wants us at the main camp. Clear up here, and let's move."

"Some of our wounded aren't going to make it a mile, the shape they're in."

"Things are tough all over," Grak snapped. "Pack up! Any who can't keep up, cut their throats and leave them."

* * * * *

Grayfen was not pleased with his ambushers. He stalked among them, his wolfskin cape swaying and flowing behind him, and they cringed as his eyes pinned them one by one—eyes as cold and bright as the rubies they resembled.

"Forty-two men lost?" he hissed. "You paid forty-two lives for a puny patrol of fifteen dinks?"

"They fought," Grak said, then recoiled as Grayfen turned and speared him with those ruby eyes—eyes like no eyes he had ever seen in a human face. "I mean—" he swallowed and added lamely "—I mean, they surprised us, sir. Some of them got through to us, and . . . and they fought like . . . like demons. And those slings of theirs . . . and their steel blades . . ." He shook his head, gesturing at the pile of weapons and armor on the ground nearby, salvaged from the bodies of the dwarf patrol.

"They fought," Grayfen snarled, his voice like a snake's hiss. "Of course they fought, idiot! Whatever else they are, the dinks are fighters! I may just send you"—he looked from one to another of them—"I may send all of you into Thorin with the first assault. You think you've seen the little misers fight, maybe you should see what they do when they're defending their homes!"

"Yes, sir," Grak muttered, keeping his eyes downward. "Only . . ."

"Not me," a man behind him whispered. "By the moons, I won't go in there with the first wave! I'm not that kind of fool."

Grak turned, wanting to silence the man, but it was too late. Grayfen had heard. Wolf-hide cape flaring, he straightened to his full height, seeming to tower above even the tall Grak. The ruby eyes glowed with an evil light from beneath arched brows the color of his silvery mane. He raised an imperious finger, pointing past Grak. "You!" he hissed. "Who are you?"

The man didn't answer. Paling, he started to turn away, then froze in place as Grayfen commanded, "Hold!"

Grayfen glanced at Grak. "That man," he said, still pointing. "Tell me his name."

"Sir, that's only Porge. He meant no disre—"

"Enough!" Grayfen cut him off. "Porge. Face me, Porge."

Ashen-faced, Porge turned to face Grayfen. Cold sweat formed on his brow as the ruby eyes bored into him. The stiff finger was still extended, pointing at him.

"What kind of fool are you, you wonder?" Grayfen's voice turned silky. "The kind who questions my command, it seems. A shame, Porge. You might have survived assault on Thorin . . . if you had held your tongue."

Beneath the constant throbbing of the distant drums, another sound grew. As though the air were charged with lightning, a sizzling, crackling sputter emerged among them. Grayfen's pointing finger and ruby eyes didn't waver, but, as the sound grew, a slow, smoky light seemed to extend from the finger, a lazy beam that approached

30

Porge languidly, then sprang at him and wrapped itself around his throat. Porge gagged, struggling to breathe. His hands clawed at the constriction on his throat, but there was nothing there to grip . . . only the smoky band of dull light. Porge gasped one last time, and his breathing stopped. His eyes bulged, his mouth gaped, and he seemed to hang from the light as his legs went limp.

For a long moment, Grayfen held him there, letting all the others see. Then he snapped his fingers, and a louder snap echoed it, the crack of Porge's neck breaking. Grayfen lowered his hand, and the body sprawled on the ground like a tattered doll.

"Get rid of that," Grayfen said contemptuously. He turned to Grak. "I accept that the dinks surprised you," he said. "You had not faced them before. Now you have. Remember what you've learned. Rest your men now. The drums are speaking. Tomorrow we move into Golash. From there, we go to Thorin."

Men were lifting Porge's body to carry him away. Grayfen glanced at them, then at the pile of dwarven armament nearby. "Get rid of those, too," he said. "We don't want to be seen with dink steels. They would be recognized."

Grak cleared his throat and nodded, glancing down at the fine dwarven sword hanging at his hip. It was of Thorin steel, exquisitely burnished, point-heavy in the dwarven fashion but razor-edged and beautiful. It was the kind of sword a man might spend a lifetime acquiring, a sword worth a small fortune anywhere else in the world.

As though reading his mind, Grayfen said, "The dinks have fine wares, Grak. Far better than they deserve. But we will change that. The treasures of Thorin will buy a thousand such swords. The treasures of Thorin . . ." As he spoke, Grayfen's ruby eyes went distant. It seemed to Grak that the magic-man was speaking not to him at all, but only to himself. "The dinks!" The soft voice became a hiss of purest hatred. "The scheming, selfish, arrogant dinks! We shall see soon enough who deserves the treasures those little misers hide in that dwarf-lair of theirs."

Grak was a callous and brutal man, but something in the mage's words and in his tone made the raider's flesh creep. Never in a long, cruel life had he heard such pure, malevolent hatred in a voice as when Grayfen spoke the name he had given the dwarves. "Dinks!"

Others beyond Grak had heard it, too. When Grayfen was gone, striding toward the main encampment of raiders in the hidden cove above the Bone River, some of the men gathered around their captain.

"What . . . what do you suppose made him that way?" Calik whispered, awed.

"I don't know." Grak shook his head. "He hates the dwarves."

"So? Who doesn't? Misers and thieves . . . why should they have all the best things?"

"He hates them more than anyone." Grak shook his head again. "Something happened, between him and them. I don't know what it was, but I think it was at the same time that he gained his magic."

"I noticed that you didn't tell him about the dwarven horse that got away."

"I told enough." Grak shrugged. "You saw what happened to Porge. Would you want to see Grayfen *really* angry?"

* * * * *

The camp of the intruders was large, sprawled across the bottom of a huge, washed-out cove above the east bank of the Bone River. It was separated by broken lands and by a rugged, seldom-traveled rock crest from the tribal lands of Golash, south of Thorin's outer fields. A hidden place, it held little comfort for the hundreds of humans assembled there.

And now, in the evening when the distant drums of Thorin could be heard like deep, chanting voices in the still mountain air, the camp was a dark, cold place. No fires were lit, nor would be again. That was Grayfen's command.

Smoke from cooking fires the morning before had almost led to discovery. It was the smoke that the dwarf scout had seen from atop Crevice Pass that had sent him hurrying back toward his patrol to report. It was because he had seen it that the patrol of dwarves had been ambushed and massacred. The intruders had orders from Grayfen not to let word of the encampment reach Thorin. Such an encampment would be investigated by Calnar soldiers, and the mage's plan would be foiled before it began.

In the gathering darkness of the cove, Grayfen made his way through the sprawling camp, unseen except by those he wished to see him. The sun was gone from the sky, and the two visible moons had yet to climb above the towering, saber-tooth peaks of the Khalkists. Only the stars in an indigo sky gave light now, and it was not a light to penetrate the shadows of the cove.

Passing among the groups and clusters of his collected people, Grayfen was only a shadow among shadows—to them. But he could see them plainly, and as he made his way toward his private quarters—a circular, slab-stone hut with a low, tapering roof, surrounded by a perimeter that none but he could cross—he studied them, assessing their readiness. Six hundred fighting men he had assembled, and each of them had recruited others. Now there were thousands.

Their weapons and equipment were a motley mix of the trappings of every nomadic culture he had encountered in two years of recruiting beyond the mountain realms. There were dour Cobar among them, huddled in their own tight groups, their woven garments bristling with quilled bolts for their crossbows and the heavy hand-darts they favored. There were burly marauders from the Baruk tribes, Sand-runners from the northern plains, hill-dwelling Flock-raiders, evil-tempered Sackmen and many who fit no particular group. There were hard-bitten fugitives from the agrarian lands to the east, refugees from the fringes of the Silvanesti forests driven out by elves—and, some said, by a marauding dragon—and a hundred kinds of wandering mercenaries willing to fight anyone's battles for a share of the spoils.

Two things bound them all together as a single force—the promise of riches when Thorin was taken and their fear of Grayfen. In recruiting, the mage had touched each of them with burning fingers and stared into their eyes with those featureless ruby orbs that were his eyes. And having touched them, he had the power to kill any one of them—anywhere—at any time he chose.

This, then, was the force that Grayfen the Mage, whom some called Ember-Eye, had amassed for his assault on Thorin. These, and his agents already at work among the people of Golash and Chandera. He was satisfied. The Balladine was beginning. The dwarves—the *dinks*—would be off guard and vulnerable. It would be the last Balladine, he told himself, and the end of the Calnar of Thorin.

Thorin would be his, and every dwarf within his reach would pay painfully and finally for the pain that lived within him each day of his life.

Grayfen made a sign with his hands, strode across the forbidden perimeter around his hut, and stepped inside, into a darkness that was not dark to him. He saw clearly in the gloom, as brightly as he saw everything—in brilliant, burning shades of red. Closing the portal behind him, he went to a plain, wooden pedestal in the center of the room and knelt before it.

With a sigh, using the thumb and first finger of each hand, he removed his eyes, easily plucking them from their sockets. Immediately, the fiery pain in his head subsided, and he rested there for a moment, letting the familiar relief of it wash over him.

With a muttered incantation, he placed the two ruby spheres on the pedestal, stood, and shuffled to his sleeping cot—a blind man groping in darkness. He found his cot and lay down upon it, wishing for real sleep . . . wishing that, for a few hours, he could be as blind as the empty sockets beneath his brows.

He was blind, but still he saw—as brightly and relentlessly as always. He saw the ceiling of the hut above the pedestal. He saw what the ruby orbs saw—always that, and never less. They lay in gloom, glowing faintly, staring at the ceiling, and the first sight in his mind was that ceiling. The second sight, captured within the orbs and always present, was of a ragged, bleeding dwarf with a slender, double-tined javelin in its hand—like a fishing spear, except that it hummed to itself and glowed with a crimson luster. As always, in his mind, Grayfen saw the image of that wounded dwarf—and as he saw it, it hurled its glowing javelin at his face.

Once, then, Grayfen had been truly blind . . . before the double-pointed spear that took his eyes gave him new ones and the power that went with them. Once, years ago and very far away, in a place called Kal-Thax, Grayfen had known the darkness. It was a dwarf who had blinded him. Now it would be dwarves who paid the price.

* * * * *

Kalil the herdsman had spent the day driving his flock up from the meadows above the Hammersong, and as the Suncradles swallowed the light of full day, he chased the last ewe into the pen and closed the gate. Though his legs ached from the day's work, Kalil was pleased. The flock had grazed well on the rich meadows. They were fat and frisky, and their wool was prime.

Far up the mountains, the drums had begun their call. Balladine was at hand. Tomorrow, Kalil would select the best animals from his herd and take them to the village, to join the trek from Golash to Thorin. Trading should be good this year; he knew the Calnar needed wool and mutton. Even after paying his trade-share to Garr Lanfel, Prince of Golash, Kalil expected to have a purse bulging with dwarven coin—and maybe a bit of dwarven steel as well.

Securing his gate, Kalil turned toward his herdsman's shack and was nearly there before he looked up and stopped, startled at what he saw. In front of his house stood a tall, gold-and-white horse, head-down and streaked with sweat. It was clearly a dwarven horse—no one but the dwarves bred and used the huge, white-maned Calnar horses. It wore a saddle of dwarven design, richly studded with steel and silver, and its loose reins dangled from its headstall.

Quickly, Kalil glanced about, his hackles rising, half expecting to see a Calnar soldier nearby. Like most of the humans of the Khalkist realms, Kalil accepted the dwarves of Calnar. He looked forward to trading with them, and he didn't mind mingling with them—on their lands—during the Balladine. But, like most humans, his regard for the Calnar was tempered by a deep-seated dislike born as much of envy as of the difference in their appearance from his own.

The dwarves were rich. He had never encountered a dwarf who wasn't rich. The dwarves made steel, and they used steel, and there was—it seemed to Kalil—a certain arrogance in the casual way the short, stubby creatures displayed their wealth. It made him feel very poor by comparison.

They were ugly little creatures, to Kalil's human perception, and they were arrogant and obviously selfish, since they seemed always to be wealthier than anyone else. The idea of a dwarf being here—at his home—irritated him as much as it startled him.

But there was no dwarf around. There was only the huge, tired horse standing in Kalil's dooryard, and he approached it cautiously. "Ho!" he said when it turned its great head to look at him with intelligent eyes. "Ho, stay! Easy now, good horse . . . stay."

When it neither bared its teeth nor backed away, Kalil picked up its reins and rubbed its muzzle with his hand. "Good horse," he crooned, noticing that the bit in its mouth and the studding on its headstall were of fine silver. He looked further. From withers to flanks hung a skirt of delicately worked mesh, with a fine saddle atop. Kalil's mouth dropped open. The saddle was smeared with dried blood, and the shaft of an arrow jutted upward from its pommel.

For a moment, Kalil had considered trying to return the horse to the dwarves of Thorin for the rich reward they undoubtedly would pay for a strayed animal. But now he changed his mind. To take a dwarven horse to the dwarves, its saddle covered with blood and a human-made arrow embedded there, would be worse than foolish. It would likely be the last thing he ever did.

He decided he wanted nothing to do with this horse. Still, its trappings were of the finest dwarven craft. The steel parts alone were worth a small fortune in human realms.

Glancing around furtively, Kalil set about relieving the horse of its burdens. Saddle, bridle, headstall, and mail skirt he removed, along with the pack behind the saddle and the saddle blanket, which was of fine, woven suede. He carried his prizes to his hay shed and hid them there. Tomorrow he would bury them—or most of them—to be recovered later.

When he came out, the horse was still standing beside his house, nibbling at his thatch roof. "Here!" he snapped. "Leave that alone!"

The horse backed away, staring at him, and then, as though it had tolerated all the human company it cared to, it turned and trotted away, up the hill.

"Good!" Kalil breathed. "Good riddance. I don't need Calnar horses here. Life is trouble enough, without dwarf trouble."

4
Portent of the Sword

The great hall called Grand Gather was the heart of Thorin Keep. Here, where ancient ogres had squared out a huge cavern for their deepest lair, the delving Calnar had begun the remodeling and expansion from which Thorin grew. Gone was the blocky, monotonous architecture of the ogres. The only remaining trace of ogre origins was the sheer size of the vast chamber.

Grand Gather had been reshaped by the dwarves into a huge amphitheater with rings of steps rising from an arena floor. It was literally the heart of Thorin, because it was from here that all the later delvings of the city within the mountain had gone forth—a busy, ever-growing sprawl of levels and ways, warrens and roads, shops and stalls, foundries, factories, smithies, and sprawling residential areas—an entire city within a mountain. Select stone removed from the delvings had gone to construct the twenty-story west wall overlooking the terraces—the only exterior wall in the entire city.

Grand Gather was enormous. Its rising rings of steps, serving as seats for assemblies, could accommodate many thousands. But now there were only a few dozen Calnar in the great chamber. High sunlight, shafting in through the great quartz lenses of sun-tunnels in the vaulted ceiling a hundred feet above, made the day within Thorin as bright as the mountain morning above the Khalkist crags. Great ranks of silvered-glass mirrors directed the light, in Grand Gather as elsewhere, so that no part of Thorin was ever dark, except at night.

When Colin Stonetooth entered Grand Gather, striding down the steps on powerful, stubby legs, some of those waiting below stood, and a few saluted. Others didn't. As chieftain of the Calnar, Colin Stonetooth had little use for ceremony, unless it served a practical purpose. Today there were no visiting delegations to impress, no games or entertainments to applaud. Nothing was scheduled here today, and the message from the captain of guards, requesting the chieftain's presence here, had been terse and without explanation.

Colin entered through the west passage, the Ten following him as they always did. They had all been out on the terraces and still wore their riding gear. The Grand Council table, a seven-sided table of polished oak wood, twelve feet across, had been placed in the center of the arena with benches around it. The five members of the Council of Wardens waited there, along with several others. Colin was surprised that all four of his children were present, as well as the delvemaster, Wight Anvil's-Cap, and the marshal of the keep, Coke Rockrend. Beyond the table, big Willen Ironmaul, captain of guards, waited with a cluster of his warriors. They formed a tight ring, some facing inward, and Colin squinted, trying to see who—or what—

they were guarding.

At the chieftain's flank, Jerem Longslate, First of the Ten, muttered, "Something's afoot, Sire. Coke Rockrend never meets with the council."

"Neither does Wight Anvil's-Cap," Colin pointed out. He raised a hand casually, and the Ten spread out, hurrying to stations around the arena where they could watch the entrances and their chieftain's back. Never in memory had the Ten been called upon to defend the life of the chieftain of the Calnar, but never did a moment pass when they were not ready to, if needed.

Colin reached the arena gate and paused there, looking from one to another of those waiting around the great table. There were wardens at five of its seven sides. The sixth was his, and it was an old mystery why there was a seventh.

The table had been crafted by a team of master carpenters more than a century ago, but even then the full council—including the chieftain—had only been six. Old Mistral Thrax, who—some said—was more than three hundred years of age, held that the seventh side was in honor of the legendary Kitlin Fishtaker, the dwarf who had stood in the path of chaos on the day when magic was born. But then, Mistral Thrax was full of stories. Only children believed the legend of Kitlin Fishtaker. What dwarf would wander the world, suffering from wounds that never healed, and carry with him an enchanted two-tined fishing spear?

What dwarf would use magic? The very idea was repugnant. Still, Mistral Thrax insisted that there was a realm called Kal-Thax, somewhere to the west, and that Kitlin Fishtaker had lived there.

Colin Stonetooth stepped into the arena and strode to the table. He looked from one to another of his wardens, then held the gaze of Frost Steelbit, chief of wardens. "Well?" he said.

Frost shrugged and turned, indicating the captain of guards, who was approaching the table.

Willen Ironmaul was young for his responsibilities but had proven himself many times over. At five feet, four inches in height, he was one of the tallest dwarves in Thorin and had the powerful build of an athlete. With a stubborn mane of thick, dark hair and a beard that seemed to defy trimming, his appearance belied the quiet wisdom of his level gray eyes.

As he approached, those eyes flicked toward Tera Sharn—as they always did when she was present—then returned to Colin Stonetooth. "Sire." He made the slightest of bows, then squared his shoulders. "I called for this meeting. You were in the fields, and I felt this matter could not wait. I hope you will approve, when you have heard the reason."

For a moment, Colin was taken aback. He had not known who summoned him, but would have assumed that it was a member of the council. For a guard captain to take such a step was almost unheard of. Still, Willen Ironmaul had earned great respect in Thorin, even among its leaders. Sometimes Colin wished that the big captain's cool, direct manner of taking charge when necessary might rub off on his own sons. "You must feel there is good reason, Willen." Colin nodded. "Proceed."

"Garr Lanfel, the prince of Golash, has sent us a puzzle, sire. The puzzle is here." Willen turned toward his clustered guards and signaled. The guards stepped aside to reveal a huddled figure in a cloak, sitting on a bench.

"Stand up!" one of the guards whispered, loudly enough for all to hear. At the command, the cloaked one stood. Colin Stonetooth hissed in amazement. It was a man—a *human* man. Standing, he towered head and shoulders above the armed dwarves flanking him.

Colin Stonetooth scowled at the hooded figure. Only rarely were humans admitted to the keep, and then only on the chieftain's orders. For Willen Ironmaul to have taken this upon himself, there must be a very good reason indeed, the chieftain thought.

"Show him," Willen ordered. The guards flanking the

man grasped his cloak and pulled it from him. The man's eyes glared at the dwarves with unconcealed hatred, but he made no sound. His hands and arms were bound with stout cord, and a gag covered his mouth.

"Sire," Willen Ironmaul said, pointing, "this man was delivered to our guards by men from Golash, by order of Prince Garr Lanfel. He was bound as he is now, and we left him so and brought him here in secret." Willen stooped, picked up a long parcel wrapped in sheepskin, and laid it on the table before Colin. "Prince Garr Lanfel instructed his men to say that this man is not of Golash. He is a stranger there, one of many who have arrived in recent days. And he was carrying this." With a sweep of his powerful arm, the big dwarf pulled aside the sheepskin. Within it lay a sword, and Colin Stonetooth's eyes narrowed as he looked at it. It was no ordinary sword, and certainly not a sword that any human should have had. It was virtually a duplicate of the blade that Willen Ironmaul carried at his back. It was of finest Thorin steel, with the distinctive floral hilt and pommel of those blades made in the fifth-level smithies, for exclusive issue to Thorin's elite guards. No such sword had ever been consigned to anyone else.

Colin lifted the blade, studied it carefully, and tasted it. Though wiped clean, its burnished steel still carried traces that were clear to the keen metal-sense of a dwarf.

The chieftain's eyes narrowed still more, and Willen Ironmaul nodded. "Aye, Sire," he said. "The sword has tasted blood recently. And not just human blood. There is Calnar blood there, too—on the hilt, guard, and pommel."

Colin Stonetooth turned, his gaze cold as he studied the visible features of the gagged human. Aside he asked, "Your border patrol, Willen? Has there been word?"

"No, Sire. Nothing."

"There is the horse," Handil Coldblade reminded them, stepping forth. As wide and sturdy as Colin himself, "the Drum" at this moment was a fierce, younger version of his father. "One of ours, Father. It was found wandering in the lower fields, lathered and stripped of its gear. Saman the

Hostler believes it is Sledge Two-Fires' mount, called
Piquin."

"Sledge led the missing patrol." Willen Ironmaul added.

At the council table, Cullom Hammerstand, warden of
trade, pulled a rolled scroll from his belt and placed it on
the oaken surface. "Heed the words of the human prince,
Garr Lanfel, Sire. He said this man is not of Golash, but is
one of many strangers recently come. Garr Lanfel is an
honorable man, Sire . . . for a human. His warning bears
out these reports of the past several weeks. Large bands of
humans have been converging, both on Golash and on
Chandera. They come quietly and blend with the humans
there."

"Many people are adrift these days," Talam Bendiron
noted. As always, the tap warden was cautious about
reaching conclusions.

"Many are adrift," Cullom Hammerstand agreed, "but
not *this* many." He unrolled the scroll, squinting at it. "By
our agents' estimates, Sire, these 'little bands' converging
on the neighboring realms now total several thousand
human males, all of them well-armed, and all arriving just
in time for the fair of Balladine. Also, in Golash they say
the strangers speak to all who will listen, spreading
vicious lies about dwarves. They seem to be doing all they
can to spread a hatred of the Calnar. And a name is used
often among the strangers. The name is Grayfen. Our
agents suspect he may be a wizard of some sort."

Colin shuddered slightly, as did most dwarves at the
mention of sorcery. Magic existed, but it was considered an
abomination. "Only in Golash?" he asked. "What of Chandera?"

The trade warden ran a finger down his scroll, read farther, then looked up. "Bram Talien of Chandera reports
strangers, as well, Sire. Though not so many."

"All of this, and this"—Willen Ironmaul indicated the
sword at Colin's hand—"are why I felt we should meet
here today."

"I agree with Willen, Father," Handil said. "Balladine is

at hand."

"And I," Tolon added. "I fear that evil approaches."

"Evil." Colin repeated the word. He waved toward the human prisoner. "Release his bonds. Let's hear what he can tell us."

Strong hands removed the cords and the gag. The man rubbed his hands, glaring at them.

"Do you speak our language, human?" Colin Stonetooth asked.

"I speak *my* language," the man growled. "But not to dinks."

"To what?"

"Dinks. Filthy *dwarves*."

One of the guards shook his head, amused that this disheveled human, who smelled as though he had never in his life had a bath, should call dwarves filthy.

"You have heard what has been said, human." Colin stood, facing the man. "What is your name, and how do you come to have this sword in your possession?"

"My name is Calik," the man snapped. "And what I have is my own business."

"What happened to the Suncradle patrol?" Willen Ironmaul demanded.

The man glared at him, tight-lipped.

"Who is Grayfen?" Handil the Drum asked.

The man's eyes narrowed with hatred, but he said nothing.

Cullom Hammerstand looked up from his counting-scroll. "How many of you are there, and what do you intend?"

Still the man stood in silence.

Willen Ironmaul glanced at his chieftain. "With your permission, Sire, I might persuade this creature to talk to us."

The man glared at him contemptuously. "It would take more than you, dink."

Colin Stonetooth sat down. "Help yourself, Willen. But try not to damage him beyond repair."

"Aye." The captain of guards nodded. Stepping away from the table, he removed his weapons and armor and strode to a clear area in the arena, clad only in kilt, shift and boots. "Send him to me," he said.

The guards pushed the man forward, and he balked. "What is this? One man, unarmed, against dozens with swords?"

"No weapons," Colin Stonetooth decreed. "And no one else will touch you. Only Willen."

"He wants to fight me? One puny dwarf? So I kill him, then what? The rest of you kill me?"

"If you defeat Willen Ironmaul, human," Handil snapped, "I will ask for your freedom. Father?"

"Agreed." Colin nodded, turning a disinterested palm.

Again the guards hustled Calik toward Willen. When he was past the table, they gave him a shove and backed away. The man hesitated for a moment, then grinned wickedly at the unarmed dwarf waiting for him. The man stood almost a foot taller than Willen and was strongly built, with long legs, long arms, and burly shoulders. "I've killed a dozen real men in the pits," he hissed. "I'll make this quick, dink." His grin widened, and he spread his hands as though in embarrassment. Then, abruptly, he crouched and lunged at the dwarf.

It was as though the man had run into a wall—into it and over it. There was a thud of colliding bodies, then Calik was on the floor beyond Willen, tumbling and skidding. He raised himself, shook his head, and blinked. Then, with a shouted curse, he launched himself again, towering over the dwarf, hard fists swinging.

Willen met the man halfway, went in under his blows, and delivered a jarring punch to his midsection. Even as the man gasped, the dwarf was behind him, kicking his feet out from under him, and several solid blows rained on him as he fell.

Untouched and unshaken, Willen Ironmaul stepped back. "Are you ready to talk to us, human?"

Enraged, Calik got his feet under him, rushed, whirled,

and aimed a lethal kick at the dwarf's head. Strong hands blocked his leg, twisting it, and Calik fell on his face. Willen Ironmaul twisted the man's arms behind him, ground his face against the stone floor, then stood and delivered a judicious kick to his ribs. "Now are you ready to talk to us?" he asked. "Everyone is waiting."

Calik's response was a sudden kick that caught Willen in the side and sent him staggering back. Snake-quick, the man pressed his advantage with a rush, a knee to the dwarf's face, and a two-fisted blow to the back of the neck that might have killed a human. Willen went to his knees, seeming dazed, and the man threw himself onto him, trying to bear him down, to get a killing hold on throat or spine. But the dwarf who had seemed dazed suddenly was upright beneath him, lifting. In an instant, Willen had the flailing, writhing man above his head, and with a heave he threw him across ten feet of empty floor.

Calik lit, rolled, and crashed against the side of the council table. Before he could move, Willen was on him, pummeling, punishing and bruising him. Calik screamed.

Willen felt small, strong hands pulling him away. Tera Sharn's voice said, "Willen, please! That's enough!"

He let her pull him back, breathing deeply to clear the battle-rage from his head. She was right, of course. The man lay groveling on the floor, obviously defeated. Willen turned toward Tera and heard a gasp as her eyes looked beyond him. Calik was not through. With a shout he came upright, grabbed the sword from in front of Colin Stonetooth, and raised it over his head. When it fell, slashing downward, its bright edge barely missed Tera. Willen pushed the girl back, out of the way, and waved off the dozen or more armed dwarves who were rushing toward him. "Stay!" he commanded. "The human has made his choice."

Willen ducked aside from the maddened human's second cut, dodged the third, and went in under the fourth. In the blink of an eye, Calik was bent over backward, the sword still waving in his hand, and Willen's short, massive arm was around his neck. With his other arm, the dwarf locked the man's shoulder . . . and pivoted, twisting.

The sound of Calik's neck breaking was almost drowned by the clang of the dropped sword falling from a dead hand.

Willen stepped away, letting the big body slump to the floor. He looked toward Colin Stonetooth. "He chose not to speak, Sire," he said.

"It is a bad omen," Tolon Farsight muttered.

"A bad business," Handil agreed. "Humans—even those friendly to us—won't like dwarves killing humans."

"I had no choice," Willen Ironmaul told him. "You saw it."

"No, it was his choice," Handil agreed. "But there will be anger."

Guards hurried forward to drag Calik away. At the council table, Frost Steelbit stood. "There are many questions, Sire," he said to the chieftain. "But the first of the questions faces us now. With what we have seen, and what we might guess, do we continue with Balladine this year?"

Before the chieftain could answer, his second son, Tolon Farsight, pushed forward. "Cancel the Balladine, Father," he said. "This business is an omen. Thorin is in danger from humans. It is best to barricade and guard, and let no human approach this season."

"The people of Golash and Chandera are our friends," Colin pointed out. "They have not threatened us."

"Humans threaten us!" Tolon growled. "Does it matter which ones? I say bar them from Thorin. The danger is more than the gain."

Colin Stonetooth gazed around at all of them thoughtfully, then shook his head. "Balladine is as important to us as it is to our neighbors," he said. "We need the humans' goods in trade, just as they need ours. Let the call continue, let the plans proceed. But"—he stood, turning away—"we shall be very careful this time. Very careful indeed. Tell the people to look to the left side of their tools."

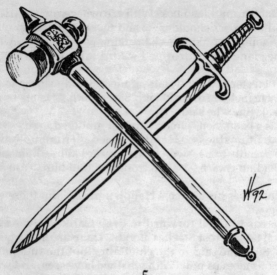

5

The Heart of Everbardin

The left side of the tools.

Every Calnar past the age of first-crafting knew the meaning of that. From the old tales came many sayings, each with a wisdom of its own. One was, "If there are enemies, raise your hammer and see it in a mirror."

The meaning was clear. In Thorin, though the finest of weapons were crafted there, few people owned swords and lances. Except for the finely made weapons carried by the guards, and the elaborate, exquisitely balanced blades carried by a few others, including the chieftain and the Ten, "weapons" were scarce. A sword was a clumsy, heavy thing, useless for any kind of work except fighting. For games and as a climbing tool a balanced javelin was far better than a lance, and bows and arrows were of no practical value in the delving of stone, the crafting of furniture and finery, the weaving of tapestries or the shaping of clay vessels.

Humans and others outside of Thorin often thought of the dwarves as being heavily armed, but that was only because most truly fine weaponry in the region came from Thorin. The best of blades, the finest arrowheads, the most valuable spearpoints and daggers, even the massive war machines that human realms coveted, all came from the foundries, forges, and shops of the dwarves of Thorin. They were a major part of the Calnar's stock in trade, because there were always so many people so anxious to have them.

It was said, among humans and other races, that the best steel was Calnar steel. The fact was, in all the realms within sight of the Khalkists at least, Calnar steel was the *only* steel. People of many races could craft in bronze and tin, and some in iron, but in these lands only the dwarves made steel.

Even the plainest Calnar trade sword would bring fifty bushels of grain at Balladine, and a Calnar steel arrowhead was worth as much as a Calnar steel coin. Humans preferred the arrowheads to coins because they had an alternate use in a pinch.

Thus, the Calnar were weapon makers for a large part of the world as they knew it. Dwarven weaponry was everywhere—except in Thorin. Few dwarves owned so much as a short sword, or cared to. To the practical-minded dwarves, a thing that was neither useful nor decorative was hardly worth having.

So there were few weapons in Thorin—as those outside of Thorin knew weapons. But there were tools. It was the nature of the Calnar: tools were as natural to them as breathing. They cherished their tools, and used them constantly.

Thus, the old saying: If there are enemies, raise your hammer and see it in a mirror.

The only difference between a hammer for driving a chisel in stone or for clearing tunnels, and a war-hammer, was in how one looked at it. An axe was for felling timber, a maul for splitting rails or squaring stone, a sling for delivering small tools and materials from one subterranean level to another, and a javelin was for securing lift-lines in climbs. But a good axe could as easily cleave bone as wood, a maul could as readily smash a shield as drive a wedge. A sling could throw missiles as well as supplies, and a well-aimed javelin could be as deadly as any spear.

A helmet was to protect one's head from falling stone in a delve. A shield was for clearing rubble and deflecting rock showers. Body armor—sometimes metal and sometimes leather—was for working in the foundries, where sparks could fly, and in the finishing shops where implements might be flung from grindstones and burnishing wheels. But these could have other uses as well.

Raise your hammer and see it in a mirror. Look to the left side of your tools. *Be ready to stop work and fight.* It was a thing that any dwarf understood. The difference between a tool and a weapon is in the mind of the user and in the circumstances of use.

Word had already spread to the crafters' galleries by the time Handil the Drum arrived there, carrying the great, deep-throated vibrar with which he had begun the Call to Balladine. The mighty drum was his own invention—a steel-banded barrel of tapered and curved hardwood slats, capped at each head by tightly drawn buffalo-hide leather. Within were other "heads" of various materials, each pitched to capture and amplify the resonance of the membrane before it. Oval openings around the center of the barrel broadcast its thunder when either head was struck.

Played atop the Sentinels, Handil's drum could be heard for miles and its echoes much farther. The Thunderer was not the biggest drum in Thorin, but it was by far the most powerful.

He carried it wrapped and muted now—as the drums always were when brought within the undermountain realm.

The sun-tunnel lighted concourse leading to the crafters' galleries was crowded, as usual, with dwarves hurrying here and there on their various errands. Handil stepped aside to let a sled crew pass. Two great Calnar horses in harness hauled an eight-foot block of hewn granite from one of the new delves while a dozen sturdy Calnar armed with prybars and mallets worked the skids. When the crew was past, Handil went on, nodding to an acquaintance now and then. Sledges rang at a side tunnel where cart rails and tow-rings were being placed for a new cable-way leading up from the farming warrens. Across the concourse, hewers and reaves were at work, fitting massive timbers into newly cut stone to expand the weavers' stalls.

The chieftain's order to be ready for trouble had put worried frowns on many of the faces in the concourse but had not interrupted the rhythm of the place. As always, there were Calnar everywhere, doing all kinds of things, and like every public part of Thorin, the great way was a bustling, flowing turmoil of busy dwarves.

Handil slowed his pace as he neared the shops. Here the corridors were even more crowded than usual, and it seemed everyone was carrying various tools and items of armor. Lines had formed as people waited their turns to sharpen spikes, fit wrist straps onto hammers, repair buckles on chest-guards, or mount horns or spikes on their helmets. Handil grinned at sight of a gray-haired, aging woman dragging a long-handled heavy maul taller than herself. In her free hand she carried a foot-long, curved spike as sharp as a dagger. A glance at the maul's head told him what she intended to do. She wanted the spike welded to the trailing face of the big splitter.

She was looking to the left side of her tools.

His grin deepened, strong teeth glinting behind his dark whiskers. The venerable mother probably had not the faintest idea of who might be an enemy, he thought, but gods help the enemy who got in the way of that tool.

"Handil? I thought I saw you here!" The voice from behind made his eyes light, and he turned. Wide-set,

serious eyes looked up at him from a broad, pretty face
framed by reddish hair. Jinna Rockreave smiled at him,
raising a finely crafted net sling. "I need a wrist strap for
this," she said, glancing at his drum. "What are you after?
Blades for your drum rings?"

"Hardly." He shook his head. "That wouldn't be very
practical. I thought I might modify the mallets a bit,
though." He studied her, seeing the pleasure in her eyes at
their meeting. It was like his own pleasure at seeing her. "It
has been too many days since we were together, Jinna. The
Call and everything . . . but I've missed you."

"And I've missed you." She nodded. "Things have been
so hectic, lately, I was afraid we might not meet until our
day of joining. I didn't want to wait that long to see you."

"Nor did I." He was still gazing into her eyes. "I . . .
well, I keep having troublesome dreams. Sometimes I
wake up thinking we might never wed at all . . . that you
might change your mind or something. You haven't, have
you? Changed your mind, I mean?"

"Not in a million years, Handil Coldblade," she chuckled, then turned serious. "What is the weapon call about?
Is there danger?"

"There could be," he warned her. "Probably not, but my
father is being cautious. Tolon and some of the elders are
concerned. There are strange humans about who seem not
to like us very much."

"Why not?"

He shrugged. "Who can understand humans? It's probably nothing, but with Balladine at hand, it's as well to be
prepared."

"I suppose. Hurry, Handil. The line is moving."

He looked around. A gap had opened in the line outside
the shops, and dozens of people were looking at the two of
them, some of them grinning openly. Many of the Calnar
knew Handil Coldblade, and *everyone* knew of him. Handil
the Drum was a famous person in Thorin, not so much for
being the chieftain's eldest son—everyone was somebody's son—but for his magnificent drum and for other

things he had invented, such as the turnable vanes which now were installed in most airshafts, allowing for pleasant temperatures in any season, and the winch-operated lift stages in the keep. Throughout Thorin, Handil the Drum was a celebrity.

Most also knew of the betrothal of Handil and Jinna Rockreave, pretty daughter of Calk Rockreave. Sight of the two young dwarves so obviously engrossed in each other was amusing to many of those waiting at the stalls.

The old woman with the splitting maul raised an eyebrow and said, "If you want to be in this line, then get a move on, or we'll go around you."

Handil glanced again at the big maul and the spikes, then stepped back. "Go ahead, mother. What you are doing looks far more useful than anything I had in mind."

"I can see what you have in mind," the woman said, glancing at Jinna Rockreave. "But the shops are hardly the place for it."

Handil grinned, conceding, and turned away. "Come and walk with me, Jinna. We can see to our tools later."

He was so absorbed in her that he didn't see the rail-setter approaching, carrying heavy lengths of steel on his shoulder, until the workman turned and his burden collided with the forward end of the great, muted drum slung from Handil's shoulder. The result was stunning, almost deafening. Even swathed, the Thunderer responded to the blow on its drawn head with a throb of sound that seemed to shake the very walls of Thorin. Here and there, little showers of dust and shards of stone fell from ceilings. People staggered, their hands going to their ears. A short distance away, timbers groaned and dwarves shouted curses as the massive, unsecured framing of the weavers' stalls shifted in its footings.

Quickly, Handil swung the drum around, wrapping his arms around the center of it to muffle its resonance. The throb died to a rumbling echo, like distant thunder. Jinna was staring at him, wide-eyed, as were others all around.

The powerful drum-tone was followed by a moment of

silence all along the concourse, then shouts and babbling as people hurried about, making sure no one was hurt and looking for structural damage in the stone walls. Apparently—and luckily—there was none. Still, Handil found a crowd of Calnar facing him as he redoubled the muting wraps on his drum.

"Someone other than the chieftain's son would be up before the wardens for sounding a drum in Thorin," a scowling carpenter snorted.

"Oh, back off, Hibal," someone else said. "It was only an accident."

"The kind of accident that could bring this concourse down upon us," a rock-cutter said. "There are rules, you know!"

Handil faced them, level-eyed, and raised a hand. "Rules are rules," he said, so that all could hear, "and no exceptions. You have my apology and my promise. I will report this to the wardens myself and take the penalty any would take." He looked at the carpenter who had first objected. "Does that satisfy you, Hibal?"

For a moment, it seemed the carpenter might want to challenge. Hibal considered it, gazing at the wide shoulders of Handil, then shook his head. "Another time maybe. I have work to do."

"Any time," Handil assured him. "Whenever you like, and I'll buy the ale afterward."

Cale Greeneye had appeared from somewhere, inquisitive as always. The chieftain's youngest son carried a long, wrapped parcel on his shoulder. As Handil turned away again, with Jinna, Cale fell into step alongside. "That was some noise you made, Brother," he said. "If you were planning to put points on the vibrar, I don't think you need to bother. That thing is weapon enough, just as it is."

"I expect I'll be hearing about that for a while," Handil admitted dourly. He nodded at his brother's parcel. "What have you there?"

"A sword," Cale said. "That same sword that the man had. . . ." He glanced at Jinna, not certain whether she knew about the human who had died in Grand Gather.

"It's all right." Handil stowed his mallets in his belt and took Jinna Rockreave's hand in his. "I'll tell Jinna what has occurred. Where are you going?"

"I'm on my way to the guards' hall to collect some armor and see about a horse. I'll need . . ." He raised a brow, looking at his brother. "Oh, you don't know, do you?"

"Know what?"

"Willen is organizing the guards for close patrols, so I volunteered to lead a search westward, to see if we can find out what happened out there. . . ." Again he glanced at the puzzled face of Jinna Rockreave, then continued. "It was my idea. The escort will be made up of volunteers."

"Anything for a journey, Little Brother?" Handil grinned. "Still, you might find something. What did Father say about this adventure?"

"What could he say? I was going, anyway. He just said to keep my wits about me."

"Good advice, considering what the wardens have learned about the wild humans. It sounds like Golash and Chandera are full of strangers. Unfriendly strangers."

"Well, those are the concern of Cullom Hammerstand's agents. I plan a far search . . . clear to the Suncradles, or beyond if necessary. I've always wanted to see what's out there, anyway."

Cale's face—a face just made for laughter, many said—turned serious. "I will miss the Balladine, Handil, and I may miss your wedding, too. So I have something here, for both of you." He opened his shoulder pouch and drew forth a small bag of fine suede. With a shrug, he handed it to Jinna.

The girl opened it, looked inside, and turned wide eyes on her future brother-in-law. "Oh, Cale! They're beautiful!" From the bag she withdrew a pair of jeweled rings, exquisitely interwoven bands of silver and copper, with gold traceries so fine that the eye could barely follow them. Each band was inset with a trio of cut diamonds.

"They're elvish work." Cale shrugged. "I've had them for years, thinking there might be a good use for them. I'd be honored if you and Handil would exchange them at your wedding. That way, it will be as though I were there to add my blessing to your union."

They stopped beneath a sun-tunnel to look at the rings, and Handil felt his throat tighten. Cale Greeneye . . . Cale Cloudwalker . . . Cale who was so different from most Calnar that he might have had elven blood in his veins had such been possible. Handil had never understood his youngest brother, even for a moment. Cale was always full of surprises—just such surprises as this. At a loss for words, Handil the Drum placed a fond hand on his brother's shoulder.

Jinna looked as though there were tears in her eyes. "Oh, Cale, of course we will. These are a wonderful gift! And you will be there with us."

"It's just a pair of rings." Cale said, embarrassed. "No big thing. Just—well, just think about me if I don't see you again before your time. I'll think of both of you, too."

Without another word, Cale turned and strode away, his wrapped sword over his shoulder. He had said his brief goodbyes—to Tolon and Tera, to his father, and now to Handil and his Jinna. He was anxious to be away, to put the familiar sights of Thorin behind him, and see what some of the distant places held.

He was certain that the sword he carried had belonged to Agate Coalglow, and they said the horse that had returned was Piquin—Sledge Two-Fires' favorite mount. It seemed certain now that the western patrol was dead, killed by wild humans. Agate had been Cale's friend, and Sledge Two-Fires was a dwarf he had admired. It seemed appropriate to Cale that he take with him something of them when he went to look for clues to their fate.

Clues, and a look at what lay beneath the Suncradles—and maybe what lay beyond.

* * * * *

It was evening when Cale Greeneye rode out from Thorin, mounted on the high back of Piquin and followed by six other young adventurers who had volunteered to go with him. The sun was setting beyond the Suncradles, and soft evening light lay on the valleys. But both visible moons were in the sky, and there was light enough for travel. The horses were fresh, and the trails open.

Cale looked back, just once, at the great outer wall of Thorin. "Thorin-Dwarfhome," he whispered. "Thorin-Everbardin, keep my soul. Welcome this one home should I never return."

Then he turned his eyes westward, where the last glow of day outlined the wavy peaks of the Suncradles. "Keep pace," he called to his companions. "There is a lot of world to see out there, and no better time than the present."

Eyes watched them all the way across the Valley of the Bone and out the Chandera Road—furtive, sullen human eyes, hidden in shadows all along a closing line which would soon be a human cordon around Thorin. Eyes watched, but no man lifted a hand. The seven armed and mounted dwarves were packed for travel, and they were going away. They didn't matter. They would be not be here to interfere with what Grayfen planned for the citadel of the dwarves.

6
The Betrayal

Bram Talien was worried. As trademaster of Chandera, he was responsible for the caravan wending its way toward Thorin, for the midsummer fair that the dwarves called Balladine. Normally, the annual journey was more a pleasure than a worry. As a trader and merchant, Bram Talien enjoyed visiting the Calnar fortress. It was a challenge to match wits with Cullom Hammerstand, the dwarves' warden of trade, and he had a deep respect for Colin Stonetooth.

The dwarves were not human, of course, but there were dwarves whose company Bram Talien preferred over that of some people he knew.

The caravan was like a traveling city. Carts, wagons,

barrows, pack beasts and laden travois by the hundreds wound upward on the mountain road in a line that was sometimes three miles long in the narrow passages, and fully half of the citizens of Chandera trudged along among them, tending stock and driving teams.

Here was the annual commodity wealth of Chandera: grains from lowland fields, spices and scents from the Bloten frontiers, hardwood timbers from the forests bounding the plains of eastern Ergoth, bonemeal and herbs, wooden baskets, tapestries and rugs, and a dozen kinds of wicker furniture. All were things that the dwarves of Thorin cherished and would trade for with their own commodities. And in special wagons near the front of the line was a real prize, something that would make the dwarven traders' eyes go wide and their bids go high.

Most of the men were armed, and dozens of them were mounted, riding guard on the train. Never in memory had a Balladine caravan been seriously threatened. Sometimes thieves would try to slip into a night camp to filch whatever they could find, and now and then a wandering band of nomads might shadow the train for a day or so, but a caravan in strength was a formidable company, and there had never been an attack. But now Bram Talien was apprehensive.

All through the land, it seemed, things were changing. Just in the past year, strangers had come among them in Chandera, and it seemed to Bram that among his own people—the subjects of Riffin Two-Tree the Wise—moods had shifted. There was talk of Chandera being "poor," and talk of fortune hunting. It was disturbing. Sometimes Bram felt as though some Chanderans were turning from the old ways and looking in strange, new directions. A sullen, angry discontent was spreading where before had been contentment.

And now there was the more immediate concern—the strangers in the distance, who clung to the caravan route as though the caravan were a flock of sheep being herded. The scouts reported large groups of people—strangers all—flanking and paralleling them, and hardly an hour passed that there were not people on the hilltops watching them.

Bram Talien had told Cullom Hammerstand's dwarven agents about the strangers on Chandera land and of his concerns. It was common for the chiefs of trade to share such information prior to Balladine. But now, two days out from Riffin Two-Tree's village, he realized that there were far more strangers in the land than he had known. They seemed to be everywhere—wild-looking, oddly dressed men who might have been assembled from dozens of different tribes—and the only certain thing about them was that they were all armed.

The land was full of movers these days, it seemed. Refugees from the south brought tales of horror, of dragons a'wing over Silvanesti, of dragonfear and dragonfire and awful magics which spread like sand on the winds: trees that danced and captured spirits, bogs that erupted vile acids, stones that exploded, and lightnings that crackled through the forests to find and strike some living thing.

How many dragons were there? Some said one or two, some said hundreds. Personally, Bram Talien doubted that any of the travelers had seen more than a few dragons, if any at all, but that did not diminish his concerns. One dragon alone would be enough to start panic and breed mass migrations.

The stories meshed in some way with the strange disappearance of elves from the realms of the eastern Khalkists. Elven parties had been common in past times. They had crossed Chandera now and then in their journeys and had shared fires with Chanderan herdsmen and patrols.

Often, in olden times, elves had even come to the dwarves' Balladine, and the goods they brought to trade were much coveted.

But it had been several seasons now since Bram Talien had even seen an elf, though Riffin Two-Tree's scouts had recently reported large numbers of what looked like western elves skirting the mountains south of Bloten, eastward-bound . . . eastward, toward Silvanesti.

Something was going on in the south, and the results in these lands were bands of migrants, uprooted tribes moving from where they had been to wherever they were going. But there was something different about the people who now flanked the Chanderan caravan. These did not look like refugees. They looked more like mercenaries.

Spurring his chestnut pony, Bram Talien rode forward along the plodding line of the caravan, feeling the wind in his beard as the horse ran. Though only half the size of the great, gold-and-white horses of Thorin, the chestnut was a good mount, as fast and strong as any in Chandera, and it was the trademaster's favorite.

Forward of the camp carts, near the front of the train, eight high-sided wagons rolled along, each drawn by a double string of oxen. Bram slowed, casting a careful eye over the wagons and their teams and rigging. Here was the special commodity with which he hoped to gain trade concessions from Cullom Hammerstand. In the high ranges on the eastern perimeter of Chandera, diggers had found a large deposit of the shiny, black firestone that the dwarves used to smelt iron and make their steel.

Cullom Hammerstand would do everything in his power to try to get the firestone for a low price. Bram smiled faintly, imagining the posturings and hand-wringing the wily dwarf would go through, trying to trade him down. Chandera would see a handsome profit this year at Balladine.

Some of the drivers and crewmen tending the high wagons turned to watch the trademaster pass, and one or two waved.

He waved back. "Tend your loads well," he called. "This year we will out-trade the dwarves of Thorin."

"We'll get this stuff there, Trademaster," a man called, "but it's your task to see we get a good price for it."

Bram nodded and started ahead again, then frowned as another voice came to him on the wind—another man, speaking to his companions. "If we had the dwarves' smelters and forges, we'd have no need to trade with them," the voice said angrily. "If we had Thorin, we'd make our own steel, and high time we did. Those selfish, bit-pinching dinks have held Thorin too long, as I see it."

Bram looked around, but whoever had spoken had turned away, and the others looked away as well. . . . Were they embarrassed at the words? Or did some among them agree?

It was troubling.

At the head of the caravan, Bram pulled up alongside Riffin Two-Tree, chief of the Chanderans. The chief rode a white horse and carried sword and shield as he always did when afield. With his iron-gray beard and studded helmet, his shoulders bulging against the seams of his leather-and-bronze coat, Riffin Two-Tree looked as fierce and formidable as he always had, until one approached very closely. Then the fading color of his cheeks, the slight moistness of his crinkled eyes, were a reminder that this man had been chief for more than fifty years, and was older—despite his stamina—than most humans ever expected to be.

"News from ahead?" the trademaster asked.

Riffin glanced around at Bram, his old eyes troubled. "We'll be at the meadows below Thorin by nightfall," he said, "but the scouts say the encampment is full—people everywhere."

"The Golash caravan is there ahead of us?"

"Not Golash." The old chief shook his head. "Garr Lanfel's train is still a day away. These are others—hundreds of armed men, like those who flank us in the hills. The scouts say their encampments fill half the valley already, with more arriving by the hour. And they carry no trade goods of any kind."

Bram Talien frowned. "What does it mean, my chief? What is happening?"

"It could mean trouble for the dwarves of Thorin," Riffin Two-Tree said. "It has the look of an invasion, and if we're not careful we could find ourselves caught up in it."

"Then we should stay back," Bram suggested. "Thorin is

Chandera's friend. We have no argument with the dwarves."

Riffin turned to look at him. "Are you sure, Bram? You have heard the talk, just as I have."

"Some of our people are discontented," Bram agreed. "It comes of jealousy, I think."

"I think it is more," Riffin rasped. "I think there are those among us who are doing their best to spread hatred toward the dwarves."

"But why?"

"To serve someone's purpose, obviously. But you are right, Bram. We will hold back until we know what is going on. I want no part in any plot against Colin Stonetooth's people . . . for more reasons than one."

Bram nodded. "They are our friends."

"Yes, they are our friends. But even if they weren't, I'd want no part of war with Thorin. Don't ever underestimate the dwarves, Bram. They would be a formidable enemy."

"Thank the gods we don't need to test that," Bram said. "Once within sight of Thorin, I'll call a halt. We'll keep our distance for a day or so, until we know—"

A shout from the rear interrupted him, and he turned. All along the caravan, flankers were closing in—the strangers, coming out of the hills, closing in on the long train like a well-organized cordon.

And just ahead, at the top of a rise, riders appeared— heavily armed men, spreading out across the road.

Riffin Two-Tree drew his shield from his shoulder and unslung his blade. All around him, Chanderan guards followed suit. Bram Talien spun his pony around and raced back along the caravan, shouting, "Alarm! Alarm! Close for defense!"

The rearward sections were already in motion, drivers whipping up their teams and carters grabbing their leads. Within moments, the long, ambling line of the caravan was a shortening, thickening thing, widening at center as the heavier vehicles pulled out right and left to let the travois, pack beasts, and sleds move in between them. Women, children, and old people were hurried forward, carrying their personal gear, into the center of the closing mass of vehicles and stock. Men not driving teams grabbed up their weapons and ranked themselves along the outer perimeter, their lines closing as the caravan became a moving oval compound, then a tightly-packed circle.

Suddenly, here and there, chaos erupted. Here a team broke free from its traces, leaving a wagon stranded. There a runner-barge overturned, spilling its load. Elsewhere two carts collided and broke down where they sat.

Bram Talien saw some of these things and drew his own blade. "Sabotage!" he muttered, heading into the crowd around a broken wagon. But armed men confronted him there, denying him entrance. A man he knew—Grif Newgrass, one of his own neighbors—raised a heavy sword and shouted, "Stand back, Trademaster. There'll be no trading this year. We've a better way to get what the dwarves have!"

Bram circled about on his mount, trying to understand what was happening, and found himself surrounded by riders, all carrying their weapons at hand. The strangers were upon them, surrounding them, and in the distance ahead, at the front of the caravan where old Riffin Two-Tree and the Chanderan guards were, steel rang on steel.

The trademaster saw a wagon driver pitch from his seat, clutching at an arrow in his throat. He saw a line of barbarians charge, with lances and swords, into a cluster of panicked Chanderan workers. He wheeled his horse and dodged a spearpoint as an attacker lunged at him. With a flick of his sword he scored the man's cheek, then drove the blade home beneath his chest-plate. The man screamed and twisted, and Bram fought to withdraw the sword. Something rang against his helmet, sending it flying from his head. He freed his sword, twisted sideways in his saddle, and started to swing at the man behind him . . . and again something hit him—this time a solid, clubbing blow against his temple.

The world went dark for Bram Talien.

* * * * *

He awakened slowly, fighting the throbbing ache in his head. When he tried to move, pain blinded him for long moments, but finally he fought it down, opened his eyes, and raised his head.

He lay in a crude tent of some kind. A fire burned near his feet, and smoke hung thick above the heads of the men who sat around it, watching him. Bram's hand went to his belt, but there were no weapons there.

The man nearest was burly and dark-bearded and looked familiar. He turned his head, and the trademaster recognized him. It was Grif Newgrass. The others were strangers—outlanders. Grif grinned and nodded his head. "You're awake," he pointed out. "That's good. Thought maybe our new friends had killed you."

With a tongue as dry as leather and a voice that was no more than a rasping whisper, Bram Talien asked, "What is happening, Grif? Who are these men?"

"Doesn't matter who they are," the man said. "Only thing that matters for you is to do exactly like you're told. You see, the old chief . . . well, he kind of met with an accident, so now the good people of Chandera need somebody to answer to. Somebody they're used to answering to. You're the trademaster, so you'll do. We'll tell you what to say to them."

"What do you want?"

"Why"—the man's beard split in a toothy grin—"we got business with those dinks in Thorin. That's what our new friends call dwarves. Good word, isn't it?—*Dinks*. They have what we want, and we're going to take it."

"Thorin's what we want," another man growled. "Time human people had that place. Our leader has plans for it. The dinks know you. You've done business with them. So you'll be our decoy and our shield."

"Why should I do what you say?" Bram struggled to a sitting position, his head ringing with pain.

The man waved a casual hand. "Show him, Clote."

Across the tent, the one called Clote stood and pulled back a wide flap, opening the shelter. Beyond was the remains of the caravan—teams and conveyances drawn into a solid ring. Within the ring, Chanderan men labored, carrying things here and there, while armed strangers—and a few Chanderan traitors—strode among them, supervising.

And in the center of the enclosure a crude fence had been erected. As men moved past it, Bram's eyes widened in shock. Within the fence were women and children. At the corners of the fence, archers sat atop short towers. At a signal from the man at the tent flap, rough men pushed into the enclosure, shoving women and children aside, then appeared at the fence holding two women, pushing them forward into view.

Bram's mouth twisted in a snarl. "Chara," he muttered. "And Corian." With a lunge, he tried to get to his feet. His hands went out, searching for a weapon—or for a throat to throttle. Grif Newgrass punched him cruelly in the stomach, then kicked his feet from under him. "You just don't understand, do you, Bram?" he spat. "Riffin Two-Tree and his soldiers are dead, and you're not in charge any more. We are."

"Told you those women would get his attention," another man chuckled. "The trademaster's wife and his daughter. Just say the word, Grif, an' I'll see to both of them, myself."

The dark-bearded one ignored him, gazing indifferently at Bram Talien. "That's why," he said, casually. "Right there's the reason why you and everybody else here will do exactly as you're told." He glanced outside, then turned again, a cruel smile parting his beard. "Oh, and don't expect any help from the Golash bunch. Grayfen's people have them, too, just like we have you."

"You'll never get away with this," Bram gasped. "The dwarves . . ."

". . . might never know what hit 'em," Grif shrugged. "Or maybe they will, and they'll fight. If so, you and your 'good citizens' will help us."

"Never!" Bram spat.

"Oh, I expect you will. After all, we're all human. When it comes right down to it, humans will side with humans against a bunch of ugly dinks."

* * * * *

Somewhere beyond the captured caravan, beyond sight of Bram Talien but not far away, the rivers called Hammersong and Bone flowed through their valley. Just across, the camps of the humans spread to the foot of the terraces, which rose in methodical, precise steps toward the west wall of Thorin Keep.

Mighty Thorin stood above it all, massive and shuttered behind great gates. Yet still the call for Balladine—the chorus of the thunder-drums—rang through the mountains. *Come trade with us*, they seemed to sing. *Come and be our guests for Balladine.*

Soon, the gates would open. Then Thorin would also be open—to attack.

In a magically protected hut among the encampments, two embers of red glowed in the dark interior beyond a low portal. Grayfen Ember-Eye rested, preparing for tomorrow. With his eyes removed, he was free of the searing pain they always brought him, and he could review his plans.

He could only estimate the strength of the dwarven fortress. Humans had been inside the place, as far as the great hall called Grand Gather, but he knew of none who had been beyond. It was reasonable to assume, though, that the great foundries and smelters lay beyond, and the shops and sleeping quarters. There would be some internal defenses, of course, but nothing that his hordes could not overcome.

How many dwarves were there? No one seemed to know, but it was assumed that there were several thousand at least. The big cavern of Grand Gather, which some people had seen, would hold several thousand. But Grayfen was not worried by that. Even if there were five thousand dwarves in that great lair, he still had the forces to outnumber them. And once inside, numbers would prevail.

The gates would open for Balladine. Once open, it required only a first assault force to hold them open until his men could get inside. And Grayfen had the means to hold the gates. The magic imposed upon him long ago by that sorcerized dwarf was a wild magic, and hard experience had taught Grayfen that his use of it was limited. But he had learned some uses, and they would serve him well at Thorin.

Resting, he wished that he could truly sleep, but darkness would not come. Resting on their pedestal, the two red orbs gazed from the hut at the red panorama beyond, and as always, Grayfen saw what they saw. In bright red hues, the scene lay there before his removed eyes—the fortress of the dwarves.

Great, planted terraces climbed the mountainside like huge steps. At the back of the uppermost terrace stood Thorin Keep, a monolithic structure of stone blocks lined with balconies and flanked by the two lower sentinel towers. The third and highest tower, called the First Sentinel, stood on the slope above the keep, a tall, stone spire overlooking all of Thorin.

Below the lowest balconies were the great gates, and behind the gates—deep within the mountain itself, beyond the stores and trade stalls—was the gigantic cavern called Grand Gather. That much of Thorin, Grayfen knew by heart. What lay beyond was only conjecture, but there was no doubt that there were smelters, foundries, and forges. The clouds of steam that rose from the mountain peak far above and beyond Thorin Keep said that they were there, somewhere below.

No human knew exactly what lay beyond Grand Gather, but that would change soon. Grayfen would know, and it would all be his.

7

Night of the Last Moons

No human knew what lay beyond Grand Gather, nor had any ever guessed the extent of Thorin. For what lay beyond the big cavern was most of Thorin. The visible face of Thorin Keep, the flanked gates, even Grand Gather itself, were only the antechambers of a huge complex where most of the Calnar lived their lives without ever seeing the world outside their mountain—or having any desire to.

Deep within the mountain, beyond Grand Gather, was an entire city built around a huge, cylindrical shaft that was the heart of Thorin. At the bottom of the shaft were the smelters, where vast, glowing fires never cooled. Above, at the next level, were foundries set in a circular cavern whose center was the great shaft. Above that, another "ring" cavern had been delved, with a ceiling that sloped upward toward the center shaft. Here were the forges of Thorin, a hundred feet below the grand concourse which was the city's central district.

The great airshaft rose through this, up and up, ringed by delved caverns at regular intervals. Near the central shaft at each level were markets and stalls, shops and storage rooms, the quarters of wardens and marshals, and the manufactories where large implements and structures were assembled. Beyond, in each ring level, were the homes of the people of Thorin.

As the day of Balladine approached, Colin Stonetooth led an inspection tour of all central levels and nodded his approval. "We have always known that the day would come when Thorin would be threatened," he told his wardens. "It is for this reason that nothing beyond Grand Gather has ever been opened to outsiders. Our greatest strength lies not in what others know of us, but in what they don't know or even suspect."

Tera Sharn, following along with her brother Tolon, shook her head. "Those people out there, waiting for the Balladine . . . they haven't been enemies. They are our neighbors."

"Some of them," Willen Ironmaul corrected. "Have you looked out at the valley, Tera? I have. Never have I seen so many humans before. There are thousands of them, everywhere one looks. If every human in Golash and Chandera were there, it would not account for half that crowd."

"I have seen," Tolon Farsight breathed. "And I do not like what I have seen."

"But Chandera and Golash are there!" Tera persisted. "Their banners fly above their caravans as always. They are at the front of the assemblage."

"With many strangers just beyond," Bardion Ledge, the waste warden, reminded her.

"Their banners are there," Cullom Hammerstand agreed, "but where are Garr Lanfel and Riffin Two-Tree? They have not come to the gates to hail us, as they did in past years. Not even Bram Talien has come, seeking ale and news. It is strange, at least."

"Ominous," Tolon said darkly.

Tera Sharn lowered her eyes, still shaking her head. "I hope there is some . . . some harmless explanation."

"I hope so, too," Colin Stonetooth laid a gentle, powerful hand on his daughter's shoulder. "I pray to Reorx and all the covenant gods that tomorrow's dawn will bring nothing more than the opening of a fine Balladine."

"But until we know," Willen Ironmaul muttered, "we keep our tools to the left." The captain of guards turned to Wight Anvil's-Cap, delvemaster of Thorin. "Are the inner gates prepared, Delvemaster?"

"They're as ready as a thing can be that has never been tested," the old dwarf growled.

"Tested?" A thin smile spread the whiskers on Colin Stonetooth's face. "Wight, if you can devise a test for something that, once fallen, can never be raised again, I'd like to see it."

The delvemaster was not amused. "Reorx grant us that they are never needed." He shrugged. "Thorin would never be the same, ever again."

"Reorx grant that none of our . . . defenses . . . ever are needed," Colin agreed. "All the same, though, when the gates are opened tomorrow, I want everything in place, just as we have planned." He raised his head, listening. Here in the higher levels of Thorin-Heart, the great ventilator shaft carried sounds from the outside world. The Balladine drums, which had continued to sing since Handil's first stroke on his vibrar, rose in a crescendo of distant thunder, then stopped. The echoes died, and silence hung over the great peaks above Thorin.

"The moons have risen," Tera Sharn said. "The call is done. Tomorrow begins Balladine."

Beyond him, throngs of Calnar were coming and going on the public way. Almost everyone in sight carried a tool of one kind or another. Even the women and many of the children were armed.

Colin Stonetooth angled across the way to where a hand-wide trough, hewn from stone, ran for several feet along a wall between two buttresses. Clear water flowed through the trough, emerging from a three-inch hole in one pillar, disappearing into a similar hole in the next. The chieftain cupped his hands, dipped some water, and drank, then muttered an oath as a three-inch iron ball rolled out of the upper hole and along the trough, showering him with droplets of spray. "Rust!" he said. "I wish the tap warden could come up with some better way of maintaining his aqueducts."

Another of the iron balls emerged, rolled languidly down the trough, and disappeared into the lower pipe.

"They work, though," Tera Sharn pointed out. "The water is always clean."

* * * * *

At the same time that Colin Stonetooth and his advisors were inspecting the dwarven city's defenses, Handil the Drum and Jinna Rockreave stood atop Thorin Keep, watching the moons rise above the mountains. Wrapped in furs against the cold, they watched Solinari edge above the crag, and Jinna slipped her hand into Handil's. "Will nights always be so beautiful?" she murmured.

He smiled down at her. "I promise it, my love. Always."

"Oh? You can keep such promises, then, Handil Moonraiser?"

"Of course I can," he chuckled. "With you beside me, there is nothing I can't do. I'll show you." He pointed upward, toward the dark silhouette of the crag below the white moon. "Watch, just there. In a moment, I shall command a red moon to rise, to follow the white one into the sky."

"Silly," Jinna giggled. "Lunitari always rises there in this season."

"Just because it always does, that doesn't mean I didn't make it happen this time, just for you."

"I see." She snuggled closer beside him. "And for how long will you have these marvelous powers, Handil Cold-blade? Long enough to see us married, I hope?"

"Longer than that," he assured her. "It is my intention to please you, my love, for as long as we both shall live."

A red glow began to form above the dark crag, where wisps of steam-cloud danced in the mountain wind, rising from the hidden warmth of Thorin's great central shaft. Gently, Handil released his hand from hers, and unslung the Thunderer from his back. With deft hands he unwrapped the big vibrar, letting its polished surfaces catch the moonlight. He handed its wrap to the girl and removed his mallets from his belt.

"I began the song this year," he said. "It is only right that I help end it."

Slinging the great drum under his left arm, he raised his mallets over its forward head, hesitated for a moment, listening to the song of the drums atop the Sentinels and the nearby slopes, then lowered them in a quick, soft tattoo on the drumhead. Instantly, the vibrar came to life, its deep voice floating outward on the air to join the song of the drums, swelling in volume as he blended his rhythm into theirs. The air above Thorin Keep seemed to throb with the powerful voice of the Thunderer, and the Sentinel drums responded, their voices blending in vast harmonies. Further drums, here and there on the slopes, added counterpoints to the fabric of sound.

Gradually, as the red glow brightened beyond the crag, Handil increased his tempo and his volume. The very mountains seemed to come alive to the sound of singing drums, and as the red moon appeared, adding its light to the white light of Solinari, the vibrar and all the other drums swelled to a crescendo that crashed and echoed among the slopes of the Khalkists. With a final tattoo of salute, Handil ceased his playing and muted the big drum under his arm, in exact synchronization with the muting of all the others, all about.

The echoes died away, and there was only the sound of

the wind in the peaks.

Handil put away his mallets and replaced Thunderer's wrap. "It is done," he said, quietly. "With the sunrise tomorrow, it is Balladine."

"Balladine," Jinna echoed, turning to look westward, down the long rank of terraces. Out there, in the upper valley, hundreds of fires winked in the night—far more than she had ever seen before. "Balladine, and our wedding, yours and mine. Moonraiser mine, let it be all of that, and nothing more."

"Anything for you," he assured her. "For as long as we live."

* * * * *

Mistral Thrax did not hear the drums end their call. At three hundred and eighteen years, Mistral Thrax was at least half a century older than any other Calnar, and he needed his sleep. It was his custom—and had been for as long as anyone could remember—to put away his scrolls when the light from the sun-tunnels began to dim, pick up his crutch, hobble the thousand yards from his cubicle to the Den of Respite, and shuffle to a table in the back, where "Mistral's bench" always awaited him.

Sometimes it was Clamp Sandhaul who brought the old dwarf his half loaf, pot meat, and ale, and sometimes one of the young dwarves who tended table in the Den of Respite. Sometimes, when he was there, even Lobard Alekeg himself served the old lorespinner. But whoever did the serving, the service was always the same—a half loaf, pot meat, and a mug of cool ale. No one in Thorin could recall Mistral Thrax ever having anything else for his supper.

And always, at the lighting of lamps, Mistral Thrax finished his ale, put down a steel coin, and shuffled out of the place, leaning on his crutch, for the thousand-yard walk home to his bed.

Rarely did Mistral Thrax dream these days. Every dream a dwarf might dream, he had dreamed long since and put away. But on this night, his sleep was troubled, and the dreams came—dark, murky dreams that made him toss and fidget in his sleep. Troubling dreams . . . bits and pieces of scene and sound: metal ringing against metal, people running and screaming, stone walls dripping red with blood, blood as bright as the pair of disembodied red eyes that seemed to glow around and through each sequence. He turned, pulled his blanket tighter around him, and tried to push the dreams away.

They faded, then began again. In a chaos of confusion, people ran and scampered around him, turning to look back with frightened faces. Then there were bloody blades ringing against scarred, dented shields, and blood . . . blood, and bright, glowing red eyes that seemed to float tranquilly through the havoc, seeing everything. A muffled crash as huge stones dropped from a ceiling, thumping into place across a tunnel way with a finality that said they would never budge again. He seemed to be looking at the sealed tunnel, and those red eyes were beside him, seeing what he saw, then turning away.

And beyond the sealed tunnel . . . somehow he could see there, too, and what he saw was thunder—shattered stone crashing down, burying everything beneath it, dust rising from rubble—then darkness and silence, as still as a grave.

Mistral Thrax thrashed about in his sleep, frightened and troubled by the dream but unable to awaken. The dark nothingness was as ominous as the chaotic visions that had preceded it, and in the darkness was . . . something—a shadow, standing as though awaiting his notice, as though seeking permission to speak.

He tried to focus on the shadow, and it seemed to him that it was a dwarf—not Calnar, but a dwarf of some other kind. The dwarf was injured somehow, and bleeding from cuts, but seemed to ignore them. In his hand, glowing slightly, was a two-tined fishing spear.

"Speak," Mistral Thrax said—or dreamed saying. "Tell me what this means."

The injured dwarf gazed at him sadly from the shadows,

then said, "When the future lies in the past, Thorin will be Thoradin. The exile will seek Everbardin, and many will follow. The way to Kal-Thax is west, Mistral Thrax. South and west. You will know the way."

Mistral Thrax tried to speak, but the stuff of dreams held him silent. The suffering phantom seemed to come toward him and to touch his forehead gently with the tip of its double-tined spear. "One needs eyes to see what cannot be seen," it murmured. "Do not be blind to the one whose eyes are not his own."

The image faded, and abruptly Mistral Thrax was awake, shivering under his blankets. In the dimness of his stone-walled room he looked about, trying to understand. *Thorin will be Thoradin?* Thorin was home. Thorin-Ever-bardin—Dwarfhome, always. Home and hope were the same word to the Calnar, and the word was Thorin.

Why had the vision spoken of *Thoradin?* Thoradin was past tense—a sad, melancholy word. Thoradin—home that once was . . . lost home . . . lost hope.

Hope, though . . . hope was a thing of the future. Yet the vision had spoken of the future lying in the past . . . and of carrying the past to the future. *Those who seek Everbardin.* . . . What could it mean, to seek *always?*

The way to Kal-Thax is west.

Mistral Thrax sat up, rubbed his eyes, and hugged his blankets around him. He felt very cold. Just a dream, he told himself. It was only a dream. He could not have really seen Kitlin Fishtaker.

8
The Attack

The first day of Balladine, as always, was the day of solstice — the one day of the year when the sun at its zenith would shine directly down the great central shaft of Thorin. For the Calnar it was the holiest and most joyous day of the year, for a very practical reason. At noon of this day, every level of the city would be flooded with brilliant light, and at the very base of the city—the deeps of the great firewell around which the smelters roared—the living flame of Thorin would be renewed by the direct, focused light of the sun, magnified and amplified by huge lenses of clear, perfect quartz high above.

For this day, the paths to the smelters were blocked. No one would enter the great pit that surrounded the firewell, or even the shielded smelters above. The carbon shields were rolled back to receive the fireflash that was the original—and secret—reason the dwarves celebrated Balladine.

Starting the day before, the lowest levels had been evacuated as always. When fireflash occurred, the heat there—even in the recesses of the smelter level, far from the firewell—would be too intense to survive. But it was only for this day, and the mighty furnace that was Thorin's foundation—a pit of pure magma—would be rejuvenated for another year.

The principle and the annual phenomenon of the solstice fireflash were as old as Thorin itself. But not older. It was no ancient ogre-work that had built the central shaft with its levels, the foundry regions, and the firewell. Some believed that the firewell itself was a gift from Reorx, but all the rest was pure dwarven craft and lay far deeper into the mountain than the old ogres had ever thought of delving.

The pit at the bottom was the very substance of Thorin, and the Calnar's greatest secret. Coal, coke, and other firestones were used in the foundries and the forges, but it was the firewell itself that gave them steel, and the annual fireflash on solstice day fed the firewell.

As usual, the big gates of Thorin Keep would open shortly before noon. Knowing nothing of the inner workings of Thorin, or of the firewell and the solstice, visitors to Balladine took it as quaint dwarven tradition that the gates always opened when the sun was overhead. In fact, though, the reason was practical, as were most dwarven traditions. Not only the obvious gates below the keep, but actually every entrance to Thorin—most of which were cleverly hidden—was opened at the same time. During fireflash, it got hot in Thorin, and the opening of ways was to air the place out.

The morning sky blazed beyond Thorin Crag when sally ports in the great gates swung open, and a company of guards emerged to take positions on the highest terrace. When the guards were in their places, trumpeters appeared and formed ranks on each side of the portal. Troops of liveried dwarves followed them, carrying banners. When this array was assembled before Thorin Keep, the trumpeters raised their burnished horns and shrilled a five-note call.

Below Thorin, on the roadways flanking the lower terraces, the caravans of Golash and Chandera were already in motion, creeping upward like great, distorted serpents—long trains of wagons, carts, barrows, and travois, with their teams in harness and their attendants flanking them.

At the sound of the trumpets, a gold-and-black banner climbed its pylon atop Thorin Keep, followed by a white banner with a blue cross. Banners arose in unison at the lead of each approaching caravan—the banners of Chandera and Golash, each accompanied by the blue cross flag of trade.

It was a ceremony as old as Balladine. The Calnar showed their colors and the blue cross. Their visitors showed their own colors and the blue cross. Each thus declared this to be a time of peace, a time of goodwill, a time to gather and mingle and exchange the goods of commerce.

At the second terrace, the human caravans turned toward each other and spread out, and even before the carriers had stopped rolling there were people at work, erecting pavilions, rolling back wagon covers and setting up shop. On the first terrace, Cullom Hammerstand and his traders led a procession of heavily laden Calnar into the open and directed the erection of the pavilions of Thorin.

Hammers rang, buntings arose, and the morning air was alive with the sounds of preparation.

As was his custom, Cullom Hammerstand went with a pair of guards to the lip of the first terrace, fifteen feet above the beginning of the second. For a time, he wondered whether his counterparts would come to exchange greetings, then he saw them, issuing from the assembling stalls to right and left—Bram Talien, coming from the Chanderan caravan, and Barak Toth from the Golash ranks. Each was accompanied by large men Cullom did not remember seeing before . . . men who wore swords at their belts and shields on their backs, and who carried bows. It was far more than ceremonial weaponry. The trade warden glanced at his own guards, who had noticed the same thing. It was obvious that they did not like what they saw.

Cullom waved a troubled salute at Bram Talien, then at Barak Toth, and raised his eyes to look beyond. Usually Garr Lanfel, the Prince of Golash, would come himself. But today there was no sign of him. Cullom frowned, wondering. Many things were strange this year, and he shared the uneasy feeling his chieftain and the others had. Balladine seemed to be opening as usual—but he knew that something was wrong.

Behind Cullom, one of his guards hissed in surprise, and Cullom glanced around. The guard, a sturdy dwarf named Sand Sakor, was turned half away, looking here and there. He seemed puzzled. "Odd," he muttered.

"Is something wrong, Sand?"

The guard shook his head. "I guess not. I felt . . . or thought I felt . . . someone touch me."

"Who?"

"I guess I imagined it, Trademaster. It was as though someone brushed past me just then. But there's no one here."

Bram Talien approached with his armed escort and stopped just below the rim. The human trader's face looked pale, and he kept his eyes down.

"Greetings, Bram Talien," Cullom Hammerstand said. "Do you bring fine works to trade this Balladine?"

"The usual, Cullom Hammerstand." The human still kept his eyes averted, though the two men with him leered and grinned at the dwarves just above. Their manner was arrogant, bordering on insulting.

"Do you have any . . . ah . . . unusual commodities this year?" the dwarf pressed. "I see large wagons there, in your caravan."

"It is only coke, Trade Warden," Bram Talien said, stiffly.

"As usual." He raised his eyes, then, and there was a plea in them. "Firestone, for your forges . . . *as usual*."

Cullom Hammerstand hesitated. The man was telling him something, giving him a warning.

The Golash contingent arrived then, and the dwarf noticed that Barak Toth's guards were of the same cut as Bram's. These were not men of Golash, any more than those with the Chanderan were of Chandera.

Barak Toth looked as frightened as Bram Talien, and Cullom Hammerstand felt a rush of intuition. The human traders were not here freely. Their guards were not their escort, they were their captors. The Chanderan and the Golash traders were prisoners!

He sensed that his own guards, behind him, had come to the same conclusion, but they kept their silence while Cullom Hammerstand thought fast. He glanced at the sky, then spoke to the humans below the terrace rim. "You who come in peace are welcome here, as always. The gates will open soon, and Balladine will begin. You should hurry, now, and make *the usual* placements."

Those below looked puzzled. One of the Chanderan's guards—or captors—demanded, "And what usual placements might that be, din . . . ah, Sir Dwarf?"

"Why, the usual. It is customary for all women and children, and the infirm, to go down to the third terrace to await Balladine . . . ah, so that our providers can serve them refreshment there while the trading begins." He glanced at Bram Talien and Barak Toth meaningfully. "It is how we always do things here, is it not, my friends?"

"Of course." Bram Talien answered, with a look of gratitude in his eyes. "We always do that . . . for their comfort."

"Then hurry them away." The dwarf nodded. "We must open the gates very soon."

Cullom Hammerstand turned away, followed by his guards, and headed for the gates. He had heeded the veiled warning that Bram Talien tried to give him and had done all he could to repay the favor. Now he had to report to his chieftain.

At his side, one of his escorts glanced back, then leaned close to whisper, "Those people are hostages, I swear. The men with them are outlanders. There is going to be some trouble."

"I know," Cullom agreed.

The other escort asked, "Do you think they fell for that business about getting the innocents out of the way?"

"I don't know." Cullom shrugged. "It was the most I could do."

"Do you think they mean to attack Thorin?" the first one wondered. He seemed astonished at the idea.

"I am afraid they intend to try."

Passing through the dwarven pavilions, Cullom Hammerstand glanced at the sky again and quickened his pace. He wanted to tell Colin Stonetooth what he had learned, before . . .

But it was too late. Even as they rounded the last pavilion, the trumpets sounded again, and Colin Stonetooth emerged from Thorin Keep, mounted on his great horse and followed by the Ten. In perfect parade drill, the group rode out from the sally port, then spread and turned their mounts, and the chieftain raised his hand. Trumpets shrilled, drums thundered, and the huge gates swung wide.

Balladine had begun.

* * * * *

The gates of Thorin were massive twin doors of hardwood timber, bound with heavy iron strap, hinged at either side of a portal twenty feet across by sixteen high. As with most gates and doors of dwarven make, the panels were a few inches narrower at top than at bottom, and the huge iron hinges were canted slightly inward. It was dwarven logic that an open door is not a door at all, so doors in Thorin were designed to close by themselves. An open door, unstopped, would swing shut by simple gravity.

Opening the great gates, though, required effort. Big, wide-arm windlasses were mounted in stone alcoves at either side of the entry corridor, with cables extending through sockets to levers beyond. A dozen dwarves at each side turned the windlasses, and the doors swung slowly outward until they stood wide. Oddly, through the turning, the gate openers, one after another, glanced around, puzzled, as though someone had tapped them on the shoulder. But there was no one there.

When the gates were fully open, they held pressure on the windlasses while others ran out to drop heavy iron pawls through ring-sockets, and into slots in the stone below. With the gates thus secured open, the openers and the stoppers stood aside, awaiting the processional of traders and barterers who would follow the chieftain out onto the high terrace. As they lined up at their posts, the pawlmen appeared as puzzled as the windlass-turners had been. Each felt that someone had touched him, though there was no one to be seen.

Only one among them even imagined he had seen anything. That one, frowning in bafflement, had the impression that a pair of red eyes had looked at him in the instant he turned.

The draft issuing through the keep was warm and becoming warmer. Far beyond, in the depths of Thorin, the sun-flare was building as the sun above the mountain neared its midday solstice. All accesses to the smelter and foundry levels now were closed, but even in the grand concourse the heat would be intense for several minutes preceding fireflash and for an hour or so afterward.

That was why Balladine always began outside, on the terraces.

* * * * *

The lookouts on the Sentinels saw the attack forming, but the sound of their horns was drowned by the trumpets blaring on the first terrace, where Colin Stonetooth had raised and then sheathed his sword—the ceremony declaring Balladine to be open. Atop Thorin Keep, Tolon the Muse heard the horns, looked up, and followed the gestures of the lookouts. From left and right, bands of armed barbarians were issuing from the cover of the caravans, racing for the top terrace and the open gates. Tolon leaned far out over the parapet, shouting and pointing.

Colin Stonetooth had sheathed his sword and was turning his tall horse toward the gates when he saw Cullom Hammerstand and two others running toward him, waving their arms. In the clamor, he could not hear them, but when Cullom pointed upward Colin saw Tolon. He looked in the direction that his son was pointing and saw the attackers—hundreds of men, armed with swords and lances, racing toward him. As he saw them, an arrow flicked past, missing him by inches, and another clanged off the half-slung shield of Jerem Longslate, First of the Ten.

"Arms!" Colin roared, pulling his sword free again. An arrow caromed off his gauntlet and embedded itself in the nearest gate, where the procession of Calnar barterers had just appeared. Colin waved them back as the Ten closed around him, using themselves and their horses as a living shield for their chieftain.

It was an all-out attack, and though the Calnar had been prepared, the sudden ferocity of it caught them off guard. A dozen dwarves fell within seconds, from arrows and thrown lances, and many more followed as the two bands of humans raced among the trading stalls, slashing and cutting.

A squadron of attackers made directly for the chieftain and ran into fury as the Ten counterattacked. Within seconds, the area near the gate was strewn with dead and dying humans, who had never realized that a Calnar and his horse—especially those of the Company of Ten—are a formidable fighting unit. Instantly, it seemed that the Ten were everywhere—swords swinging, shields ringing, and iron-shod hooves slashing with deadly precision. The first humans to reach Colin Stonetooth's guard never had a chance.

"Back!" the chieftain called. "Retreat in order! Stoppers stand by the gates!"

He glanced around, deflecting an arrow with his shield, and stared.

At each gate, the pawlmen and the windlassmen beyond were on their knees, some even rolling on the ground, each clawing at his throat. Even in the turmoil, the sounds of their agony and the breaking of spines could be heard. Among them, for an instant, was just a suggestion of a pair of glowing red eyes.

The gates would not be closed. A magic had been done, and once open, the massive portal remained open.

Colin Stonetooth and those around him held their ground for a minute, and then for another, letting all the Calnar who could retreat through the gates. There were not many left to retreat. Cullom Hammerstand, trade warden of Thorin, lay dead almost at the feet of Jerem Longslate's war-horse. His escorts lay beside him. Everywhere the terrace was strewn with corpses, and many among them were dwarves.

Some came from within to try for the gate pawls and were cut down as they appeared.

Three armed humans erupted through the living shield of the Ten, aiming for Colin Stonetooth. Two of them died under the hooves of his great, gold-and-white horse, and the third was split from neck to waist by the chieftain's sword.

Everywhere along the thin line, attackers fell in their own blood, but for each one down, a dozen others charged forward. There were far too many of them to stop.

"Through the gates!" Colin Stonetooth ordered, and the Ten responded, backing their mounts, cutting and slashing, still protecting their chieftain in retreat.

Inside the great tunnel, Willen Ironmaul and three companies of guards reached the portal. They spread across the entrance in phalanx, and the chieftain and the Ten backed through their ranks, still fighting. Those humans pressing them suddenly found themselves confronted by dwarves on foot, armed with javelins, swords, and axes—a solid wall of shields, with mayhem flicking forth among them. The charge was stopped, but only for a moment. Beyond the shrieking, falling men were hundreds more, pressing to attack.

Grudgingly, the dwarves of Calnar retreated into their gaping shelter with its useless gates, and a torrent of howling barbarians poured in after them.

9

Battle of the Keep

The first invaders past the gates charged into the dimness of the great tunnel below Thorin Keep, then hesitated, slowing and searching as others piled in behind them. "Where are they?" men shouted. "Where did they go?"

Where moments before there had been ranks of slowly retreating dwarves, now there was no one. The dwarves had simply disappeared. But the confusion was only momentary. Among the marauders were men who had been within Thorin—agents of Grayfen who had lived among the neighboring tribes and had attended previous Balladines. They knew the ways of the fortress.

As men milled around in the subterranean roadway, peering at side tunnels and rising stairways cut into the stone, Sith Kilane and Bome Tolly pushed forward to take command. Kilane pointed down-tunnel with a bloody sword. "That way lies their arena, called Grand Gather. The keep is above us, up those stairs. We will split up here. Some of you follow Bome Tolly to Grand Gather. The rest come with me, up to the keep."

Led by men who knew the way, the hordes divided and went in pursuit of the Calnar. Some, out on the terraces and around the gates, paused to loot the bodies of the dead, but most swarmed around and into the underground city. Many among them had waited years for just such a chance—to conquer and loot the fabled treasures of Thorin. Howling with bloodlust, their war cries ringing through the corridors and halls of Thorin Keep, those following Sith Kilane thronged onto the twin spiral stairways and raced upward, spreading and searching at each level.

Steel rang upon steel, and Thorin Keep echoed with the sounds of combat as human raiders encountered companies of dwarven guards at each level. The stairways wound upward, parallel spirals of hewn steps bending around monolithic pillars of dressed stone which rose within a vaultlike shaft. Everywhere they looked, the invaders saw more and more finery—tapestries gracing tiled walls, furnishings of the finest craft, bolts and swaths of exquisite cloth—and the higher they climbed the finer were the treasures displayed. The humans had thought the dwarves to be wealthy. Now their eyes glowed at the very richness of what they saw.

Guards met them at each level, fought and retreated, heavily outnumbered. Kilane noticed vaguely that his followers were fewer than they had been. Many had stopped at each level, anxious to steal what they could before someone else beat them to it.

It was fewer than a hundred invaders who took the rising stairs toward the highest level of the keep. Kilane halted them halfway up, raising a hand for silence. Somewhere nearby were faint rumblings that seemed to come from within the very stones.

"What is that?" someone behind him snapped. "It sounds like winches!"

Kilane raised his hand again, hushing them, trying to identify the sound. It did sound like winches being operated—a low, continual rumbling sound with a metallic, rattling undertone. Like cables on pulleys. He didn't know what it was, though the noise from below had decreased, and he heard it clearly now. For a moment longer, the sound continued. Then it stopped, and an eerie stillness came over the vertical shaft with its two stairways.

In the silence, another sound grew. Far below, metal grated against stone, a series of sharp, hissing noises, each ending in a final-sounding thud. It seemed to go on and on, then ended with a heavy, metallic thump that echoed up the shaft. Around and behind Kilane, men gazed about in confusion. A dozen or so on the second stairway crowded the rim of the stairs, peering downward, and a man screamed as he lost his balance and fell, disappearing into the gloom below. A long moment passed, then the rest heard him land—not with a thud, as on the stone floor of the entry tunnel, but with a ringing, rattling thump, followed by clatters of small things falling.

From somewhere below, voices came: "Gods! That one is done for!" "What is that down there? What did he hit?"

And from farther down: "They've closed the shaft! Look at that, will you? We're sealed off in here! There are iron bars clear across, wall to wall. The whole stairshaft is blocked off at the second level!"

Sith Kilane swore under his breath. It had been expected that the dwarves might have some surprises, but to slide cage bars across the whole shaft?

"We'll have to go on," he told those behind him. "The dwarves are just ahead. They've sealed themselves in here with us. Find them! We'll make them let us out!"

With anger added to their energies, the horde of humans sped upward, a spiraling mass of armed men racing around twin pillars of stone, and came out on the highest enclosed level of Thorin Keep. Overhead, skylights flooded the wide hall and the corridors beyond with brilliant light.

And they were alone. There wasn't a dwarf in sight, anywhere. The invaders spread out to search. Sith Kilane stalked the bright halls in a fury. All the way up Thorin Keep, there had been dwarves ahead of them. They had seen them, had clashed with their rear guards. They had been in hot pursuit. There had been dozens of dwarves . . . many dozens of them. But now they were just . . . gone.

"There must be secret passages!" Kilane shouted. "Find them!"

Long minutes passed in frantic search, then one of the men swept aside a tapestry on the back wall of one of the stair pillars and gawked at what he saw there. He shouted, and others came to look. It was a doorway, cut into the stone of the huge pillar. A small doorway—to humans—less than six feet high and about four feet wide. The closed door was of finely finished wood, highly ornamented.

Men pushed at the door, pried at its edges, and strained against it, but it would not move.

"Stand back!" Sith Kilane ordered. Raising his bloodstained sword in both hands, he swung downward at the center of the door. The blade struck and broke. The impact made Kilane's teeth rattle. With the others, he peered at the gouge in the wood where his sword had hit it.

The wood was a veneer. Beneath its decorative surface, the door was solid metal.

* * * * *

When the humans first entered the stairways of the keep, Tolon the Muse had made up his mind—the invaders might get in, but none of them would ever get out alive if he could manage it. With guards fighting delaying battles at each level, Tolon rushed to get all the dwarves in the keep to the highest level, where the lift-stages opened. The human mob was still far down the stairs when Tolon assembled his survivors and opened the lift doors.

He held position there, on the upper level of the keep, while people streamed past him, entering the lifts nine at a time, packing the suspended stages one after another for their trip downward through the hollow pillars surrounded by the stairs.

Many of them were injured. At the lower levels the guards had fought, had held the stairhead long enough for other dwarves to stream upward ahead of the invaders. Some had died, and many were bleeding. Tolon had no idea how many Calnar had been in the keep when the attack came, but he guessed there were more than a hundred. Yet, when the last of them arrived in the upper hall, and he herded them toward the cable-lift, he counted fewer than fifty who had made it to the top. Grieving and dark-browed with a smoldering anger, the second son of Colin Stonetooth saw the last of them into the lift stages and shared the next stage with two injured guards. He sealed the portal behind him as he stepped onto the platform. Could the humans break through that door, into the lifts? He didn't know. It depended upon the tools they could find. But it would not be easy.

In the meantime, he had a surprise for them.

Normally, only Colin Stonetooth himself could have ordered the keep sealed and had his orders obeyed. But the chieftain was not here, and looking at the fierce scowls of the armed Calnar with him—the remnants of an entire company of keep guards—he knew that they would follow his plan.

How many of the invading humans were in the keep? There was no way of knowing. Hundreds, probably. But it didn't matter. Tolon had made up his mind that those who were there—who had invaded the very home of the leaders of the Calnar—were not going to leave.

Tolon did not know where the rest of his family was now. He had seen his father, retreating with the Ten on the first terrace, making for the gates. The chieftain must be inside now, maybe in Grand Gather or beyond. He had last seen Handil on his way to Grand Gather, carrying his drum as always, with Jinna Rockreave beside him. Cale Greeneye, of course, was gone—off on some adventure of his own choosing, with the pretext of seeking a lost patrol—and Tera Sharn had been on her way to the main concourse earlier in the day. Tolon wished them all well and muttered a prayer to Reorx for their safety as he lent a hand at the stage winches, inching the endless belt of the lift downward.

Of the family of Colin Stonetooth, only Tolon was present here, where human barbarians streamed upward through the keep. For here and now, Tolon the Muse would take charge of defenses.

"All able guards off at second level!" he called, his voice carrying downward to the stages below. "We'll make for the winch chamber."

Beside him, one of the guards grinned darkly. He had been thinking the same thing himself.

Not in living memory had the keep been sealed, but the mechanisms were sleek and ready. It was typical of the Calnar, with their loathing of rust and tarnish, that all metal artifacts in Thorin were kept in good repair. This included the racks of iron bars—some of them thirty feet long—in the winch chamber at second level, and the two-inch-wide holes drilled into the stone of the frontal wall at eight-inch intervals. Beyond the wall was the keep's big stairshaft, and in its opposite wall, or in the stair pillars themselves, were sockets—one for each hole in the frontal wall.

Working swiftly, Tolon Farsight and ten sturdy dwarven guards lifted the long bars, fed them through their sleeve holes, and drove them home. Beyond the stone, each bar emerged into the stairshaft, slid across, and thumped into its socket. It took them less than two minutes to put all of the bars in place. Dimly, from beyond the stone, they heard a scream, and some of the bars rattled in their sockets.

With the bars in place, the eleven lifted a great, hewn timber and dropped it into iron stays at each end of the line of sockets. The mass of it completely covered the holes, sealing off the bars beyond. Now nothing more than eight inches wide was going anywhere past the second level of Thorin Keep.

With that done, Tolon led his guards back to the lift shaft, where his other charges—fewer than forty dwarves from the keep, mostly women and wounded guards—waited in the shadows.

From far above, they could hear the sounds of humans at the top level, beating on the steel door there, trying to force it open.

"I'm glad Handil isn't here to see this," Tolon muttered, staring up the great shaft with its endless, vertical row of lift stages. "This lift is his pride and joy. Next to that vibrar of his, it's the best thing he ever invented."

From a cabinet at the base of the shaft, they took tools—prybars and wrenches—and began dismantling the lift belt.

The last coupling had just been pulled when they heard the upper door, far above, crash open and the shouts of humans ringing down the shaft. By sound alone, they could almost see the humans up there, crowding into the chamber, beginning to haul on the pulley cables to descend.

Tolon pointed at the giant pulley wheels on each side of the lift base. "Spring the cables," he said.

Guards on each side hefted prybars and slipped them under the rims of the wheels.

"Everybody stand back," Tolon said. The little crowd shuffled away, into the shadows beyond the lift port.

The guards secured their prybars, heaved at them, and the cables jumped from their tracks on the wheels. The guards threw themselves back, one falling and rolling, as pandemonium erupted above. Abruptly the lift shaft was a chaos of falling debris—uncoupled stages slamming down, crushing the stages below, loose cable whirring and slapping in the confines of the shaft . . . and piercing screams. As the dust settled, Tolon tried to make out how many of the invaders had come down with the lift debris.

But it was impossible to tell for sure. There wasn't enough left of the men to sort out the pieces.

"So far," Tolon the Muse muttered, "so good."

The keep was sealed, and the humans within it would wait. With the lifts destroyed, there was nowhere for them to go.

Tolon led his little band into a side tunnel and sealed its entrance behind them. It was only a service way, a maintenance tunnel for the elaborate water system that supplied this part of Thorin. But it led to where he wanted to go.

A hundred yards of dimness, and the dwarves emerged into a narrow, ill-lighted cavern where rough wooden shelves lined the walls. Tools of all sorts were on the shelves, and Tolon easily found what he was looking for. There were hammers, delvers' shields, and slings. And in a corner was a rack of three-inch iron balls. The heavy balls were intended for aqueduct cleaning, but Tolon had another use in mind. Every tool had a left side.

Leaving his injured in the hidden cavern with some of the women to care for them, Tolon and his guards made packs of sacking and filled them with cleaning balls. Each took a pack, a pair of web slings, a hammer, and a shield, and Tolon led them up a dark, winding tunnel that opened into a maze of windshafts. He looked back and found he had more help than he had expected. Fully a dozen of the dwarven women had armed themselves as the guards had and followed along.

Tolon nodded his approval. "Everybody pick a shaft," he told them. "Follow it to its end, and feel free to kill any human you see."

Some of the shafts led to the upper walls of Grand Gather, some to the vents of the first concourse, and some to the intakes on the outer wall of the keep. The airshafts would be almost impossible for a human to negotiate, but to the Calnar they were easy. The vents—always high above the floor beyond—would make fine ambush holes, and there wasn't a dwarf in Thorin who was not deadly accurate with a sling.

Aqueduct cleaners! The ubiquitous three-inch iron balls would be lethal weapons when propelled by delvers' slings. It was, however, unfortunate that one of the first humans killed by an iron ball that day—out on the first terrace—was Bram Talien of Chandera. The trader had just put a sword through the gullet of one of his captors and was trying to get back to his family when the ball smashed his skull. Shena Brightiron, whose sling propelled the missile, was a young Calnar maiden whose home was deep within Thorin, near the markets. In her entire life, she had seen only two or three humans, and to her they all looked alike.

They were the enemy.

10

Bloody Solstice

Reinforced by members of Willen Ironmaul's elite guard, Colin Stonetooth and the Ten held the human onslaught at the gates for long minutes, while the lower keep households, pavilion workers, and a hundred others who had survived the first rush fled toward Grand Gather and the city beyond. Then with the corridor behind them clear, the chieftain and his fighters wheeled and raced away, past the stairways to the keep, into the winding, rising corridor that led to Grand Gather. Behind them, growing numbers of invaders stumbled over their own dead at Thorin's gaping portal.

It would take the humans' eyes moments to adjust from the sunlight beyond the gates to the dimness within, and

Colin needed that time to spring his next defense. There was nothing he or his warriors could do about the keep, except to hope that those within could hold out long enough to escape. Tolon was there . . . Tolon with his dark moods and his devious mind. He had been atop the keep when the attack began and had not emerged with the refugees.

Colin prayed to Reorx for his second son, at the same time baring his teeth at thoughts of the sort of havoc "Tolon the Muse" might dream up for those humans unfortunate enough to face him.

He did not know where Handil was, or Tera Sharn. Somewhere in the city, he hoped, away from the invaders. The chieftain feared for them. Tera—thoughtful, logical Tera! Faced with murderous enemies, Tera might try to reason with them. It would be her way. He understood well the reliance upon reason and logic that guided his daughter. It was her legacy from himself, and now he cursed the tendency. Tolon had been right. Colin should not have counted on reason and logic. Because he trusted his friends among the humans, reason had told him to trust humans. He had been wrong, and now Thorin was paying the price.

And Handil! Where was Handil? Colin did not doubt his oldest son's courage, or his ferocity in battle. Handil was a fighter, for all of his indifference to rule. But what could one do against invaders, with a drum?

Within moments, the humans would be after them, and Colin Stonetooth cursed his own stubborn naivete as he spurred his horse on. There had been warnings. There had been ample warnings. But he had chosen to believe that Balladine would be respected. Pools of lensed daylight showed the path ahead, where the entry to Grand Gather was now in sight at the end of the big, rising tunnel.

The tunnel ahead was empty, except for a company of Willen's guards at the arena portal. Just beyond, large, square shapes, surrounded by workers, were slowly moved. Those who had made it past the keep would be there now, and Willen would be setting his trap for the pursuers. It had seemed an excessive thing when they had first discussed it—eight-foot cubes of stone on low rollers, in place to block the portal. Now Colin realized that it would not be enough. The stones would delay the humans, but not stop them. The invaders were simply too many to be held.

Colin glanced back for the first time since passing the keep. Jerem Longslate rode just behind, his bearded face grim beneath his polished helm, and behind him came the Ten.

But they were no longer ten. At a glance, Colin saw that Chock Render and Balam Axethrow were missing. They were dead, then. Only death could separate any member of the Ten from his chieftain.

Abruptly, the chieftain's tall horse shied and spun half around to lash out with its rear hooves. Colin clung to his saddle and raised his blade, peering around.

There was no one there, just himself and his escort. But the other horses were excited, too, as though they could see an enemy that their riders could not. Colin gave his mount its head and muttered, "Schoen, attack!"

The big horse turned, reared, and lashed out with front hooves, slashing at empty air, its ears laid back. The scream of its battle cry echoed from stone walls, and beneath the sound was another, like scurrying footsteps . . . like someone scooting away, trying to escape the flailing hooves. And for an instant, two bright orbs, like glowing eyes, turning away. Then there was nothing. Schoen pranced and bristled, the golden hide beneath his white mane quivering. But whatever the horse had seen, or thought it saw, was gone.

"Did you see anyone here?" Colin asked. "Or anything?"

"No, Sire," Jerem Longslate said, as the others shook their heads. "The horses did, though."

Behind them, the sounds of pursuit grew. The invaders were in the tunnel, and some were now in sight, rounding the bend a hundred yards back—a howling, kill-crazed torrent of humans filling the big space from wall to wall. There were hundreds of them, and more behind.

"To Grand Gather," Colin rasped. He spurred Schoen, and the horses thundered to the portal, past the guards there and into the vaulted space of the great assembly hall. Behind them, guards' slings whistled. There were cries from the charging human mob as thrown missiles scored hits there. Colin Stonetooth drew rein and wheeled, pointing with his bloody sword. "The stones will not hold them! There are too many! Willen!"

Instantly, Willen Ironmaul was there, beside his leader's horse. "Aye, Sire!"

"Turn the stones, Willen. Face the rollers outward."

A lethal grin spread across the big dwarf's face. Willen understood instantly, and the idea pleased him. "Aye, Sire. Workers! To your prys! Turn the stones!"

Spotting Frost Steelbit among the milling crowds nearby, Colin shouted, "Frost! Take charge of the wounded and the weak! Get them out of here, into the concourse. We'll make a stand there, at the inner gate!" He swung down, and Jerem Longslate and the others also dismounted. The horses were led away, toward the far portal of Grand Gather and the city beyond. There would be no further need of horses now. What must be done would be done afoot.

Wight Anvil's-Cap, the old delvemaster, appeared at Colin's side. "Has it come to that, then? Must we close the inner gate?"

"I am afraid we have no choice," Colin rasped. "This is no barbarian attack. It's an invasion. Nothing less will keep those people out of Thorin."

"Reorx help us," the delvemaster muttered. "No one knows whether that thing will even work. It has never been tried."

"I know that, Wight. Pray that it does, because if it fails, we'll be fighting that mob in the streets of Thorin itself." He turned away, toward the portal. The second of the two huge blocks of stone was just being steadied in place, pointing outward. Beyond, the howling of the human tide was deafening. Arrows were flicking through the opening, between and around the stones. "Willen, is it ready?"

"Ready, Sire."

"Then let them go and close these doors."

At Willen Ironmaul's command, burly dwarves stooped behind the stones, heaved at prybars, and the stones moved. For an instant they seemed to hang suspended in the portal, then they pitched outward and began to roll down the corridor beyond, their rollers rumbling as they picked up speed, twin juggernauts bearing down on the packed masses of humans charging upward.

"Close and bar those doors," Colin ordered. The oaken gates slammed, dimming the screams from beyond, where tons of polished stone paved trails of carnage through the human ranks. Colin Stonetooth didn't stop to listen. "Retreat!" he shouted. "To the inner gate!"

By the hundreds dwarves ran, around and across Grand Gather's arena, some stopping to help the wounded littering the area. The barrage of arrows from the invaders had done damage. Everywhere, people were down. Abruptly, Colin Stonetooth spotted Handil in the crowd, coming toward him against the flow, carrying his drum. Jinna Rockreave was with him, her eyes wide and a web sling clasped in her small fingers.

"I heard, Father," Handil said. "In the city they say a thousand humans have attacked us."

"A thousand?" Colin shook his head. "Many thousands, I'd say. Too many to fight off. Thorin must be sealed." He turned as a resounding crash echoed through the great chamber. The doors from the keep tunnel had burst open, and wild-eyed, howling humans were pouring through. "To the inner gates!" he snapped. "Hurry."

An arrow whisked past his head and sank into the back of a fleeing stone-mover. Other arrows followed, and Jerem Longslate and his men pressed around the chieftain, shielding him. One of them gasped and fell, a shaft protruding from his exposed side. He had used his shield for the chieftain, not for himself.

"Come, Sire!" Jerem Longslate urged. "There is no time!"

"Come on!" Colin shouted at Handil as the guards hurried him away, their shields at his back.

Handil turned and hesitated. Beside him, Jinna Rockreave spun her sling and released it. The stone—the size of a fist—sang across the arena and took a bearded man full in the face. He fell backward, carrying others with him.

"Jinna, come on!" Handil shouted.

"All right," the girl nodded. "Just one more . . ." And then she was on her back on the stone floor, an arrow standing from her breast.

Handil dropped to his knees beside her. "Jinna!"

At the touch of his hands she shuddered and gasped. "Don't . . . don't move me, Handil. The pain . . ."

With a cry of agony, Handil the Drum crouched over his beloved and raised stricken eyes toward the far portal. His father was there, beckoning to him, and workers were chipping out the stone at each side, where the stops of the inner gate were concealed.

"Handil," Jinna whispered, "go now. Leave me. You must. The humans . . ." Gasping with pain, she held out her hand and dropped something into his.

Tears misted his eyes as he saw what it was—an exquisite ring, embedded and twined in the elven style. The gift from Cale Greeneye. Arrows whisked around him, and a thrown axe hummed past his head as he slipped the ring on, then drew its mate from his belt and placed it carefully on Jinna's finger.

"For as long as we live," he murmured, gazing into her stricken eyes, seeing the blood that seeped from her nose and mouth. "For as long as we live."

Humans were rushing toward him now, weapons raised for the kill. In the distance he heard his father's voice, calling his name, and then a crash like thunder. He glanced around. Where there had been a portal—had always been a portal, opening onto the great concourse of Thorin—now was solid stone, twenty feet thick. The inner gate had worked. Thorin was safe behind a wall of stone that no human could penetrate.

Jinna no longer moved, and he realized that she had stopped breathing. Distractedly, barely aware of the howling tide of murderous humans sweeping down on him, Handil the Drum stood, swung his vibrar under his arm, and stripped away its wraps. An arrow buried itself in his thigh as he drew forth his mallets, but he hardly felt it.

The nearest humans were only yards away now, rushing at him, but when he turned to them, they slowed, stunned at what they saw in his eyes. In that instant, a few of them may have realized that they were looking at their own deaths. Unhurriedly, standing over the body of his beloved, Handil raised his mallets and brought them down, and the Thunderer began to sing.

No Call to Balladine was this, no glad song of the high peaks. The rhythm of the big vibrar was a dirge, and it filled the great hall of Grand Gather with sound so intense that humans reeled back from it, many dropping their weapons to clap hands to their ears.

Another arrow struck Handil, and then another, but they meant nothing to him. The mallets increased their tempo, and the vibrar thundered.

And all around—above where the sun-tunnelled ceiling arched away, around every wall and in every rise and ramp of Grand Gather—hewn stone took up the vibrations and began to disintegrate. The cavern roared and bellowed, and huge chunks of broken stone showered down from above, crushing everyone and everything beneath them. An entire sun-tunnel slipped free of its collar somewhere and plummeted to the arena floor, shattering into bright, piercing shards which flew in all directions. Humans milled and screamed, many turning back the way they had come. But the entryway had collapsed, and there was nowhere to go.

A raging human, crazed by fear, ran at Handil with a

raised sword and impaled himself upon the lance of another human trying to get away. An axe struck Handil in the hip, and he fell, then raised himself on one knee, never missing a beat.

The song of the vibrar built upon itself like contained thunders rolling back and back, echoes becoming great choruses of echoes.

"As long as we live," Handil the Drum muttered to himself, building his beat to a crescendo. And the entire roof of Grand Gather collapsed inward, millions of tons of cold stone filling and forever sealing what was now only a silent tomb.

Clouds of dust and debris rose from the mountainside above Thorin Keep as a chasm opened there. The great monolith called First Sentinel, standing just at the edge of the collapse, teetered and swayed, then disintegrated and fell into the hole, raising more clouds of stone-dust.

And above it all the sun of Krynn approached the zenith of its solstice day.

* * * * *

Just as no human had ever guessed the magnitude of Thorin, neither had any human ever known—or even suspected—about the inner gates. Most of the Calnar themselves were only vaguely aware that, suspended unseen in a hall-sized slot above the east portal of Grand Gather, was a gigantic hanging wall of solid granite held in place by cable-braced props. Old Mistral Thrax might have remembered the tremendous task of creating this massive deadfall, had he ever had cause to think about it, but few others beyond the leaders of the Calnar had known it was there. It was plastered over and unseen, and had never been used because once released it was unlikely that it could ever be raised again.

But now, in their last moments, the invaders in Grand Gather had learned of it. And now all those beyond, in Thorin proper, knew of it. Where had stood the door to

Grand Gather, now was an impenetrable wall. As Wight Anvil's-Cap had said, Thorin would never again be the same. The keep, the outer tunnels, even Grand Gather, had always been a facade. Now they—or what was left of them—were cut off forever from the city beneath the crag.

The Calnar had removed themselves from invasion by sealing the only entry that any but themselves knew about. Within Thorin now were only Calnar—except one. Raging and unseen, one walked among them who was human . . . or had once been human, before encountering a dwarf imbued with wild magic from the Graystone itself.

Grayfen stalked the great concourse of Thorin, unseen as long as he shielded his eyes. Only he, of all the human forces, had got past the inner gate before it came crashing down, and the rage that boiled within him was a burning, insane fire. The dinks had tricked them! Long years of planning and intrigue had come to nothing. He was in Thorin, but not as a conqueror. He was a shadow among those he hated most, trapped with no way out.

The glowing orbs that were his only eyes burned in his head, their presence a pounding pain that never relented. He longed to remove them, even for a few minutes, but without them his magic would not work, and he would be seen and killed.

In his rage he struck out around him. A dozen times in as many minutes he touched some passing dwarf, then did the magic he had learned and watched, unseen, as the dwarf died in agony, clawing at its throat.

But that only tired him, and did no good. He could not kill them all.

The magic! He knew there was more that it would do, more than he had learned. Too often, when he had tried to devise spells, they had turned on him with painful results. Yet now, in his rage, he knew there was a thing he could do, and the magic itself seemed to tell him how. Revenge! The magic whispered it. Revenge upon Colin Stonetooth, whose fault it was that he was trapped.

The rage boiled and coalesced within him and became

arcane words that molded themselves to his tongue. "*In morit deis Calnaris*," he whispered. "*Refeist ot atium dactas ot destis!*"

As though the magic itself instructed him, he spoke the spell and knew what it meant. To the leader of the dwarves, exile. To his seed, death!

It was all he could do. Yet, somewhere ahead must lie the fabulous treasure that everyone knew the dwarves had. The subterranean city was far bigger than he had suspected, and far brighter. The radiance of the place seemed to increase with each passing second, and to eyes that could not close, that could never not see, it was intensely painful. And the place was incredibly hot. He felt as though he were in a furnace. Despite the pain, he went toward the brightness. That must be where the treasure was.

Most of the dwarves he saw now were hurrying in the other direction, and as he emerged into a great, circular chamber filled with blinding light, the only other creature there was a hobbling, ancient-looking dwarf with a crutch, who glanced his way and then stopped to stare. Grayfen shielded his eyes and went on. Just ahead, in the center of the chamber, stood a shaft of brilliant light. It seemed to come out of the floor, or from above, and where it stood the floor ended at a precipitous pit.

The treasure, he thought. The treasure of the dinks! It must be there! Agonized by brilliant light, tortured by intense heat, Grayfen approached to the very lip of the pit and heard a sound. He turned to see the old dwarf with the crutch directly behind him.

"The dream was real," the ancient creature hissed. "You are the one Fishtaker showed me. You are the enemy!"

"You see me?" Grayfen gasped.

"As clearly as though you were alive," the dwarf said.

"I *am* alive," Grayfen snapped, starting to raise his hand. "It is you who are . . ."

The motion was never completed. More quickly than the man could have believed, the old dwarf raised his crutch and heaved it like a javelin. The foot of it thudded into the mage's belly with such force that it doubled him over. Hard old hands clawed at his face, and suddenly he was blind. His eyes were gone, clenched in the dwarf's hands.

The mage lashed out, searching, and took one step back . . . into searing nothingness. His scream as he disappeared into the shaft of light was drowned by a hum of vibrance as the sun of Krynn reached zenith above the central light-shaft of Thorin, and fireflash occurred—the fireflash of Balladine.

Mistral Thrax threw himself aside, face down, his smoking cloak shielding him from the instant of searing heat. When he got to his feet again, staggering, most of his beard was burned away, his clothing smoldered, and he felt as though he were one solid blister. But he opened his hands and stared at what they held. The eyes of Grayfen had been red, glowing orbs. Now in the old hands of Mistral Thrax lay a pair of black spheres, like marbles made of jet. But beneath them, on his palms, were red marks—like drawings of a fishing spear, done in glowing red.

Staggering, he picked up his crutch and turned away, not looking back at the shaft of brilliance that hummed happily now from mountaintop to the magma pit below.

He had things to do. First, a mug of cold ale at Lobard's, then he must find Colin Stonetooth and tell him of the portent of his dream—of seeking Everbardin, and of Kal-Thax being to the west.

11
The Exiles

Snowcaps lay heavy upon the Khalkist peaks when Colin Stonetooth led his procession down from the warren ports and
around the towering bulk of the mountain to the devas-
tated slopes that once had been the proud face of Thorin.
Ogres looked down from the heights as the long line
passed below, and growled impatiently. But no ogre cared
to confront such a force as this—more than a thousand
determined dwarves, some mounted on the great Calnar
horses and some afoot, but all heavily armed and packed
for travel.

Not in even the longest memory had there been such a
sight, anywhere on Krynn. Humans migrated constantly—
small, nomadic bands roaming here and there—as did

many of the other races. But a migration of dwarves was a thing none of them had ever seen before, and even the ogres in the cold heights shook their heads in wonder at the sight of a tribe of dwarves on the move.

On the slope above the sinkhole that had once been the mountain roof of Grand Gather, Colin Stonetooth halted them for a last look at the place that had been their home for as long as they could remember. Where once had been clean, wind-shaped mountainside, now there was the collapsed pit, its sides a deep cone of rockslide leading to the entombed depths below. Beyond, at the lower end of the hole, was the stub of the First Sentinel, a broken shaft of stone standing in its own rubble. And farther down, a stark silhouette against the umbers and golds of the valleys below, was the roof of the keep, still littered with the drying bones of human savages . . . mute testimony to the silent death within.

The forces of Sith Kilane—at least a few of them—had lasted for weeks, imprisoned in the keep. Some had made it to the roof, to be picked off by dwarven marksmen with slings. Some had shouted and pleaded from the balconies until sling-stones or javelins brought them down, and some—after days of suffering—had jumped. The remainder of the ill-fated invasion forces had died of thirst or starvation, their corpses still within, ignored by the dwarves. The keep remained sealed, and maybe it always would.

Above Thorin, Colin Stonetooth took a last, sad look out over the lands he had ruled, then leaned from his saddle to clasp the hard hand of his second son, Tolon Farsight. "You are Chieftain of the Calnar now," he said, "by your own choice and the choice of those who remain here with you. I wish you hot forges and good trade."

"And to you, Father." Tolon nodded. "Wherever the roads take you. May you find your Kal-Thax, and may the majesty of the Calnar make of it a fine nation."

"Not Calnar," Colin muttered, looking away. "The Calnar are of Thorin. You are the Calnar now. We will take another name, for other places."

"Oh? What name?"

"What our human neighbors—when they were neighbors—called us, because of where we lived. *The Highest*. We will take that name with us, Tolon. From this day, those of us who seek Kal-Thax are the Hylar."

"Hylar." Tolon thought it over and nodded. "A good name. May it serve you well, Father. May you find the way."

Colin tipped his head, indicating Cale Greeneye, who sat nearby in the saddle of his great horse, Piquin. Cale and his scouts had returned a few days after the battle of Thorin. They had returned to a place very different from the Thorin they left.

"Your brother will lead us safely to the plains," Colin told Tolon. "He has scouted that far and will scout for us beyond, as we travel. Ah, don't look so downcast!" The old chieftain shook his head. "You know I must make this journey, my son. There is no place here for a former chieftain, and now it is your turn. Guide your people well and wisely."

"All because of an old dwarf's dream," Tolon muttered.

"Not only that," Colin said. "I failed in my judgement. I trusted friends and was blind to enemies. You were right, Tolon, and I was wrong. A chieftain cannot fail his people to such an extreme and remain chieftain. The laws apply to all, and the law decrees exile. I choose to make my exile a quest for prophesy, and those who follow me do so of their own free will.

"Those of us who go from here, Tolon," the old chief added, "have lost Everbardin in Thorin. We must find it elsewhere, if we find it at all." Once more he clasped Tolon's hand, then reined Schoen around and trotted away, downhill toward the far valleys and the Suncradles which rose beyond. With a wave at Tolon, Cale Greeneye reined after him, followed by Jerem Longslate and the Ten, which included several new members who had been chosen to replace the brave dwarves who had died defending their chieftain.

Willen Ironmaul directed his guard companies to the flanks, then paused to gaze at Tolon the Muse. "Consider Sheen Barbit for your guard captain, Tolon," he suggested. "He is the best of those who choose to remain. Will you try to reopen trade with Golash and Chandera?"

"Trade, yes," Tolon said. "But not Balladine. The Calnar will never again forget that humans are savages, no matter how friendly they appear."

"Live long and well, Tolon Farsight," Willen said, formally, then wheeled away.

Beside him, on her own mount, Tera Sharn glanced back at her brother. They had said their goodbyes earlier in private, for each knew the parting would be forever. Tera nodded and turned to look ahead.

Skirting the edge of the great sinkhole, Colin Stonetooth and the Ten in the lead, the people who were now Hylar began their journey. Three and five abreast, the procession was more than two miles long.

Among them were drummers, and as the first of these came abreast of the sinkhole he loosed his vibrar and began a slow, steady beat—a dirge, or a salute. Then others behind him joined in, and, as the procession crept past the sinkhole, the mountains echoed the steady, minor-key thunders of great drums saying a last farewell to the greatest drummer of them all. For the Hylar, as for the Calnar, there would always be the memory of Handil the Drum.

The procession wound downward, past the death-stink of the silent keep and out onto the war-littered terraces. On a hillside in the distance, a little band of humans raised their hands in salute, then turned away, and Colin Stonetooth knew that Garr Lanfel, the Prince of Golash, had made a final gesture in honor of a friendship that would never be again.

Down the terraces, toward the valleys of the Hammersong and the Bone, the new clan of the Hylar marched to the sound of its drums, eyes raised to the Suncradles and the distances beyond.

Never once did Colin Stonetooth turn to look back at what had been Thorin-Everbardin. But some did, and their whispers were bittersweet on the winds.

"Thoradin," they muttered. For the people who were now Hylar, Thorin was gone. What remained was Thoradin—a memory of the past.

Part II:
The Tribes Of Kal-Thax

The Land of Kal-Thax
Kharolis Mountains

Century of Wind
Decade of Oak
Year of Brass

12
Land of Conflict

The smoke of a hundred morning fires hazed the early autumn air above the eastern foothills of the Kharolis Mountains. As far as the eye could see, peering eastward from the slopes beyond, little wisps of smoke rose to the north and south, a solid crescent of smoke that rose skyward, then feathered on the breeze to lie like low clouds in the distance.

For weeks it had been like this. Hardly a day passed without sign of the bands of human wanderers who pressed westward, across the plains of central Ansalon until they came to the rising spires of the Kharolis Mountains. And always, then, they pushed toward the great pass below Cloudseeker Peak, and their camp smoke hazed the foothills below. Slide Tolec had learned to predict when the next human assault would come simply by the smoke over the foothills.

Except for a few remote camps of ogres and goblins, the people out there were a mix of human-kind. Most of them were refugees and wanderers, bands and whole tribes driven westward by the spread of the dragon wars far to the east. They sought places to rest, places to hide, places to resettle, but they were not welcomed in the hills and plains east of the mountains. That was part of the far-reaching realm of Ergoth, and the Ergothians didn't want hordes of strangers crowding into their land. Thus the knights and armed bands of wardens from Ergoth pushed the travelers onward, toward the mountains.

Refugees and displaced tribes—many of them he had seen at close quarters, when they came up the slopes only to be driven back by dwarves—appeared harmless enough, except for being human. The dwarves of Kal-Thax had learned long ago what happened when humans were allowed to scatter through these mountains. In certain seasons and in certain places—fertile valleys here and there—they managed to survive, for a time. They would spread and multiply. But then the food supplies and the shelter suitable for humans would be too little. The seasons would change and there would be famine, and then the raiding and the looting of the Einar—the dwarves—would begin.

Slide had thought about the harsh sanctions the dwarves had created. No other races were welcome in Kal-Thax. Kal-Thax was for the Einar. Kal-Thax was for dwarves and no one else. Like every dwarf in Kal-Thax, Slide agreed that it was a necessary law, especially where humans were concerned. If humans could just pass through, some had reasoned, maybe it would not be necessary. But humans did not "pass through." They would come in, if allowed, and they would spread and colonize, and the old troubles would begin again.

A shadow fell across the ledge where Slide squatted, and a wide-shouldered, bandy-legged figure draped in furs scrambled down from the ledges above to drop lithely—and almost soundlessly—beside him. Slide scowled behind his mesh faceplate. It was only one of the many unnerving habits of Glome the Assassin, this penchant for showing up silently and always unexpected. Slide said nothing, though. Those foolhardy enough to offend Glome the Assassin sometimes wound up dead.

For a second, Glome crouched beside Slide Tolec, studying him with quick, close-set eyes beneath a heavy brow that seemed to radiate the force of his presence and the strength of his arms. Then he turned and peered off into the distance, toward the plains where the smoke mounted from alien fires. Only for a moment did he scan the human camps. Turning to his right, he shaded his eyes to look off southward across the expanse of the high meadows which were the crest of a mighty shoulder of Cloudseeker Mountain. In that direction too, there was smoke—not as much as on the distant plains, but nearer by miles. A camp was there, and there were hints of movement and bright colors.

Glome pointed. "Daewar," he growled. "They camp on Theiwar territory."

"They've been there for a week." Slide shrugged. "They are here to help us repel the outsiders. Beyond them are Vog Ironface and the Daergar, as well."

"Forget about the humans," Glome growled. "I think it is time we dealt with the Daewar. We have wasted too much time."

Without another word, Glome turned and disappeared into the caves behind the ledge—silently, as usual.

Slide shivered slightly. Even now, with thousands of human invaders massing at the foot of the mountains, Glome still dwelt on his primary ambition, to wage war against the Daewar.

Or was that his real ambition, Slide wondered, to fight the Daewar? Or was it just a means toward some greater, darker ambition lying within the assassin's mind?

No one really knew where Glome had come from. Somewhere in Kal-Thax, of course, from one or another of the many little bands or villages of the widespread Einar, but

117

no one knew exactly where. Glome had not been Theiwar originally. He had just appeared one day, shortly before the time the old chieftain, Crouch Redfire, disappeared.

No one knew what had become of Crouch Redfire, but Glome had walked into the home lairs of the Theiwar and established himself immediately as a leader, through bullying, threats, and—many suspected—outright murder in several cases. He had an uncanny knack for seeking out all the malcontents in the tribe and getting them to accept his lead. Within a very short time, Glome had a substantial following among the Theiwar. Some had thought that Glome intended to take over as chieftain, but the succession had already been claimed by Twist Cutshank and—surprisingly—Glome had backed him against challengers. Twist Cutshank was a strong, brutal person—not overly smart, but crafty in his way. Now Twist was chieftain, and Glome was his chief advisor, and Slide Tolec wondered what Glome's ambitions really were. He had the feeling that they went far beyond merely being chieftain of the thane of Theiwar.

Slide turned his gaze eastward again, toward the distant smoke. Always, outsiders had come in the warm seasons—humans and others—trying to enter the closed land of Kal-Thax. But never had he seen so many.

Refugees from distant wars—yet among them would be the raiders and the looters, humans who found in the chaos of war the excuse and the opportunity to take what they could get.

And there were other camps out there, too, other smoke apart from the human crescent facing the pass. Far north, barely visible, was smoke from the dark, oily fires of what might be a goblin encampment. And nearer at hand, on high ridges aside from the human camps, were the little tendrils of what might be ogre fires.

Slide Tolec felt little sympathy for any of them. They did not belong in Kal-Thax.

Squatting beneath the stone overhang that shaded the Theiwar outpost caves, Slide peered outward, estimating the fires, and idly fingered the blade at his side. The numbers were increasing out there. Soon they would come, some of them at least, trying once again to penetrate the mountain lands.

There were so many this year! Slide felt that maybe it was well that the Daewar had come—from their own lairs far north on the hidden face of Sky's End Mountain—to aid in the defense. Slide had no more use for the arrogant, jovial "gold-molders" than did any other Theiwar. The Daewar were upstarts—only within the past century had they formed a thane—and yet they seemed to thrive. And they didn't hesitate to display their success. Every Daewar he had ever seen wore a fortune in the finest of armor and the gaudiest of attire.

And they could fight! While the Theiwar were expert at sabotage and ambush, and while none could match the dark-sighted Daergar in a night attack, few would dare to challenge the gold-molders in direct battle. The old Theiwar chief, Crouch Redfire, had badly weakened the Theiwar when he tested them by sending them into Daewar territory. The Daewar captain, Gem Bluesleeve, and his "Golden Hammer" elite troops had decimated the Theiwar raiders.

The term "gold-molder" was intended as an insult—implying that the Daewar were as soft and malleable as the bright metal that was the color of their hair and beards, and which they favored for ornamentation. But only an idiot or a suicide would so insult a Daewar to his face.

Though Slide resented the brightly clad sun people, now, seeing the smoke of the human campfires above the foothills, he was glad that the Daewar were here, and that they were part of the treaty of exclusion which kept Kal-Thax closed to aliens.

From the shadows behind him a deep voice rasped, "Slide! Have you gone to sleep there? What do you see?"

Scowling, Slide turned slightly to glance back into the depths. "I'm looking at what you told me to look at, . . . Sire. The outsiders are massing more and more in the foothills. They will be coming soon."

"Soon?" Twist Cutshank's voice mocked him. "Soon? What does 'soon' mean? This morning? Today? Next month?"

Slide stifled a sigh of disgust. How did the chieftain of the Theiwar expect him to read the minds of humans? "Today, maybe," he answered. "There are at least a hundred fires out there now. They'll have to move soon or starve."

"A hundred fires?" He heard the stomp of heavy boots and knew that the chieftain and others wanted to see for themselves. "All together?"

"No, they're scattered over many miles. But they've discovered now that they can't pass the gorge, and the cliffs of Shalomar block them to the south, so they are massing below the pass. Like they always do, except now there are many more."

As Twist Cutshank emerged onto the shelf, adjusting his mesh faceplate over craggy, sullen features, Slide moved aside for him, as people usually did. Twist Cutshank was not tall—he stood barely more than four feet high—but he was massive, with huge shoulders and almost no neck at all. His arms were as thick and knotty as the boles of mountain pines, and at least as long as his stubby, powerful legs.

"Fugitives," he rumbled, then shielded his eyes against the morning sun to peer into the distance. "Rust!" he said. "There must be thousands of them!"

"I told you," Slide Tolec muttered, then raised his voice. "They'll be coming soon, up the valley."

That was the one certainty, here in the eastern border lands of Kal-Thax. Intruders, when they came, would push westward across the foothills and into the wide, climbing valley that pointed toward the crest of Cloudseeker Mountain. It was the route they always followed. The way to Kal-Thax from the east was like a funnel. Across the plains of eastern Ergoth, migrants held to the narrowing "corridor" of wild lands, avoiding the northerly routes which led to the human city of Xak Tsaroth, where thieves and slavers waited to take their toll, and avoiding the ice barrens to the south. From the wilds, they slipped into the settled regions and were harried there by knights and companies of armed wardens, protecting the villages.

Reaching the foothills, the wanderers quickly found that the Grand Gorge was impassable to humans, and the Cliffs of Shalomar were unscalable by humans. So they set their eyes on the three crags atop Cloudseeker—those massive, upright fangs of stone that the dwarves called the Windweavers—and entered the narrowing valley that was their only route. And there, for more years than even the dwarves could remember, they were attacked and driven away or killed.

It was the only thing that every thane, tribe, and band of dwarves in Kal-Thax agreed on: Kal-Thax was closed to outside races and must remain so.

The "funnel" led directly into the territory of the Theiwar and was the reason that the Theiwar had become the first thane—or organized, land-holding nation—in Kal-Thax. Originally just small tribes of Einar, the Theiwar were cliff-dwelling people and had found fine profits in waylaying the humans and others who occasionally wandered into these mountains. Ambush, slaughter, and looting of outsiders had become a major industry in times past, and Thane Theiwar had profited from it.

Most travelers from the bog-lands and the plains never realized they had entered Kal-Thax until they were many miles up the rugged path among the foothills, and none realized that the path toward the three crags was a trap. Just below Galefang, the largest of the Windweavers, the path veered southward between high walls, directly into the canyon below the Theiwar caves. By the dozens and the hundreds, strangers had died there, and the Theiwar had looted and disposed of their bodies.

But it was different now. This time the intruders were a massive force, and the Theiwar did not have the field to themselves. The Daewar had come, arrogant as always, bypassing the Theiwar encampment without so much as a by-your-leave for trespassing on Theiwar grounds, and now were encamped right out on the promontory—a shoulder of the mountain, in the middle of the pass—as though to take charge of all defenses. A few miles beyond the Daewar camp, Slide knew, were hordes of grim, squinting Daergar, hiding their faces from the bright sunlight that hurt their dark-seeker eyes. They had come from their dimly lit tunnels and their precious mines to join in the defense of Kal-Thax. Here and there also were bands of the wild, erratic Klar, brandishing their bludgeons and waiting for the chance to bash a few human skulls.

In all, it was a grim and deadly array of dwarven fighters, none of the groups on very good terms with any of the others, but all determined that outsiders would not enter the mountain realm.

Slide wondered, though silently, what kind of fighting force they all might be if they could for once get together and act in unison. It was a foolish notion. Never in all the centuries since the Theiwar—and then the Daewar and Daergar and, to some extent, even the Klar—had become organized thanes, never had they acted in unison on any issue except the pact to keep aliens out.

In the distance to the east, the smoke of the human camps was trailing away on the breeze, and Slide, peering through his mesh faceplate, saw the beginnings of movement there. It was what he had expected. Someone in the foothills had taken charge, and now the humans—some of them at least—were on the move, heading up the pass.

He squinted, and Brule Vaportongue edged up beside him, his face hidden by the Daergar mask he wore. Brule was half Daergar and shunned the daylight.

"What do you see?" Brule asked. "Are they coming?"

"They're coming." Slide nodded. "By evening, the Daewar out there will be up to their eyeballs in humans."

"The gold-molders have placed themselves to take the first assault," Brule rasped. "So let them take it. We can attack from the flank, after they've slowed them down."

To one side, Glome the Assassin turned and spat, "Shut up over there. We have better things to think about than fighting humans." He turned back to Twist Cutshank, and all the rest turned to listen.

"The time is here to deal with the Daewar," Glome told the chieftain. "My spies have been on the slopes of Sky's End, as I told you. The citadel there is poorly guarded. The gold-molders are spending all their time delving into the mountain behind their fortifications. The spies believe they are expanding their city, deeper into the mountain."

"They can still fight," Twist Cutshank rumbled. "Don't forget the beating we took last time we tried an attack, Glome."

"That?" Glome growled. "That was no attack. That was a fiasco. Your old chieftain, Crouch Redfire, was an idiot, trying to raid Daebardin when Olim Goldbuckle and all his troops were there."

"So what makes it different now?" Twist glared. "A Daewar patrol on the defense line?"

Glome pointed southward, toward the Daewar camp. "Patrol? That is no mere patrol out there. I got close and looked around. That is Goldbuckle himself, with Gem Bluesleeve and most of his army. That isn't a hundred or so Daewar out there. That is a thousand or more—right out in the open, on Theiwar territory."

"So what are you suggesting?" Twist stared at Glome. "That we withdraw and go loot Daebardin while their prince is away?"

"More than that," Glome said. "First let them get bloodied by the humans. Let the Daewar take the brunt of today's assault—and tomorrow's, if there is one. Then, when Goldbuckle is weak, we can easily finish him off. After that, nothing stands between us and the treasures of Daebardin."

"Treasures none of us have ever seen," Twist pointed out. "We're not even sure they *have* treasures."

"Of course they have treasures!" Glome snapped. "Look at them! Every Daewar you ever saw wears a fortune in armor alone. And if they didn't have treasure, why would they have been delving all these years over on Sky's End? The rubble heaps below their citadel are enormous! They must be building an entire city under that mountain. Why would they do that, except to fortify, to protect vast treasures?"

"I'd like to see that undermountain city," Twist Cutshank admitted. "Treasures, huh? Maybe so."

"That place must be huge by now," Glome nodded. "A fortress for a king, possibly?"

"King? There are no kings in Kal-Thax!"

"But maybe Olim Goldbuckle wants to be one," Glome purred. "Have you thought about that? About the possibility of bowing before a bloody Daewar? Maybe *that* is why the gold-molders dig. Maybe when they have their fortress completed they intend to conquer all the thanes. Would you enjoy having that rusty gold-molder's foot on your neck, Twist Cutshank?" Glome turned, looking at the others. There were dozens of Theiwar on the ledge now. "Would any Theiwar willingly bow to a Daewar king?" he asked. "I say Olim Goldbuckle intends to be king of Kal-Thax, and if we want to stop him, we must strike first!"

It was a powerful argument, and none could deny it. Slide Tolec's brows lowered, though, as another thought crossed his mind. Maybe someone in Kal-Thax *did* want to become king. But was it the prince of the Daewar? Or was it, just possibly, someone else?

Twist Cutshank was gazing at Glome. "Are you suggesting we betray a defense, Glome?" he asked. "That would be breaking the pact."

"We won't let humans in," Glome explained. "We'll just let the Daewar do all the fighting."

"And if the humans get past them?"

"Then we will turn them back. But either way, this may be our chance to be rid of Olim Goldbuckle."

"What of the Daergar?"

"What of them?" Glome snorted. "Vog Ironface knows the Daewar threat as well as we do. The Daergar will join us when they see what we are doing."

Slide Tolec had his doubts about that. The treaty of the thanes was a sacred thing, and the Daergar supported it loyally. It was in their best interests. Should outsiders settle within the mountains of Kal-Thax, the first prizes they would seek would be the Daergar mines.

Still, there was a bond of sorts between the Theiwar and the Daergar. Many times in the past, they had fought each other. But the rise of the powerful, populous Daewar to the north, in their stronghold on Sky's End, had brought a tenuous peace between Theiwar and Daergar. Each recognized a more dangerous enemy, and hostility between the cliff-cave people and the dark-dwellers was set aside for an uneasy alliance, and for trade. The Theiwar mined the steel-hardening black stone of Cloudseeker's lower slopes, and in return acquired the swift, dark-metal Daergar weapons, which most of them preferred over anything the Theiwar crafters could forge.

Twist Cutshank squinted out across the bright, high lands, toward the climbing foothills to the east. The smoke had diminished in the distance, but now everyone could see the movement of massed humans pouring over the far crests. Even at such a distance, sunlight glinted on the steel and bronze of weapons. After a time, the Theiwar chieftain hissed, "There are horsemen leading them!"

Slide Tolec's eyes watered as he tried to make out details in the distance. There *were* horsemen there—hundreds of them, it seemed, and they were of a type he had seen before. "Cobar!" he said. "The raiders from the northern plains."

"Very well," Twist Cutshank decided. "It shall be as Glome says. Instead of flanking the Daewar positions, we hold back. Let the gold-molders take the full brunt of the attack. Maybe the humans will deal with the Daewar for us . . . but if any get through, then we and the Daergar must turn them back."

13

The Defenders

Olim Goldbuckle knew very well the threat that Kal-Thax faced in this season of massive migrations. For a month, his Daewar scouts had surveyed the border slopes as more and more humans—and not a few ogres and goblins—arrived there, some fleeing the dragon war in the east, others taking advantage of the chaos to seek new lands or treasures.

The Daewar prince had huddled with his advisors as the reports came in, assessing what was happening in the human realms beyond Kal-Thax and what it meant for the dwarves. It seemed that displaced people by the thousands or tens of thousands were spilling across the wide, unguardable eastern borders of the human realm of Ergoth and migrating westward toward the sparsely settled southern hills which bordered on the mountain barrier of Kal-Thax. Many of them, the dwarves assumed, would be caught by the patrols of the overlords of the human city of Xak Tsaroth and sold into slavery—either there, or transported to the distant barbarian lands of Istar by trade caravans.

But others—especially the wily Cobar, Sandrunners, and Sackmen of the northern plains—would know about Xak Tsaroth and avoid it, swinging southward through the hills. The Daewar spies confirmed this. By far the most dangerous of the human masses streaming across Ergoth— harried and herded by the knights and by companies of armed citizens—were those closing in on the funnel pass east of Cloudseeker Peak.

Traditionally that was Theiwar territory, and the Theiwar had dealt with outsiders penetrating the borders there. At times they were aided by the Daergar, protecting their mining areas. But now, Olim Goldbuckle knew, the force of the human numbers was far more than the primitive Theiwar—or even the dour, crafty Daergar—could counter.

"The humans must be stopped before they reach Cloudseeker," the prince of the Daewar told his captain, Gem Bluesleeve. "We are bound by the pact of Kal-Thax to assist our neighbors in the defense of the realm."

"Especially of Cloudseeker." Gem nodded, his eyes twinkling.

"Most especially of Cloudseeker," Olim agreed. "You might say we have a deep interest there." He chuckled. "Those Theiwar! They claim their mountain and cling to their cliffs, never wondering what might lie beneath their feet. What a waste, if such marvels were to go unused. How goes the delving?"

"Slate Coldsheet estimates another month before we break through into the caverns Urkhan found," Gem told him. "But you know how the delvemaster is. Always conservative. If he says a month, we might be there in a week."

"So near," Olim breathed. "Years of tunneling, Gem. It would be tragic to come so close and then lose everything because the Theiwar failed to hold back a bunch of humans. The Theiwar aren't inclined to explore, Gem, but humans are. They must be stopped. Get the army ready to move, all except the home guard. We are going to the front passes to help our neighbors keep intruders away."

"That's Theiwar territory," Gem reminded his prince. "They might not appreciate the Daewar army showing up there."

"We shall try not to be too noticeable," Olim said. "Possibly we can make many seem like few. But either way, I don't intend to ask Twist Cutshank's permission to evoke the Pact of Kal-Thax. It is our right . . . and our duty."

So, now, on a bright autumn day, most of the Daewar army was spread along the center rise of the high promontory above the funnel pass, as thousands of human marauders swarmed up the slopes toward them. The promontory was a vast, high meadow flanked by jutting cliffs and broken steeps that narrowed, closing in as the elevation rose toward the level crest that was a jutting shoulder of great Cloudseeker, which stood in the distance behind like a gigantic, three-horned head draped in a sloping cowl.

From the moment the humans—still tiny with distance—began their drive up the pass, it had been apparent that they were led by swarms of riders, roughly clad, fierce-looking men who pummeled their dark horses as they toiled up the grade toward the promontory. There were hundreds of them, and beyond and around them came footmen—a motley assemblage of men from many lands, all with one thing in mind. Their reasons may have been many and varied, but they came on grimly, all determined to break the blockade of Kal-Thax and enter the mountains beyond the midlands.

Gem Bluesleeve watched curiously as the throng came nearer, shading his eyes with the upturned visor of his gold-embossed helmet. It was not the first time he had seen humans making for Kal-Thax. Many times, over the years, Daewar patrols had watched as Theiwar ambushers waylaid travelers coming from the eastern lands. At times, when the groups of trespassers were large, Daewar had even joined in the defense to throw them back. And there had been times when Daewar had even intervened before an ambush, when it was obvious that the interlopers were only poor travelers, lost or outcast, whose only real crime was being in the wrong place.

Some among the Theiwar had fumed and threatened each time a Daewar unit interfered, and there were hard feelings between the thanes because of it. But the Daewar had paid little attention. To the Theiwar, slaughter and looting of trespassers might be a thriving business. But to most Daewar, murder was senseless and embarrassing if there was nothing to be gained by it and if the intruders could be turned away with words.

The mass of humanity coming up the pass now, though, was nothing like the little groups and bands of travelers of past years. This was a massive raid, with the look of a full-scale assault led by mounted looters. Gem stepped to his prince's side to point out the spreading, tactical maneuvering of the climbing humans.

"These are not here by accident," he said. "Those horsemen, in the lead, are men of the Cobar plains. The Cobar do not just wander about, as do some tribes. The Cobar are raiders and looters."

"Mounted intruders," Olim Goldbuckle mused. "Has there ever been a mounted attack before?"

"Not that I've heard of," Gem admitted. "Many humans have horses, but these mountains are not horse country. Not even the knights of Ergoth would try to enter here on horseback."

"And yet the Cobar do," Olim noted. "What do you make of that?"

"They know we're here." Gem shrugged. "Those other people with them may intend to invade Kal-Thax and carve out human kingdoms. But the Cobar do not intend to settle here. They come only to raid, to pillage, and then to return to their plains."

"It will be difficult, fighting horsemen on this level ground," Olim said.

"Then let's not meet them here," Gem suggested. "Let's go out and meet them on the slopes. If I'm to face horsemen, I'd prefer to have the uphill advantage."

Olim gazed around, studying the terrain. "The pass is wider over there," he pointed out. "We will be spread thin. But then, we are not alone." He gazed northward, at the craggy cliffs which were the Theiwar border camps. "Flash signals to Twist Cutshank of the Theiwar," he said, "and to Vog Ironface of the Daergar. Signal my greetings and say that we will hold the middle pass. Ask that they position themselves on our forward flanks, the Theiwar to the north and the Daergar to the south. Among us, we should be able to persuade the humans that they are not wanted in Kal-Thax."

The signals were flashed. Daewar "callers" were positioned on pinnacles of stone using mirrors of polished brass to catch and relay the sunlight in common code. A response and agreement came from the south, from the Daergar placements under the steeps there, but there was no answer from the Theiwar. When his callers reported this to Gem Bluesleeve, he passed it on to Olim Goldbuckle. "There is no question the signal was seen, Sire," he assured the prince. "With a high sun, and the air clear, the flashes are unmistakable."

"Twist Cutshank is sulking," Goldbuckle decided. "He is probably miffed that we came onto his territory without his invitation."

"But can we count on them to do their part?" Gem asked, worried.

"We'll have to," the prince said. "He has seen what is coming, and, savage or not, he knows what it will take to hold this pass. To fail would be to break the Pact of Kal-Thax, and even Twist Cutshank wouldn't do that."

With the sun high overhead, the Daewar army broke

camp and moved out, cresting the promontory in plain view of the oncoming, quickly spreading human force. In their glistening armor and bright cloaks, the Daewar were an impressive display of presence atop the long rise, and there was visible hesitation among the bands of footmen climbing among the mounted Cobar horsemen. But not for long. The Cobar rode among them, swinging whips and the flats of blades, and the advance resumed.

By the time the sun was above Sky's End to the north, the human force was less than half a mile away and could be seen clearly. Most of the humans were on foot—a motley assortment of men from many tribes and homelands, clothed in whatever garb they had brought or had found in their wanderings. The weapons they carried ranged from staffs and cudgels to every kind of blade, and their shields and armor were as varied as their clothing. Some had metal shields and bits of metal armor. Far more wore heavy, studded leathers and even whole furs of various animals. There were shields of braced hardwood, shields woven of reeds, and shields of tanned hide stretched over wooden frames. To the finely equipped Daewar, they wouldn't have seemed especially dangerous—except that there were thousands of them.

The riders were a different story. As Gem had said, the Cobar were a fierce people, and their raiders knew how to fight. They handled their horses expertly, and the weapons they carried—slim lances, curved swords, and dagger-studded fighting shields—looked deadly.

At Gem's orders, the Daewar spread into a long, double line along the crest of the promontory. It was a well-tested Daewar strategy for defense. Spreading from center, the dwarves took positions every ten yards, two defenders at each station, one kneeling behind his shield with sling and hammer at hand, the second a step forward and to one side, shield high and sword in hand. At ten-yard intervals, with sling-stones to cover the gaps, the defense was virtually a wall. And, faced with horses, Gem had added an extra touch. Each station was equipped with cable and a throw-net.

When the lead humans were less than a hundred yards away, slowing for assembly, Olim Goldbuckle stepped forward and raised an imperious hand. "You have crossed into the land of Kal-Thax!" he called. "Entry here is forbidden! Turn around and go away!"

For a moment there was no answer, then a Cobar horseman with owl feathers adorning his helmet stepped his mount forward. "I claim that one's armor!" he shouted, pointing at Olim. "See how pretty he looks, like a shiny little toy person! And that cloak, with the flower designs, I'll take it, too!"

Laughter arose from the ranks of his followers, and others took up the cry, looking along the line of dwarves, picking out and claiming various weapons, bits of armor, and personal gear, shouting taunts and derision. Stolidly, the prince of the Daewar stood his ground until the noise died away. Then he called, "You have had your warning! Kal-Thax is closed to you! There is nothing here for you except defeat and death!"

Something in the dwarf's tone made Owl Feathers hesitate. He had never fought dwarves before. They didn't look very dangerous to him, but he had heard they could be full of surprises. Turning, he gave quick orders to the nearest riders and waited while they were passed along. Then he raised his sword, glanced each way along the line of his men, and slashed it forward.

Even on the steep grade, the Cobar horses were quick. From a standstill, they surged into a pounding charge in a spearpoint formation that flashed toward the center of the Daewar line. Fifty yards now separated them, then forty and thirty, and abruptly all of the Cobar riders sheathed their swords and unslung their riding lances as they bore down on the waiting dwarves. Behind them, the charging human footmen were a howling mob, brandishing their weapons as they ran.

The Cobar charge closed to twenty yards, then fifteen, and the riders raised their lances. Short, sturdy spears with

iron heads, the lances came up, held level, then shot forward as the riders flung them in unison directly at each
pair of dwarven guards ahead of them. And as the spears
flew, the riders hauled on their reins, wheeled their horses,
and raced off at right angles to right and left, veering back
to circle around the mobs of charging footmen.

Thrown spears clanged and thudded against dwarven
shields, a ringing tattoo of metal on metal that echoed
from the cliffs and the distant peaks. Most were deflected,
but here and there a spear got through and a Daewar
guardsman reeled backward, impaled.

"Slings!" Gem Bluesleeve shouted. From the long Daewar line, deadly stones shot out, driven by humming
slings, but the targets they found were not the mounted
raiders. Instead, they crashed into the leading wave of
footmen, mowing them down as a scythe mows standing
grain. The riders were away by then, circling around
behind the footmen to drive them forward into the dwarven lines.

One wave of sling-stones did its work, then another, and
then the Daewar found themselves hand to hand with
thousands of howling, slashing humans, some attacking
fiercely, some just trying to get through, away from the
mounted demons behind them.

The Daewar line wavered from the sheer force of the
attack. But minute by minute it held, and then the tide of
battle began to turn. The Daewar line surged outward,
each pair defending and countering, moving carefully over
the fallen bodies of human attackers—and of dwarves. As
the line bowed forward it opened, and Gem Bluesleeve's
elite "Golden Hammer" company charged through, a
solid, moving wall of shields, thudding hammers, and
flashing blades.

Swift and deadly, moving as a single being, the Golden
Hammer drove through the mass of human attackers,
scattering them in panic. Then the dwarven battle force
turned, circled, and drove through again, and yet again as
the Daewar on the holding line pressed relentlessly

forward in their wake.

It was too much for even the fiercest of the marauders. They couldn't get past the ranked shields to attack, they couldn't block them because of the weapons snaking out to draw blood or crush bone at each thrust, and they couldn't throw weight of numbers at them in screaming charges. Each time some tried, the dwarves went in under the weapons of the taller humans and bore them down, screaming.

Olim Goldbuckle and his personal guard were everywhere in the conflict—attacking, repelling, and organizing new tactics. In a swirl of fighting, milling confusion, the dwarven units seemed almost aloof to the panic around them. With methodical, determined dwarven logic they pressed and pounded, slashed and cut until what had been a massed assault was a broken, scattered battle, humans blindly fighting and trying to get away all along a mile-wide field.

Olim Goldbuckle found himself abruptly unoccupied as the latest gang of humans fled in panic, and signaled to Gem Bluesleeve, who polished off a barbarian, gave quick orders to his company, then hurried to join his prince.

Olim had climbed to the top of a boulder and was surveying the field. Carnage was everywhere, and some scattered fighting still went on, but Olim was looking for something else. "Where are the horsemen?" he snapped as Gem reached the boulder.

Gem looked around. He hadn't seen a horseman since the fighting started. He climbed up beside his prince. Far south, near the steeps, companies of Daergar in iron masks were methodically attacking bands of humans who had fled in that direction, turning them away from the rising lands. Gem looked to the north and muttered an oath. There was no one on that side—only a few fleeing bands of humans with his own people in pursuit. "Where are the Theiwar?" he hissed. "They should be over there on our forward flank. That side of the pass is wide open!"

Olim shaded his eyes. "Have they betrayed us? Have

they let the outsiders through and betrayed the Pact of Kal-Thax?"

He had barely spoken when shouts erupted on the near lines, where pairs of Daewar turned to point westward, up the rise.

Coming over the crest were human riders—hundreds of them, with the owl-feathered barbarian in the lead.

Gem cupped his hands. "Turn!" he roared. "Turn and defend!"

Swiftly the Daewar line reversed itself, regrouping in the two-at-ten-yards pattern to meet the charging riders.

The horsemen thundered toward them, but not as riders attacking in a charge. Instead, they seemed to be fleeing from something. Then, above and behind them, Theiwar warriors came over the crest. There was blood on their dark swords, and on their dark-steel armor, and through their mesh face-plates clamored their battle cries.

"They ambushed them!" Gem gasped. "The gods'-rejected Theiwar! They let those people through the lines, then ambushed them!"

"I don't believe it," Olim rumbled. "Twist Cutshank is stupid, but he isn't *that* stupid!"

"See for yourself, Sire. They are pressing their attack."

"Pressing, yes," Olim growled. "Right down on our lines. Defend! Defend!"

"Nets and cables!" Gem shouted, signaling. Jumping to the ground, he ran to help.

Like a ragged juggernaut, the Cobar swept down on the thin Daewar line. Sling-stones stopped a few, and thrown nets attached to anchored cables brought down a few more, but the human riders had the slope to their advantage. Slashing and ripping, they went through and over the Daewar line . . . and didn't even slow down. Once in the clear, most of them kept on going. For now, they had had enough of dwarves.

One, though, hauled rein on the slope just below Olim's boulder, turned, and screamed a cry of hatred. Owl feathers rippling in the wind above his helmet, the Cobar leader heeled his mount, raised his sword in both hands, and charged the Daewar prince.

Two blades flashed as one in the sunlight. The human's blade sliced toward Olim's head and was deflected by an iron shield on an arm that, inch for inch, was far stronger than any human's. Olim's whistling blade came around in a wide arc and caught the human in midsection, just below his belted chest-plate. It almost cut him in two.

As Owl Feather flopped to the ground, dying, Olim straightened and scowled at the blood on his bright sword. Oddly, in that moment he noticed—or realized consciously for the first time—that human blood was precisely the same color as dwarven blood.

Just up the slope, so near that he could see their dark eyes behind their mesh masks, half a hundred Theiwar warriors clustered as though to flee. Chasing after the human riders, they had become separated from their main forces and now found themselves practically in the middle of the Daewar defenses—far too close for comfort. Raising his sword in command signal, Olim shouted, "Gem! Circle those Theiwar! Capture them!"

Gem Bluesleeve barked commands, and companies in the Daewar line headed up-slope at a run, encircling the confused Theiwar who turned to flee only to find themselves ringed by Daewar blades and shields. Gem Bluesleeve strode into the ring and ordered, "Theiwar! Lay down your arms! You are prisoners!"

From atop his rock, Olim watched, anger glinting in his blue eyes. If these Theiwar behaved themselves they would not be hurt, but he didn't want any of them reporting back to Twist Cutshank just yet.

The Theiwar treachery—letting humans through the line and them turning them back upon the Daewar—had been a vicious trick, but Olim suspected there was more to it than just Twist Cutshank's peevishness. Now he intended to find out.

14

The Price of Treachery

The autumn sun had gone behind the peaks, and twilight lay upon Kal-Thax when Theiwar watchers saw a little band of brightly clad dwarves making their way northward. They were obviously Daewar, but there were fewer than a hundred of them, and many appeared injured.

Within minutes, Twist Cutshank himself was on the spotting ledge with Brule Vaportongue and a dozen others. "The plan worked," the Theiwar chieftain gloated. "The humans cut them to pieces. Those are all that are left."

"That's Goldbuckle himself in the lead," Slide Tolec noted, pointing. "I know him by his floral cloak."

"It worked!" Twist repeated, a fierce grin parting his

whiskers. "Glome was right. The Daewar are defeated. All we need to do is finish the job. Mark their route and get ready. I want Olim Goldbuckle's head on a javelin tip. With him gone, we'll have no problem taking over that stronghold of theirs."

"You mean to ambush them?" Slide asked. He was surprised and a bit shocked at how few Daewar survivors there seemed to be. It didn't seem right, somehow, that the human horsemen could have done so much damage— could have killed so many. And yet, there they were, no more than a hundred battered, slow-moving Daewar. And no returning Theiwar had reported anything of what occurred after the horsemen returned to the battle. In fact, there were quite a few Theiwar missing, as well.

"Of course we ambush them," Twist grunted. "That's part of Glome's plan. Then we go take over that fortress they've been digging. No Daewar will ever again think of being king of Kal-Thax!"

"You really think the Daewar wants to be a king?" Brule Vaportongue asked.

"You heard Glome," Twist snapped. "Why else would the Daewar have been digging a fortress all these years under Sky's End?"

Glome himself was not there, and Slide realized that the assassin had been gone most of the day. It was as though he had shown up just long enough to persuade Twist Cutshank to start a war, then disappeared. Brule crouched on the shelf, staring out at the approaching Daewar, and the frown on his V-shaped face was as puzzled as Slide's own. Still, when Twist Cutshank proceeded to organize his ambush and set out with his troops, they both remained silent. Something was very wrong here, and they both felt it. But they didn't know what it was, and they knew the chieftain would not listen to their vague suspicions. It seemed the only person Twist listened to, now that he was chieftain, was Glome the Assassin.

By evening light the Theiwar ambushers were concealed along both sides of a narrow draw along which the

Daewar must pass. Twist Cutshank crept to a stone out-cropping and watched them approach. They were near now, and the Theiwar's eyes fixed on the gleaming helmet and floral cloak of the Daewar prince. Soon, he told himself. Soon, the Daewar will be dead.

"I don't care how many of the gold-molders you kill," he called softly. "Kill them all, for all I care. Just make sure that prince dies. Whoever's blade draws Goldbuckle's blood will have first choice of prizes when we enter the Daewar delves."

Directly behind him a deep voice growled, "Well, I suppose that's clear enough."

Twist spun around, his mouth open. Six feet away, Olim Goldbuckle, bare-headed and without his regal cloak, gazed at him with angry, hooded eyes. Beyond, all along the ambush canyon, Daewar fighters—hundreds of them—were surrounding and containing the surprised Theiwar in their hiding places.

"Twist Cutshank," the Daewar prince rumbled, "I accuse you of treachery, betrayal, and of intentionally breaking the Pact of Kal-Thax. Do you submit to judgment of the thanes, or do you wish to challenge me?"

With a roar of rage, Twist Cutshank drew his curved, dark-steel blade and launched himself at the prince of the Daewar. His sword flashed downward at the golden, unprotected hair of Olim's head . . . and missed as the Daewar dodged aside, thrusting with his bright blade.

Twist felt the cold steel rip through the strapping between his breastplates, and felt the icy fire of it entering his chest. He tried to raise his blade again, but somehow lacked the strength even to hold it. It slipped from his fingers, and he sagged to his knees.

"I kind of thought you might choose to challenge," Olim Goldbuckle said quietly. With a heave, he turned the blade and sliced, severing the Theiwar's heart within him. When he withdrew his sword, Twist Cutshank pitched forward and lay still.

Wiping his sword clean, Olim strode back into the

canyon and looked around at the captured ambushers. A Daewar guardsman stepped forward to hand him his helmet and help him with his cloak. When he was fully garbed again, Olim raised his voice. "You Theiwar," he said so that all could hear. "You listen too much to the wrong people. First you followed Crouch Redfire, then you followed Twist Cutshank, and now you must find someone else to follow. Twist Cutshank broke the pact, and now he is dead. Can anyone here tell me why he chose to betray his allies?"

At first there was no answer, then from the guarded lines a broad-shouldered Theiwar of middle years stepped forward. "I can tell you, Daewar," he growled.

"And who are you?"

"I am Slide Tolec."

"Then tell me, Slide Tolec," Olim urged. "Did your chief so hunger for bloodshed that he would carry out a betrayal and plan an invasion? Did he think the Daewar so rich that it would be worth the cost?"

"He believed that you have treasures," Slide Tolec said. "Many think so. Do you?"

"Not like your leaders seem to think," Olim snapped. "Was that his reason for this day's treachery?"

"Part of it," Slide admitted. "But mostly he feared that the Daewar plan to rule all of Kal-Thax."

Olim frowned. "Rule Kal-Thax? Why did he think that?"

"Why else would you be delving a new fortress?" Slide glared at his captor. "Oh, we know what you have been doing over there on Sky's End. We have eyes. We have seen the dumps of your delving. You must be digging out an entire city underground."

"Delving a . . ." Olim stammered, abruptly at a loss for words. "You think we are delving a . . ." He clamped his mouth shut and looked away, stifling a laugh. A few yards away, Gem Bluesleeve stood in open-mouthed astonishment.

Doing his best to conceal his delight, Olim turned back

to Slide Tolec. "What we do under Sky's End is our own business," he said sternly. "If, as you say, we are delving a fortress city there, then that is not the Theiwar's concern."

"It is if you plan to rule Kal-Thax from there," Slide Tolec said stubbornly. "You can kill those of us you have captured if you want to, but we are only a few. There are many others who will avenge us. And if we die, the rest will know why we died . . . because the Daewar intend to rule! No Theiwar will ever bend the knee to a Daewar king!"

"And if I told you that we have no such intention, would you believe me?"

"Would you, if you were us?"

"Probably not," Olim admitted. "Very well. The chieftain who led you in this folly has paid with his life. We came here to protect the Pact of Kal-Thax. We will come again when humans again press the borders, and we will keep coming as long as there is threat from outside. Tell whoever is your next chieftain to expect that and to get used to it."

"You . . . you are letting us go?"

"What would it accomplish to kill you?" Olim turned his back and shook his head, stifling a grin of delight. Then he straightened his face, put on his sternest expression, and snapped at his captain, "Gem! Don't just stand there gaping. We must be on our way."

Gem Bluesleeve blinked at his prince. "But, Sire, what he said about our delvings—"

"So, they've figured out what we're doing." Olim quickly cut him off. "Building ourselves a fortress. Well, we couldn't keep it secret forever, could we?"

"Couldn't . . . ?" Gem paused, then squared his shoulders. "Ah . . . no, Sire. It's hard to keep a fortress secret."

* * * * *

The slopes remained clear of intruders—it would be a while before humans or anyone else stirred up the courage

DRAGONLANCE Dwarven Nations

to try another assault on the mountain realm—and Slide Tolec led a party from the border outpost back to Theibardin, the maze of hollowed-out caves that ran around two of the faces of Cloudseeker, high on the huge mountain's crest.

It was the home realm of the Theiwar, and Slide had a grim intuition of what they would find when they arrived there. Instinct told him that Glome the Assassin had known, before it ever happened, that the Daewar stragglers had been decoys, and that Olim Goldbuckle was coming to call in force. Somehow, Slide felt, Glome had forseen the fate of Twist Cutshank, had even aided and abetted it.

It was no real surprise, then, to arrive at the Theiwar home lairs and find that Glome and his followers had taken control of the place. Glome had declared himself chieftain of the Theiwar and was proceeding with plans to attack, invade, and loot the Daewar's new city under Sky's End. The plan was simple and straightforward. Somehow, Glome had enlisted the help of the Daergar by persuading Vog Ironface that the Daewar intended to take over all the mining in Kal-Thax. With a combined force of Theiwar and Daergar—and as many of the wild, erratic Klar as they could round up—Glome intended to take the old Daewar citadel on the slopes of Sky's End's, which was—his spies assured him—the only entrance to the Daewar's new delvings.

With the citadel held, Glome reasoned, they could lay siege to the underground city until they starved the Daewar out and forced a surrender.

When Slide Tolec and Brule Vaportongue first heard of the plan, they glanced at each other in astonishment. For the first time, it occurred to both of them that Glome the Assassin might truly be insane.

But after a glimpse of Glome himself, his eyes shining with a zealot's fervor and an avenger's rage—and surrounded by his hundreds of ardent followers—Slide and Brule wisely decided to keep their mouths shut. Glome was chieftain now, but not like any chieftain who had ruled before.

Glome did not accept criticism, and had repealed the law of challenge. Now, for any Theiwar to speak against the chieftain or his plans, the penalty was death.

Part III:
A Taste of Chivalry

The Valley Lands
Southeastern Ergoth

Century of Wind
Decade of Oak
Fall, Year of Brass

15

A Knight to Pass

The route of the seekers held southwestward as days became weeks and weeks became months. Across the central pass of the Suncradles and for five days beyond, the route had been charted by Cale Greeneye and his six companions in their search for the lost patrol. But everything west of that was uncharted country, and Colin Stonetooth led his people into it without ever looking back. Behind them was Thoradin; ahead—so said the prophecy of Mistral Thrax— was Everbardin.

No longer of Thorin, they were no longer Calnar, but still they were of those once called "the highest," because of Thorin's lofty place high above the human realms. In the dwarven manner of speech, the term was "Hylar." So, having no other name for themselves, they took the name Hylar and carried it with them. For them, Thorin was now Thoradin, and Thoradin was of the past. Somewhere beyond the hills and plains of the middle realms lay the future.

Perched in the saddle of the great horse Piquin, with six other young adventurers at his back, Cale Greeneye scouted far afield as the tribe of Colin Stonetooth plodded onward toward a distant place none of them had ever seen—a place called Kal-Thax, which might be nothing more than legend or the dreams of old Mistral Thrax. Through the foothills leading down toward the Ergothian realm, the Hylar trekked, a thousand homeless households on the move. The steady beat of their marching drums was a promise and a warning to any who heard . . . a promise to the Hylar people that the prophecy of Everbardin would be fulfilled, and a warning to all others that these were a people who looked to the left sides of their tools.

Many times the dwarves had halted the journey—to rest and gather food, to perform marriages and funerals, once for the birth of a baby to one of the younger women, and sometimes just because a hill demanded to be delved, a forest cleaned of underbrush, or a vein of ore to be mined and smelted.

Now, as the procession entered even more new lands at a place where steep ravines crisscrossed a jumbled, broken countryside, they no longer resembled the serene, practical, and ensconced people they had been within Thorin. Their features were the same. They were still a short, sturdy dwarven people with dark hair and proud, thoughtful eyes, whose males' trimmed beards were back-swept as though they faced into a wind and whose females were strong and usually beautiful. But now much of their attire was of the fabrics they had crafted along the way, and their armaments were more obviously warlike than they had favored in Thorin.

Three times the Hylar had been attacked—twice by roving humans and once by ogres—and their lessons had been learned well. They were a weathered and travel-wise group now, and most creatures gave them wide berth in passing.

At the rock-strewn top of a deep ravine that was as wide as a small valley, Cale Greeneye and his scouts drew rein, shading their eyes against the quartering sun of Krynn. The ravine walls were steep, though shelved with natural trails angling downward, and below were groves of trees lining a ribbon of bright water.

Cale studied the landscape, gazing carefully up and down the canyon, then gestured. "Let's take a look," he said. "That may be a good place to pass the night."

He jerked around, then, as a voice only feet away said, "That's exactly what you'll have to do if you intend to cross that stream, but it won't be easy."

Cale squinted, then frowned as a small figure stepped out of shadows between two slabs of upthrust stone. The creature was no taller than a dwarf—not as tall as most— but was distinctly not a dwarf. He was slim and fine-boned, with a face that might have belonged to a half-sized elf and a great cascade of brown hair tied up in the back with a leather thong.

"A kender," Cale Greeneye rasped, looking down from the height of Piquin's saddle. "By Reorx! Are you people everywhere?"

"Not me," the kender shook his head, eyes widening in surprise. "I'm just right here, at least right now. Of course, before I came here, I was at . . ."

"What did you mean, crossing the stream won't be easy?"

"Oh, that's because of the knight," the kender said, shrugging.

"What knight?" Cale demanded, raising his voice in irritation.

"Oh, I don't know. Any night really." The kender looked from one to another of them, gazing happily up at the frowning faces high above him. "You don't live around here, do you?"

"Of course not!" Cale snapped. "We're just passing through."

"I didn't think so," the kender said. "You're dwarves, and there aren't any dwarves around here that I know of. But if you plan to pass the knight down there, like you said, then you'd better have a pretty good plan, because he won't make it easy for you."

"Who won't?"

"The knight."

"*What knight?*"

"The one down there at the bridge. And you don't need to shout. I can hear you just fine. I have good ears. Do you know, I can hear insects breathe? Have you ever listened to a pond beetle breathing? It sounds just like an angry minotaur, except a lot smaller. Sand scorpions sound pretty neat, too, but you have to be really careful, or they'll sting you on the ear. My cousin Chiswin had one ear twice the size of the other for three weeks because he was listening to . . ."

"Gods' rust!" Cale Greeneye hissed. "I only asked you a simple question! And you're babbling on and on, and I haven't learned anything yet. Don't you ever shut up?"

"Sure." The kender nodded and raised a curious brow. "You talk a lot yourself, for a dwarf. Are you sure you aren't from around here? I believe those are the biggest horses I ever saw. And all seven of them are the same color. The knight's horse is pretty big, but not that big, and it's a horse of a different color. Sort of light brown, like . . ."

Cale took a deep breath. "*What knight?*" he roared.

"I just told you. The one down there at the bridge."

"There . . . is . . . a . . . knight . . . at . . . the . . . bridge?" Cale spoke very slowly and distinctly, waving back his companions. Two of them had drawn their axes, out of sheer exasperation.

"There sure is," the kender assured him. "His name is Glendon."

"And what is this Glendon doing there, at the bridge?"

"He's waiting for people to try to cross the stream."

"Why?"

"So he can stop them. It's what he does, you know . . . or, rather, I guess you don't know, not being from around here." Abruptly, the kender scampered directly under Piquin's belly and peered up from the other side. "Aha! I wondered how you dwarves get on and off these big horses. Now I see. You have a little roll-down rope ladder. That's pretty clever."

Cale was fighting the reins, barely keeping his startled mount in control. Piquin's ears were laid back, his eyes rolling, and his jaws fighting the bit. The other horses, sensing his panic, shied and back-stepped, and for a moment all the dwarves had their hands full.

"Rust and corruption!" Cale yelled, baring his teeth in a snarl. "Don't you know better than to run under a horse?" Furious, Cale brought Piquin under control, slipped off his spurs, loosed the hitch on his mounting ladder, and scurried down. He turned, the reins in one hand, the other balled into a fist. "I won't stand for . . ." he stopped, looking this way and that. The kender was nowhere in sight. "Now where did that little tarnish go?"

"Who?" a voice asked, from above.

Cale swung around and looked up. The kender was sitting in his saddle, high atop Piquin. "You!" the dwarf roared. "Come down from there!"

"Oh," the kender said. He scampered down the ladder, agile as a spider on a web. "That's all right, I was just curious. But I guess that was bad manners, considering that we haven't been introduced or anything. My name is Springheel. Castomel Springheel. You can call me Cas if you want to. Who are you?"

"Cale Greeneye," Cale growled. "And you stay away from my horse!"

"I'm pleased to meet you," the kender said brightly. "And these others?"

With an impatient hiss, Cale gestured. "That's Mica Rockreave, Gran Molden, and Coal Bellmetal. The three over there are Flint Cokeras, Pim Bouldersfield, and Shard

Feldspar. Did you hear what I told you?"

"Plain as day," Cas nodded. "It may be a pleasure to meet all of you,"—his brows drew together thoughtfully—"but then, of course, it may not. It's too early to be sure. What kind of dwarves are you?"

"Hylar," Cale announced proudly.

"Really? Never heard of them. Are you going to try to pass the knight today?"

"If he's in our way," Cale assured the little creature. "You say his name is Glendon? What's the matter with him?"

"You mean, aside from being a human?"

"I mean, why does he want to stop people from crossing the stream? What's on the other side?"

"Nothing much. It's about like this side, only it's the other side instead."

Cale closed his eyes tightly and counted to seven. Then he asked, as politely as he could, "Why doesn't he want us to cross his . . . his berusted bridge?"

"I'm sure it's nothing personal," the kender assured him. "It's just that he made a vow. He said he is testing himself. I guess that's something knights do."

Shaking his head, Cale Greeneye clambered back aboard Piquin and hauled up his mounting ladder. "Pim," he said, turning, "you and Coal go back and report what we've heard. The rest of us will go down and see about that knight."

"Oh, good!" Cas Springheel grinned. "I'll go tell Glendon that you're coming. He'll be delighted. There hasn't been anybody for him to test himself on since those wandering ogres two days ago." The kender turned and scampered away.

"What ogres?" Cale called after him. "What happened?"

"Nothing much," the high voice drifted back up the slope. "They didn't get across."

"Rust!" Cale muttered. "I should know better than to try to talk to a kender. *Anybody* should know better." With a sigh of disgust, he reached toward his saddle horn, then stopped. "Where's my other spur?"

"Your what?" Mica Rockreave squinted at him.

"My other spur! I had two of them just a minute ago. Now there's only one."

* * * * *

The kender was out of sight by the time the mounted dwarves reached the valley floor, where great, gnarled trees swallowed the path. With drawn blades and loosed shields, they rode into the shadows, their eyes darting around for any sign of danger. But for all its ominous appearance, the grove seemed peaceful enough. Birds of a dozen colors and a hundred voices livened the tops of the trees, and where afternoon sun slanted through breaks in the foliage canopy bright flowers grew.

The path wound downward, the woods spreading and becoming more open. Around a bend Cale led them, then around another, and drew rein. Ahead the forest ended, and brushy slopes led downward to the bank of a rushing stream less than a hundred feet wide at this point. Lying across the stream was a great, gray tree trunk, weathered with age. Its top surface had been hewn level, making a smooth wooden path five feet wide with graded gravel approaches.

But it wasn't the hewn timber bridge that held the dwarves' attention. It was the figure atop it. The man—he was apparently human, though not even the slightest part of his face or body was visible—wore an assemblage of oiled chain mail and polished armor that covered him from plumed helm to steel-shod toes, from gantleted hands to plated shins to shrouded breastplate. His cloak and plume were deep blue in color, and the stitchwork device at his breast, like the lacquered emblem on his oval shield, was a red falcon in stoop on a field of gray. Besides his shield, he carried a banded mace at his back, a black-hilted sword at his side, and a long, tapered lance tipped with an iron ball upright in its saddle-boot.

153

The horse beneath him was almost as heavily—and elaborately—armored as he was, from spiked foreplate to skirts of mail.

As the dwarves reached the bridge approach, the man raised his shield toward them. His voice sounded deep and hollow, resonating from the closed face-plate of his helm. "Turn away!" he ordered. "None may cross here, upon my oath and honor."

Cale's glance picked out something else then. On the far bank, just to one side of the bridge, the kender sat grinning, cradling his knees as he watched with bright-eyed interest. The dwarf pointed. "If none may cross, then how about him?"

The man didn't turn. "That is a kender," he said. "Kender don't count."

"We do, too!" Cas Springheel objected from the far bank. "Some of us do, anyway!"

The man ignored him, his visage fixed stonily on the four mounted dwarves facing him. "Turn away," he repeated. "None may cross here, upon my oath and . . ."

"You already said that," Cale Greeneye snapped. "What is this oath you speak of?"

"My oath," the knight said. "My oath, upon my honor. I have sworn to hold this bridge."

"Why?"

For a moment, the man was silent, as though considering a question too preposterous to deserve an answer. Then he said, "Why not? It's as good a bridge as any."

"And if we decide to cross?"

"I will oppose your crossing."

"And if we cross anyway?"

"That is most unlikely."

"But if we do?"

"Then upon my honor, I would owe you a debt of service."

"What does that mean?" Mica Rockreave demanded.

"It doesn't matter what it means," the knight said, patiently, "for you shall not cross."

"I've had enough of this," Cale Greeneye muttered. He drew his axe, spurred Piquin with his one remaining spur, and crouched in his saddle as the tall horse thundered onto the bridge, straight at the motionless knight.

Cale had no idea what happened next. All he saw was a glimpse of the oval shield rising, the lance tipping downward, and the armored horse turning daintily, quartering to lean toward him. One moment he and Piquin were bearing down on the armored man, and an instant later the two of them, dwarf and horse, tumbled with resounding splashes into the rushing water below the bridge. Cale's own shield and his axe flew from his grip, and his chest felt as though a Thorin smith had rearranged his ribs with a hammer.

Piquin thrashed about for a moment in the cold water, then got his bearings and headed back to shore, angling downstream on the current. For Cale, it was less simple. Massive and solid as any true dwarf, he went straight to the bottom and felt his boot soles crunch against gravel. He bent his knees and pushed upright as hard as he could, springing from the streambed. His head cleared water for only a second, but it was long enough to gulp in a deep breath before he sank again. Then, half walking and half swimming, he began his submerged journey back to shore.

He was fifty yards downstream when Gran Molden grasped his hand and helped him from the water. Piquin was already there, soaking wet and watching curiously. Cale shook himself, spat water, and cleared his eyes, then turned to glare upstream. The bridge was still there, the armored horse still stood upon it, and the hooded knight still sat his horse, motionless as though nothing had happened. Flint Cokeras and Shard Feldspar sat in their saddles, gaping.

"Rust and tarnish!" Cale snarled, then bent to cough up water. When the spasm passed, he grabbed Piquin's reins and stormed upstream to the foot of the bridge. Striding to the very butt of the tree-bridge, he faced the stolid knight and demanded, "How did you do that?"

"Properly," the knight said. "It's a matter of proper training."

"Well, we're still coming across!" Cale raised his hand and sliced downward. "Shard! Flint! Put an end to this!"

Instantly, two powerful dwarven horses thundered past him, their riders wielding shield and blade. Side by side, they filled the narrow bridge. Beyond them, Cale saw the knight dip his lance, saw the shield rise, and saw the armored horse turn slightly and brace itself, as though kneeling. The dwarves hit the obstacle with a crash, and their tall horses loomed above the human's shorter animal. Then the lance swept around in an arc, the emblazoned shield thrust upward, and the warhorse reared high, directly between its opponents.

Dwarves and golden horses seemed to fly in all directions, ending with resounding splashes on both sides of the bridge, and the knight resumed his position. "I did that properly, too," his hollow-sounding voice called to Cale. "In all modesty, I am really quite good at what I do."

It took a while to get Flint Cokeras and Shard Feldspar back on dry ground. When all were accounted for, the dwarves huddled together for a moment, then separated and began unpacking the gear from their saddles. On the bridge, the knight waited patiently. Beyond him, the kender danced up and down the riverbank, trying to see what was going on.

Cale's companions rummaged through packs and came up with delving tools, a pick and shovel, and a finely made light winch fitted with a length of good Thoradin twist cable.

While Gran Molden stood guard with a loaded sling, the others went to work at the foot of the bridge. Within moments they had a sizeable hole dug alongside the log butt and were fitting their winch to the timber.

"What are you doing over there?" the knight called, sounding puzzled.

They ignored him. While Flint played out cable from the winch, Cale carried its end downstream and spliced a loop around the trunk of a sturdy tree. He returned, thrust pry-bars through the winch sockets, and three strong dwarves put their backs to the task of reeling in cable.

For a moment, nothing happened. Then the timber bridge shuddered, and the knight shouted, "You can't do that!"

By then, though, they had. The entire bridge tilted, slid into the freshly dug hole alongside, and knight and horse disappeared into the river. For long seconds there was no sign of them, then a horse head bobbed to the surface downstream, and an unarmored head with flowing red hair surfaced near it.

Repacking their goods, Cale and his companions climbed aboard their horses and rode in stately procession across the slanting bridge to the far bank, where a delighted kender was clapping, dancing around, and calling encouragement to the man trying to follow his horse out of the water downstream.

"You did it!" the kender burbled to Cale Greeneye. "You actually made it across!"

"In no particular modesty," Cale told him, "we are very good at what we do, too."

The man had gained the shore. Without his armor, which he had left somewhere beneath the water, he looked thoroughly human and thoroughly drenched.

"Bring him up here," Cale Greeneye ordered. "I want to find out about that 'debt of service' business." He looked around, remembering his missing spur. "Where did that kender go?"

Castomel Springheel was nowhere in sight. His sharp ears had caught the sound of distant drums, and he was on his curious way to see where the sound came from.

16

A Debt of Service

The arrival of the hylar had transformed the quiet little valley into a
bustling, busy place. There were dwarves everywhere:
dwarves at work straightening the tipped bridge; dwarves
making fires and setting up lean-tos; dwarves tending
stock, unpacking provisions, and scouting sentry posts;
dwarves on fold-out ladders grooming dozens of the huge,
gold-and-white horses; dwarves with nets and hooks
retrieving arms and armor from the rushing stream; dwarf
women tending dwarf children; dwarf foragers beginning
a harvest of hay and wild grains from the fields above the
stream; and a very old dwarf with a crutch, who muttered
dourly to himself as he padded around here and there, trying to find a quiet place to rest.

Glendon Hawke felt totally out of place among them, but there wasn't a thing he could do about it. They had his horse, his arms and armor, all of his clothing except the brief under-kilt he wore . . . and they had him. A ring of grim-looking dwarves with weapons in hand surrounded him. Nobody had told the man that he was a prisoner, but it was clear that he wasn't going anywhere, even had his honor permitted it.

The evening breeze had dried his hair, and it fluttered around his cheeks like locks of spun copper as he turned toward a procession of dwarves coming through the ring of guards. One was Cale Greeneye, the one who had demanded and accepted his pledge of service. Following him were a regal-looking older dwarf with fierce features and shrewd eyes, a heavily-muscled younger dwarf who seemed inches taller than most of them, a strikingly pretty female in traveling robes, and the old dwarf with the crutch. There were others, as well, but these held back as the first five approached.

Cale Greeneye looked the man up and down, an ironic twinkle in his eyes, then turned to the older dwarf standing beside him. "Sire, this is the human I told you about. His name is Glendon Hawke . . . or *Sir* Glendon, I suppose, though he doesn't look much like a sir right now. He calls himself a knight."

"I *am* a knight," Glendon muttered. "Not of the orders, of course, but no less a knight. I am a free lance."

"Sir Knight," Cale completed the introductions, "this is our chieftain, Colin Stonetooth, my father. And my sister, Tera Sharn. And this is our captain of guards, Willen Ironmaul. The venerable one there is Mistral Thrax. Please tell them what you have granted to me."

Glendon took a deep breath. "I have pledged you my service," he said grudgingly.

"Why?"

"Because my honor demands it. You bested me at the bridge, even if you did so by foul means." Standing very straight, the human looked down at his new masters, accepting his fate. He was at least a foot taller than any of them, even the massive Willen Ironmaul. But his pledge was his honor, and he had given his pledge.

"Right." Cale Greeneye nodded. "And I have committed your services to my father."

The chieftain was studying Glendon with unconcealed dislike. Now he glanced at his son. "This . . . this *human* is going to teach us to fight? I have my doubts, as I told you."

"He has skills, Father," Cale assured the chieftain. "I have seen them."

"Yes, I know. With lance and shield, on horseback. What else?"

"He told me he has studied every sort of combat. I tested him with simple swords. He disarmed me with one parry."

The chieftain gazed at Glendon again, curiously. "You disarmed my son?"

"Of course," the man said. "He doesn't know how to use a sword. No offense intended, though. He is quick and strong, and can learn."

The dwarves glanced at one another. Among them, Cale Greeneye was reckoned a fine swordsman—almost the equal of Jerem Longslate, who had never been bested either in trial or in combat.

Colin Stonetooth turned his head, catching the eye of the captain of the Ten. "I should like to see that for myself," he decided. "Jerem?"

"Yes, Sire." Jerem Longslate handed his shield and buckler to one of his companions. "Simple swords?"

"For now." Colin Stonetooth nodded. "Do you agree?" he asked Glendon Hawke.

"I am at your service," the man shrugged.

"Do you want your own sword?" Cale asked him.

"It doesn't matter," the knight said. "The skill is in the hand, not in the blade."

Cale pulled his own sword and turned it, presenting the hilt. "Then use mine," he said.

By the time the rest had stepped back, clearing a wide

circle, Jerem Longslate had stripped himself of armor and robes. Wearing only his kilt and boots, carrying only his wide sword, he strode forward to face the man who towered over him. "Are there any particular rituals or rules?" he asked.

"None." The man shook his head. "A demonstration is all that was requested. Just attack me, whenever and however you like." He hefted Cale's blade, testing its weight. It was balanced differently than his own. Its weight was forward, toward the point. Well suited, he thought, to short arms with powerful wrists and shoulders. Turning half away from Jerem Longslate, he held the blade upright, gazing at its surface.

After a moment, Jerem barked, "Well, are you about ready? I'm waiting."

The human didn't even look at him. "Why are you waiting? I invited you to attack."

Jerem frowned, then shrugged. He raised his own blade before him, circled two steps to the right, and abruptly ducked and lunged, a movement almost too quick to see. Taking the man at his word, he went straight for the heart . . . and stopped. Somehow his sword was not where it should be. It was still in his hand, but now pointed off to one side. The clang of struck steel rang in his ears, and something sharp was poking at his throat. It was the human's blade.

"You see," Glendon said, critically, "you made two mistakes there. The first was in thinking that I did not see you. The second was that midriff thrust. I hardly had to parry at all to knock it aside. If you intend to defeat a person in combat, you shouldn't give him such advantages."

The man pulled back his sword, and a tiny drop of blood trickled from beneath the dwarf's whiskers. Jerem glanced over at his chieftain. "It was a fluke, Sire. May I try again?"

"As you please," Colin Stonetooth nodded.

This time the captain of the Ten gave no advantages. With a flurry of whistling cuts and thrusts he attacked the tall human . . . and found himself flat on his back on the hard ground while his sword spun upward, flashing in the evening sun. At the top of its arc the sword steadied, then fell point-downward directly toward him. At the last instant, a long arm stretched above him and a long-fingered, human hand caught the falling blade.

Jerem rolled away and got to his feet. Glendon Hawke calmly flipped the dwarf's sword, reversed it, and handed it back to him. "That was much better," he said approvingly. "If you would like to learn that disarm-deck-and-skewer trick, I'll teach it to you . . . after you have mastered some basics."

Colin Stonetooth spread his hands, looking at his grinning son. "Very well, Cale," he agreed. "The man can instruct us. What does he want in return?"

"To be released from service when his task is done, and to have his belongings returned to him. He asks no other reward. He said his pledge is bound by honor, not by trade."

"A noble human," Colin said, wonderingly.

Glendon Hawke heard the comment. "Nobility, like chivalry, is a condition of knighthood, . . . Sire. Skill alone is only the pattern of the tapestry, not the fabric. Disciplines of hand and mind must be woven from the heart."

"We can stop here for a while," Colin decided. "It will do us no harm to learn what this man can teach us."

Off to one side of the camp, noise erupted—a flurry of booming sounds that settled quickly into a fast, rhythmic beat. Colin Stonetooth put his hands to his ears, and Cale Greeneye shouted, "Somebody get that kender away from the drums! And while you're at it, search him! I want my spur back!"

All around, dwarves glanced at one another and shook their heads. Everyone knew about the kender. Through all the history of Thorin, wandering kender had appeared now and then among the Calnar—usually during Balladine, when bright baubles lay everywhere for quick hands to take.

Kender had never been welcomed at Balladine. But no one had ever devised an effective way to keep them out. And, once present, there was no good way to get rid of a kender short of killing him or boring him.

There was an old saying among the dwarves, accepted as just one of those unpleasant facts of life: *Kender happen*.

* * * * *

"It is a contamination of magic," Mistral Thrax explained sadly. "The old scrolls tell of it, those handed down by the earliest smiths. It was the god Reorx—they say—who created the powers of chaos, in the form of a faceted gray stone. And all in its path became infected by its evil."

"Old tales." Colin Stonetooth shook his head. "Why would the greatest of the gods, the creator of all metals—and maybe the creator of all of us as well—have despoiled the world with . . ."—his beard twitched as he curled a lip in disgust—"with *magic*? Surely, Mistral, you don't believe that?"

The ancient shrugged and turned his palms upward. On each calloused palm a symbol glowed dull red—a Y-shaped design that might have been a twin-tined spear. "I don't know now what I believe," he said. "But this is real, and it came from the magical eyes of a human who used sorcery. And I believe my vision of Kitlin Fishtaker was real . . . and I know the way to Kal-Thax. How would I know the way to Kal-Thax if I weren't touched by . . . by magic?"

They sat atop a stone bluff, watching the combat drills in the fields below. The human knight, Glendon, had started teaching Willen Ironmaul's guards the skills of his craft, and now he was surrounded by fully half the Hylar nation—men, women, and even children—all anxious to learn the arts of strategy and weaponry. Colin Stonetooth noted to himself that his Hylar had come a long way since Thoradin. No longer was the left side of the tools just an occasional interest. Many of the tools they carried now—

things like swords and maces—were tools with no other side but the left.

Glendon Hawke might not have been happy with the turn of events that brought him here, teaching the means of combat to hundreds of fascinated dwarves, but he had admitted to the chieftain that he had never encountered students more apt. The Ten had been the first instructed, and Jerem Longslate had learned the sword so well that he could now disarm the teacher one time out of three. They were also learning the fine art of shield-play and the strangely human arts of the lance. The giant Calnar horses had proved surprisingly adept at lance-charging and were learning along with their riders.

In many ways, the dwarves surprised Glendon. As they learned, they adapted their new skills to their own circumstances and often improved on them. One example—the sudden wheeling of a rider to pick up a footman, then charging into battle with each dwarf clinging to one side of the high saddle, hammers or axes swinging in great arcs—had come as close to killing the knight as any tactic he had ever seen. Had he not dived facedown into the dust the first time Willen Ironmaul and a guardsman demonstrated that, he was sure he would have been beheaded.

The field below the bluff rang with the clang of steel on steel, an energetic counterpoint to the ringing of hammers on anvils off to one side, where dwarves were shaping new shields crafted after Glendon Hawke's own. There were also bits of armor in the making and sturdy axes suited both to woodcraft and to war. Some of the craftsmen were also beating out battle-helms more suitable for outdoor wear than the old delving helmets most of the Hylar had worn.

Colin Stonetooth watched his people moodily. They were changing, becoming a nation unlike the Calnar from whom they had separated. He hoped the differences would not one day bring their downfall. As a tribe, the Hylar were becoming more formidable by the day, under the tutelage of the somber human knight. But, as with the

Calnar of their origins, they were not a prolific people. A male and female who wed tended to wed for life and rarely produced more than three or four children.

We are becoming fighters, Colin Stonetooth thought, watching. Let us not become so enamored of our new skills that we put too much trust in them. No matter how dangerous we are, one by one, we are not destined to be numerous.

As though reading his mind—a tendency the old dwarf had developed of late and which Colin found startling and distracting—Mistral Thrax said, "Yes, we have a destiny. I do not see it clearly, but the new skills will aid in it." He stared at the marks on his palms, looking puzzled, then muttered, "In Kal-Thax. Our destiny. Not to be all, or even most, but to lead . . . others?" He shook his head. "I do not understand, my chieftain."

"Nor do I," Colin admitted. "Tell me more about the old scrolls."

"They are very old," Mistral Thrax mused. "Several centuries, at least. Perhaps more. And some of them speak of that mystical gem, the faceted gray stone. They say that Reorx himself created it and placed it on Krynn. It was delivered into the keeping of a human king."

"Why?" Colin's brows went up in outrage. "A *human*? Why a human? If Reorx had done such a thing, why not give it to dwarves? We are the primary people of this world, after all."

"They don't say why." Mistral Thrax shook his head. "But they do say that the humans lost the thing."

"Well, of course they did! Who would trust any human with anything of importance? Even a god should know better! At least, no self-respecting dwarf would ever actually try to *use* such powers."

"Gnomes set it free," Mistral Thrax said. "At least, so the scrolls say."

"Gnomes? That's even worse than it being in the hands of humans!"

"Oh, they didn't get it. Gnomes can't do anything right.

They just set it loose, and since then there has been magic on Krynn. So the scrolls say."

"And this?" Colin indicated the marks on the old dwarf's hands. "You think it comes from that?"

"The legends of the scrolls tell of Kitlin Fishtaker, a dwarven spearman who traded river fish to the humans of that place. They say he was there when the gray stone was released and tried to knock the thing down with his spear before it could get loose. The stone punished him. He was permanently contaminated with magic and became an outcast because any who touched him also would catch the disease."

"Folk tales," Colin Stonetooth rumbled.

"Maybe." Mistral Thrax shrugged. "But I saw Kitlin Fishtaker in a vision, and I saw the man who couldn't be seen in the attack on . . . Thoradin. And the eyes I pulled from his head were not eyes. And now I, too, am contaminated."

"And so we wander across the vast lands in search of a place we have never seen, called Kal-Thax." Colin planted his chin on his fists moodily. "It's just as well, I suppose. After what happened, I could no longer stay there, and all the rest here came with me by choice. So, having somewhere to go is better than having nowhere to go, even if the place we aim for is only a legend itself."

"Kal-Thax is there," Mistral Thrax assured him. "In those mountains ahead."

"I see no mountains," Colin snapped.

"But you will, my chieftain. I see them already . . . more clearly, sometimes, than I see what is around us here."

On the wide field below, Glendon had his charges lined up in double rows, facing each other. He raised a hand, stepped back, and several hundred Hylar—men, women and children—began happily pounding away at one another with padded swords and shields.

Castomel Springheel drifted through the defenses of the Ten to appear beside Colin Stonetooth. Grinning his delight, the kender surveyed the drill field. "They'll never believe this back in Kendermore," he told himself. "Dwarves going to knight school! I wouldn't believe it myself, if I wasn't right here to see it."

Part IV:
Urkhan's Legacy

The Great Caverns
Beneath Cloudseeker Peak

Century of Wind
Decade of Oak
Early Spring, Year of Copper

17
The Undermountain

The mountain peak called Cloudseeker was not the tallest of peaks in Kal-Thax. Its broad summit, from which the Wind-weavers thrust upward like giant sharks' teeth, was lower by a thousand feet than soaring Sky's End, to the north. But Cloudseeker was far wider. From the foot of its north slopes where Sky's End began to climb, to the sloping fields and the high-walled, closed valley that marked its southern base, Cloudseeker was nearly fifty miles across by horizontal measurement.

The caves and shallow warrens of the Theiwar strong-hold, called Theibardin or "Theiwar-Home," occupied only a small area below its crest. Above, the three great crags of the Windweavers jutted skyward, surrounding an immense sinkhole lake that was frozen over in most seasons but which provided constant seepage of moisture into the very heart of the mountain. Few, if any, Theiwar had ever ventured into the resulting deep caverns, but Daewar explorer-spies, far more venturesome than the dour, single-minded Theiwar, had crept into them by various routes, charted portions of them, and returned to Daebardin with wondrous tales.

Beneath the crags, they said, were deep caverns that ran for miles, converging into an enormous chamber dominated above by a giant stalactite a thousand yards high and even wider at its top, standing like a giant pillar above a subterranean lake big enough to be called a sea. The great stalactite was of living stone, and on the charts they called the sea Urkhan, in honor of a Daewar explorer who had died there on the expedition.

The Urkhan Sea was at least seven miles across, north to south, and was surrounded by dozens of square miles of natural caverns eroded into shale layers surmounted by harder stone. Throughout these, fresh air flowed from natural vents around the base of the peak and wafted upward to numerous open seeps around the Windweavers that served as exhausts. And many of the deep warrens were lighted by quartz strata, admitting daylight from miles above.

Only a bit of the marvel had been explored, but it was these reports and these charts that had enchanted the old Daewar regent, Bole Diamondcuff, and after him the prince, Olim Goldbuckle. Visions of an impregnable fortress, of a subterranean realm which might one day be a kingdom, blossomed for them both. Long before the spread of chaos from the east became obvious, it was Goldbuckle's decision to drive a road right through the heart of Sky's End, into the deeps of Cloudseeker, and relocate Daebardin into the subterranean heart of the mountain that the surly Theiwar thought of as their own.

To the ambitious and energetic Daewar dwarves, the golden people of Kal-Thax, the only valid claim the

Theiwar had was to the part of the mountain they actually occupied and used, which was almost none of it. "Use it or lose it," was the Daewar philosophy where territory was concerned.

So the great secret road went forward, a level tunnel twenty feet wide and fifteen feet high, driven through the granite heart of Sky's End from Daebardin on the north, into the porous underlayers of Cloudseeker. As it neared its end, the Daewar made preparation to move to new quarters.

The hidden opening beneath Galefang, where Olim Goldbuckle led his expedition after the defense of the eastern border and the punishing of the Theiwar chieftain, was only a little, wind-scoured tunnel in the face of a cliff. But set into its back wall were iron doors, and beyond the doors was a wide, spiral shaft leading downward to the roadhead far below.

Hundreds of Daewar worked there, in gloom illuminated by oil wicks, forge glows, and torches. Expert delvers, the Daewar had averaged nearly thirty yards a day for almost ten years, digging away at the solid stone while winch-driven cable carts strung with dozens of almost inaudible bat-bells hauled the rubble back along the lengthening tunnel to dump it below Daebardin's slopes. The resulting skirt of broken stone now was a slope in itself, extending almost to the great chasm which separated the base of Sky's End from the foothills and the breaks and plains of the wastelands beyond.

Sealing the high doors behind them, Olim Goldbuckle and his legion descended into the depths of Cloudseeker, where delvemasters studied their charts while picks and drills chipped away at stone that was softer than most they had encountered before and different in color.

Emerging into the roadway, Olim Goldbuckle climbed atop a laden cable-cart and picked up a piece of the stone rubble. He looked at it, sniffed it, and tasted it, then tossed it back and swung down. Above him, bat-bells tinkled merrily. The bells were tiny silver devices which the

Daewar had invented long ago to drive away the flocks of blood bats which sometimes invaded digs. But now they had another use as well. Although most people—even dwarves—could hardly hear the bells, they had found that echoes in stone could resonate them. By "thumping" stone in a delve, and counting the times the bells responded, they could tell how far it was from one side of the stone to the other.

Olim ignored the tiny sounds now, brushing his hands. "Gypsum," he said to Gem Bluesleeve. "We are near the caverns."

"Very near, Sire," a delvemaster looked up from his spread chart. "Nearer than we thought. We could break through at any moment."

"Into what?" Olim squinted at the chart.

"According to Urkhan's calculations," the delvemaster said, "there is a great natural cavern ahead. The one he called the first warren. It connects to other caverns beyond, and eventually to the subterranean sea."

"I hope we break through above sea level," Olim noted.

The delvemaster drew himself up, as one deeply offended. "Would you like to calculate the elevations yourself, Sire?"

"Of course not." Olim smiled. "I trust your calculations above all others, Slate Coldsheet. Just keep doing the wonderful job you do." He turned away, muttering to Gem Bluesleeve. "That's the problem with delvers, Gem. By the time they are wise enough to chart a bore, their sense of humor has been drowned out by the ringing in their ears."

Followed by some of his guard, Olim went forward to where the boring was in progress. The ring of hammers on iron drills, the splitting of stone as foot-wide slabs were broken away with prybars, and the clank of picks and mauls as the rubble was broken filled the wide tunnel with a chorus of sound. Beneath its tempo was the crunch of shovels, the low thunder of rubble raining into high-sided carts, and the ever-present, rhythmic tapping of mallets as spikes were set to steady the cart rails that followed along behind the dig.

The carts were wide, low-wheeled vehicles chained together by threes and fives, and a constant parade of them had been rolling back to the far side of Sky's End for the past ten years to dump rubble. At intervals, where the tunnel was wider, empty returning carts were diverted to side-rails to make way for the full ones.

Working in shifts, with hammer drills and prybars, the Daewar delvers could extend their tunnel as much as fifty feet in a day's time, even in the toughest rock. Now that the substance was softer, they were moving faster than that, though some additional effort was required for occasional shoring as they went. The first vertical fault they had encountered, a seep in soft, porous stone, had cost them a dozen lives and three days' delay because of a cave-in. Now they took no such chances.

A lantern-bearer going before him, Olim Goldbuckle went all the way to the front, where a fresh layer of stone had just been levered away, adding another foot to the tunnel's almost fifty miles of length. Drillers and drivers, cutters and prisers stepped back as the prince approached, and a sweating young Daewar with bulging forearms and whiskers of spun gold pointed at the new-cut face of the tunnel. "Softer by the minute, Sire. And we have sound."

"We are that close?" Olim's brow creased. "Let me hear." He knelt at the sheer wall of the fresh cut and sniffed the stone, then pressed his ear against its surface. The young driver stepped forward, attached a string of bat-bells to the surface, raised his hammer, and delivered a smashing blow to the stone inches from his prince's head. The bat-bells quivered and tinkled, and Olim counted his heartbeats, then grinned as a muted echo came back to him, ringing through the stone itself.

"Twenty feet," he judged. "Not more than that." He stood. "Gem, bring a company of fighters forward. I doubt if there is a Theiwar within miles. They don't have the patience or the inclination to explore what is beneath their very feet, but let's take no chances when we break through.

If there happens to be anyone there, we don't want reports going aloft just yet."

"Yes, Sire," Gem Bluesleeve agreed. "If they knew we were tunneling into their mountain, rather than building a city under ours, they might be rather upset." Gem hurried back the way they had come to select his company of warriors. He would head it himself.

Olim followed him, away from the resumed clamor of the dig. He had a few hours to wait before the tunnel broke through into the first of the giant caverns charted by Urkhan and his band. He wanted to eat, and to rest, and to give some thought to what should be done once the tunnel was completed. He didn't really expect to find anyone at the end of it. The Theiwar were not explorers, and who else could have stumbled onto Urkhan's discovery?

Once fortified, not even dragons or magic would be likely to invade such a place. Olim shivered slightly at the thought. He had never seen a dragon and never expected to. But there was magic in the world, and, like all of his kind, he considered magic an abhorrent thing, an evil that only humans or other lesser races would even think about exercising. Even the primitive Theiwar and dark-dwelling Daergar . . . even the wild-eyed Klar abhorred magic. There were legends, of course, of a dwarf who had become involved with magic in some way, but to Olim Goldbuckle the idea was unthinkable. Yet, there had been times of late when Olim's dreams had been troublesome. Several times, in his sleep, when he dreamed of the great undertaking now at hand, a spectral, shadowy figure had been there in his dreams—a figure that whispered words to him. "The Daewar are chosen," the specter said, "to carve out a place." But then it added, "But others will come to guide your race." Each time, Olim had awakened shaken and puzzled. What others? What did it mean?

As an attendant handed him a loaf and a bowl, Olim Goldbuckle's gold-whiskered face contorted itself into a scowl. "Guide my race?" he muttered. "None but Daewar shall rule Daewar!"

"Sire?" The attendant blinked at him, startled.

"Nothing!" Olim growled. "Bring me ale."

"Yes, Sire." The attendant hurried away, and Olim perched on the wheel of a sidelined cart to have his meal.

Had he been human, or even elf, Olim Goldbuckle might have dismissed the dreams as something imagined . . . as something simply beyond understanding. But Olim Goldbuckle, prince of the Daewar, was a dwarf. And like most full dwarves, his practical mind had no use for the unintelligible nor any patience for things indistinct. He could not ignore the dreams or simply forget them. Especially not the latest one.

"You will know them when they come," the phantom voice had added, this last time. "You will know them by the drum."

Olim was still thinking about dreams when distant shouts echoed back along the tunnel, and messengers came running. "We're through, Sire!" they shouted. "We have entered the first warren, just as Urkhan's charts promised!"

"Send runners northward," Olim ordered. "Withdraw all Daewar from Daebardin and start them this way. Prepare to seal this tunnel when all have passed through. We will establish residence and claim this place as soon as we have looked around."

* * * * *

The warren was an immense natural cavern, softly lighted by a high ceiling that was, in some places, pure quartz. More than half a mile beneath the surface, it was as Urkhan's explorers had described—a vast, elongated chamber almost two miles across at its widest point and four miles long including a narrowing, funnel-like "tail" that curved away to the east. Here and there, stalactites hung from the high ceilings, their shapes as varied and fantastic as candle-beads. Beneath each was a waiting stalagmite, tall sentinel spires like the bases of trees in a giant forest.

"Marvelous!" Olim Goldbuckle exclaimed as he led his guards through the new opening into the silent cavern. Faint echoes of his voice drifted lazily back to him, and in the distance something moved—something very large, slowly raising what might have been a head, to listen.

Some of the Daewar clasped their swords, but an old delvemaster hurried forward to thrust an unrolled scroll under the nose of his prince. "Tractor worm," he said, pointing. "As Urkhan described. They are large creatures. Very strong. But slow, dull-witted, and docile. The explorers supposed that they might be useful, if they could be controlled."

"Tractor worm," Olim repeated. Quickening his stride, he hurried toward the movement, dozens of Daewar following him as more entered the cavern behind them.

The thing was huge, at least thirty feet in length, and it turned what appeared to be its head toward them as they approached. No eyes were visible, nor ears. Instead, its "face" was a cluster of waving tentacles surrounding an orifice that opened and closed rhythmically. Olim stepped closer, peering at the creature. He raised his shield and waved it from side to side. The creature did not respond. "It's blind," he said.

At the sound of his voice, the thing turned toward him, its tentacles quivering. "Ho!" Olim rasped. "It can hear me."

Beside him, Gem Bluesleeve stepped aside and cupped his hands. "Ho, worm!" he called. Immediately, the raised end of the thing turned toward him. He stepped farther to the side and called again. Again the worm responded, turning to face him. "It hears," he called to the others. "Watch!" Turning, he hurried away, quartering around the creature until he was off to one side of it. Then he called, "Ho! Worm! Here I am!"

Obediently, the thing turned toward him, this time moving its entire body in a slow, methodical arc to face him. The dwarf chuckled. "I have this thing's full attention," he called. "See? Now it is coming toward me!" He scampered away a hundred feet and turned to call once more. The huge worm increased its speed, its gray, banded body rippling as it flowed across the uneven floor of the cavern. It was faster than it had seemed, and Gem backpedaled, staying a good distance from it. Its pace was that of a walking dwarf.

"He has its attention, all right," Olim noted to the others watching. "Now I wonder what he intends to do with it."

"Or how he will get rid of it," the old master delver Slate Coldsheet added. "The captain should have read these scrolls. Urkhan's party reported that the worms tend to become . . . uh . . . attached to people. They follow and try to get close. The danger is that they might actually crush a person by their weight. Some of the explorers were nearly exhausted by the time they managed to elude their pets."

"I could use some help here, I think!" Gem Bluesleeve called, walking briskly in the distance while the giant worm chugged along behind him. "I don't know how to make this thing stop!"

"Some of you drillers," Olim said, gesturing, "see if you can get some grapples on that thing."

Gem was quite some distance away now, coming around in a long circle, trying to head back to the others. Behind him, the worm followed happily, its banded length rippling in the subdued light, its tentacled face waving merrily.

Carrying chains, throw-lines, and rock-harness, several dozen drillers and delvers fanned out to approach the monster from its flanks. It seemed not to mind them at all. Its full attention was focused on Gem Bluesleeve, and it seemed to desire nothing else in life than to reach him. Gem kept walking, trying to keep that from happening.

Flanking the worm, teams of dwarves managed to get sling-harness attached to it at various places and grasped the halter-lines, setting their heels. The worm neither slowed nor turned. It continued its methodical pace, following Gem Bluesleeve. Behind and along its flanks dozens of sturdy dwarves were dragged along, their steel soles carving ruts in the hard floor.

"Tie off those lines!" Olim Goldbuckle roared. Gem was approaching now, looking very worried, and the worm wasn't far behind him.

Scrambling, the delvers spread and raced outward, carrying their cables. Two modest stalagmites were within reach, and they snugged the lines there, then watched in awe as the cables came taught, strained, and hummed, and the stone of the stalagmites began to crumble. The worm slowed, but surged forward again as one of the restraints burst in a shower of limestone dust. But other cables held the monster now, attached to sturdier uprights, and it tugged futilely at its bonds for a moment, then subsided.

"Tractor worm," the old delvemaster remarked, shaking his head. "We should have a few of those things hauling our ore-carts."

Behind Olim there was a clatter as something fell to the stone floor. Out in the cavern the tractor worm, which had been resting quietly on its tethers, suddenly raised the front half of its huge body upright, whistled a sound that might have been either a scream or a roar, and surged against the lines. Cables parted, and the worm shot free to roll over on the floor.

More quickly than seemed possible, it turned, raised itself, and dived straight at a group of drillers trying to back away. The great creature's body smashed down on them, then it roared and raised itself again, flailing about like a creature gone berserk.

"The bat-bells!" the delvemaster shouted. "Someone dropped the bat-bells. That's what it hears!"

Dwarves scurried about, collecting the spilled silver bells and thrusting them into clothing to muffle their sound. Out in the cavern, Gem Bluesleeve brandished his sword and shouted. "Ho! Worm! To me!"

Again the worm turned, away from the drillers, heading for Gem. Other drillers and several guardsmen raced toward it, throwing cables and stone-nets.

Then, as abruptly as it had reacted, the creature subsided. All the bat-bells had been muffled, and it no longer heard their clamor. Racing around the thing, delvers and guards bound it in a thick mesh of steel cables and ran anchor lines to several large stands of stone.

Where it had attacked, two delvers lay dead, smashed into the stone floor by the mass of the monster. Several others limped away, injured but still able to move.

"Keep those delving bells silent!" Olim Goldbuckle ordered. "Get them out of here. Take them back into the tunnel." Then he swung around to face the delvemaster. "You still think those worms might be useful, Slate?"

"If they can be controlled," Slate said. "They react to sound, and if there are some sounds that . . . I don't know. We'll have to work at it."

Gem Bluesleeve approached, visibly shaken. It had been on impulse that he had distracted the raving worm from the delvers, calling its attention to himself. Now he was wondering just what he—sword and all—could have done had the thing not stopped.

Olim Goldbuckle looked at his captain and frowned, then sighed, shaking his head. It would do no good to admonish the guardsman for risking his own life. It was just the way he was.

Gem approached, started to speak, then simply shrugged.

"If you are through playing with your worm," Olim Goldbuckle told him, "I believe we should get on with exploring these caverns."

Slate Coldsheet glanced at his chart and pointed. "Straight south, Sire. A mile or so, then the cavern narrows for another mile, past which is some kind of crevice. Beyond should be another cavern—not quite as wide as this, but longer. From there should be a tunnel to Urkhan's sea."

18

The Blood of Ambition

By the double light of Krynn's moons the raiders converged upon the nighttime slopes of Sky's End, and Glome the Assassin stood atop a ridge, watching in satisfaction.

As chieftain of the Theiwar of Theibardin, now that Twist Cutshank was dead, he had been able to assemble the tribes of Theiwar to council. Once gathered, it had been an easy accession for Glome. No subtlety had been involved in his becoming chieftain of the Theiwar. A few beatings, a few assassinations, and now he was the undisputed leader of thousands of dwarves who must do his bidding. He had summarily repealed the rights of contest and of challenge.

More than that, his army of invasion now included a

thousand or more Daergar from the Thunder Peaks, and a sizeable group—no one knew how many—of wild Klar, erratic and unpredictable but as determined as the rest to have a share in the treasures of the Daewar. It was the reward that Glome promised, in return for their support in the invasion of Daebardin, the stronghold beneath Sky's End that none of them had ever seen. They had never seen it because no spy had ever managed to get past the Daewar guards. But the growing fan of rubble on the mountainside beneath the Daewar citadel told them that it was by now an extensive delve, and where Daewar delved, there were treasures.

All the clans knew of the wealth of the Daewar. The proud, arrogant gold-molders did more than display their wealth throughout Kal-Thax. They flaunted it. It was in the bright finery of their apparel, the burnished sheen of their armor, the adornment of their ox-carts, in the very way they carried themselves when they walked.

Many Theiwar and Daergar had seen the insides of Daewar pavilions at trade camps, and it was a joke among the other tribes that the Daewar so enjoyed their comforts that no Daewar would travel a mile without a ton or so of carpets, crystal-wear, and gold-inlaid furniture for his comfort while roughing it in the wilderness. A joke, it was, but not one told with laughter. It was one of the reasons that so many of the other dwarves hated the Daewar.

The Daewar were rich, and flaunted their wealth.

For that reason—and because he had convinced many of them that the Daewar intended to conquer them, it had been easy for Glome the Assassin to recruit an army to invade Daebardin. The opportunity to loot the Daewar was promise enough for most of them.

The Daewar had made a fatal error by delving into Sky's End. Their old citadel on the shoulder of the mountain was small, but it was also well-placed and difficult to attack. Now, though, the Daewar were under the mountain—with only one way out. It was a perfect situation for a successful siege. Their subterranean city would be a trap for them once Glome's army held the citadel.

If any among the invaders suspected that Glome the Assassin had reasons of his own for this venture—that he in fact intended to make himself king of all Kal-Thax—they were wise enough not to mention the idea.

So now they gathered on the night-dark slope of Sky's End, thousands of armed Theiwar, Daergar, and a smattering of erratic, fanatical Klar, and just below them were the ramparts of the old citadel of the Daewar.

"I see no guards," Slide Tolec muttered. "Where are they? There are always guards."

"And always lights at night," someone else noted. "The gold people are night-blind. But I see no lights."

It was true. On the slope below, the spired citadel stood in darkness, silhouetted against the moonlit rubble-fields beyond. Only moon-shadows moved on its ramparts, darknesses among the patterns of red and white moonlight, sliding slowly inward as the moons Solinari and Lunitari crept higher in the spangled sky.

"Is it a trap?" one of the Daergar captains asked. "Do they somehow know we are here?"

"They know nothing," Glome snapped. "The Daewar are tricky, but they don't read minds or see in the dark. We have moved only by night since we assembled at the pits six days ago."

"Then where are their guards?" the Daergar growled, his voice muffled by the slitted iron mask he wore. Some of the Daergar removed their masks at night, when the light did not pain them, but some chose to wear them even then, and the effect was disconcerting when they spoke—a voice coming from a faceless ovoid of dark metal whose only feature was a narrow slit in front of the hidden eyes.

"It doesn't matter where they are," Glome said. "Visible or not, they will be dead soon enough. Are the trundles prepared?"

"They've been in place since just after sunset," Slide Tolec reminded him. "And they have been loaded for an hour. You can see them as well as we can."

The trundles were Glome's own plan—long, pegged-down nets that spanned a quarter mile of slopes above the Daewar citadel. The nets had been carried all the way from Theibardin and were set in place after darkness fell. Once they were in place, teams of dwarves had begun filling them with stones weighing forty to sixty pounds each. Hundreds of tons of stone now bulged the nets, and the keeper cables were as taut as iron bars.

"Then give the signal," Glome commanded. "We are ready."

"Hold!" someone called. "Look!"

Below the trundle nets, there was movement on the slope. At first it was furtive, hidden by shadows. Then into the moonlight ran a crowd of dwarves, leaping and shouting, heading downhill toward the silent Daewar citadel. There were a dozen or more of them—ragged, wild-haired creatures waving various weapons as they ran. Their cries were shouts of hatred, wild war cries that echoed from the slopes.

"Rust and tarnish!" Glome swore. "Those Klar . . . what do they think they're doing?"

"Who knows what Klar think?" a Daergar warrior rumbled from behind his featureless mask. "But they will ruin everything."

"No, they won't," Glome decided. "Slide! The signal!"

Slide Tolec put a short trumpet to his lips and blew a blast, then another. All up and down the net line, dwarves raised heavy axes above the keeper cables, and when Slide's trumpet sounded again, they sliced downward. With a crash that grew like thunder, the nets collapsed and tons of stone plunged down the slope, picking up momentum with each yard. The dust that rose above the landslide was a dense cloud, billowing upward in the garish light of the moons. Beyond it, the thunder of falling, crashing stone drowned out the screams of the dozen or so Klar trapped ahead of the fall.

Again Slide Tolec sounded his trumpet, and the battle cries of thousands of Theiwar and Daergar rose above the tumult of falling stone crashing down upon the Daewar citadel. A torrent of dark shapes on the mountainside, Glome's army charged down the rock-scoured slopes, following after the chaos they had unleashed.

Parts of the citadel still stood, broken spires thrusting skyward in the moonlit dust, but there were great holes in the structure where walls had fallen under the torrent of stone, and the Theiwar, Daergar, and remaining Klar poured through them, fanning out to occupy the old stronghold of the Daewar. Shouts of "Kill the Daewar!" rang and echoed, then died away in confused silence. Somewhere a querulous voice called, "Where are they? There's no one here!"

For more than an hour, in angry silence, the invaders searched level after level of the Daewar's mountainside city. They found nothing. The place was completely deserted. Not so much as a rug or piece of furniture remained.

It was by tracing the tracks of the ore carts back into the stone of Sky's End, that they found the sealed gate where the fresh delving of the Daewar had begun. It was a circular slab of solid granite, twelve feet in diameter, set into the neck of a tunnel.

"The delvings." Glome the Assassin decided. "They have completed their new city under the mountain and withdrawn to it." He pointed at the granite slab. "Bring it down," he commanded. "The Daewar are on the other side."

They brought out their tools and set to work. Outside, beyond the wrecked walls of the old citadel of Daebardin, daylight came and went and came again as determined dwarves chipped away at the edges of the plug gate. Finally, though, it was loose and they attacked it with prybars. After a moment, the thing teetered outward and fell as dwarves scampered aside, then drew their weapons and poured through the opening.

Beyond should have been an underground city, a city filled with Daewar and Daewar treasures. Instead, there was only a tunnel—a huge, track-floored tunnel that receded southward toward the heart of Sky's End.

A cluster of dark-blade-wielding Daergar turned to stare with blank, iron faces at the leader of the Theiwar. "So they are here?" one of them hissed. "Where, Theiwar?"

"Deeper," Glome decided. "The Daewar prince said they were delving deep. We must follow this tunnel. Their new city is ahead somewhere."

"It had better be," a Daergar rumbled.

Mile after mile the tunnel ran, deeper and deeper into the stone core of the mountain. Almost featureless, except for widened caverns at regular intervals, where the telltale marks of pulled spikes—where cart-track had been pulled up—spread into double pairs. Here, in the Daewar's delvings, the ore carts had been able to pass, laden carts rumbling outward, empties heading back into the mountain. With something like awe, the Theiwar studied these marks, as they studied the precise chiseling of the walls where stone had been removed a few feet at a time to bore the tunnel.

The huge tunnel, driving straight into the heart of a mountain, was impressive. It was not a thing beyond their understanding—many Theiwar were fair tunnelers—but it was a feat far larger than anything they had ever attempted, and the farther they went the more they realized the enormity of what the Daewar had done. If this mighty tunnel were no more than a road leading to their underground city, then what must the city be like?

After a few miles, Glome's army began to shrink as individuals and small groups, mostly Theiwar, held back, waited for the rest to pass, then quietly turned and went back the way they had come. It had occurred to many of them that if there were a city at the end of this road there must be far more Daewar than anyone had thought. The idea of attacking a tribe that outnumbered them, on its own ground, gave many a Theiwar second thoughts about the whole venture.

Few of the Daergar turned back. Driven by the intense,

single-minded stubbornness of natural miners, the Daergar would go on, and some of the wild, erratic Klar with them.

Far into Sky's End, Slide Tolec noticed that the Theiwar were far less numerous than they had been, and he edged aside, looking back along the great tunnel. Pretending to adjust his boots, he knelt beside a wall while the mixed army—still several thousand strong—marched past him.

When they had all gone by, he stood and glanced around. For a second he thought he was alone, then a shadow moved nearby, and a familiar voice said, "You, too, Slide Tolec?"

Brule Vaportongue stepped from shadows into the dim light of Slide's oil-wick. "You have realized it, too, then?"

"Realized what?" Slide snapped the words. The half-Daergar dark-seeker had startled him, and he resented it.

"That it is time to leave this place." Brule shrugged. "No Daewar fortune awaits us here. Only death. This road is not the entrance to a city. It is exactly what it seems. A road. The Daewar built it, and the Daewar have gone where it leads, and Glome the Assassin is going to his death."

"You fear the Daewar?" Slide sneered.

"Not as much as I fear my half-kin." Brule shrugged again, not reacting to the taunt. "I know the taste of the stubbornness that drives the Daergar. It is what Glome played on to get them to follow him. But I know a thing about that stubbornness that even Glome does not know."

"And what is that?"

"The blood call of the Daewar," Brule Vaportongue said, "can be opened, but not closed. My half-brothers there"— he waved in the direction the dwarven army had gone— "seek the blood of the Daewar. But if they are denied it, they will find other blood. The Daergar are like their blades. Once drawn, they will not be sheathed again until they have tasted blood."

Thoughtfully, Slide Tolec gazed down the tunnel where the sounds of Glome's invasion were fading. Then he adjusted his pack, weapons, and belts and turned away. "I'm tired of this," he said. "I'm going home."

"Good choice." Brule Vaportongue nodded and fell into step with the Theiwar.

* * * * *

Glome's dwindling army was twelve miles into the heart of Sky's End when it reached the second blockade, a grating made of four-inch-thick bars of forged iron, beaten together in hammer welds.

Glome pounded on the barricade in a rage. "Cart track!" he shouted. "Rust and corrode the Daewar, they've made a gate of cart track!" Panting in frustration, he gestured angrily, "Open it!"

Other Theiwar and several Daergar came forward to peer at the gate, holding up torches. The light shone through the grating, gleaming on metalwork beyond where a pair of cable winches sat, beyond reach as were the spike-locks which sealed the gate to its deep slot in the cavern floor.

"We can't open this," a Daergar said. "It can only be opened from the other side."

"Then cut it!" Glome roared.

"With what?" the Daergar asked, his voice a silky purr as he turned to face the Theiwar leader. "We brought no forging tools. No steel chisels or saws, only delving tools. You said that was all we would need."

"Well, I didn't know about this!"

"You didn't know about a lot of things, Theiwar," the Daergar purred. "You have wasted our time." The blank iron mask turned slightly away then back, and Glome barely got his shield up in time to catch the dark-steel blade slicing toward his throat.

"Defend!" Glome shouted, blocking another cut with his own blade. "The Daergar have turned on us!"

In the blink of an eye, the big tunnel was a tumult of clangs and clatters, shouts and screams as dwarf attacked dwarf, hundreds on each side, their shadows huge on cavern walls in the murky light of fallen torches.

Glome dodged and parried, hampered by the fighting all around him. He thrust, cut, and spun, shield and sword flashing alternately as weapons and defense. All around him, Theiwar and Daergar were locked in ringing, mortal combat, and bright blood pooled on the tunnel's stone floor. For long minutes Glome stood his ground, clearing space around him again and again, his booted feet treading the bodies of fallen allies and fallen enemies. Then he was borne down under a concerted rush of Daergar, with Theiwar defenders piling onto them from behind.

The battle raged before the mute iron gate, then spread back up the tunnel as dwarves fled, and other dwarves pursued. Hundreds lay dead in the howling darkness as blood-washed torches sputtered out, and a time came when the darkness was a silence as well.

The echoes faded northward as the battle continued there, going away, and in the wide cavern before the Daewar gate, nothing moved except the flickering small flame of a dropped lantern.

Then there was movement. Fallen bodies piled on the floor shifted, and shifted again, and a head was raised cautiously. For long moments the figure was still except for a blank, featureless face turning this way and that. Then he pushed bodies aside and climbed out. From helmet to boots he was drenched with blood, even the slitted iron mask dripping gore. Across its eye-slit was a deep furrow where it had deflected a sword cut.

He stood, looked around at the silent death littering the tunnel, then turned to the iron-bar gate and growled deep in his throat. With a curse he pulled away the mask from his face and flung it aside, then stooped to find his shield and blades.

The Daewar would pay for his humiliation. Someday, they would pay. Let them think—for now—that Glome the Assassin was dead. Let them all think that. They would learn otherwise some day. It was not the way of Glome the

Assassin to die. It was his way to kill.

Through murder and manipulation, Glome the Assassin had become chieftain among the Theiwar of Theibardin, and being chieftain had given him a dream.

Glome intended to be king of all Kal-Thax, and it didn't matter to him who he had to kill to get there.

19

The Deeps

The Daewar explorer-spy, Urkhan, had died trying to chart the wonders beneath Cloudseeker Mountain. But in dying, he had given birth to a dream. Now Olim Goldbuckle looked upon the gigantic, dimly lighted cavern that was Urkhan's legacy, and wondered for the first time whether even he, the prince of all the Daewar, were dwarf enough to make the dream come true.

To eyes accustomed to the contours of mountainsides and the limitations of delves, the cavern was mind-boggling. Even after seeing its wonders a hundred times, it was still breathtaking. Miles wide, its lower perimeter was a series of rocky shores running down to a clear-water subterranean lake. From the east shore, where the Daewar had begun the delving of quarters, the far shores were barely visible, even where the quartz light shafts were strong. But rising above the center of the lake was a funnel-like pillar of stone, widening toward the top where it blended into the great, vaulted reaches of the cavern's ceiling.

Half a mile high, and wider than that at its top, the stalactite seemed a monumental pillar upon which the entire mountain might rest. In the varying light, the serrated surfaces of the thing glistened wetly, and water dripped from nodules along its sides.

"It is living stone," Gem Bluesleeve breathed for the dozenth time, gazing in awe at the huge pillar in the distance. "The waters that created it still nourish it."

"No waters created that," old Slate Coldsheet rumbled. "It is a god's work. Only Reorx could have managed such a creation."

"Reorx had a little help from that big sinkhole between the Windweavers, then," Olim Goldbuckle said. "Water creates stalactites, and the water must come from there."

"Where does the wind come from?" Gem Bluesleeve asked, pointing out at the wave-flecked surface of the lake. "In all the days since we moved Daebardin here, the air has never been still."

"The vents," Olim Goldbuckle said, then glanced at Gem. "Oh, you hadn't heard the scouts' reports? It seems there are natural vents around the mountain's flanks. They don't know how many, yet, but one of them is south of here, right in the bottom of that walled valley that the Theiwar call Deadfall. And there are high shafts at the crest. Mica Diamondtoe believes there are upward vents around the sinkhole up there, right at the base of Galefang, and that it is the winds on the Windweavers that create the draft down here."

"If there are vents that admit the wind," Gem frowned, "then there are vents that will admit enemies."

"As we find them, we will grate them." Olim nodded. "Just as we did the road from Sky's End." He looked upward, where the sounds of delving and building were concentrated. Above the east shoreline of the big lake, the cavern walls rose in a series of stairlike levels, and it was here that the Daewar were digging in. Three separate levels of delvings were under way, and more were planned. Everywhere up the wall were Daewar—thousands of them visible at any time—digging away at the porous levels of stone, piercing into the depths beyond the natural cavern, hollowing out cubicles that connected with other cubicles. Places for people to live, places for exchanging goods, places for councils and gatherings—the beginnings of a city.

From the delves, along a series of roads and tunnels, ore carts rumbled, carrying select rubble from the delves to other, distant caverns which would be farming warrens when their fields were perfected. It was in those caverns that Daewar daredevils were harnessing the power of the tractor worms to draw sleds to crush the stone that would be the basis of topsoil when it was completed.

In the meantime, foraging parties were roaming the caverns, gathering tons of edible fungus, various kinds of meat that no one questioned too far, and a dozen varieties of vining fruits which grew naturally in these subterranean realms, wherever there was light from a quartz layer.

"It is magnificent," Olim Goldbuckle said, surveying his new realm. "It goes beyond anything that any of us dreamed."

Slate Coldsheet shook his grizzled head, frowning. "This place is big, right enough. But I'd feel better if I knew how people are supposed to live here."

The others looked at him curiously. "Like people live anywhere else, old one," Gem said. "By using what we have found."

"But what have we found?" the old delvemaster spread his arms, turning. "A place. A place with water and worms."

"And fresh air and sunlight," Gem added.

"And—Reorx willing—defendable against invasion," the prince pointed out. "What is bothering you, Delvemaster?"

"Food and fuel," Slate said flatly. "Oh, our foragers are feeding us now, but those supplies will run out. And wood. We need timber, Sire. We will always need timber, and no forests grow beneath mountains."

Olim scratched his beard, looking up at the delves. Without timber for beams, they would be shallow and unreliable. Doors would be a problem, as well, and furnishings.

"And rich ores," the delvemaster continued. "There are no real lodes here, Sire. And no way to reach the rich veins to the south."

"We can still trade," Olim told him. "Our road will serve."

"Fifty miles of tunnel, going the wrong direction? And that isn't all." The old dwarf pointed downshore, where long lines of Daewar were operating a bucket brigade. They were carrying water from the lake to the delvings, where it was lifted by ropes. "In Daebardin, Sire, we collected water from above. Cisterns and flows. Here we have to carry it from below. It is not efficient. Your people don't like it."

"Oh? They are grumbling, then? And what else don't they like?"

"Many of them don't like it here," Slate told him. "Gil Gemcrust and his weavers are upset because there is nothing to weave. The artisans wear gloomy faces because the forges are cold. The woodcrafters . . . most of them are there in the water line because they have nothing else to do. And not an hour ago I heard Winna Redthread complaining that the only grain left in the stores is oats."

"Winna Redthread!" Olim spat. "That female would be desolate if she didn't have something to complain about."

"It is the delvers, too, Sire. And their families. There is much discontent. They say people are supposed to delve into mountainsides, not from the bellies of mountains. They say people are supposed to live inward from outside, not outward from inside."

Olim Goldbuckle felt a growl coming on, and stifled it to

a rumble in his throat. Leave it to a gray-headed delve-master to burst the bubbles of dreams! Impatiently, he turned away. "We'll think of something," he said.

It was a logging crew, outbound through the great tunnel, that found the remains of the Theiwar and Daergar who had died fighting each other beyond the iron grate. Hundreds of bodies littered the siding cave, and others beyond. The Daewar wandered for a mile or more, gawking at the fallen dwarves, then turned around and went back to report.

Gem Bluesleeve led a company of warriors to investigate, all the way back to the north slope of Sky's End. There he found the wreckage of the citadel and surmised what had occurred.

Olim Goldbuckle listened to the reports with his council, then sent parties to remove the bodies in the passage and to reseal the tunnel at its far end.

"Sky's End is behind us," he told the council of thane elders. "We came from there to here and will not go back. We will find other ways to the outside. We will explore the paths of Urkhan. If there are not suitable routes from these caverns, then we will drill our own routes, just as we drilled our passage here."

Late autumn lay on the Kharolis Mountains when Daewar explorers probing upward broke through into some old, nearly deserted lairs of the Theiwar—lairs that had been worn out and largely abandoned, high on the south shoulder of the peak called Cloudseeker. A few Theiwar were there, and a few Daewar fell to stones and dark blades in the first moments of penetration, but the defense mounted by the Theiwar was pitifully small. In this entire cave system, only a few hundred Theiwar remained, mostly women and children and the very old. But among them at the time were some Theiwar leaders arranging for food supplies. The Daewar troop that followed the delvers through, led by Gem Bluesleeve, subdued and disarmed them with little effort.

And it was then that Olim Goldbuckle learned that the

human intruders had regrouped and attacked again out on the eastern slopes.

Along a wide front, up through the foothills from the plains, thousands upon thousands of humans now mounted an invasion upon Kal-Thax. Pushed westward by the dragon war in the east, shunned and harried by the organized realm of Ergoth, new hordes of humans—and other races among them—had found themselves blocked by the domains of the dwarves and had reacted as humans do. They had fallen back, milled around in confusion until there were enough of them massed there, then they had organized themselves and attacked.

With only the Theiwar, Daergar, and Klar to patrol the eastern borders of Kal-Thax, the invaders had pushed far into the passes, farther than they ever had managed to go before. Taking advantage of the latest war between Theiwar and Daergar—with Klar intervening on both sides—the humans and their allies had established a cordon from Grand Gorge to the Cliffs of Shalomar and begun a series of bloody raids against the dwarves.

A tenuous treaty stood now between the Theiwar and the Daergar, linked in their defense of Kal-Thax against the outsiders. Most of the warriors of both tribes were on the eastern slopes, fighting.

"Rust!" a thunderous Olim Goldbuckle roared when he heard this report. "Rust and tarnish! Daewar, to arms! The Pact of Kal-Thax calls!"

Before him, three Theiwar captives stood in wide-eyed awe, staring around them at the immense cavern to which they had been brought blindfolded.

"What . . . what is this place?" Slide Tolec asked finally.

At his arm, a Daewar guard grinned. "It may be your last, best hope, Theiwar," he whispered. "If we do not beat off the outsiders this time, you and your kind had better hope that our prince will allow you sanctuary in New Daebardin."

* * * * *

The war that raged along the east slopes of the Kharolis range was more than a war. It was an ongoing clash between the stubborn, immovable determination of the dwarven nations who had sworn in the name of Reorx to allow no outsiders into Kal-Thax, and the desperate, irresistible drive of thousands upon thousands of displaced creatures who had nowhere else to go.

The first Daewar company to pour down the slopes of Cloudseeker to reinforce the ragtag army of Theiwar, Daergar, Klar—and, now and then, even clots of terrified Aghar, the reclusive gully dwarves, caught up in a skirmish—ran headlong into the fury of a band of ogres fighting alongside humans. Outnumbered a dozen to one by the Daewar, the ogres yet managed to decimate the company before taking to their heels. In that one clash, seventeen Daewar died and four others were wounded. Five ogres were killed, one captured, and none knew how many were injured.

From their towering captive, Gem Bluesleeve learned that the ogres had fled a place called Bloten, driven out by a dragon seeking a base from which to fly against elves in the east.

All up and down the slopes of the Kharolis Mountains, dwarves were fighting against humans, ogres, and—beneath the Cliffs of Shalomar—even some squadrons of goblins. The dwarven lines held day after day, but Olim Goldbuckle of the Daewar, Slide Tolec of the Theiwar, and Vog Ironface of the Daergar all knew that they could not hold for long unless they could somehow turn from defense to attack. Autumn lay upon the mountains, and the advancing ices might give the dwarves a brief reprieve—but only if they could hold the invaders east of the frontal ranges. If the outsiders made it into the high mountains and found shelter in some of the deep valleys hidden there, then by spring, Kal-Thax would be indefensible.

It was Olim Goldbuckle's captain, Gem Bluesleeve, who led the first assault down the slopes, hoping to break the cordon.

With three hundred Daewar and a hundred each of Theiwar and Daergar behind him, Bluesleeve—leading companies of his elite Golden Hammer guard—attacked downslope in phalanx pattern, and the humans there, mostly wild Sackmen from the northern plains, found themselves faced by a moving wall of iron shields from which naked blades flicked like snakes' tongues. For a moment, the humans held the line, but only for a moment. Flanked by howling, slashing Klar, the phalanx punched through the human defense and spread into a broad wedge of swords and shields, marching across the bodies of fallen foe.

In disarray, the Sackmen fled down the slopes, and the dwarves pursued . . . and ran headlong into something few of them had ever seen before.

Running as though from death itself, the mass of humans spread across the rising plains and disappeared behind a line of tall, ominous figures—fighters of Ergoth, armored from head to toe, sitting upon armored horses, and bringing long lances down for a charge.

On the open ground, the dwarves were no match for mounted Ergothians led by knights. More than a third of Gem Bluesleeve's command fell there, before the rest escaped back up the slopes. The line of armored riders pursued only as far as the rising ridges and stopped there. But one of them raised his faceplate to call after the Golden Hammer, "Stay in your mountains, dwarves! Defend yourselves there if you will, but do not bring your problems to us!"

Below the retreating dwarves, the armored ones turned methodically and began sweeping the plains, turning Sackmen back toward the mountains.

Atop a spire, Olim Goldbuckle watched the rout and shook his head sadly. "We have lost our one advantage," he told Slide Tolec. "Those people do not want our enemies any more than we do. Kal-Thax is lost, and there is nowhere to turn but to the deeps beneath the stone."

"We Theiwar have no deeps," Slide said. "What of us?"

A few feet away, a featureless mask turned toward them. "Nor do we, Daewar," the voice of Vog Ironface said, sounding like hollow thunder. "Unless you think we can defend mineshafts."

Olim looked from one to the other of them, then fixed his level gaze on the Theiwar. "You once told me that you believed we were creating a fortress," he reminded him. "Do you remember?"

"That was a trick," Slide frowned. "You let us believe that, to divert us from what you were really doing."

"Nonetheless." Olim shrugged. "We now have deeps, and there is room there for Theiwar"—he glanced aside, dislike plain on his face as he looked at the dark slit in front of Vog's eyes—"and even for Daergar. The Daewar will not be the ones to break the Pact of Kal-Thax. But the deeps we have found are ours, and only Daewar shall rule there."

The Daergar started to answer, then stepped back with a gasp as the air behind Olim Goldbuckle crackled, and a figure appeared there—an ancient, tattered form leaning on a two-tined spear. Eyes that were like darkness gazed out from beneath a mane of silver hair. The phantom shimmered, varying from translucent to almost transparent. It seemed to stand before them, but its feet didn't quite touch the ground.

"The highest of the deep shall rule," a cold voice whispered. "Only the highest of the deep."

Olim stared at the apparition. It was the figure from his troubling dreams. "You!" he muttered.

"Yes," the cold voice said, then seemed to be talking to no one at all. "Delve the deeps of dwarvendom. Those who rule have yet to come. You will know them when they do. You will know them by the drum."

Dumbly, Theiwar and Daergar gawked at the apparition. Then Olim Goldbuckle choked out, "Who, then? What drum?"

The figure turned slightly and became transparent. "That drum," it whispered, still turning, toward the plains beyond the mountain slopes. "That drum." It turned a bit more and was gone.

Yet on the freshening east wind, sweeping across the seething plains below the Kharolis Mountains, there was a sound. Faint with distance, far beyond the massed confusion of invaders below Kal-Thax, still it was there, and they all heard it.

The rhythmic, heartbeat sound of marching drums.

The dwarves weren't the only ones who heard the distant sound. Down through the foothills, marauders turned their faces eastward, and out on the plains a rank of Ergothians wheeled and rode away, seeking the source of this new thing.

Gem Bluesleeve saw his chance, and he took it. At his command, hundreds of Daewar stormed down the slopes, with Theiwar and Daergar at their flanks. Confused and surprised, and without the Ergothians behind them, human companies on the slopes turned and fled. Within hours, the Golden Hammer had established a defense perimeter below the shoulders of the high peaks.

Part V:
The Life Tree People

The Eastern Border
of Kal-Thax

Century of Wind
Decade of Oak
Fall, Year of Copper

20

Forging Bonds

High mountains were visible in the distance when the Hylar made long camp on the banks of a wooded stream. Though still far away, the mountains stood blue in the western sky and called to them, like echoes of Thoradin in their hearts.

While the campsite was being cleared and fires prepared, Colin Stonetooth and others climbed a knoll and looked to the west. Tera Sharn stood at her father's shoulder as he tested the winds with ears and nose, the knelt to look at the soil beneath the lush grasses. He pulled a sprig of grass, chewed on it thoughtfully, then scraped earth from beneath and tasted it. The land was rich and fertile, as much of southeastern Ergoth was. But it was land suited to humans more than to dwarves.

But beyond, where the high mountains rose blue in the autumn light, the vista that tugged at him and the winds sweeping down from there spoke of high meadows and honest stone, of steeps and caverns and mineral deposits . . . of dwarven places.

"We will remain here long enough for the animals to graze and the foresters to lay in stores," Colin Stonetooth decreed. "Let the crafters work their forges and the weavers work their wools. When next we set out our anvils, it will be within those mountains yonder."

"Kal-Thax," said Mistral Thrax. "Kal-Thax is there, in those mountains. The place of Everbardin."

"Then tell our bonded knight to lay out his fields and complete his drills," the chieftain said. "He is human and will not go to Kal-Thax, but we will not pause again until we are there."

The site of the camp was well chosen. It offered ripe fields for harvest and graze, wood for fires and forges, and water for bathing and the tending of stock. The Hylar had come far in learning the ways of combat under the tutelage of Glendon Hawke, but there were still more drills to be accomplished, and time was needed for that.

But there was still another—and primary—reason why the great caravan of the Hylar stopped. It was time for the wedding of the chieftain's daughter, Tera Sharn, and the captain of guards, Willen Ironmaul.

Through a thousand miles of wilderness, and even before in the place that had been Thorin, the people had watched the romance between the robust guardsman and the dark-eyed princess develop. Handil the Drum had become legend among the Hylar, and Tolon the Muse was far behind, ruling a place the Hylar would never again see. Cale Greeneye was well-loved among his father's people, but was strange to them, preferring other ways to dwarven ways.

That left Tera Sharn as one for the people to idolize, and idolize her they did. For his part, Willen had traveled the past hundred miles with a wide, silly grin parting his whiskers and sometimes acted as though his head were lost in the clouds.

It was time for a wedding, and the Hylar set it up in great style. In a clearing they erected a large, ornate forge with crested stone arches above it representing the strength of mountains, and four silver-inlaid bellows, representing the four seasons' winds that sang across high peaks.

Throughout one morning, most of the tribe worked to make things ready, the women shouting orders, the men running here and there, doing as they were told. Foresters selected wood for the ceremonial forge—seven varieties of wood, representing the seven precious metals: hickory for steel, symbol of flexibility and wisdom; oak for iron, for strength; maple for tin, for unswerving devotion; cedar for copper, the metal of the heart; ash for nickel, for endurance and faith; multi-colored pine for bronze, symbolic of blendings, and yellow hedge for gold, representing the lasting comforts of home and family.

A ceremonial bronze hammer had been forged for the occasion, and a set of copper tongs with rosewood grips.

When the sun was high in the bright sky, the entire tribe assembled around the forge, in which bright coals glowed cherry-red. The Hylar guard—trimmed, shined, and brushed, each warrior mounted on his best tall horse—spread in formation to line a pathway, along which road came Colin Stonetooth and the Ten, followed by a dazed-looking Willen Ironmaul flanked by guardsmen. Sedately, they rode to the forge clearing and dismounted.

For a moment there was silence, the only sounds those of the breeze, songbirds, and an excited kender voice saying, "Wow! Would you look at that! It's . . ." The voice stopped abruptly as strong dwarven hands were clapped over the kender's mouth. Softly, then, a drum was tapped. Then another, and another, picking up the rhythm. All around the clearing, drummers tapped a soft riff on muffled vibrars as another pathway opened and a dozen dwarf girls came through, strewing handsful of steel coins and arrowheads. Behind them walked Tera Sharn, wearing her finest kilt and lace sandals, a bodice embroidered with sunbursts, and a long, quilted cloak of the finest web-silk fabric. Her hair was tied high on her head and adorned by a copper comb.

Several of Willen Ironmaul's escorts stepped close to him, ready to support him in case his knees began to shake.

Colin Stonetooth strode to the forge and raised his hands. "People of the people," he intoned. "People of the highest place, people of the Hylar! Gather now in the sight of Reorx, maker of all people, Reorx who must certainly watch over these, his most beloved people, who were created last and best—"

"That isn't right!" a high voice protested from aside. "Dwarves aren't the . . ." Hard hands muffled the kender again, and a deep voice whispered, "Get that little nuisance out of here!"

"Who were created last and are therefore best," Colin Stonetooth elaborated. "People of the Hylar, observe and witness. Two among us have chosen to bond as husband and wife. Willen Ironmaul, Captain of the General Guard, has chosen Tera Sharn, ah . . . my daughter. And she has chosen him as well. Does anyone here assembled wish . . . or dare . . . to challenge?"

On cue, Tera Sharn raised a flower-garlanded javelin—ornate but nonetheless deadly—and held it high, turning full circle, her eyes meeting those of each unmarried young woman in the crowd. One of the guards nudged Willen Ironmaul, who seemed to snap out of a trance and raised his sword, where every male in the crowd could see it.

There being no challengers, Colin Stonetooth nodded. The bride and groom put down their weapons, joined hands and stepped closer to the forge, feeling its pleasant heat on their faces. At its foot stood a gold-embossed eighty-pound anvil, wrapped in ribbons. Willen squatted, hoisted the anvil and set it on the forge's rim, between the ceremonial hammer and the ceremonial tongs.

One of the guard escorts and one of Tera Sharn's pretty attendants stepped to the couple's sides and reached beyond them with long, iron tongs. From the coals they lifted small, slim ingots—one of silver and one of gold, heated and glowing. Carefully, they laid these atop the anvil, one across the other, and stepped back.

Tera Sharn picked up the rosewood-handled copper tongs and gripped the hot ingots at their center. She lifted them, looked up at Willen and recited, "May the halves of our joining be equal and strong." She returned the heated ingots to the anvil.

Willen stared down at her, trying not to grin. He lifted the hammer. "And may they never be separated," he said. With one swift blow, he smote the joined ingots, forever welding them into a single metal cross—the cross of the pillars of the world.

A rousing cheer went up from the crowd, and Colin Stonetooth raised his hands to silence it. Then he looked at Willen and Tera. "Will you exchange tokens?" he asked.

Tera Sharn reached into her bodice and pulled out a pendant and chain, beautifully crafted from nickel steel. Standing on tiptoe, she reached high and dropped the loop over Willen's head, letting the pendant settle on his breast. It was a single star. "For my love," she whispered.

Willen, red-cheeked above his swept-back beard, reached to the pouch at his belt and fumbled inside it. "And for mine—" he started, then stopped, his eyes widening as he fumbled in his pouch. Suddenly he turned, pushed through the crowd, and strode to the side of the clearing, a thunderous frown on his brow. To the dwarves holding the stifled kender he said, "Give me that little thief!"

The instant his mouth was free, Castomel Springheel hissed, "Thief? Who are you calling thief, you over-grown—"

Willen grasped the little creature, lifted him, turned him upside down, and shook him as one might shake out a cleaning cloth. The kender yelled, and things rained down from him, from the large pouch at his belt, from other, hidden pouches, from the neck of his green shirt, from everywhere. A pair of bright daggers clattered to the ground, followed by a spur, a dozen or so bright beads, various bits of stone, some rolls of foolscap, a chunk of hard bread, a bit of cheese, an egg, a ruby clasp, a pair of bracelets, a chained pendant. . . .

"There it is," Willen rasped. Dropping Castomel Springheel unceremoniously, he picked up the pendant, turned a fierce scowl on the sprawled kender, then strode back to the forge carrying his token.

Behind him, voices were raised in surprise and anger. "That's my clasp! I wondered where that was." "Whose spur is this?" "Those are Mica's bracelets, he's been looking all over for those!" And a high-pitched kender voice, "Keep your hands off that cheese! That's my lunch!"

At the forge, Willen resumed his place as though there had been no interruption. He slipped the pendant's tooled chain over Tera Sharn's head. "For my love," he said.

As his pendant was a star, the one he gave to her was a finely engraved oval of rich, pink granite. They smiled at each other. By this exchange, she promised him heaven and he promised her the world.

Once more, Colin Stonetooth raised his hands. "These two people are husband and wife!" he proclaimed. Then, "Well, why is everybody still standing around? Go about your business!"

At the far side of the clearing, towering over the dwarves around him, Glendon Hawke removed his light helm and ran long fingers through his red hair. He was impressed. He had seen human weddings, and some had been quite elaborate, but he had never seen a ceremony more thoroughly symbolic or better performed than this. "Sometimes dwarves are almost human," he muttered.

Beside him a burly Hylar swung around. "You watch your mouth!" the dwarf said.

Nearby, Cas Springheel reassembled his scattered belongings, muttering under his breath. "If that's how they're going to act, I can take a hint," he said. "I've been kicked out of better places than this." Smoothing down his clothing, he returned his pack sling to his shoulder, picked up the fork-ended walking stick he had been toying with lately—he had an idea that a fine weapon could be made from it—and executed an angry bow to no one in particular. "Please don't be offended by my departure," he piped. "I'm only leaving because dwarves are really dull. Especially when they get up on their high horses."

The direction he chose in leaving took him through most of the milling crowd, and his pack was bulging nicely again when he stalked out of the Hylar camp.

* * * * *

It was four days later that Cale Greeneye rode in at a gallop. Past the drill fields he spurred, and ranks of armed Hylar stopped their weapons practice to watch him pass. At the center of the compound he brought Piquin to a sliding stop before Colin Stonetooth's hut. The chieftain appeared at the doorway as his son vaulted from his saddle, not bothering with the mounting ladder.

"Sire!" Cale's eyes glittered with excitement as he pointed westward. "Humans coming this way. Mounted and armed, and in force. Three hundred or more! They know we're here and are heading for us."

"Are they hostile?" Colin beckoned, and the Ten hurried off to collect and saddle their horses.

"I'd say so," Cale nodded. "Gran Molden crept close enough to hear some of them talking. They've been in a fight with dwarves, somewhere west of here. They were trying to go up into the mountains, and the dwarves attacked them. Gran says the humans know we are dwarves and are out for revenge, as though they think we're the same ones who attacked them."

"They don't know one dwarf from another," Colin rumbled, shaking his head. He had known humans who had been friends. People almost as civilized as dwarves. People

DRAGONLANCE Dwarven Nations

he had trusted, so much that he had not wanted to believe there were enemies among them. Now, it seemed, humans were usually the enemy. "Just as we sometimes fail to distinguish one human from another," he muttered. Despite all that had happened, he still found himself clinging to the idea that there were decent humans, humans with a sense of—he sought a word and it came to him—a sense of honor. People like the strange knight among them now.

Like Glendon Hawke. Colin turned to look for the human and found he was already on his way, long legs sprinting, curious to find out what was happening.

"Sir Knight," Colin faced him, cross-armed, "your kin are coming to call. Where do you stand?"

"What kin? Describe them."

Quickly, Cale Greeneye described the humans approaching beyond the near hills. "They are dark, hairy men," he said. "They wear some armor, but it is rough-cut and tarnished. They wear ornaments in their hair and on their helms and braid their beards. Some wear leather cloaks, split at the back. They have many sorts of weapons. Their horses are small, quick, and wiry, and are painted with symbols."

Glendon listened intently, then shook his head. "No kin of mine," he said icily. "Not Ergothians, not even from the northern realms. They sound like Cobar. Hill people from the east. No better than Sackmen and Sandrunners, most of them. But they are ferocious fighters, and they take what they want if they can." He glanced around at the dwarves nearby. "My guess is they want your horses, your arms, and your armor . . . and any other valuables you have. Cobar are notorious robbers, and you people wear fortunes on your shoulders."

"Gran Molden says they're angry," Cale told him. "They've fought dwarves west of here."

"They tried to enter Kal-Thax, then," Glendon nodded.

Colin spun toward him. "You know of Kal-Thax?"

"Of course," Glendon shrugged. "Doesn't everybody? It's where the dwarves live. Well, most of them, anyway."

"Why didn't you tell us about Kal-Thax?" Mistral Thrax rasped. "That's the place we're looking for!"

Glendon shrugged again. "You didn't ask."

"Well, we're asking now!"

"Kal-Thax is in the Kharolis Mountains," the knight said. "West of here. The dwarves there deny entrance to all outsiders. They are fierce and pretty primitive—except maybe the bright-colored ones. They seem fairly civilized sometimes, though they are as hostile as the rest to anybody trying to cross their borders. If the Cobar tangled with them, I can see why they'd be angry."

"Two of those coming are different," Cale said. "They wear full armor, like yours, and there are pennants on their lances. Crossed swords on fields of white."

"Knights," Glendon breathed. "And they ride with Cobar?"

"Not with them," Cale corrected. "They are off to one side. It's more as though they are watching them than riding with them."

"Ah." Glendon nodded. "I thought as much."

Again, Colin Stonetooth asked, "Where do you stand, human? By your oath, are you with us or against us?"

"By my oath," the knight said, "I am neither. I pledged to teach your people what I can. I have done that. There is no more that I can teach. I will take no part in your test."

"Test?"

"The Cobar, Sire. You cannot escape them, and I think they will attack you. It will be interesting to see what you have learned from my efforts."

"*Interesting*? By Reorx, I . . ."

"I will stand aside and watch," the knight said flatly. "I have kept my bargain with you. Now will you keep yours with me?"

"What?"

"To release me from service and return my belongings to me."

Glendon glanced westward. A haze of dust was visible, rising above the nearest hill, and on the hilltop were mounted humans, more and more of them.

"Keep your belongings," the Hylar chieftain rasped. "You already have them back anyway. I'll release you when I know more."

The Cobar men came at a charge, heading for the heart of the dwarves' camp, and were within a hundred yards when a hail of sling-stones whistled through their front ranks. The charge broke in momentary confusion, then regrouped, the marauders wheeling to continue their attack. But they were met by a solemn rank of armored dwarves mounted high on great horses. Before the men could charge again, a counter-charge bore into them, and men and horses fell before the disciplined fighting dwarves like wheat to the sickle.

Thundering through the ranks of the Cobar, wheeling and driving through again, Willen Ironmaul's guards pressed the humans, giving them no time to regroup and no room to maneuver. In precision drill the Hylar fighters whirled and swept, this way and then that, cleaving and punishing the marauders. And at each clash, the weapons were different. Lances first, then swords, then one of the tactics that Glendon Hawke had never taught them, a swerving charge on wheeling mounts which seemed to have no riders—until they turned, and the dwarves clinging to the horses' sides lashed out with deadly hammers and axes.

And through it all, a continuing roil of drums set the pace and called the plays.

Colin Stonetooth and the Ten were everywhere, a separate, compact fighting machine of iron hooves, edged shields, steel blades, axes, and hammers.

Upstream, at a ford on the creek, Glendon Hawke lowered his faceplate and tipped down the point of his lance. "Sirs!" he called to the two bright-armored knights across from him. "This is not a good time to cross this stream, I assure you!"

They hesitated, trying to recognize the blue-plumed figure challenging them. He was not one of them, by his dress, but his posture spoke of great skill and his manner was like their own. One of them raised a hand in careful salute. "You side with dwarves against humans, Sir Freelance?"

"I take no sides here," Glendon called back. "And do you, Sirs, side with Cobar? Against anybody?"

"Of course not!"

"Then by your leave, Sirs, let us just watch the test . . . me from here, and you from over there."

The battle was over in minutes. With splendid precision and great skill the Hylar swept the field until the only humans upright were those running away. At a trumpet call the Hylar regrouped. There were some missing, but only a few.

"Let them go." Colin Stonetooth waved after the fleeing humans. "They can spread the word that it is best to leave Hylar alone." He turned to glance at the stream, where Glendon Hawke still held the ford. The strange knights were turning, riding away.

Followed only by the Ten, Colin Stonetooth rode down to the stream and wheeled to face Glendon. "Why did you intervene?" he demanded.

"I did not intervene," the knight said calmly. "And neither did anyone else. Congratulations on your test. I can teach you nothing more. Do you release me?"

Without answering, Colin Stonetooth wheeled his mount and started back to camp. "Bring that human to me at supper," he told Jerem Longslate. "And bring the thing the steelmaster has prepared."

* * * * *

In the evening, Glendon Hawke was brought before Colin Stonetooth, and again the entire tribe assembled. The knight looked around him at a sea of solemn, expressionless dwarves and frowned. He had expected the Hylar to keep their bargain, but who knew what dwarves were likely to do. He felt disappointed, though. He had thought—he had been so sure!—that in learning the skills, they had also absorbed the aspects of chivalry—the sense of rightness and honor that were part of the skills. It should be as clear to them now as to him, he thought, the way of the lance—the difference between right and wrong.

Colin Stonetooth gazed up at the man icily. "Kneel before me, human," the dwarf said. "I'm getting a cramp in my neck."

With a shrug, Glendon complied. He would not bow, but he would kneel.

Colin Stonetooth held out his hand. "Give me your sword," he demanded.

Glendon hesitated and heard the whisper of half-drawn blades all around him. Slowly he drew his sword, reversed it, and handed it over. The Hylar chieftain took it and set it aside, then reached around, picked up a wrapped blade, and held it before him, peeling the fabric away.

Glendon blinked, and his eyes went wide. In size and shape the sword was almost identical to his own. In length and taper, in shape of pommel and curve of guard, it was an exact twin. But there the similarity ended. This sword was exquisite, a work of the finest craft he had ever seen. Its blade glistened in the light, its razor edges as finely honed as a cleric's shaving blade. Its hilt was of polished blackwood, inlaid with fine, elaborate patterns of silver and gold. And in the crest of its nickel-steel pommel was a perfect blue-white diamond the size of a cloak button.

Colin Stonetooth held the sword out to him, hilt-forward. "We have learned from you, Sir Glendon Hawke," the dwarf said. "I think we have only begun to realize how much we have learned. Your pledge is kept, and with this token I complete mine. You are free of service, Sir Knight. And this sword is yours. It is the finest of our craft. It will never fail you. Take it and go, with the thanks of the Hylar."

21
Elven Encounter

The mountains rose ahead and on both sides as Cale Greeneye and his adventurers scouted the trail, just within sound of the marching drums. Here the rising plains formed a natural pathway, funneling between high ridges toward the thrusting peaks westward. Ahead and beyond, range after range of mountains rose into the distance, each more distant silhouette bluer than the one before and rising higher into the sky.

The western plains seemed jammed with people—humans, mostly—but their encampments were scattered and aloof from one another and well out from the rising mountains. Cale and his scouts had encountered no trouble in slipping through, and now the foothills rose around them and the mountains ahead.

It was a majestic vista, crowned by the farthest and highest of the ranges ahead. There were the highlands and the peaks rising above them. On the right, blue with distance like a snow-crowned monarch, the tallest peak seemed to pierce the very sky, to shear it away as though there were no sky beyond.

To its left and straight ahead as the valley pointed was a massive mountain that seemed to dominate the view. Not as tall as the sky-ender north of it, it was far wider and was topped by three giant crags like great fangs or spearheads. Mists rolled and swirled around these spires, as grain rises in a broth when stirred by a spoon. Drifts of cloud danced there like threads weaving themselves in tapestries.

Farther south, bending away beyond the flank of that cloud-stirring mountain, was yet another giant rise, a rugged, saw-toothed eminence capped by double peaks.

"Those three crags up there"—Mica Rockreave pointed ahead—"stand like beacons, inviting us onward."

"Too inviting for my taste." Gran Molden frowned. "If I were going to lay a trap for travelers, that's where I would put it, because that's where they would go."

"Are you thinking of laying a trap, Gran?" Cale Green-eye teased.

"I'm thinking of avoiding the traps of others," Gran snapped. "See how this valley narrows ahead, climbing toward that widest crest? And how the cloud-comb crags beckon? Anyone coming this way would be tempted to take that path."

"Let's not forget what the knight told us," Coal Bell-metal put in. "Kal-Thax is a sealed land. No outsiders are allowed in, and those who try to enter rarely return. The people of Kal-Thax don't want visitors."

"He also said the people there are dwarves, like us."

"He said they are dwarves. He didn't say they are like us."

"Well, dwarves or not,"—Flint Cokeras tapped a hard fist against his armor-plated chest—"no one is going to

218

stop the Hylar without a fight."

Cale Greeneye shook his head, tightening rein to ease Piquin's long stride. "You're always spoiling for a fight, Flint. But why fight, if you don't have to? Look over there, on the flank of that ridge."

They looked to the right, shading their eyes. "What do you see?" Flint asked.

"Look closely," Cale said, pointing. "There. On the slope. There is fresh stone there. Bits of stone have been moved, and the pattern is upward, like a trail. Someone else has distrusted this valley. They've made another trail, going the same way, but with better cover."

"Wise, I'd say," Shard Feldspar squinted, beginning to see what Cale saw. "But who would lay a trail so dim? No dwarf did that. And no human would ever be able to follow it. Maybe we'd better take a look."

Cale turned, listening. The faint, distant drums told him that the main march was still miles away. "All right. We have time." Nudging Piquin, he led to the right, the others following.

The upward trail was dim indeed. But for Cale's knack for seeing what was out of place, they would not have been able to follow it. Upward it led, along the flank of a rising ridge, concealed from view except for those upon it. The only signs that anyone had ever gone this way were so subtle that only a sharp-eyed dwarf might have seen them—a bit of stone turned slightly from alignment with its imprint, a smudge on a ledge where something had scraped against the rock, a bit of gravel sunk more deeply in sand than its own weight would account for.

At a bend, Cale climbed down from Piquin's saddle and squatted to taste the stone of an outcrop. "Well, *someone* has been along here," he said. "But I can't tell who."

He was just reaching for his mounting ladder when Gran Molden's tense voice said, "Don't move, Cale. We have a problem."

He turned slowly and froze. A dozen or more lithe figures stood on the trail, above and below them. Without sound, they had appeared there, only yards away, and the dwarves found themselves looking down the shafts of deadly arrows in drawn bows.

Cale gaped at the somber archers. For an instant, he had thought they were humans. But now he knew better. "Elves," he muttered. Slowly and carefully he stepped away from Piquin, raising his hands away from his weapons. The other dwarves, in their saddles, did the same.

From uphill, more and more elves appeared, emerging soundlessly from the brush and stones of the mountainside. The dwarves stared around at them, intensely aware of the steady arrows trained on them from all sides. They had seen elves before. In past times, a few elves had come to Balladine to trade—aloof, stately people in the flowing robes and spider-silk-fine garments of the Silvanesti, and now and then a silent, furtive Kagonesti from the deep forests south of the ledgelands.

But these were different, somehow. Their garments were mostly soft leathers and rough weaves, blending with the colors of the land. Their features were neither the cold, aloof faces of Silvanesti nor the weirdly painted, intense faces of Kagonesti. These were elves, but another kind of elves.

"Hold your arrows," Cale said cautiously. "We mean no threat to you."

"Nor will you ever, dwarf," the nearest one said icily. The drawn bow aligned itself on Cale's throat, and he could almost feel the broad, razor-edged arrowhead piercing his flesh.

Then another voice came, softly but with authority. "Hold, Demoth! These people are not of Kal-Thax."

Cale turned. Among the elves now above them on the rise—hundreds of them, it seemed—one had stepped forward. Lithe and graceful as a perfect sapling in fall, she paused with one slender, soft-booted foot on a rock and gestured. "Look at their horses," she said. "Have you ever seen horses like these beyond the Khalkists? These dwarves are Calnar."

The one called Demoth relaxed his bowstring slightly. "Then what are they doing here?"

"Maybe we should ask," the female suggested. She looked from one to another of the dwarves with wide-set, slanting eyes. "What *are* you doing so far from home, high-dwellers?"

Cale found his voice and lowered his arms a bit. "We have no home. We were Calnar once, but no longer. Now we are Hylar, and seeking new delves."

She looked beyond him, into the distance. "Those drums are yours, then?"

"They are ours. Mistral Thrax has had a vision of Ever-bardin, and the people of Colin Stonetooth have followed it." He glanced at Demoth's bow, took a deep breath and lowered his arms, taking a demanding stance. "And why are elves in this place? And in the name of Reorx, why do you point arrows at us?"

The female elf gestured. "Lower your points," she said. All around, reluctantly, bows were lowered and draws relaxed. She looked at Cale again. "My name is Eloeth," she said. "There is more to it than that, but Eloeth is enough. And you?"

"Cale Greeneye," he said. "Son of Colin Stonetooth, once chieftain of the Calnar, now leader of the Hylar."

"The Calnar of Thorin," she said. "I have heard the drums of Balladine."

"Thoradin," he corrected. "Thorin is Thorin only for those who remained. We search for Everbardin."

"Well, have a care searching these mountains," she suggested. "Look down there."

Cale turned. He could see nothing where she pointed.

"Come up here where I am," she said. "Then look."

Cale clambered up the rise to stand beside the elf girl. She was taller than him by several inches, though she looked to weigh only a fraction of his solid bulk. She pointed again, and Cale turned. From here he could see the valley beyond the trail—the same valley he and the others had turned from, but higher, deeper into the mountains.

The valley floor was littered with death. He shaded his eyes, squinting. The largest of the silent forms looked like horses. Or most of them did. A few looked like dead ogres. And scattered everywhere were other, smaller things. He stared.

"Only the latest of many battles," the elf told him. "Kal-Thax is under siege and is not a safe place to travel."

"You're here," Cale pointed out.

"We have our own ways," Eloeth said. "There is dragon war in Silvanesti. Our cousins need us there, and all we can bring with us. To go east we must cross Kal-Thax. So we do."

He looked around, trying to estimate their number, but it was impossible. The elves had a way of moving a bit and becoming very hard to see, camouflaged against the terrain. But there were a lot of them.

"We are one of many parties," Eloeth said. "And we are looking for allies." She looked again at the other dwarves, noticing their armor and their weapons. "I don't suppose any of you would be interested in fighting dragons?"

"Of course not," he said. "Not that we couldn't, if we wanted to, but only humans and kender turn to new ventures before the old ones are complete." He paused, looking eastward, then added, "There are a lot of humans between here and where you're going. They might be better mannered if they had something constructive to do. Maybe some of them would join you to fight dragons."

"Humans?" she raised an exquisite eyebrow.

"I know," Cale shrugged. "But they aren't all bad. I know a knight who might help. His name is Glendon Hawke. He's a great fighter, and he is back there somewhere, in the direction you're going."

"Would he join us?"

"I haven't any idea," Cale told her. "But you could talk to him. If he won't help, maybe he knows somebody who will."

"Thank you," the elf girl said. "In return for that, I give

you a suggestion. If you want to get into Kal-Thax without going through a war zone, turn north. That mountain over there—the highest one—is called Sky's End. Go around to the north of it. There's a dwarven place there that has been abandoned. And the rises below it are deserted right now. Since the early snows, the broken lands are virtually impassable . . . for humans, at least. You could begin your search there for . . . what is it you call what you seek?"

"Everbardin," he said. "It means hope. And home."

"Everbardin," she repeated. "To us, Qualinesti means hope—or new hope. Silvanesti means home." She backed away. "Go in peace, Cale Greeneye. You and we are not at war . . . though everybody else around here seems to be."

Cale clambered down to the trail again and climbed aboard Piquin, then looked around in surprise. Where there had been dozens, or maybe hundreds, of elves, now he saw only a few—then none. The lithe, silent beings had gone their way, fading into the landscape. His companions also were staring around in confusion.

"Well," Cale decided, "you heard what she said. Let's veer north and take a look at that next peak."

"You trust that elf?" Gran Molden stared at him.

"Why not?" Cale glared back. "I gave her some advice, and she responded. That's one thing about elves. They are straight traders." From a high place where they could see the Hylar procession, Cale signaled, using his burnished shield as a mirror. Across the miles, the response came, and they saw Colin Stonetooth's tribe change course to follow them. Then they headed for the slopes of Sky's End.

When the dwarven scouts were gone, shadows moved on the hillside, and what had seemed a vacant slope became a large band of western elves trotting down a hidden trail. At the lead, the elf called Demoth asked, "Why would you counsel dwarves, Eloeth? They are nothing to us. Especially here, in Kal-Thax."

She smiled slightly. "Why not? Those were unusual dwarves, Demoth. They found our trail, when no one else ever has. Besides, I have a hunch about that one . . . that

Cale Greeneye."

"What hunch?"

"I don't know. I have a feeling we'll see him again. Come on. Let's have a look at these 'Hylar' with their marching drums, then see if we can find a knight named Glendon."

* * * * *

In the shadow of a great peak, through broken, tumbled lands bounded by a deep, vertical gorge, the people called Hylar entered the realm of Kal-Thax. Old Mistral Thrax extended his red-palmed hands upward. "There," he told Colin Stonetooth. "Up there, above the stonefall."

"Those bead-eyes from the mage?" someone asked. "Do they guide you, Mistral?"

"My hands guide me." The old dwarf shrugged. "I haven't seen those bead-eyes since the day that kender left. But this is the place where our search begins."

Here the entire lower face of the mountain was a massive fan of stone rubble, miles wide at the bottom. Dwarves climbed through it, poking and tasting. "Hewn stone," they reported. "From fresh delving, very deep."

Above, high on the mountainside, they found the remains of an elaborate citadel, partly destroyed by rockfall. Within and behind it the Hylar studied walls, passageways, cubicles, and ledges, learning what they could of those who had created this place. They were dwarves, obviously, and the cuttings of the stone spoke of a numerous, energetic people whose tools, primitive by Hylar standards, were nonetheless of fine quality.

And the place was only recently abandoned. So where had they gone?

Wight Anvil's-Cap, a master delver, studied the rubble below the delvings. Frost Steelbit, who had been chief of wardens in Thorin, studied the patterns of the wrecked citadel. Talam Bendiron, who once had been tap warden, puzzled over the placement of seeps and cisterns. Then they conferred with Colin Stonetooth.

"This place was called Daebardin, and its people the Daewar," Frost said. "But the runes have been scratched over, indicating that they packed up and left."

"These Daewar are primitive in some ways," Talam said. "They do not have the knowledge of water-tunneling, so they have to live near a natural source. But our tampers have sounded out this peak and its only water is outside, on its face."

"Yet they went inward," Wight reported. "This delving-stone is from a tunnel that goes south into the mountain. The rubble indicates a straight dig, directly into the stone heart of the peak, with no consistent layers . . . as there would be if they had widened their digs or delved a living space."

"They are people of the sun," Frost Steelbit puzzled. "The architecture of their citadel shows that. They do not like the dark deeps, and they don't know how to build sun-tunnels, yet they penetrated a peak with no natural quartz for light. Why would they do that?"

"There has been fighting here," Jerem Longslate noted. "It looks like war between tribes. Some of those who battered the citadel were dark-seekers. Others were of a cliff-dwelling type."

"But not those who lived here," Frost persisted. "These are puzzling people. Not as primitive as those around them seem, though as Talam said, there are many things they haven't discovered. Still, the people who built this place are fairly civilized, it seems."

"Possibly these are the ones that knight mentioned," Colin suggested. "The ones he called the bright-colored dwarves. He said they are better organized than most in Kal-Thax."

"Obviously," Frost agreed. "They are fine delvers, which means they have fine organization. But they are sun people. Why would they dig into darkness?"

"Possibly to reach a place where they knew there would be light," Colin mused. "We know where their tunnel begins. I think we should find where it ends."

"It will take a while to break through the seal they set in their tunnel," Wight Anvil's-Cap said. "It is only stone, but cleverly done—a hinged plug, of all things! Balam Platen wants to study how it was made. He believes that such a gate, using the proper metals to shield the stone, would be impregnable."

"Let him study to his content." The chieftain nodded in agreement. "There will be time to explore the tunnel. Right now, there are other things to do. We must establish residence in this land, of course. After that, I think we should take a look at these mountains and maybe meet some of our new neighbors."

Since this place was obviously dwarven, and obviously abandoned, Colin Stonetooth claimed it and the adjoining slopes for the Hylar, thus establishing his tribe as a legitimate resident nation in the realm of Kal-Thax and laying a foundation for diplomatic negotiations—once they found someone to negotiate with. In a solemn ceremony, he proclaimed all of the north side of Sky's End and the valley below as far as the great gorge as Hylar ground. As was dwarven custom, the Hylar claimed the site of their stronghold, enough land around that to support the stronghold, and enough beyond that to establish a wide perimeter for privacy and defense.

Armed companies were sent out to mark the boundaries with runes and cairns. Thus did what had been Daebardin become the first Hybardin.

Most of the tribe—now a thane, as the runes they found said land-holding tribes were called—went to work on the old citadel and the hewn caves behind it to create temporary quarters. Cale Greeneye and his scouts explored the nearby countryside and had a look beyond the peak where armies of dwarves—unaware as yet of the Hylar— patrolled the frontal ranges facing east. Colin Stonetooth and the elders laid their plans, and Willen Ironmaul readied the Hylar Guard for an expedition to neighboring slopes.

And while all this was under way, Tera Sharn involved herself in the repair and general tidying up of her people's new home.

Working with other women and the older children, she was carrying bales into the delves for counting when she stopped suddenly, her eyes widening. For an instant, she thought she had seen someone—a strange, ancient, glowing dwarf, watching her. Like the person of Mistral Thrax's dream. It was only for an instant, though, and then the vision was gone.

Then she knew something that she had not known before. Dropping the packs, she spread her hands on her small midriff and a slight smile creased her cheeks.

When the work was done, she went looking for Willen Ironmaul. "We have a secret, my love," she told him. "The first child to be born in this new place—the first child of the Hylar realm—will be your child and mine."

It was the following morning when the chieftain of the Hylar set out to meet his new neighbors. Flanked by the Ten and followed by an army of hundreds of Hylar who wore armor fashioned for the skills learned from a human knight, Colin Stonetooth crossed the shoulder of Sky's End and headed for the Windweaver crags.

22
The New Neighbors

Except for the deserted slope north of Sky's End, which was virtually impassable for humans, the only ready access into the Kharolis Mountains from the east was along a narrowing foothill range extending from Grand Gorge to the Cliffs of Shalomar. North of that, for hundreds of miles, the gorge and its precipitous canyons guarded the mountain range. To the south, the cliffs did the same. And in both directions, encroaching winter was narrowing the approaches day by day.

All of the assaults by outsiders driven by the eastern wars, therefore, had been along a sixty-mile front between the gorge and the cliffs, where several valleys ran deep into the mountains, with pathways beyond.

As the strongest force among the tribes linked by the Pact of the Kal-Thax thanes, the Daewar held the central range, with Theiwar on their north flank and Daergar— defending their mines from other dwarves as much as defending Kal-Thax from intrusion—on the south. Here and there among them, usually wandering the lower slopes, were bands of wild Klar, and there were even some Aghar here and there, driven upward from lower regions. No one had any idea where the Aghar were from day to day, because of the tendency of the gully dwarves to pack up and move every time anyone noticed them.

On this day, things were quiet along the front. Fresh snows lay on the peaks and in the high valleys, and biting winds carried laden clouds eastward. Although the distant plains seethed with humans and who knew what else, there had been no concerted attempts to invade—and thus no real battles—for more than a week. There was some skirmishing, but most of it now was between Theiwar and Daewar troops, or between Theiwar and Daergar, or Daergar and Daewar. Also, a group of Klar, crazed by mercury vapors after a "spirit floating" ceremony in some deep, hidden hole, had tried to attack a Daewar patrol and been wiped out, which had led to harsh words between some Daewar commanders and the Daergar miners who provided the hated tamex—the false metal—to the Klar.

On top of everything else, nearly a dozen dwarves in the reserve lines—dwarves of various tribes—had been found mysteriously murdered in recent days, killed silently, and robbed of some of their garb or armor. Some of the missing items included a Theiwar sloped helmet with face mesh, several kinds of cloaks, shrouds, and kilts, a Daergar iron mask, a Daewar winter mantel. It was as though some assassin were methodically prowling the darkness, collecting a variety of clothing.

Olim Goldbuckle was at a loss as to what was going on, and his counterpart chiefs—Slide Tolec of the Theiwar and Vog Ironface of the Daergar—seemed as puzzled as he was.

It was a minor thing, but troubling.

On this morning, though, there were other things to think about. Daewar scouts came pounding in from the rear lines and pointed toward the high crags where spotters were stationed. Bright signals were coming from up there, and Olim read the flashes carefully, then turned to peer northwestward, shading his eyes. "By Reorx's hammer!" he spat. "They've gotten behind us!"

There in the distance, on the high slopes beyond the Theiwar camps, an army snaked its way down the flank of a rise—hundreds of armored figures astride tall mounts, and many hundreds more afoot, carrying javelins and pennants, all moving steadily toward the widespread defense lines.

"Signal Slide Tolec!" Olim Goldbuckle commanded. "Those people are almost on top of him. Tell him to defend!"

Burnished mirrors flashed in the wintry sun, and even in the distance they could see the Theiwar camps coming alive to face the new danger.

"Who are they?" Olim growled, trying to see details across the miles. "Are those horses? What kind of horses could traverse these mountains in winter?"

Gem Bluesleeve was beside him, squinting younger eyes. "See their armor, Sire! It is like the armor of those knights we met on the plains. And their horses are armored, too."

"Knights?" Olim squinted harder. "Up here? How did they get here? And how did they get above us? Horses are useless in this season. They can't negotiate mountain passes in winter!"

"Those seem to," Gem pointed out.

"Well, whoever they are, the Theiwar see them now. They will deal with them."

In the distance, bands of dark figures ran from the Theiwar camps toward the path of the intruders and disappeared over a glistening rise. Olim assumed an ambush was being laid. The Theiwar were very good at ambush.

The strangers, whoever they were, were about to learn just how good. Olim smiled grimly as the army on the mountainside marched around a curve and out of sight—directly into a prepared Theiwar defense.

For a time, there was nothing to see. Whatever was happening on the north flank miles away, was hidden from the Daewar camps. Minutes dragged by as Olim Goldbuckle stared into the distance, imagining what Slide Tolec's troops must be doing to the intruders.

Then, distant but strong on the wind, came a sound, and Olim paled beneath his whiskers. Errant winds gusted, driving curtains of snow across the slanted lands, but on the wind came the sound of marching drums.

The blowing snow drifted past, and figures seemed to rise out of it. Hundreds of armed, armored figures, some mounted high on tall, golden horses. They were well past the Theiwar camps and were closing fast on the Daewar line.

* * * * *

Colin Stonetooth paused for a moment as the Hylar cleared the twisting, snow-packed path and emerged into a low, rough canyon between caprock-topped cliffs. Beside him, Jerem Longslate nodded. "Those were ambush signals, all right," he said. "And there is the ambush, just ahead. There . . . and there, up in the rocks. They are hiding from us, waiting for us to come to them. Definitely an ambush."

"Hardly a greeting committee," the chieftain agreed. He turned and beckoned. When Willen Ironmaul rode up beside him, he pointed ahead. "Those people Cale saw from the promontory. Some of them are in this canyon now, waiting to ambush us. Do you see them?"

"Aye, Sire." The big guardsman nodded. "I see where they are."

"I want to talk to them," Colin Stonetooth said. "Have someone round them up and bring them along. We will go on to where those large groups are assembled, down on the pass."

"Yes, Sire." Willen wheeled his giant horse and pranced back to give his orders to the guard companies. "We have found some of our neighbors," he said. "First section, take a foot company and gather up that ambush. Sections two and three, go have a look at those camps beyond. Gather up whoever's there and rejoin us over where all those brightly clothed people are." He circled his arm above his head. "Companies forward!"

"Sometimes your son-in-law sounds just like that human knight," Jerem Longslate said to Colin.

"Sometimes you do, too," Colin reminded the First of the Ten.

Jerem shrugged. "Well, the knight was the one who taught us."

* * * * *

Beneath a slanting sun, the canyon lay in silence, only the mountain winds whispering through it. Then there were the echoes of steel-shod hooves on stone, the creak and clink of armor, the sounds of booted feet marching.

"They're coming," a Theiwar whispered in the shadowed clefts below the caprock. "Ready?"

"Ready," other quiet voices responded.

Dark in the shadows they waited, and the intruders appeared at a bend, coming toward them. Slide Tolec frowned, easing forward for a better look. They were dwarves! But what kind of dwarves? And riding horses! They looked like no one he had ever seen—sturdy, dark-maned people with horned or plumed helms, edged shields at every shoulder, and wide, tapered blades at hand. They fairly bristled with weaponry.

Most of the strangers had trimmed beards that seemed swept back, as though they faced a wind. Again, Slide gaped at the tall golden-and-white horses and shook his head in wonder. He had seen horses, but he had never seen dwarves ride them. And such horses! They were half again the size of any horses he had ever seen.

Behind the company of mounted dwarves came foot-men, a hundred or more of them, marching in perfect precision as though someone were calling the step. They moved as though a drummer were pacing them.

Slide had never seen such people. Dwarves or not, though, they were intruders. This was no new thane sprung from the Einar masses. These people were from somewhere other than Kal-Thax!

The column came directly below the ambush, and Slide Tolec raised his arm and sliced downward. From both sides of the canyon, a hail of stones and missiles crashed down on the strangers below. Thrown stones, sling-stones, bolts from throwing sticks, and several axes descended upon the intruders like raining death . . . descended, ricocheted aside, and rattled on the stone floor of the canyon.

Slide stared down into the chasm. At the instant of attack, even as the stones had rained down, the mounted dwarves had wheeled, separated, and pounded ahead, their tall horses hardly breaking stride as they angled up the snowy slopes. Directly below the ambushers, the canyon floor was a solid carpet of metal shields, covering every part of every intruder. And even as Slide gawked, the shields parted in neat rows, each shield tilting, and a barrage of iron balls whistled upward, driven by deadly, humming slings. Singing like angry hornets, the hail of balls smashed into the shallow caverns, throwing shards of broken stone, caroming this way and that among the Thei-war. There were shrieks and howls, and several dwarves plunged from hiding to roll down the crusted slopes where sturdy shields stopped them and strong hands disarmed them.

Slide Tolec stared in amazement. Once before, he had seen an ambush turned. But never like this! The strange dwarves moved and struck in perfect unison, wasting no effort. It was as though they were fierce, deadly dolls all dancing on a single string. The carpet of shields tilted again, turned to the sides, and a forest of iron-tipped javelins bristled there, held in strong hands on cocked, powerful arms.

Slide saw movement above and glanced upward. The caprock above the far canyon wall was lined with burly figures astride tall horses, all looking directly across at his hiding place. He started to retreat farther into the depths, but from directly overhead a lance point was thrust downward, pinning his sleeve to the stone beneath his arm.

A deep voice called, "You in the holes! Come out, and be quick about it!"

* * * * *

Pushing a thousand or more fleeing Theiwar ahead of them, scattering bands of Daergar and Klar as the wind scattered the drifting snow and gathering them, too, into their herd, wedges of Hylar warriors led by mounted elite guards moved in on the main camp of Olim Goldbuckle's Daewar army and surrounded it. At a dozen points, Kal-Thax dwarves tried to charge the strangers, to break their lines, but they were repelled expertly and easily each time. There were few casualties in the attempts. Most were simply pushed back, pushed inward until the main camp—a quarter mile square at the head of a promontory looking out at the distant plains—was filled almost solidly with panicked dwarves, staring around in confusion.

Gem Bluesleeve attempted to rally a counterattack by the Daewar, a running wedge of shield-bearers thrown directly at the line of strangers. But the lead shields met lance-tips wielded by mounted dwarves, and the attack collapsed upon itself. Footmen flanking the riders charged forward and drove the Golden Hammer's best warriors back into the crowded campsite. A hundred yards away, a howling charge by masked Daergar did no better.

Olim Goldbuckle knew a hopeless situation when he saw one. The Daewar leader climbed up on a rock, spread his hands, and bellowed, "Hold!" Then he dropped his shield to the ground, loosed his sword and dropped it, and stood empty-handed and defiant, his fists on his hips. "We are taken!" he shouted, looking this way and that at the solid line of strange dwarves facing him fifty yards away. "We yield! Who are you people, and what do you want?"

Directly ahead of him the line parted and a plume-helmed rider pushed through, accompanied by ten others flanking him in tight formation. The leader reined in his tall horse, sat in silence for a moment facing Olim Gold-buckle, then slung his great hammer and raised his visor. The face revealed there was as weathered and tough as mountain stone, framed by dark, clipped hair and a trimmed, back-swept beard with touches of silver in it. "Name yourself!" he demanded.

Olim squared his shoulders in defiance. "I am Olim Goldbuckle, Prince of Thane Daewar of Kal-Thax!"

Eyes like ice studied him. "Are you the leader of all these warriors?"

Some distance away the crowd rippled as a masked warrior in dark furs pushed through. Without removing the slitted iron mask below his conical helm, he faced the stranger. "I am Vog Ironface!" his hollow-sounding voice called. "I am Chieftain of Thane Daergar of Kal-Thax!"

And on the other side, a wide-shouldered dwarf in bronze-studded leathers stepped up onto a cask and pulled aside his mesh visor, squinting in the sun. "I am Slide Tolec!" he spat. "I am Chieftain of Thane Theiwar of Kal-Thax!"

Near the east perimeter a wild-haired figure in uncut furs and wrapped boots pushed past others of his kind to face the line of shields. "Bole Trune!" he shouted, snarling in rage. "I am Klar! I lead Klar of Kal-Thax!"

Somewhere in the crowd, a small, quavering voice was raised. "Where Highbulp?"

"Dunno," another answered. "What want Highbulp for?"

"He s'posed say who he is," the first voice explained.

"Let Highbulp sleep," another suggested. "He don'

know who he is half th' time, anyway." Then that voice rose higher, "Aghar! This place, whatever! Highbulp's name Faze I or somethin' !"

The armored, mounted dwarf with the plumed helm and swept-back whiskers looked around, surveying the thousands of encircled beings before him. "You are many tribes," he said. "Do you war upon one another here, or just upon strangers?"

Olim Goldbuckle gritted his teeth, scowling at the armed one. There was a quality about the strangers—and particularly about this one—that annoyed him, but at the same time puzzled him. They seemed more aloof than hostile, more curious than combative, but he had seen them effortlessly throw back every attack made against them. "We war upon whom we please!" the Daewar roared. "Now you know who we are! Who are you?"

"I am Colin Stonetooth," the stranger said evenly. "We are the Hylar. We are new-come to this realm, but we have come to stay. We claim equal rights and will defend them if we must."

"Intruders!" Vog Ironface shouted, his voice echoing through his slitted mask. "You are not of Kal-Thax!"

"We are of Kal-Thax now," Colin Stonetooth said, his voice deep and level. "We have made due claim, and the territory we hold is ours."

"You are not part of the pact!" Slide Tolec called, his broad shoulders hunched as he pushed closer to the line of shields. "Kal-Thax belongs to those who defend it!"

Colin Stonetooth inclined his head, looking down at the angry Theiwar. "And what is this pact?" he asked.

"A treaty! A covenant of thanes, to defend Kal-Thax against intruders."

"Against what intruders?" the Hylar prodded.

"All intruders!" Vog Ironface snapped. "You and all the others!"

"We are not intruders," the Hylar said, slowly. "We came here, yes. But now we are here, just as you are. What intruders?"

Olim Goldbuckle shook his head, not liking the logic of the newcomer but understanding it. The strangers were indeed dwarves, and if they had laid proper claim to territories here—which he somehow was sure they had—then they were part of Kal-Thax, like it or not. Finally, in the silence, he raised his arm and pointed toward the far plains. "Those intruders," he said. "Especially the humans! They are out there and they threaten Kal-Thax. We are allied in its defense."

"Then we, the Hylar, will join in your pact." Colin Stonetooth nodded. "For those humans out there, we have no more love than you do."

"You will help to defend Kal-Thax?"

"Of course we will," the Hylar assured them. "I wonder, though . . . exactly what is it that we must defend?"

"Kal-Thax!" Olim Goldbuckle tipped his head, staring at the Hylar. "These mountains are Kal-Thax."

"And you allow none to pass through?"

"*Pass through*? Those are mostly humans out there, Hylar. Humans do not 'pass through.' Humans invade! They encroach! Wherever humans get a foothold, eventually there will be none there but humans." Olim Goldbuckle spread his hands. "Our people learned that, long ago. If humans get into Kal-Thax, they will stay."

Colin Stonetooth gazed around at the highland vistas. "Humans cannot live in mountains like these," he said. "We have dealt with humans, too, and we know them. They are not trustworthy, on the whole, but these mountains need no defense against them. Humans would starve here."

"There are valleys in Kal-Thax," Olim said, stubbornly. "They would settle in the valleys and build colonies. They would multiply and expand. In the end, they would try to wipe out the dwarves. That's how humans are. They must be kept out of Kal-Thax!"

"There are many kinds of defense," Colin Stonetooth replied. "I have seen great tides of wanderers out there, on those plains. Even the strongest dam will break if there is not a controlled release . . . a way for the flow to pass beyond. Has that been considered?"

"It has been considered enough!" Vog Ironface shouted. "Are you . . . you *Hylar* with us or not?"

"We are here to stay, if that's what you mean. No humans or anyone else will drive us out. We seek Everbardin here, in Kal-Thax." Colin Stonetooth leaned forward in his saddle, gazing from one to another of them. "Do any of you question that we can defend what we choose to defend?"

There was no answer to that. Of all the dwarven troops standing cordon along the eastern flank of Kal-Thax, nearly a third were here, ringed and helpless, held hostage by a few hundred strangers with strange skills.

"Then so be it." Colin Stonetooth nodded. "We do not want war with people of our own kind. You, Olim Goldbuckle! I ask your pledge of peace and a council of Thanes. Do you agree?"

Olim shrugged. "I agree," he said.

The Hylar turned. "You, Slide Tolec! Do you also agree?"

The Theiwar squinted at him, hating him but helpless to contest his will. Then he spread his hands. "I agree," he said.

Colin turned to Vog Ironface. "And you? Will you show me your face and agree to what I ask?"

"I will agree," the hollow voice rumbled. "But I will not blind myself for your pleasure."

"A dark-seeker," Colin muttered curiously. Then he nodded and turned toward the wildly clad Klar. "And you, Bole Trune of Thane Klar?"

The Klar seemed taken aback at the idea that anyone would ask for his promise. But he shrugged. "I agree," he said. Turning, he scowled fiercely about at others of his kind. "My word is given! I kill any Klar who breaks it!"

From somewhere, deep in the crowd, a wavering voice offered, "Highbulp prob'ly ag . . . agr . . . go 'long with that, too, when he wake up. That okay?"

With a gesture, Colin Stonetooth backed his mount away, and the line of shields withdrew, companies of

Hylar moving in perfect unison to a tattoo of drums.

Olim Goldbuckle frowned. Drums! So these were the ones! He snapped his fingers, and a Daewar picked up his sword and shield and handed them to him. "You called for a Council of Thanes!" he called to the Hylar leader. "When and where?"

"When the passes are blocked by winter," Colin called back. "But first"—he turned, scanning the foothills below the line of defense—"I believe we could give those people out there something to think about until spring."

Without waiting for a response, the Hylar leader wheeled his horse and headed eastward at a trot, his ten bodyguards flanking him purposefully. Behind him, companies of mounted Hylar spread and followed in a widening spearhead formation. Hylar footmen formed precise companies and followed, trotting along behind and among the mounted units. Within moments the Hylar army had become a deadly wedge of armed dwarves, banners aloft and drums singing, heading for the camps of the humans on the ridges below.

Olim Goldbuckle looked after them, then slung his shield and raised his sword. "Well, you heard him!" he roared. "Let's go chase some humans!"

Within moments the hundreds of Hylar in the lead were followed by thousands of Daewar, Daergar, and Theiwar, with bands of Klar running and howling along their flanks. By the time this wall of dwarves reached the lesser slopes, entire camps of human intruders were scurrying about in panic, turning to flee to the plains beyond.

In the highlands camp, only a few dwarves remained—a tumble of gully dwarves heading for cover, a few stragglers from other tribes, and a cluster of a hundred or so armed figures watching the assault from above.

These were a mix of kinds—mostly Theiwar, but with some Daergar among them. They clustered around an individual who might have been anything. Silently he had mingled with the others of all the camps, unnoticed except by those who chose to follow him. Though his face was obscured by Theiwar mesh, the clothing and armor he wore were an odd collection of Daewar, Daergar, Theiwar, and even Klar garb. He could have passed through any of their camps unnoticed, and had.

Now he stared after the receding Hylar force, and his eyes burned with hatred. "I do not agree," he muttered. "Glome the Assassin will not be herded like those sheep, by a band of strangers."

Glome had plans of his own, and no one, not even these strange Hylar, were going to stand in his way.

23
A Call to Covenant

Methodically, relentlessly, the combined dwarven armies of eastern Kal-Thax—led by a few hundred Hylar—swept the passes and valleys below the highland range, driving vast numbers of humans and other races ahead of them. Within days, the entire border from Grand Gorge to the Cliffs of Shalomar was secured and free of most intruders.

There were clashes of arms during those days, but they were few and brief. A band of roaming goblins, taking advantage of the human disarray to raid a camp of nomadic Sackmen, found itself instead faced with the blades and shields of the Golden Hammer, Gem Bluesleeve's Daewar strike force. Trapped between their human victims and the marching dwarves, the goblins tried to fight free. Very few survived to flee alongside the very people they had first attacked. A fighting unit of wild Sandrunners from the northern plains stood off two companies of combined Daergar and Theiwar for a day, then was massacred by Daergar in the dark of night.

And at the very edge of the foothill range, miles from the rising mountains to the west, a company of Ergothian knights and footmen—accompanied by various other natives of the land of Ergoth, trying to turn the flood of outlanders being forced back into their lands—confronted Willen Ironmaul's elite guard at the crest of a low ridge. Twice, the human forces hit the line of mounted dwarves, and twice they were thrown back—as much by the ferocity of the Calnar horses as by the stubborn determination of the dwarves who rode them. Then, as they regrouped, Willen himself rode out from his lines and raised a hand in salute toward a familiar figure. The knight who rode forward to meet him wore a blue cloak over his mail, and a blue plume on his helm. The red falcon in stoop upon his breast was the same as it had been when last they met, and the sword he carried was an exquisite, dwarf-crafted blade with a diamond in its pommel.

"Ho, Sir Knight!" the dwarf called as Glendon Hawke approached. "Must we now test ourselves against our teacher?"

"Ho, Sir Dwarf!" Glendon retorted. "Have you found your Everbardin in those mountains?"

"We have found the place to begin our quest." Willen nodded. "And people of our race—or fairly close—to share it if they will."

Three knights bearing the insignia of an Ergothian lord had ridden forward, stepping their mounts past Glendon's, edging the free lance knight aside. "And now you return here, driving outlanders before you?" one said. "These Cobar and Sackmen do not belong here, Sir Dwarf. Why do you bring them to us?"

"They do not belong in Kal-Thax, either," Willen pointed out. "And if they tried to stay in those mountains through the winter—even if we would allow it—they would starve or freeze before spring. Is that what you humans want?"

"Of course not!" the same knight snapped. "But we can't have them overrunning our lands. And if we push them north, toward Xak Tsaroth, the overlords there will put them to death, or send them off to Istar to be sold as slaves. We want no part of such business."

"Then why not do something about the reason they come here?"

"What reason?" Glendon straightened in his saddle, resting his lance, ignoring the glares of the pennanted knights at his interruption.

"The dragon wars in the east," Willen said. "Cale Green-eye has met elves who believe the dragons can be defeated, if the elves can rally enough support."

"Yes, I know about the elves. They came looking for me. They said I was recommended by dwarves. They also have spoken to the lords of eastern Ergoth."

"And will you help them?"

"Some have already gone," an Ergothian knight said haughtily, "and others are considering it."

"And you, Sir Glendon?"

"It is difficult to say no to an elf named Eloeth. But I was needed here first. A village has employed me as its . . . well, its champion." He glanced aside at the knights, two of whom were frowning at him. "Well, people can't wait forever for the leaders of Ergoth to come to agreement with those bullies in Xak Tsaroth!"

Willen wondered what that was all about, but no explanations seemed forthcoming. He shifted, to point behind him, where laden clouds flowed among the Kharolis peaks. "Winter is at hand up there, human. And we are up there. There is nothing more you and your countrymen can do here . . . unless it is to assure the slaughter of people of your own kind."

"Cobar and Sackmen?" a knight sneered. "Sandrunners and Morion bandits? They are not of our kind!"

"They *are* human," Willen Ironmaul pointed out. "You

can deal with them or drive them away, but not to the west. Not now."

One of the three pennanted knights—a burly, gray-bearded man in battle-scarred armor—had said nothing, only listened curiously. But now he raised a gloved hand. "The dwarf is right," he said. "Within a week, the passes up there will be closed. These migrants would stand no chance. It may be that the time is at hand for duty to bend the knee to honor on this front." He turned to gaze at Willen Ironmaul, and the big dwarf felt the impact of cold, gray eyes as direct and forceful as those of Colin Stonetooth himself. "You may retire from the field, Sir Dwarf. You have accomplished what you came to do. For now."

Without waiting for a reply, the gray knight wheeled his mount and rode away, his two companions following him obediently. Willen stared after him, then asked, "Who was that?"

"That," Glendon said, "was Lord Charon, and I imagine you are the first dwarf he has ever honored with a word." The falcon knight raised his hand in salute and backed his sturdy horse away. "Farewell, Sir Dwarf. But heed carefully what you have heard. Lord Charon said, 'For now.' You will have no further intrusions while the snows last. But with spring . . . well, as I said, these people aren't our people, and when they can go, they will go where they will."

* * * * *

When snows filled the passes below the Windweavers, Colin Stonetooth led his warriors back to the promontory of the camps. Cale Greeneye and a group from Hybardin awaited him there with news.

For some time Colin Stonetooth conferred with Mistral Thrax, beside a fire where the old dwarf sat swathed in furs. Then the chieftain called the rest to him for their reports.

The sealed tunnel behind the old Daewar stronghold on

Sky's End had been opened, and Wight Anvil's-Cap had led explorers into it. The tunnel was a marvel of delving, they reported—nearly fifty miles in length and blocked at intervals by heavy grills made of iron railing, which the metalworkers in the party had removed. At the tunnel's end was a system of natural caverns deep beneath the surface. There, keeping themselves hidden, Hylar scouts had seen dwarves—Daewar, by the runes on the walls—doing things with what appeared to be giant worms. Beyond were other guarded tunnels.

The explorers had turned back to await the chieftain's orders, but Wight Anvil's-Cap was convinced by what he saw there that the huge cavern they had seen was just the first of many. He was excited by the possibilities. The cavern was miles in dimensions, and sky-lighted by quartz strata—not as well lighted as Thorin with its sun-tunnels, but light, nonetheless. There was fresh air, ventilation, and—in the judgment of Talam Bendiron, who knew of such things—there seemed plentiful water somewhere near.

"Light at the end of the tunnel," Colin mused. "I was right, then. The sun-people tunneled through darkness because they knew there would be light."

And there was more to the report. Cale Greeneye and his roving scouts had followed a group of Daewar returning from the slopes, and had seen them enter a hidden gate at the foot of a cliff on Cloudseeker Mountain, beneath the Windweaver crags. The gate was due south of the opening on Sky's End, and Wight Anvil's-Cap calculated that it was a second passage, leading downward to the same tunnel he had explored. In the same vicinity, only a few miles away, were the high, shallow caves where many of the Theiwar seemed to be concentrated.

"It appears that the sun-lovers tunneled beneath their neighbors," Cale noted, "as though they knew what they would find there."

Colin Stonetooth made a mental note to never underestimate the Daewar or their prince, Olim Goldbuckle.

Stepping away from the fire, where Wight Anvil's-Cap was helping Mistral Thrax brew a mix of herbal tea and hot ale, he beckoned to his youngest son and pointed eastward. On the slopes below, large groups of dwarves were trudging upward toward them—several distinct groups, shunning each other but all coming the same way.

"Our allies are returning," Colin said. "Soon it will be time for the council they promised. I think we should council in the caverns that Wight has spied below. It will be a delicate matter, though. Our Daewar friends might resent intrusion."

"Not to mention the Theiwar resenting the Daewar's intrusion under their mountain." Cale grinned. "And those people of the iron faces—the Daergar—they seem to resent everybody, just on general principle."

"Complex relationships make for complex negotiations." Colin shrugged. "I will send Willen and his elites north with these people, to approach from there through the long tunnel. The foot companies will accompany me to that hidden gate, and I shall call for the thanes' council there. Reorx grant me the wisdom, maybe I can get all of these various people to talk before they begin to fight."

"Reorx grant you a *lot* of wisdom to do that," Cale said, seriously. Then, "What do you want of me, Father?"

"Take your scouts, and any other volunteers you can get from Willen's troops. Set lookouts on the peaks. With the borders of Kal-Thax closed now, when the drums call, these tribes and many others—those Einar you have seen—will come. Some may be combative at first, and I want no surprises. Once we are gathered—and at peace—I would like a thorough exploration of this region. I leave that to you."

"That is duty of my choice." Cale nodded, then raised an eyebrow. "Father, since leaving Thoradin, have you ever wished to return?"

Colin frowned. "Why do you ask that?"

"Because I never have," his son said. "I think I was always restless there, as though I were trapped by the city itself. Now I find—and some of the others do, too—that I have no real liking for caverns and tunnels, for stone ceilings and walls. I wonder if I—if a lot of us—are really true dwarves. Some of us prefer the axe to the hammer, and prefer the sun to the stone."

Colin rubbed his beard thoughtfully then said, "No dwarf may tell another what he will be, Cale. For my part, the proper way to live is in good delvings, beneath the standing peaks. But not all are so inclined. You are a true dwarf, Cale, but some prefer the sun to the stone. In Thorin . . . Thoradin . . . in your grandsire's time, when they were still constructing the sun-tunnels, some people preferred to set the outer sleeves rather than the inner. There was a name for them, which was said with great respect. They were called the Neidar."

"Neidar?" Cale gazed at his father. "Knoll-dwellers?"

"The outside crews built cabins for themselves," Colin explained. "Usually on knolls on the mountainside, where the winds would sweep away the winter snows. Over time, many of them developed a fondness for the open sky. When the work was done, some of them would have remained outside by choice had it not been for the ogre wars. Many of our people still prefer the axe to the hammer . . . just as you and your companions do."

"Neidar," Cale mused. "Maybe I *am* Neidar, then. I like the mountain's sides better than I like its belly." He nodded, started away, then turned back. "Father, those caverns beneath Cloudseeker . . . they mean more to you than just caverns, don't they?"

"They may," Colin said quietly. "Mistral Thrax has told me . . . from whatever strange wisdom he holds in his hands . . . that there lies Everbardin."

* * * * *

Group by cautious group, the massed tribes of Kal-Thax withdrew from the now silent foothills, marching up the funnel passes toward the Windweaver crags. Led by the newcomers, those who called themselves Hylar, they had driven away the outsiders encroaching into their mountains and in all likelihood had the mountains to themselves now, until spring. It was time to go home and get on with their various schemes and plans.

Keeping distance between themselves and the other tribes, the Daewar angled northward above the promontory, the Theiwar headed west toward the crest of Cloudseeker, and the sullen Daergar turned south toward their mines. The wild, undisciplined Klar were here and there, going their own directions.

But they were all still within sight of one another when a sound grew on the mountain winds—a strong, strange, compelling music that was more than just the rhythms of marching drums. It was a signal, and a song. The dwarves of Kal-Thax had never before heard the eerie, beautiful drum-song of the Call to Balladine. But they heard it now, and there was no doubt what it meant. Colin Stonetooth had done what he promised. He had driven the human invaders away from Kal-Thax for the winter. And now he called his new neighbors to do as they had promised. The drum-song was a call, and a summons. It was time for the Council of Thanes.

Vog Ironface and his Daergar warriors heard the call and turned masked faces toward it, locating the source. From the heights of Cloudseeker it came, from the icy region of the Windweaver crags. Theiwar territory. Were the strangers aligned now with Theiwar? If so, then they were aligned against the Daergar.

"Come on," Vog Ironface rumbled, his voice hollow and sullen behind his slitted mask. "If we are betrayed, let's learn of it now."

Slide Tolec heard the sound, directly ahead, seeming to come from his own caves, and a cold dread touched him. The Hylar! The strangers, new-come to Kal-Thax, who had demonstrated their military might and then had withdrawn, to lead a sweep to clear outsiders from the slopes of the realm. Had it all been a ruse? With everyone preoccupied, had they come back here and invaded Theibardin? Were the Hylar now in control of Theiwar lairs?

He remembered Crouch Redfire, who had first organized the Theiwar into a power in Kal-Thax, and Twist Cutshank, who had listened to false counsel and almost destroyed them. It was like something those two might have done, to carry out such a betrayal.

"Theiwar!" Slide Tolec shouted. "Forward! Prepare to attack!"

And just north of the Theiwar, Prince Olim Goldbuckle and his Daewar army heard the call and checked their weapons. The sound of drums was coming from below Galefang, where the Daewar's secret entrance to the subterranean world below Cloudseeker lay. The Hylar had found the way to Urkhan's caverns! They would invade New Daebardin! Olim drew his sword and sliced it forward in the cold mountain air. "Daewar to me!" he roared. "Flanks left and right! Double-time!"

"The Theiwar!" Gem Bluesleeve called, pointing to the left where Theiwar were pouring over a ridge, angling upward toward Galefang. "And there! The Daergar are coming!"

"Shields and blades!" Olim ordered. "Get ready to fight!"

On rises and ridges all around, bands of fur-clothed Klar heard the drum-call and saw the armies of Daewar, Theiwar, and Daergar heading for the source of it. "Rust and rot!" Bole Trune growled. "I give my word, I let no one break it. Klar! Fight!"

A mile or so away, huddled under an outthrust shelf of stone, small faces turned toward the sound of the drums and one of them asked, "What that noise?"

"Drum," another said. "Like before."

"What before?"

"Before! When we get all surrounded an' say okay we do council."

"When all that happen?"

"While back, Highbulp. You were havin' nap, maybe

didn' notice."

"Well, what it mean?"

"Prob'ly mean we s'posed to go where noise is."

"Why?"

" 'Cause we said okay we would."

"Oh."

There were other ears, too, that heard the song of the drums. For miles around, in caverns and valley shelters, in fields, mining camps, and snowy pastures, the Einar by the thousands turned to listen and wonder. Unaffiliated with any tribe, though they shared ancestors with all of them, the common folk of Kal-Thax heard the call and came out from tiny villages, cave complexes, and remote shelters to follow the strange, hypnotic sound—the commanding, lovely Call to Balladine.

Some of the Klar arrived first at the cliffs below Gale-fang. They howled down the slopes, in Klar fashion, then stopped in confusion as they saw the solid wall of iron shields facing them there.

The Daewar came then, pushing up through a snowy draw, bright garments brilliant against the white of new winter. In the thousands, they far outnumbered the Hylar foot companies and the eleven mounted Hylar waiting under the cliffs, but Olim Goldbuckle remembered the encirclement of the border camps and the precise, efficient way in which these outland strangers had made themselves part of Kal-Thax. They hesitated, and when the Hylar line made no move, they pulled back to wait.

The Theiwar came cautiously, ready to counterattack invaders in their country, but when they saw the assembly below the cliffs they were confused. Nobody was attacking anybody. Gathering to one side of the massed Daewar, they clustered around and behind Slide Tolec, their hands on their dark blades, and waited.

By the time the Daergar of Vog Ironface arrived on the scene, others were arriving, too—small groups of puzzled, cautious Einar from the nearer slopes, and even a little tribe—or tumble—of Aghar, creeping along a gully to peer out at what was happening beyond.

By dusk, thousands and tens of thousands of dwarves waited on the slope of Cloudseeker, below the towering crag called Galefang, nearest of the Windweavers. It was what Colin Stonetooth had counted on. There was such a crowd now, that no one—not even the well-armed Daewar—could start trouble without risking a free-for-all in which *everyone* would be outnumbered.

The sheer numbers, and the complexity of the groups, made it simply impractical for anyone to attack anyone. And to most dwarves—even the unpredictable Klar—the primary test of any situation—the primary test of *anything*—was its practicality.

Mounted on his great horse Schoen, and flanked by the Ten, Colin Stonetooth rode to the top of a shoulder in full view of everyone on the slope. With great ceremony, he removed his helm and shield and handed them across to Jerem Longslate, First of the Ten. Then he drew his sword and hammer and—as he had seen Olim Goldbuckle do to signal a talk—he dropped them on the ground.

The drums ceased their song, and in the silence Colin Stonetooth said, in a voice that carried to the fringes of the great crowd, "We are the Hylar. We are newly-come, but we are of Kal-Thax now, just as are all of you. So know this: in the spring, or the next spring, these mountains may be overrun by humans. Unless we—all of us, in unison—take measures to prevent it, we will all fall before the tide of human migration, if not this year, then the year after."

Olim Goldbuckle stepped to the head of his legions and raised his arms. "You speak of measures, Hylar!" he called. "What measures?"

"We will show you," Colin said. "Among us, we have the means to create a stronghold which no human horde can penetrate." He pointed. "You, Vog Ironface! Your people have the raw materials that will be needed, in your mines. The ores to make the metals for a mighty stronghold. And you, Slide Tolec! Your people know these passes better than any. And you, Bole Trune of the Klar.

Organized, your people can save themselves from the humans by helping to save all the rest of us."

Olim Goldbuckle cupped his hands to shout, "And the Daewar? What do you think we can offer to your plan?"

Colin Stonetooth gazed at the Daewar prince and suppressed a smile. "You, Prince Olim, have the place."

"What place?" Olim snapped.

"He's right!" Slide Tolec yelled. "The Daewar have a great, secret cavern somewhere. I have seen it."

"That place," Colin Stonetooth nodded. "A place that all can share, and by right must share. The Daewar because they found it first, the Theiwar because it is in their claimed territory . . ."

"In Theiwar territory?" Slide Tolec demanded. "Where?"

". . . the Daergar because they have the materials to build it into a stronghold," Colin continued, "the Klar— and the Einar and any others who care to, because they can assist in its construction and in its defense."

Olim Goldbuckle was fuming. How did the outlander know of his secret place—of Urkhan's findings? "And what of you, Hylar?" he shouted, angrily. "You tell us all that we might offer—what we can do with our own resources—but what of you? What do you offer?"

Colin Stonetooth spread his hands in an eloquent shrug. "We know how," he said. Then his voice became commanding as he turned toward the ranked Theiwar. "Slide Tolec, we are within your people's borders. Do you grant us permission to go underground?"

Startled at the polite, ceremonial question, Slide glanced around at his followers, then nodded. "I give permission," he said. "We'd like to see what the Daewar found here, too."

Colin turned to the Daewar prince. "Olim Goldbuckle, the gate behind me, in the cliff, is of Daewar crafting. Will you honor your neighbors by inviting us through it, in peace?"

"And if I don't?" Olim demanded.

"Then we'll take it down ourselves!" Slide Tolec shouted.

"This is Theiwar territory!"

"I already have a company of warriors below," Colin said mildly. "It would be better if you invited us in."

Olim Goldbuckle, the master of maneuvering, knew when he was outmaneuvered. "We will open the gate," he conceded.

"I call a Council of Thanes!" Colin Stonetooth announced so all could hear. "To be held in Thorbardin!"

Every eye in the crowd turned to him in puzzlement. "Where?" some asked.

Even Jerem Longslate stared at his chieftain in surprise. "*Thor . . . bardin*, Sire? Is this the name of our Everbardin?"

"In honor of the past." Colin nodded. "And of the future."

Part VI:
Thorbardin

Thorbardin
Beneath Cloudseeker Peak

Century of Wind
Decade of Hickory
Early Spring, Year of Zinc

24
The Covenant and the Assassin

By the time snows lay deep upon the Kharolis range, the mountain called Cloudseeker swarmed with dwarves, outside and in. The Council of the Thanes had lasted seventeen days, and scribes would be at work for years to come, recording and interpreting all that had been decided.

With the Ten at his back, Willen Ironmaul's guards positioned at strategic points, and several companies of footmen at his call, Colin Stonetooth of the Hylar could have dominated the proceedings. But he was wise enough not to. This place beneath the peaks, which he had named Thorbardin, would be his clan's Everbardin, and the Hylar chieftain was determined to keep resentments to a minimum among those who would share its space. So Colin

Stonetooth had a huge, seven-sided table crafted and placed on a wide, flat ledge on the shore of the Urkhan Sea, and brought the leaders of the thanes together there.

Each prince and chieftain chose his own place at the table, and Colin Stonetooth was the last to be seated—even after Faze I, Highbulp of Clan Aghar, who was so awed by the proceedings and the presences around him that he did the only thing he could think of to do. He laid his head on the great table and went to sleep.

Olim Goldbuckle chose the bench on the east, with his back to the brightest part of the great cavern, where the Daewar already had significant delvings going on. Vog Ironface of the Daergar chose a southern seat, Slide Tolec of the Theiwar a bench on the north, with Bole Trune of the Klar on his left, and the little Aghar Highbulp snoring on his right, and two benches remained. A heavily bearded dwarf named Grist Stonemill, selected by the Einar to speak for them, took the one on Faze I's right, and Colin Stonetooth sat down beside the Daewar prince.

The Ten stood behind him, and others moved forward to stand behind their leaders—Gem Bluesleeve and his Golden Hammer guards behind the Daewar prince, Brule Vaportongue and a dozen Theiwar behind Slide Tolec, eight masked figures behind the Daergar chief, a collection of unshorn Klar behind Bole Trune, several Einar behind Grist Stonemill, and a strange-looking little figure called Grand Notioner behind the sleeping Faze I.

"In the place from which we Hylar came," Colin said, "we used a seven-sided table for matters of council, and none knew why, because only six sides were needed. Now I see that seven is, indeed, the proper number." He looked from one to another of them. "Reorx attend us here," he said. "Give us the wisdom that we must have."

"Reorx attend," Olim Goldbuckle muttered, and others at the table nodded.

And so began seventeen days of debate and council, during which everything from the name of the place to a list of agreements for public and private use of its resources was worked out.

The Daewar would keep and hold the easternmost shore of the Urkhan Sea, where an arm of it curved around a bend in the cavern. The quartz above made it a brightly lighted bay, the brightest natural place in the immense system. They would claim this shore and the stone beyond it, where they were already delving their city of New Daebardin.

The Theiwar would claim the northwest shore and the stone beyond it, as far as the entrance to the cavern Urkhan had called the first warren. The Daergar would own the south shore where the quartz-strata light was dimmest and would turn their rubble heaps over to the Aghar, who preferred surroundings such as rubble heaps from other peoples' delves.

The Daewar would have preferred that both Daergar and gully dwarves be as far from them as possible, preferably clear across the sea. But Olim consented, since the bend in the natural cavern would block any view of unsightly digs from the Daewar city.

The Klar, those of them who chose to make homes in the subterranean chamber, would claim and hold the deep regions at the east end of a second natural warren where an arm of the sea had its shores.

Most of the Einar wanted no part of the caverns, preferring shallower digs. Those who did, though, were given leave to affiliate themselves with whichever Thorbardin clan suited them. For the rest, who were now beginning to adopt the name Neidar, which they had heard from Cale Greeneye and his adventurers, a pledge was made. The Neidar would remain outside to tend the fields and flocks that needed the seasons and the sun. In return for supplying the deep lairs with grains, meat, and lumber, they would have right of entry into Thorbardin any time they chose to do so and protection against their enemies by the armies within the stronghold.

The seventh place at the table, henceforth, would be the Neidar seat.

The two largest warrens would be common ground for all the thanes. Leveled and improved by workers using the giant tractor worms, they would be enriched with topsoil from outside—and with the fertilizers that Bardion Ledge, once waste warden of Thorin, knew how to process. The warrens would become subterranean farms.

The Urkhan Sea itself would be common property to all, and Talam Bendiron was already at work designing a system of counterweight-powered aqueducts to do away with such primitive and wasteful procedures as bucket brigades.

Each city would be as self-contained as it wished in such things as forges and shops, markets and housing, town customs and enforcement. But a system of tunnel roads and cable-cart ways would connect all the cities and would have common usage.

Frost Steelbit and Gran Molden revealed intricate plans for a gated entry to the south, utilizing the Daewar's hinged plug concept and Daergar iron for sheathing, combined by Hylar craft. The new gate would give ready access to the best Einar fields and provide access for metals from the Daergar mines.

It was suggested that a second such gate be placed at the northern end of the underground realm, but that was set aside for later consideration. It was also suggested that the great tunnel the Daewar had bored through Sky's End might be converted to a trade route—assuming things beyond Kal-Thax eventually settled down enough to allow trade with the outside.

The armies of the thanes would be separate but would be at the common call to defend Kal-Thax against the threat of humans, ogres, or anything else that might threaten. And the Hylar agreed to train the troops in the ways that they had learned.

There would be exploration to determine whether a magma pit could be created to power foundries, as in Thoradin. There would be surveys of places suitable for installation of sun-tunnels and a complete mapping of the natural ventilation system, which seemed to flow from a deep, walled valley to the south—that same valley the Theiwar called Deadfall—with exhausts high above, among the Windweavers themselves.

So many plans and ideas were discussed, so many measures decided in those seventeen days, that hordes of scribes were kept busy just jotting things down for later enscrollment.

And somewhere along the way, Olim Goldbuckle glanced at the tomes of his scribes and turned to frown at Colin Stonetooth. "We have overlooked something," the Daewar said. "Every thane but one has an assigned place for its delvings. Where will the Hylar live?"

Before Colin Stonetooth could respond, a voice behind him said, "There. There is Hybardin."

They turned. Behind the Hylar chieftain's bench, old Mistral Thrax leaned on his crutch. His free arm was outstretched, pointing upward, and the palm of his hand glowed dull red. As though there were no one there but himself, the ancient dwarf muttered, "It is the Life Tree. The Life Tree of the Hylar. There shall be Hybardin."

He was pointing out across the sea, at the great stalactite standing above the waters, its upper reaches blending into the distant ceilings of the cavern.

"Mistral Thrax has spoken." Colin Stonetooth nodded. "That will be the home of the Hylar. We will build our city within it."

Olim Goldbuckle's frown deepened. "The highest of the deep?" he muttered.

Colin glanced at him. "What?"

"Nothing," the Daewar prince snapped. "But now I have a question, and perhaps the Hylar have a suggestion about it. We have avoided this subject until now, but its time is here. Who will rule Thorbardin?"

All around the table they went silent, casting suspicious glances at one another.

Colin Stonetooth took a deep breath. It was the question he had dreaded, the one which could bring all their plans down around their ears. No Daewar was willing to be ruled by a non-Daewar, nor any Theiwar by a non-Theiwar, nor any Daergar by any but a Daergar.

"There are no kings here," Slide Tolec hissed. "Are there any who would be?"

"I am prince of the Daewar," Olim Goldbuckle noted.

"But not a king," Vog Ironface rumbled. He turned toward Colin Stonetooth, and for the first time removed his mask. The features behind it were sharp and chiseled, like the face of a fierce fox. "And you, Hylar? Would you be king?"

Colin Stonetooth shook his head. "The Theiwar is right," he said. "There are no kings here. Nor need there be any. Should the day ever come when Thorbardin needs a king, then—trust Reorx—a king may arise. But that day is not now. I would have Thorbardin governed by pact, not by power."

"Then there must be such a pact," Slide Tolec said.

"A sworn alliance," Olim Goldbuckle mused. "A solemn covenant, forged from our oaths and our honor. A Covenant of Thanes."

Aside, where a grim and silent group watched the proceedings, one sneered. "No king," he muttered. "So they say. Yet the Hylar says there may be a king one day. I say that day will come much sooner than they think."

And around him, others nodded while a few muttered, "Glome shall be king. Soon there will be enough of us."

Glome the Assassin no longer looked as he had a season past, when for a brief time he had led the Theiwar. He had assembled a collection of disguises, which let him seem to be anything he chose to be. Today he seemed a Daewar footman, with a cloak covering his helm. It was part of the power he held over his followers. He could be anyone, it seemed. And he could go anywhere.

His followers were mostly Theiwar and Daergar, but among them now were a number of rebellious Daewar, disgruntled at the upside-down world to which their prince had led them, and a fair number of Klar, angry at the bullying of Bole Trune. The group was a subversion—a growing, ragtag band held together by a common belief that Glome the Assassin would prevail in Kal-Thax. Not everyone was happy with this council of thanes or with the kind of future their leaders envisioned. Many had been recruited simply by the promise that Glome would wind up in charge here, and that his friends would be rewarded. Never had there been a king in Kal-Thax, but there would be. And great wealth would go to those who made him king.

"Not Daewar," Glome had told them. "Not Theiwar, not Daergar, not Klar. The king will be all of these . . . as I am all of these. I will be king."

"Our leaders do not lead," a Theiwar growled. "The Daewar prince, the mighty Daergar . . . even Slide Tolec of Thane Theiwar has surrendered to these Hylar. They give away our rights. They make pacts which will leave us as weak and soft as porous stone. They abandon the old customs because the Hylar have made them afraid. It is time for a king in Kal-Thax. A strong king,"

"Glome is strong," another muttered. "Glome deserves to be king."

For now, though, Glome and his supporters bided their time, waiting for their opportunity to strike.

* * * * *

When all of the articles of the covenant had been debated and the final arguments resolved, Colin Stonetooth had a forge set on the shore of Urkhan's Sea, and dwarves of all the thanes gathered for the Hylar ceremony of binding and bonding. Ingots of seven metals were heated on the glowing coals, and a great anvil was wreathed in the woods of the stone. Atop the anvil, the ingots were laid one upon another, so that their shape was the shape of a star. Then, one after another, the leaders of the thanes struck with hammers, bonding the metals together into one single artifact.

Colin Stonetooth's was the final blow, and his hammer rang echoes from the distances of the subterranean land. When he raised the hammer after striking, no ridge or seam remained on the surface of the joined ingots. There upon the forge lay a perfect fourteen-pointed amulet, smooth and gleaming from perimeter to perimeter.

"It is a covenant," Colin Stonetooth intoned, and around him the others echoed his words. "It is a covenant . . . covenant . . . covenant."

"Joined in seamless bond," Colin said, and the voices around echoed, "Bond . . . bond . . . bond."

"The Covenant of Thanes," Colin said. "Thanes . . . thanes . . . thanes," the voices echoed.

"A solemn pledge of all here gathered. A covenant of the forge . . . forge . . . forge . . . forge."

"The Covenant of Thorbardin!" He laid aside his hammer, and the vast distances of the mighty cavern whispered the echoes, "Thorbardin . . . Thorbardin . . . Thorbardin!" With his calloused bare hand he picked up the hot amulet from the forge, turned, and strode to the lapping shore. With a heave, he threw the amulet far out over the water, and a puff of steam arose where it sank beneath the waves.

"Forever," Colin Stonetooth whispered. "Thorbardin forever."

* * * * *

When word came to the old fortress on Sky's End that the Hylar would move one last time, Tera Sharn—now round-bellied with the child within her—assembled her belongings and began the loading of packs as the Hylar people waited for their escort. It was nearly fifty miles through the great tunnel to the place her father had named Thorbardin, they said. It would be a long, dark journey, but she was prepared. Her child would be born in Ever-bardin.

Other arrangements had been made, though. It was

more than an escort company that arrived at the north end of the tunnel. Willen Ironmaul came with most of the Hylar guard and a string of Calnar horses pulling Daewar carts. It was Colin Stonetooth's desire that his people should make the journey to their new home in comfort, and it was Willen's desire that his wife, carrying their child within her, should ride in ease and style.

One last time, then, the Hylar people packed their goods and their belongings and set out for the place which would be home.

"The last journey," Willen promised Tera. "Everbardin is found, and your father waits there for us. The Hylar will not move again."

"The last journey," she repeated. "It is well, my love. And the other people? They are there, too?"

"The thanes are bonded," he assured her. "Only Colin Stonetooth could have managed it, but manage it he did."

* * * * *

Despite its immensity, the great central cavern of the lake now teemed with activity. Dwarves were everywhere, it seemed: dwarves planning, delving, firing up forges, hauling stones and ores; dwarves huddling together in thought; dwarves arguing and squabbling; dwarves with hammers, bores and chisels. The cavern sang with the music of doing.

The Daewar were superb delvers, but had little of the arts of construction. The Theiwar knew the uses of bracing and the laying of walls, but knew little of tunneling. The Daergar were miners and could trace the patterns of stone better than any of the rest. The Hylar were skilled at invention and at the directing of light, wind, and water. Little by little, though, as they wandered about one another's digs, the skills began to blend, and the great natural cavern began to be a constructed place, suitable for a mighty stronghold.

Colin Stonetooth had gone with Wight Anvil's-Cap to

see the stone-cutting methods of the Daewar, then had left the chief delver there, taking notes, and had strolled away to look at the scrolls where Talam Bendiron was showing a cluster of Theiwar how to channel water into their lairs. Beyond, the Hylar chieftain inspected a glass furnace where mirrors were being crafted and sun-tunnels planned. Then he strolled on, accompanied only by the Ten, and paused at some distance to gaze out across the lake, where the great stalactite stood above the distant waters like a pillar supporting a world. His eyes rose slowly, following the contours of the huge, living stone monolith as it widened in the distance above. It was an awesome sight, like standing beneath an enormous mushroom, and he nodded. "Mistral Thrax was right," he said. "It is where the Hylar belong. My people will be comfortable there."

"Aye," Jerem Longslate agreed. "It is the Life Tree of the Hylar."

"The heart of Everbardin," Colin muttered, then gasped as a javelin seemed to blossom from his breast. Thrown by a strong arm, the shaft pierced him through, its thud drowned by a chorus of shouts as a flood of dwarves raced from shadows below the stepped cliffs to fall upon the Ten.

"Defend!" Jerem Longslate roared, drawing his blade as he unslung his shield. Beside him, Colin Stonetooth sank to his knees, his hands clawing at the javelin in his chest. His lips moved, but no sound came from them.

"Ring and defend!" Jerem shouted, deflecting another javelin with his shield. "Our chief is down!"

The Ten gathered around their fallen leader, shields up and blades at the ready, as the horde of attackers hit them like storm waters on a rocky shore. Shouts of "For Glome!" and "Glome the King!" rang in their ears, and their Hylar blades lashed out and came back dripping blood.

25

Sealed in Blood

Glome had awaited his time, and the opportunity had come. For days he had watched the leaders of the thanes succumb, one after another, to the strange new ideas brought forward by the outlander strangers who called themselves Hylar. He knew why the thanes' chiefs were so malleable. It was because they were afraid of these new dwarves.

But Glome was not afraid of them. He had seen them fight, and he knew that a headlong attack in force was not the way to defeat them. But such an attack was rarely his way. Strong and brutal, devious and opportunistic, Glome the Assassin had risen to power among the Theiwar because he did not take foolish chances. His chance here, he knew, would be to catch the Hylar unwary and wipe out their leadership.

The opportunity came when the Hylar chieftain, satisfied that the foolish covenant between the leaders of the clans was a solemn pact, dismissed his soldiers and sent them off to bring the rest of the Hylar people to this cavern.

To the crafty mind of Glome, it was the height of stupidity, that the Hylar chieftain so trusted in a thing as fragile as a promise. Promises, to Glome, were simply things said to lull an antagonist long enough to strike him. He could hardly believe it when he saw the mounted guards of the Hylar vanish into the Daewar's tunnel, followed in force by the footmen, carrying construction tools, and then saw Colin Stonetooth wandering along the lake shore accompanied only by his ten bodyguards.

For a moment, he suspected a trap. But it was no trap. The Hylar trusted those he had dealt with and had left himself undefended. It took only minutes for Glome to rally and place his supporters, and it was Glome himself who launched the attack and saw his javelin pierce the light breastplate of the Hylar chief. Then, by the hundreds, the rebels fell upon the bodyguards and bore them down.

For long minutes, the scene at the lakeshore was noise and confusion as attackers climbed over one another for a chance to use their weapons. Then at Glome's roar of command the rebels backed away and stared at the huge pile of dead and dying dwarves. There were a hundred or more of them, piled like twitching dolls on the place where the Hylar bodyguard had gone down. But even as they stared at the pile of bodies, the pile shifted. It surged upward, corpses rolling away, and a half-dozen dripping Hylar shields protruded above it. In a moment, the shields had warriors behind them, a tight ring of armor on a hill of death, and those rebels who were close enough felt the sting of whistling blades from among the shields.

In a panic, the attackers fell back. Some turned to run, but Glome's shout stopped them. "Attack!" he ordered. "They are only a few! Cut them down! Bring out the body of their chief!"

It was easier said than done. By threes and fives, rebel dwarves charged the Hylar defense, and by threes and fives they fell, adding to the carnage.

Still, the numbers were overwhelming. A Hylar guard went down with an axe in his back. Another fell to sword cuts and another to a thrown hammer. Glome heard distant shouts and saw dwarves coming from everywhere—Theiwar, Daergar, Klar, and, beyond them, bright ranks of Daewar.

Only one Hylar remained now, standing among the dead, turning this way and that, his sword and shield as blood red as the piled death at his feet. It was the one called Jerem Longslate, the one known as First of the Ten.

Two Theiwar rebels rushed him, one from each side, their dark Daergar blades swinging. He seemed barely to move, but one of the attackers thudded into the cutting edge of his shield while the other's sword flew from his grasp, twirling upward, then fell back upon its owner, point first.

Missiles whined around him, caroming off his shield, helm, and gauntlets, yet still he stood. Shouting crowds of covenant dwarves were closing rapidly on the throng of rebels. With a curse, Glome grabbed one of his own fighters by the back of the neck and charged the lone Hylar, thrusting his follower ahead of him like a shield. At the last instant, he flung the rebel forward upon the Hylar's sword, ducked, and rolled beneath him, stabbing upward.

It was over then, and, as Jerem Longslate fell, Glome the Assassin kicked and rummaged among the bleeding bodies until he found the Hylar chief, Colin Stonetooth. The Hylar was dead, still carrying Glome's javelin in his breast. With a heave, Glome lifted the body and held it high above his head, turning to face the dwarves rushing toward him from the digs.

"The Hylar is dead!" he shouted. "See! He is dead! He who made you betray the old ways is gone, and the pact is broken!"

While Glome's followers crowded around him, wide-eyed, the thousands from the digs crowded them, pressing forward to see what was going on, yet holding back from the dripping blades of the rebels.

"I have saved you all from the outsider!" Glome shouted. "I, Glome, have freed you! The covenant is done! Kal-Thax is restored to its rightful owners!"

The crowds surged as more new arrivals pressed in, stunned faces gawking at the scene before them. Glome thought he saw awe and respect in those faces, and he began to gloat. He had done it! He had won! "See me!" he shouted. "I am Glome! I am Theiwar, and I am Daewar, and I am Daergar, and I am Klar! I am your savior! I have killed the Hylar! Kneel before me! Kneel and call me king!"

Still holding the lifeless, blood-drenched body of the Hylar chieftain above his head, Glome turned slowly, letting them all see. He turned and hesitated. Slide Tolec stood before him, staring at him with stunned eyes. "Kneel before me, Slide Tolec of the Theiwar!" Glome demanded. "Kneel, and I may have mercy upon you."

"Glome," the Theiwar said. "Glome, what have you done?"

"I have killed the Hylar," Glome repeated. "The false covenant is broken."

"Broken?" Slide shook his head, slowly. "You have broken nothing, Glome, except a pledge. You were Theiwar once. I am Theiwar, and I gave my pledge. You have broken it."

Behind him, Glome heard another voice, hollow and angry. "And mine!" Glome turned to stare at the featureless mask of Vog Ironface.

"And mine!" another voice called, from where a large crowd of Daewar had gathered. "I gave the bond of the forge, murderer. The pledge of Olim Goldbuckle."

Now crowding toward the assassin were a large group of wild Klar, with Bole Trune in the lead, brandishing a heavy club.

"People of Kal-Thax!" Glome shouted, desperation in his voice. "Your leaders have betrayed you! The outlander

Hylar led them in false directions! Cast them aside and support me! I will be your king!"

Many in the crowd hesitated, unsure of what to do, their sheer numbers blocking those who pressed toward Glome and his band. Then from the lake's edge a dusty Daewar delver, his working hammer still in his hand, shouted, "Look! Look at the water!"

Those near him turned. From the stacked bodies at Glome's feet, blood had flowed downward to the water's edge—Daewar blood mingling with Theiwar blood, Theiwar with Daergar, Daergar with Klar, and all of them with Hylar—and as the runnels of gore reached the lapping water of Urkhan's Sea, the water turned pink, then red, the stain spreading outward from the bank.

Nearly a hundred yards it spread, then the waters there seemed to roil upward, like a rising tide. The surface broke, and a figure arose from it, to stand as though suspended just above its surface. A tattered, pained figure with white hair and whiskers outlining a sad, ancient face. As though walking on the ground, though its feet were inches above the lake's surface, the apparition made its way toward the shore as dwarves scattered and backed away ahead of it. When it was at the shoreline, it sagged tiredly, leaning upon its twin-tined spear, and raised a hand, palm forward. Its fingers opened and exposed a fourteen-pointed amulet.

In a voice that was like the winds in the tunnels, it said, "The covenant was forged by fire and tempered by water. Now it is sealed by blood." The phantom lowered its hand and straightened. Raising its spear, it pointed the tines directly at Glome, who stood transfixed, still holding the dead Hylar chieftain above his head. "You, Glome. Do you know now that you have completed the thing you thought to undo? Until this hour, Thorbardin was only a promise. Now Thorbardin lives."

The figure turned away and was gone. All along the shoreline, eyes wide with awe stared where it had been, then turned. Growls erupted here and there in the crowd and became a roar of anger as mobs of dwarves—all kinds of dwarves, armed with hammers, chisels, stones, or whatever was at hand—surged toward the cluster of rebels surrounding Glome.

With a cry, Glome dropped the body of Colin Stonetooth and retreated, pushing through his pressed followers, heading for the dimness of the tunnel that led to the first warren. "Hold them back," he screamed at his followers. "Defend! I order you to defend!"

Confused and frightened, the rebels milled about, some facing the oncoming horde, some trying to run. For a moment, it seemed they would hold where they were, wielding swords and lances against the motley tools of the mob. But a path opened through the mob, and a solid mass of Daewar warriors charged through. Gem Bluesleeve's Golden Hammer had arrived from New Daebardin.

The rebels turned, separated, and fled in panic, thousands of howling dwarves on their heels.

In dark shadows near the warren tunnel, Glome the Assassin lay hidden as the chase went by, then crept upward to the cleft where the tunnel began. Behind him, diminishing in various directions, were the sounds of conflict—of his rebels being run down by an enraged mob. But that didn't really matter to him. All he wanted was a place to hide, a means of escape. He was almost at the cleft when a lone figure stepped from the shadows to face him.

"I know you, Glome," Slide Tolec said coldly. "I knew where you would be."

Slide knew Glome too well to give him a chance to strike. Even before the assassin could raise his sword, the Theiwar chieftain lunged at him, and the axe he swung nearly cut Glome in two.

Some of the rebels made it as far as the Theiwar digs before they were cut down. Others fell at the lake's edge, and others beneath the jutting cliffs that blocked the northwest shore. A hundred or more of them, rallied by the best among them, made a stand at a place that had no name and were methodically cut to pieces there by Daewar footmen, Daergar swordsmen, Theiwar blades, and Klar stone axes.

Two former Daewar, hunted down in the first warren later, were disarmed and chained by Gem Bluesleeve's guard. From somewhere, delvers brought little silver bat-bells and hung them from the prisoners' chains. From a distance, the Daewar watched as a rampaging tractor worm located the source of the sound and smashed at it until the bells no longer sounded.

Olim Goldbuckle himself went to the road tunnel to meet the returning Hylar, and Willen Ironmaul and Tera Sharn saw a thing there that no living dwarf had ever seen. The prince of the Daewar of Kal-Thax had tears on his cheeks as he told them what had occurred.

* * * * *

On a bright winter morning, the bodies of Colin Stone-tooth and the Ten were carried in solemn procession along the great corridor that was the source of winds, and the winds seemed to hush their whispers as the drums of the Hylar beat a requiem.

They were buried with great honor in the deep, walled canyon that the Theiwar had always called Deadfall. But as Olim Goldbuckle called upon Reorx and all the other gods to recognize and honor those being buried there, he gave the place a new name.

From that day forward, the place would be known as the Valley of the Thanes.

And high above, all around the crests of the great walls of the valley, lifeless figures dangled from iron spikes. The bodies of Glome and his followers had been taken out of Thorbardin and given to Cale Greeneye and his Neidar adventurers. It was Cale's tribute to his father, that the bodies of his murderers be hung where their lifeless eyes could look down upon what they had done, and from where—when their bones decayed and fell from the spikes—they would be lost among the rubble of the cliffs.

For a time, Tera Sharn's grief at her father's death kept her to her quarters, and Willen Ironmaul stalked the Hylar digs, hard-eyed and lonely, tormented by guilt that he had not been there when his chieftain—his beloved wife's own father—needed him. Yet the time of grieving eventually passed, and the two were together again. Still, at times Willen caught her eyes upon him, brooding and speculative, deep with thoughts she was not ready to share.

* * * * *

In a way, the death of Colin Stonetooth had bonded the clans closer, as though the bloody, senseless act of Glome and his followers stood as an example of everything evil and pointless about the old ways, when tribal rivalries had overshadowed all other interests. Now Daewar, Theiwar, Daergar, and Klar had fought shoulder to shoulder against enemies from within, and they saw one another with wiser eyes.

Still, it was as though the heart had gone out of Thorbardin. Colin Stonetooth had been that heart. Now the thanes went about their delvings grimly and separately, each tribe progressing at its own rate as they tried to build homes within the great cavern of the underground sea. The Daewar delved rapidly, but to no great depth. The Theiwar hollowed out lairs that were little more than caves within caves, and the Daergar stayed to the dark places, unwilling to come near to anyone else.

The population of Thorbardin had grown greatly as Einar from the outside came to join this or that clan, but the increased numbers of dwarves only made food scarce, as no real systems of production and trade had yet been perfected.

Then, on a morning when the sun of Krynn shone radiant down the quartz veins and the subterranean lake sparkled with its light, a sound arose that brought people from their labors and their lairs. The Hylar drums were singing again, that same quickening, pulsing beat that they had played before on the slopes of Cloudseeker. The music the Hylar named Call to Balladine.

The drums were muffled, here deep beneath the mountains, but every ear in Thorbardin heard the call and most responded. By the thousands, following the lake shore, they went to see what was going on.

The table of seven sides was erected again on the scrubbed stone of that same shore where Colin Stonetooth had died, and behind it waited a dozen Hylar drummers and Olim Goldbuckle, Prince of the Daewar. When the thane leaders were present, Olim asked them solemnly to take the seats they had claimed before. When they were seated, Tera Sharn came to stand at her father's place at the seventh side. With Willen Ironmaul at her shoulder, seeming to tower over her, she gazed silently at one and then another of the four chieftains gathered at the table. When her gaze rested on Olim Goldbuckle she asked, "You ordered the drums?"

"It is how the thanes were first called." The Daewar shrugged, his blond whiskers glowing in the subdued light. "I thought it appropriate, and the drummers agreed. We have things to discuss at this table, and now we are assembled." He glanced around. "Well, most of us are."

The Aghar were absent this time, because the entire tribe had wandered off somewhere and had not yet been found. And most of the Einar had retired to their valleys to prepare for spring.

But the Daewar prince was there, and Slide Tolec, with Vog Ironface of the Daergar, and the Klar leader, Bole Trune. The Hylar drums had called, and they had responded. With wide, dark eyes as wise as her father's, Tera Sharn regarded them one by one. Then she asked, "You . . . all of you . . . avenged my father. Why?"

There was silence for a moment, then Olim Goldbuckle said, "It was not vengeance. We joined to keep the peace of the covenant."

"Glome and his followers would have brought chaos upon Thorbardin." Slide Tolec nodded. "In Kal-Thax, we have seen the face of chaos. We have despised one another and have paid the price for it."

"The Hylar, your father," Vog rumbled, "brought wisdom here."

"I see," Tera said. "And now my father is gone."

"Which is why we are here at this table today," Olim said. "Who will lead the Hylar now?"

Behind Tera, Willen Ironmaul said proudly, "Our people have asked my wife to take her father's place."

"You, and not your brother?" Vog raised his mask, looking at the young dwarf woman curiously. Even to his Daergar eyes her beauty was obvious, as apparent as the fullness of her belly. "Your Hylar would follow a female chief?"

"My brother Cale Greeneye favors the open sky above his head," Tera said. "He is Neidar and has no wish to lead. He has told our people that."

"What have you told your people?" Olim asked.

"I have given them no answer," she said. "Though I have thought about the matter." She hesitated, collecting her thoughts, then said, "Colin Stonetooth, my father, was a wise person. He looked always ahead, and never back. And because of that wisdom, he made a mistake . . . twice. He trusted the right people, seeing the path ahead, but he failed to see the wrong ones behind. At Thorin, which is now Thoradin, it was humans who betrayed him."

A resonant growl came from Vog's mask, but Tera raised a small hand. "Not all humans," she said. "Those my father trusted as friends were—as much as they could be— true friends. But others were not. And then here, where we found others of our own kind, he trusted. He trusted and was blind to the enemies who stalked him."

"As we all were," Olim nodded.

"I am my father's daughter," Tera said. "His blood is my blood, and his ways my ways. Sooner or later I would make the same mistakes he made, because I see as he saw. Therefore I will propose another for chieftain of the Hylar, but I believe I would like for each of you to approve before I do."

They stared at her blankly. "Why ask us?" Slide Tolec tilted his head. "Each thane in Thorbardin is independent. The Covenant is clear about that."

"So it is," she agreed. "But there is much to do here if Thorbardin as my father envisioned it—and as each of you envision it—is to be built. Old differences among the clans must be recognized, and different ways respected, but the Council of Thanes must act as one on matters of the future. To do things which have never been done before, all must work together. This Council alone can make that occur. Therefore I ask your approval before I say to my people that my husband, Willen Ironmaul, should be their chief."

Behind her, Willen's mouth dropped open. "Me? Tera, I am no chief! I'm just a soldier. I wouldn't know how to . . ."

Tera looked around at him and slipped her hand into his. "No one is a chief until the time comes to lead," she said.

Slowly, a grin spread across Olim Goldbuckle's wide face, parting his golden whiskers. "You are your father's daughter," he said. "I wonder if your Hylar suspect how fortunate they are."

"I would welcome Willen Ironmaul to this table," Slide Tolec said solemnly. "I know as well as anyone that being chief comes of necessity more than by design."

Vog Ironface hesitated, then raised his mask. Glinting ferret eyes in a face that sloped like a fox's studied the big Hylar guardsman, and he nodded. "I have seen you fight," Vog said. "There is more to your strategies than strength and precision. There is something unseen. What is it?"

"It is order." Willen shrugged. "The teacher who taught us how to fight also taught us why and when. He said that skills without honor—which I think is nothing more than order of the heart—are like a forge without fire."

"Honor is order?" the Daergar mused. "Order of the heart. Interesting. Wisdom"—he glanced at Tera—"and honor. Willen Ironmaul, Vog Ironface will welcome you to this table."

"As will I," Olim Goldbuckle chuckled. "Maybe some order of the heart is what is needed to get us all moving forward again."

At the far side, Bole Trune rose to his feet, drew his cudgel, and placed it on the table before him. Then he turned to Willen Ironmaul. "Klar have trusted Hylar," he rumbled. "Bole Trune trusts you."

A few days later the muffled drums said that Willen Ironmaul had been named chieftain of Thane Hylar of Thorbardin. And in the song of the drums was a resonance that echoed in the hearts of dwarves of all the thanes, quickening their steps as they worked. Purpose, they felt, had been restored.

26
The Road to Reason

Through the final weeks of winter forges rang beneath Cloudseeker Peak, and the vapors rising above the Windweavers were warm from the fires far below. Though the clans of Kal-Thax had acted in unison for centuries to defend against intrusion into their lands, this was the first time in history that they had actually worked together to achieve something positive, and deep in the heart of the mountain, their combined skills began to show visible results.

To the Daewar's genius at delving were added the Hylar arts of stonecutting and masonry, and the delves were no longer limited in their expanse. With the introduction of lift platforms, like those invented by Handil Farsight, the difficulty of working from level to level in a dig was almost eliminated. The dark steel of the Daergar proved excellent for the making of rails and cables, and the dwarves began construction of a series of subterranean roads to connect the centers of all the separate towns of Thorbardin and to accommodate cable carts to and from the warrens.

Boats were crafted from lumber brought by the Neidar or traded from the region's independent Einar, and wharves were chiseled into the slopes of the lakeshore. From there, cables were strung out to the base of the great, living stalactite above the water and fixed there. From here would begin the construction of the Hylar's delves, working upward through the stone and—eventually—downward from the mountain's peak through shafts that would later accommodate sun-tunnels.

Most of what would someday exist here was still in the minds and on the scrolls of the crafters, but it was begun and there would be no stopping it.

The thane leaders envisioned Thorbardin as a fortress, a stronghold from which the dwarves could issue forth at will to protect their fields and valleys. No longer could all of Kal-Thax be, simply, closed. It was far too large, and too accessible, for the growing press of outsiders to be entirely kept out. In times long past, when intruders were few, that might have been possible. But now it was not a practical option, and the dwarven people were nothing if not practical. Still, the realm could be held against settlement, and this was the intention of the new covenant.

Some outsiders would get in. Some might journey across Kal-Thax. But with the fortress of Thorbardin dominating the realm, none would take root there.

An option of a different sort was proposed by Tera Sharn and presented by Willen Ironmaul. If the tide of outsiders could not be stopped, they suggested, then why not turn it, as a shield turns a lance?

They puzzled over the idea and how it might be accomplished, and it was Olim Goldbuckle who came up with the answer. "Since we don't want all those people coming here," he suggested, "maybe we could give them somewhere else to go instead. Most people—humans in particular—are more likely to follow a road than to cross it."

Thus, even before the first thaw of spring was felt in the valleys, Cale Greeneye rode out from Kal-Thax with a company of Neidar volunteers to scout the internal ranges, and Willen Ironmaul rode eastward with a hundred mounted Hylar warriors led by his new guard captain, Sand Sakor, and accompanied by Gem Bluesleeve and his Golden Hammer footmen. On behalf of the Council of Thanes, Willen intended to have a talk with whoever was in charge in southeastern Ergoth. The humans who lived there were as beset by the flood of refugees from the east as the dwarves of Kal-Thax were.

During the Hylar migration, they had seen human citadels scattered here and there across the countryside. Homes and fiefdoms to the knights of the lords that governed the land, some of these were no more than manor houses perched atop ridges and rocky hills overlooking the fields and herds of their supplicants. But there was one that Cale Greeneye had seen from a distance and reported. It was a great, walled keep atop a high bluff and was obviously the home of someone important. It sat several miles north of the field where the Hylar had defeated the Cobar raiders, and Willen suspected that the place was the seat of that gray knight who had spoken warning to him on that day—the one Glendon Hawke called Lord Charon. For Calnar horses and sturdy Daewar footmen, the place was not too far away, and the man had seemed to be in charge. Willen decided he would be the one to see.

Two days out from the lower slopes, the dwarf troop entered tilled fields and meadows, with little villages visible here and there among them. A few miles farther and the great citadel was in sight. It was as Cale had described it—a tall fortification of gray stone, with ramparts and parapets where banners flew. It was not a great structure by Hylar standards, but better than most things Willen had seen built by humans.

He wasn't sure what protocols were involved in approaching a human stronghold to discuss business, but he had observed back in Thoradin that humans were very much like dwarves in their thinking, except for their inability to really concentrate on anything for very long. So he took the direct approach. With his troops at his back, the new chieftain of the Hylar of Thorbardin simply headed for the place and assumed he would be noticed soon.

The first to notice the dwarves were villagers at a little place where thatch-roofed huts crowded along what seemed to be the beginning of a road. At first glance there were no people visible, either in the village or thereabouts in the crusted fields where the melting snows had left gray-white patterns atop the dark mud beneath. No one was stirring, but there was smoke above the huts, so Willen had a trumpeter blow salute, then led his troops right into the center of the place. Here and there shutters parted, and doors opened a crack. Shadowed eyes stared out at the short, armored creatures perched on the tall horses, then shutters slammed and doors echoed to the sounds of bolts being dropped into place. From somewhere a flimsy arrow—like a quarrel from a badly strung crossbow—arced in the sunlight and glanced off Willen's helm.

He raised his shield and quartered around in his high saddle. "Here, now!" he roared. "There's no call for that!"

Somewhere nearby, a great squawking and flailing erupted. It sounded like foxes in a chicken coop. At one flank of the dwarf troop, a shutter opened momentarily and something flew out, bouncing harmlessly off the armor of Sand Sakor. Sand looked down at the fallen object, then looked up at his chieftain. "It's a potato," he said in disbelief. "Somebody threw a potato at me."

Gem Bluesleeve strolled forward to ask, "Would you like for us to haul those people out where we can see them?"

"Go away!" a muffled human voice called from within

one of the huts. "Go away! There's nothing here for you!"

And another voice, even more muffled, said, "Hoodlums! Can't they just leave us alone?"

And another, "Wait, Mullin! I don't think these are the same hoodlums. Look how short they are. Do you think those might be dwarves?"

"Dwarves don't ride horses, idiot!" the first voice chided.

"Are those really horses? How'd they get so big?"

The sound of chickens in panic came again, then stopped. Willen shook his head. "We mean no harm!" he called. "We're just passing through. We're looking for the home of Lord Charon."

"You see?" a voice insisted. "They're the same ones. The hoodlums looking for Lord Charon."

"They can't be the same ones. Those were bigger and their horses were shorter, and besides, those already know where Lord Charon is."

"Then these are more of the same." The voice rose again. "Go away and leave us alone!"

"Rust!" Willen growled. "All right! We'll go away! Just tell us if that citadel ahead is Lord Charon's keep!"

"Of course it is," a querulous voice snapped. "What else would it be?"

"Thank you," Willen Ironmaul said. He flicked his reins and headed out of the village.

Behind him, the hidden voices chattered, "I tell you, Mullin, those are dwarves!" "Nonsense! Why would dwarves come here? And what would dwarves want with Lord Charon?" "Well, I think it's more of those same hoodlums from Xak Tsaroth." "There aren't any dwarves in Xak Tsaroth, it's a human city." "Then maybe the hoodlums are getting shorter there."

"What do you suppose that was all about?" Sand Sakor wondered.

"I can probably tell you what it was about, if you want to know," a high voice said from below.

Willen glanced down and frowned. "You!"

"Of course I'm me," Castomel Springheel assured him. "I've been me most of my life, except maybe the time when that old mage turned me into a goat for a day and a half. I wasn't quite myself then."

The kender was trotting along happily, almost under the hooves of Willen's great horse, Shag, and was carrying a brace of chickens. "If you're looking for Lord Charon," he said, "that's his stronghold up there on that hill. But then, if you're looking for the Tariff Overlord's people, that's where they are, too. Except they're outside. Lord Charon doesn't invite them in." The kender's brow lowered in disapproval. "They steal anything they can get their hands on."

"Like someone else I've met," Willen snorted.

Cas glanced up at him. "Who?"

"Never mind. Where did you get those chickens?"

"What chickens? Oh, these?" the kender glanced at the birds dangling from his hands as though surprised to find them there. He shrugged. "I don't know. I was just thinking about supper, and sure enough, there were some chickens just waiting around. I don't suppose they belonged to anybody. If they did, they didn't say so. How about letting me have a ride on your horse?"

"Absolutely not!" Willen rasped. "I prefer you down there with your hands full of chickens."

"That's all right," the kender said happily, glancing around. Behind and flanking the mounted Hylar, Gem Bluesleeve's foot troop had been keeping pace. Now, though, at a hand signal from Willen, all of the Daewar had veered aside and were streaming off at an angle to the left, disappearing by threes and sixes into a ravine that wandered between fields. "Where are they going?" When no answer came the kender shrugged. "Well, if those people can run like that, with all that armor on, then I guess I can't complain."

The hillside below the citadel looked like a travelers' camp. There were cook-fires, and tents, and a makeshift corral with a dozen or more horses in it. At a glance, it seemed there were several hundred human males camped there, and that they had been there for a while. On the parapets above, where pennants flew, liveried guardsmen patrolled.

"Those are Lord Charon's household troops," Cas Springheel chatted, pointing a chicken-laden hand toward the heights of the citadel. "Lord Charon isn't very happy about the Tariff Overlord in Xak Tsaroth sending all these people out here to collect taxes, so he doesn't let them in. But at the same time he doesn't want to drive them away because the Tariff Overlord of Xak Tsaroth is recognized as a legitimate civil authority in Ergoth, though Lord Charon personally considers him a buffoon."

"So what are they doing?" Willen asked.

"Nothing," the kender said, trotting along beside the large horse. "It's kind of a standoff."

"Humans," Willen muttered, shaking his head.

Trumpets sounded then, atop the citadel, and Willen knew that they had been noticed.

A hundred yards from the citadel, the mounted column of dwarves halted. The guards atop the tower had doubled in number, their heads and shoulders visible against the sky, but no weapons were being brandished. They seemed to be just watching. The high gates of the keep remained closed. But in front of them, on the hillside, were nearly a dozen mounted humans in heavy armor, and a broad, double rank of armed footmen—hundreds of them—with pikes and longaxes. As the dwarves halted, a rider stepped his mount forward from the center and gazed at them. Without turning, he bellowed, "By the gods, I think these are dwarves!"

"I assure you, sir, that we *are* dwarves. We are here to call on Lord Charon, and since you are not him, I advise you to stand aside."

"Stand aside?" The man seemed astonished. "*Stand aside?* Do you know who I am, dwarf?"

"No," Willen admitted. "Who are you?"

"I," the man drew himself up in his saddle, almost parting the layers of armor at his midsection, "am none other than Shamad Turnstreet, deputy to the Overlord of Tariffs of the city of Xak Tsaroth. And you dwarves," he pointed an accusing finger, "are liable both for the general tariff decreed for the rural provinces and for special penalties as border-crossers and illegal aliens. If you don't have the money, I am authorized to seize your horses, arms, and valuables."

"About the time the moons rust over, you will," Willen said evenly. "I am Willen Ironmaul, Chieftain of Thane Hylar of Thorbardin and Kal-Thax, and I am here to see Lord Charon on official business for the Council of Thanes. Now stand aside."

"Impudence," Shamad Turnstreet spat. "I do not take impudence from dwarves." He raised an imperious hand. "Seize these creatures!"

The other mounted humans rode up beside him, loosing shields and lances, and the line of footmen spread for a charge.

"You are making a mistake, Shamad Turnstreet," Willen called. "Consider yourself warned."

"Insolence!" the human roared. He lowered his face plate. "Forward!" he ordered.

The footmen closed ranks and charged. Just behind and looming above them, armed riders lowered their lances, raised their shields, and charged, closing on the line of footmen who spread to let them through.

"If that's how you want it," Willen muttered. He signaled, and his troop spread into spearpoint formation. "Hammers and shields," he called, and swept his arm forward.

With a resounding crash and din, the two lines met. Lances and pikes glanced off dwarven shields as the spear formation of dwarves swept through, and as each point was deflected a heavy hammer descended casually—almost delicately—upon the headgear of its wielder. In seconds, the entire dwarf troop was through the line of humans, wheeling about in precise coordination to survey the field behind them. Everywhere were sprawled, tumbled men rolling around in confusion, holding their heads in their hands, getting to their knees to search for their dropped weapons. In the distance, eleven riderless horses pounded away toward the outlying fields. Delighted laughter floated down from the high ramparts of the citadel on the hill.

"I told you people to stand aside!" Willen Ironmaul shouted. "Now let well enough alone!"

But up on the hillside above, an outraged voice shouted, "A fluke! It was a trick! Regroup and attack!"

Shamad Turnstreet had directed the assault but had not taken part in it. Now he sat his saddle on the slope above, waving his arms in rage. "Attack!" he called. "Attack!"

Reluctantly, his troops got to their feet, picked up fallen weapons, and reassembled themselves, this time in a spearpoint formation as the dwarves had done before. All the humans except their leader were on foot now, but the charge they leveled at the dwarven ranks bristled with deadly points and blades.

Willen's troop touched reins, and the tall Calnar horses spread and reformed, an outward-curving line like open arms waiting to greet the assault. And abruptly, there were no riders in any of the saddles. Each Hylar clung now alongside his mount's shoulder, shield placed to protect both horse and rider.

Gawking in confusion, the human rush slowed for a moment, then regained its force. Battle cries rang out, drowning the voice of Shamad Turnstreet, who was looking past his troops at what was behind them.

At the moment the human line hit the dwarven defense, Gem Bluesleeve's Golden Hammer hit the human line from the rear, crushing the charge against the Hylar line as a pestle crushes orestone in a dwarven miner's mortar.

Again, no dwarf was touched by a blade, and again every human in the attack was rapped sharply by dwarven hammers. This time, the blows were less delicate. Some who fell would not get up again without assistance.

The dwarves backed away disdainfully. "Pick up your

wounded and get out of our way!" Willen ordered the humans. "We have business here, but it isn't with the likes of you!"

It was all too much for the blustering Shamad Turnstreet. With a cry, the Deputy Overlord lowered his lance, spurred his mount, and thundered down the hillside, directly at the exposed back of Willen Ironmaul.

Shag's ears turned at the sound, and the Calnar horse sidestepped as the human's lance flicked past the dwarf. In an instant, Willen dropped his shield and hammer, braced his booted feet against the saddle's foretree, and leaned out, his strong hands closing on the armored shoulders of the human as he hurtled past. With a heave, the dwarf wrenched the human loose from his saddle, dropped him clattering to the ground, and fell atop him. Willen rolled the man over on his belly, squatted atop him, and methodically removed his weapons, his helmet, his back-plate, his gauntlets, and his armor skirt.

Gathering up all these implements, Willen stepped away and said, "Tariffmaster, go back to the city where you belong. For the inconvenience you have caused to representatives of the Council of Thanes of Thorbardin and Kal-Thax, I hereby levy your horse and your armor as taxes. Now get away from here before I decide to collect further tariffs."

Roars of laughter rang down from the ramparts of the citadel. It sounded—and looked—as though the entire household were up there now, taking in the show.

When the tax collector from Xak Tsaroth had gone, half-naked and followed by a stumbling, wretched band of associates, the gates of Citadel Charon opened and knights rode out, parting to make way for the gray knight Willen had met before—Lord Charon himself. The human rode to within a few yards of Willen and stopped. "Greetings, Sir Dwarf," he said. "That was a lively entertainment, though you have thoroughly humiliated an official of the Ergothian realm."

"Official?" Willen gazed at the man. "That was only a

hoodlum. Lord Knight, I am here as a representative of—"

"I know." Charon nodded. "I heard. And what is the business you wish to discuss?"

"A road," Willen said. "A common road, a joint venture by Ergoth and Kal-Thax. A road northward, through the pass at Tharkas to the lands beyond. A road to help you get rid of the refugees who plague you and to keep them from spreading into Kal-Thax."

"A road," Charon said. "Well, it is a thing we can talk about . . . along with the price of dwarven tools and whether those big horses of yours might interbreed with plains stock. But before we sit to table, Sir Dwarf, I have a question."

"Sir?"

"You humiliated those buffoons from Xak Tsaroth. Oh, I don't mind, personally. Turnstreet plays at chivalry, but he is, as you say, nothing more than a hoodlum. But tell me, Sir Dwarf, had that been me who attacked you . . . would you have played such games with me?"

"No, sir," Willen said seriously. "I would never play games with you, Lord Knight. It would be far too dangerous. Had *you* attacked me, I would have killed you as promptly as I could."

Not far away, Castomel Springheel was foraging happily through the remains of the hillside camp. He had somehow come into possession of Shamad Turnstreet's hammered breastplate and had thought of a fine use for it. If he could find some fat or a little lard, the iron shell would be just the thing for frying his chickens.

27
Tharkas Pass

From the flanks of Sky's End, Cale Greeneye and his company wound north and west through steep-walled canyons and vast valleys hidden within the high Kharolis, where whole villages of Einar turned out to gape at this strange band of explorers led by dozens of dwarves mounted upon huge horses. Most of the people of these mountains had never seen horses before, and none had seen horses like the Calnar breed.

Those who traveled with them were just as remarkable. The Hylar were strange to the Einar and seemed wise and worldly. But others were obviously Daewar by their golden beards and bright clothing, and there were even a few Theiwar in the group—young adventurers who had joined the Neidar scouts as much out of boredom as anything else.

For many of the remote Einar, it was a strange idea—that people of various tribes and cultures could blend as a group and join in a common cause. Many also were fascinated by the name the adventurers had adopted for themselves. *Neidar*. Knoll-dwellers, or hill-dwellers. For the pastoral dwarves, oriented as all dwarves to the comforts of home and hearth, it was a rich name—a name that spoke of living preferences. A far better word than Einar, which meant only unaffiliated.

At each encounter, Cale told the Einar of the planned fortress of Thorbardin, located beneath Cloudseeker Mountain, and extended the invitation of the Council of Thanes to those who cared to join in the great venture—to affiliate themselves with whichever undermountain tribe appealed to them and become part of Thorbardin. He also told them that, for those who chose to stay on the land, rather than under it, their herds and crops would bring good prices in trade at Thorbardin, where such basics as food and fibers were much needed.

At each morning's departure, Cale looked back at the people with whom they had stayed the night, wondering what his passing through would bring about. Many, he was sure, would go to see for themselves what was going on under Cloudseeker—out of curiosity, if nothing else. Some would choose to stay, to join the Daewar, or the Theiwar, or Daergar, to be a part of the great undertaking that was Thorbardin.

A task of monumental proportion, the chance to be part of something grand . . . the opportunity to craft and to build, to work with stone, metals, and timbers, to use tools to one's content—all of these would be great temptations to any dwarf, and Cale understood that. He wondered how many thousands—or tens of thousands—of new residents Thorbardin would have by the time he and his company returned, just from what they had told people as they journeyed through the land of Kal-Thax.

He almost wished he could be in the subterranean caverns to see the reaction of those Einar who came to look. They would be astonished at least. They would gape and gawk in wonder as new ideas smote them from every side. Just as Glow Coppertoe, who had been Daewar all his life, was astonished in the early days of the exploration when Cale had sat his mount at the rim of the Grand Gorge and said casually, "This will need to have a bridge built across it."

To the Daewar, the idea of building a bridge across such a chasm was startling. But then, historically the Daewar were delvers, not builders. And they had never seen Thoradin.

Willen Ironmaul was off to the east, establishing a diplomatic relationship with the humans there with the idea of building a road northward. It was the mission of Cale Greeneye and his Neidar to determine a route for the road. If Willen succeeded, humans would soon be at work, grading and crowning a way from the plains of southeastern Ergoth to the breaks where the heights of Kal-Thax began. But they would go no farther than the Gorge. Humans would not be able to span such a canyon, to build such a bridge. But dwarves could, if they knew how. And the Hylar, who had been Calnar, knew how.

Cale mapped a route under the very slopes of Sky's End and up across the first pass into the heart of the mountains, heading northwest. In the distance, Daewar lore said, was a pass at a place the Daewar called Tharkas. Some of the Einar they met verified that. Some had actually seen it—a deep cleft between almost unscalable heights. And beyond were other lands—human or elf, or both, none were quite sure—where refugees from the eastern wars might settle in and make new homes . . . and from where, in the words of Olim Goldbuckle, trade might flow once they got settled.

No human would ever settle in Kal-Thax. The Covenant of Thanes made that clear. But then, why would humans want to settle in the dwarven high country if they could find places suited to humans just beyond?

To Cale, as to all of the Council of Thanes, it seemed the perfect solution to the problem of refugees piling up on Kal-Thax's eastern border. Simply build a road across Kal-Thax and let them use it. No one really cared if foreigners traveled *through* Kal-Thax, as long as they minded their manners, left the dwarves alone, and didn't pause too long in the mountains.

So, let them cross, and let them settle the lands beyond. Who would mind that?

On the ninth day out from the last Einar settlement, wending their way among peaks and crags that became higher, rougher, and more forbidding with each mile northward, the explorers came out on a high, grassy shelf and caught their first glimpse of Tharkas Pass. Spring had laid its first touch on these climes, and a soft haze lay in the hollows beneath snow-capped peaks that receded into blue distance. But beyond the farthest visible slopes rose a mammoth, saw-toothed ridge of mountains, standing above the marching peaks the way the eastern Kharolis peaks stood above their foothills.

To the mountain-dwelling dwarves, an unreachable summit was almost unthinkable. Like the Hylar, the children of the tribes of Kal-Thax learned to climb as soon as they learned to walk. But now the explorers paused in awe, staring at the mighty wall that was the north border of Kal-Thax. It seemed to run from horizon to vertiginous horizon, losing itself in the maze of steep peaks that flanked it. Only at one point was it broken—by a deep, slanted rift as though a huge axe had cut away a wedge of it.

"Tharkas Pass." Cale pointed and turned abruptly at the melodious voice that responded from the slope above him.

"That's what dwarves call it," the voice said. "We have another name for it, but not many dwarves can pronounce it—or want to."

Cale and those with him squinted, their eyes roving the forested slope, and then there was movement there, and Cale's eyes brightened as he raised a hand in salute.

"Eloeth!" he called. "We meet again!"

The dwarf felt he would never get used to the way these elves could appear and disappear, camouflaging themselves and blending into their surroundings. Where moments ago there had seemed to be no one, now the wooded slope above the shelf was alive with slim, graceful creatures clad in leathers and weaves that were the colors of the wild lands.

Two of them he recognized from an earlier meeting—the slant-eyed Eloeth and, not far behind her, the somber, smoke-haired male called Demoth. Both carried bows, but while Eloeth's was slung at her shoulder, Demoth's was at hand. He held it casually, but the notched arrow was ready to draw and release.

"Cale Greeneye," Eloeth said, returning his wave. "Your company has grown since last we met. How fare the Hylar? I have heard you found your Everbardin."

"You have heard?"

"We hear many things," she said, perching on a broken tree just yards away. "For instance, we hear that the drumbeater dwarves have allied with the tribes of Kal-Thax and now are seeking an alliance with the humans of eastern Ergoth."

"Not so much an alliance." Cale frowned. "More like a joint project. We might build a road."

"Through Tharkas Pass?"

Cale gazed at the wall of peaks in the distance. "Where else? A road that dead-ended at those mountains would do no good."

"And do you know what lies beyond Tharkas?"

"Some other land." He shrugged. "Someplace where humans might go, so they won't need to bother us."

Eloeth shook her head slightly. Cale couldn't tell whether the expression on her face was a smile or a grimace. "Other lands, indeed," she said. "That 'other land' is the home of my people. It has been, ever since some of us began to drift away from Silvanesti. Do you think that we want those you will not allow in Kal-Thax? The western forests are not a dumping ground for dwarves' spare humans, you know."

Cale stared at her, at a loss for words. It had never crossed his mind—or anyone else's, apparently—that there might be people beyond Kal-Thax just as reluctant to absorb hordes of refugees as the dwarves were.

"Well?" Eloeth prompted.

"Well . . . we have come this far to see Tharkas Pass. I would like to see it."

"Don't you think you have come far enough beyond your own lands?" Demoth challenged, striding down the slope to stand beside Eloeth. Behind them other elves— hundreds of them, it seemed, changed positions subtly, backing the challenge.

"This *is* our land!" Mica Rockreave bristled, at Cale's flank. "We have joined in the Covenant of Thanes, and you people are the trespassers here, not us. Kal-Thax is ours, and Kal-Thax goes all the way to Tharkas Pass."

"Does it?" Eloeth smiled knowingly. "Who says so?"

"Olim Goldbuckle said so," Cale put in, trying to wave down the short-tempered Mica Rockreave. "The Daewar have made a map of Kal-Thax. The boundaries are clear."

"Dwarven maps are like dwarven minds," Demoth purred. "They claim everything and clarify nothing. Realms are not bound by lines on maps, dwarf. Realms extend to the reach of those who control them and no farther."

"Dwarves control the lands from the south plains to Tharkas Pass," Cale explained. "At least, that's how it is supposed to be."

"Dwarves are—" Demoth started, then subsided as Eloeth raised an elegant hand. Cale turned to scowl at Mica Rockreave and put a finger to his lips. The last thing the young Neidar wanted to do, on a scouting mission, was to start a war with the elves.

"Demoth is right," Eloeth said softly. "Not in a hundred years or more has their been a dwarven patrol exercising presence this far north. You are eighty miles beyond the natural limit of Kal-Thax where people live and use the land. This is all wilderness out here, and just beyond that pass lies the enchanted forest we call home."

"And beyond that?"

"Beyond?" She shrugged. "All sorts of places. Human realms, mostly. Western Ergoth is nearest and largest. Why?"

"Just curious," Cale assured her. "But I would still like to see that pass. Do you object?"

"I suppose we can show it to you," Eloeth said, standing. "It won't hurt for you to see it."

"Thank you," Cale Greeneye bowed slightly in his tall saddle, then turned another frown on Mica Rockreave and those around him. "Just be still and let me handle this!" he whispered.

"But these elves are . . ."

"These elves are going to show us Tharkas Pass. Come on. Let's go."

* * * * *

Cale was astonished at how quickly they covered the miles up to the great pass. Following the hidden ways and traveled trails of the elves, most of which he would never have known were there except for the sight of throngs of silent-footed elves trotting along ahead of him, they seemed to bypass all of the rough places and travel only the best paths. The sun of Krynn was still in the sky when the party climbed the last rise and entered a huge, magnificently walled cleft in the mountain ridge. For a mile they traveled between wide-set stone steeps which climbed into the high mists, then the path angled downward slightly and—abruptly—the walls opened out.

The view was breathtaking. The path curved downward, following natural slopes—downward and away to lose itself in distance. And beyond, spreading to the limits of vision, was a tremendous, forested plateau, a solid carpet of new-greening trees that rolled away toward the horizon. From the mouth of the pass the forests of the elves seemed to begin several thousand feet away and to go on from there forever.

"Beautiful," Cale breathed, climbing down from Piquin's high back to stand beside Eloeth. "That's where you live, huh?"

"That is the place we call home." She nodded. "From where the forest begins, as far as you can see."

"From where the forest begins?" Cale pointed. "Down there?"

"That's right."

Cale smiled delightedly, then turned, facing his own companions, and raised sturdy arms. "On behalf of the Council of Thanes and the people of Kal-Thax," he roared, "I hereby claim all the lands we have traveled, to and including this place where we stand, as part of Kal-Thax. Kal-Thax extends to this point!" He unslung his hammer, drew an iron spike from his belt and knelt. With one resounding blow he drove the spike into the stone of Tharkas Pass.

Demoth was beside him then, spinning to face him, his bow raised threateningly. "Stop that!" the elf demanded. "What are you doing?"

Cale stood and gazed at the elf levelly. "I have done what you yourself suggested. I have just clarified what dwarven maps—and dwarven minds—claim. Everything behind us is Kal-Thax, by right of my claim and my stake."

Demoth stared, still holding his bow tensed. "You can't do that," he said.

"I just did," the Neidar pointed out. "And if you have any doubt of the reach of those who claim the realm, then please notice that *we* have reached here with your blessing. And if you raise that bow, elf, I swear I will feed you my hammer a pound at a time."

"Demoth!" Eloeth was there, pushing down the male elf's hands and his bow. "Let it alone! It's only a claim, and means nothing unless it is ratified and enforced." She turned to Cale. "Clever," she said. "You obtained my warrant that this place is beyond our homeland, so you have taken nothing that we have a right to defend. You are full of surprises, Cale Greeneye of the Hylar."

"Of Thorbardin and Kal-Thax," he corrected, "though I—and my friends—are more Neidar than Holgar."

"What?"

"It is a manner of speech. It means we prefer the outsides of slopes to the insides of them. But I have one more surprise for you, if you will permit. On that pack horse are two kegs of good ale, and we have the haunches of a mountain bison. If you and your company will share a fire with us this night, I'd like to hear how the wars go in the east."

"But what of this claim business?"

"Oh, that's all done. I've made the claim on legitimate grounds. I suppose it's up to my leaders, and yours, to get together sometime and decide what to do about it." He turned again, gazing off across the distant forest. "Western Ergoth lies beyond, you say? Where?"

She pointed northward. "There, and westward beyond the forest."

"The new road might have to be longer than we anticipated," Cale said. "But it could serve elven purposes, too, you know."

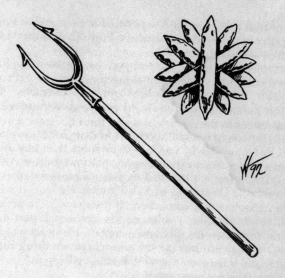

28
Father of Kings

Willen Ironmaul felt a touch of elation as he and his personal escort—named the Ten in honor of those who had served Colin Stonetooth—emerged from the first warren into the great cavern of Thorbardin. His mission to the lands of eastern Ergoth had been a success. He knew Tera would be pleased. His immediate desire was to go straight to the new Hylar delvings and see her, but a reception committee was waiting for him at the cable-way.

"The drums told us you had returned." Olim Gold-buckle grinned. "Business first, Sir Chieftain. How went your visit to the human lands?"

"Very well, I believe," Willen said. "Not only will they build a roadway to the mountains, following Cale's route, but the knights have agreed to patrol it at their end to stop the migrations toward Cloudseeker. Lord Charon gave me his oath and his hand on it."

"Marvelous!" The Daewar slapped the big dwarf on his armored back and started him along the shoreline path to Daebardin. "I have called for the Council to assemble," he said. "Now, how about trade? Did you discuss trade with the Ergothians?"

"They will trade grain, dyes, and fibers for tools and glass." Willen nodded. "I agreed to no more than that, but if it goes well we can expand upon the commodities. Oh, and Lord Charon is prepared to discuss more extensive trade with the Overlords in Xak Tsaroth. He feels it will give his people a nice edge there, if their clerks can act as agents for things like woolen goods, embossed plating, leathers, and ironware. Oh, and gemcraft. His exact words were, 'Those pestilent city-dwellers love anything that sparkles, and if they can't steal it, then they'll buy it.' "

"Did you discuss weapons?"

"They know we can make better weapons than they can, but I didn't discuss trading in weapons. I felt that should be a Council decision."

The Daewar prince glanced at Willen shrewdly. "A wise notion," he said. "We should go slowly in providing humans with fine weapons. But that may come later. The more secure we become in Kal-Thax, with Thorbardin as our fortress, the less we shall need to worry about our goods being turned against us."

Through the outer Theiwar digs they walked, and Willen was taken by the extent of the delving that had been done just in the time of his journey. Many of the delvers working there, he noticed, were Daewar.

"We're doing some bartering of skills," Olim noted. "We do what we're best at, they do what they're best at, and we all come out ahead."

Everywhere, as far as could be seen around the lakeshore, the great cavern bustled with activity. By the hundreds and by the thousands, the people of Thorbardin were working to build cities and homes for all of the emerged thanes.

Past the Theiwar digs, the little procession entered a wide tunnel and emerged into Klar territory. Here the delves were different—lower and wider, with stout barricades for walls. The Klar had their own ideas of architecture, and their own ways of doing things, but here again, Willen noticed a mix of races. Much of the delving was being done by Daewar, much of the hauling by Theiwar and quite a few Hylar were involved in the masonry of the heavy walls. The place was being built for Klar, but there weren't many Klar to be seen.

"More barter?" he asked.

"Of course," Olim chuckled. "The Klar don't care for construction, so they're working the warrens while this goes on. They do have a way with worms."

Across a waterway, where cable-ferries plied, they entered a brighter territory. Hylar designers were supervising the installation of a mirrored sun gallery for the Daewar beneath one of the mountain's quartz shafts.

"The other chiefs will meet us in my assembly hall," Olim Goldbuckle said. "But I think there is time for a bit of ale first."

Willen started to nod, then turned abruptly, looking out across the waters of the subterranean sea. Out there, where the huge mass of the "living stone" stalactite stood above the water, drums were speaking. He listened for a moment, then handed his packs to the nearest of the Ten and grabbed Olim's arm. "Hang the council meeting!" he said. "I have to go home! Where are your docks?"

With the chieftain of the Hylar in charge, and the prince of the Daewar in tow, the two sprinted away, leaving their stunned escorts to stare after them.

"What was that all about?" a Daewar guard stammered.

"The drums!" A Hylar grinned. "Our chief is about to be a father."

Mistral Thrax had heard the drums, too. Now, as he hobbled from his temporary cubicle in Daebardin down to the shore of the Urkhan Sea, the echoing clamors of the great cavern seemed to take on the sound of them, and he hopped faster, flailing his crutch as he ran. The palms of his hands, which had once touched magic, tingled and itched, and he felt the lore of past and future gathering around him.

Tera Sharn's child was due, and the drums called, and Mistral Thrax wanted to be there. A child was borning, and the child was of the seed of Colin Stonetooth.

At the pier below Daebardin's main way, Mistral Thrax hobbled across to where a cable-boat was tied. The boatman—like most boatmen working the new cable-ways from the shores out to the lower end of the great stalactite that was being delved for the Hylar—was a sullen-looking Theiwar. The Theiwar had proven adept at handling cables and winches, and many—unlike most dwarves of other clans—could swim. Thus they often bartered service in the cable-ways, and particularly the waterways. Their skills they bartered for the skills of Daewar to delve living spaces for them, of Hylar to construct walls and doors, and for materials from the Daergar mines and forges.

It was a system that had evolved in recent times, this trading of skills among the clans, and most of the dwarves felt it worked well enough, except for the resultant necessity to deal with people for whom centuries of enmity were not easily forgotten. Daewar delvers riding the boats or cable-carts tended to ignore the Theiwar who operated them, as though they were not there. The Theiwar, in their turn, did all they could to make their Daewar passengers uncomfortable.

As for the Daergar, delivering loads of ore to the furnaces and foundries, they simply ignored everybody unless someone happened to bump them or get in their way. Hardly a day went by in Thorbardin without some major dispute that in many cases had to be resolved by the Council of Thanes. Already, plans were being drawn for a Hall of Justice, because of the pugnacious attitudes of the people who had come to live—more or less together—in

Thorbardin. And there were more people each day, as Einar from outside came to join the undermountain clans.

At pierside, Mistral Thrax poised himself on his crutch, then hopped down into the big cable-boat, causing waters to lap along its sides and drawing a frown from the Theiwar at the winch.

"What do you want?" the boatman snapped.

"What do you think I want?" Mistral growled back, seating himself in the stern. "This is a boat, and I'm a passenger. I want to go to the stalactite."

"Well, that's good," the Theiwar said, "since that's the only place this boat goes. Hardly worth the effort, though, just for one old gimper. Gonna work, might as well have a load." He glared at the old Hylar, and lounged pointedly against his cable housing.

"I didn't ask your opinions on the subject of efficiency!" Mistral glared back. "Get that winch going!"

"What will you give me to take you across?" the Theiwar asked.

"It's what I'll give you if you don't that should concern you!" Mistral raised his crutch like a cudgel.

The Theiwar sighed, then cast off his moorings and grasped his winch handles. "At least you're no gold-molding Daewar," he muttered. "I hate taking orders from Daewar."

Mistral lowered his crutch as the boat began to move. "If you don't like this job, why do it?"

"It beats digging rock," the boatman allowed. "There's a team of delvers slaking out a dig for me and my family in Theibardin. So I'm over here hauling this scow." A trumpet sounded, and he looked up. "Oh, now that's more like it," he said, reversing the winch. Immediately, the boat stopped and started going backward, back toward the Daebardin pier.

Mistral turned. There were people at the pier, waving frantically. Among them were Willen Ironmaul and Olim Goldbuckle, a brace of panting guardsmen, and a pair of aging Hylar women carrying bundles of cloths. There were also several Daewar women, and a Theiwar woman carrying copper pots.

As the boat approached the landing, the crowd pushed forward. "Hurry up, Chard!" the Theiwar woman called to the boatman. "We are wanted over there!"

Even before the boat had nestled against the dock, people were piling aboard, pushing and shoving for space. The last to board were the chieftain of the Hylar and the prince of the Daewar. "Hurry, boatman!" Willen snapped. "It's time!"

The Theiwar gazed at him impudently. "And what time is that?"

With a surge and two strides, Willen was in the bow, pushing the Theiwar out of the way. The big Hylar took the winch-handles in hands like iron sledges, and the boat plowed water as it headed out across Urkhan's Sea.

"You and your attitudes!" the Theiwar women snapped at the boatman. She brandished her copper pots at him. "Don't you know what these mean?"

He stared at her stupidly, then his eyes widened. "Ah?" he said. "Ah! *That* time!" Staggering forward, he joined the Hylar chieftain at the winches, and the boat fairly raced for the tip of the stalactite in the middle of the lake.

Mistral Thrax frowned, shoving for space between two of the females. The women always know, he thought, the women with their cloths and their serious expressions, the copper pots for heating water—probably they knew even before the drums sounded from the Hylar quarters. It was time for a child to be born. His palms tingled and itched, and he clung to a wale to keep from being pushed overboard as the women shifted their positions in the boat impatiently. "Hurry!" one of them demanded. "Can't you people pull faster?"

Muttering an oath, Mistral Thrax tapped his crutch against the timbered deck, then stared at it, blinking. For an instant, the crutch had seemed to glow. And in that instant it had seemed not like a crutch, but more like a fishing spear—a spear with twin tines. Mistral looked up.

Apparently, no one else had noticed anything. He noticed that other boats were coming from other piers around the big lake, all pulling toward the center.

Approaching the giant stalactite was like approaching an upside-down mountain suspended from the sky. It was a huge, glistening mass of stone, rounded at the bottom where it almost touched the little island beneath that was its twin stalagmite, rising from the water. The distance between the stone surfaces was less than ten feet, and they were coupled now by a masonry shaft where the Hylar had installed a lift-belt, of the kind Handil the Drum had perfected in Thorin. The lift rose upward, into the main shaft where delving had begun and where the first quarters of the Hylar had been installed.

The boat creaked and nestled into a stone quay made of rubble from the delving above. Guards hurried forward from the lift to secure the lines, then stepped back as Willen Ironmaul stepped ashore and turned to lend stout hands to the others debarking. "How is my wife?" Willen asked.

"Very well, Sire," a portal guard assured him. "But those with her say that her time is at hand. The child comes soon."

Willen headed for the lift, but the women crowded ahead of him. "You wait your turn," one of them snapped. "She needs us now more than she needs you. Just stay out of the way."

"Here!" the Theiwar woman thrust her copper kettles at the chieftain of the Hylar. "Make yourself useful. Bring water."

He handed the kettles to a guard. "You heard her," he said. "Bring water." As the lift stages disappeared up the shaft, carrying the women, Willen swung aboard the next stage and Mistral Thrax scrambled on beside him, clinging to Willen's breastplate to keep from falling. Behind them, Olim and others crowded toward the next stage.

Upward through its shaft the lift-belt rumbled, and they stepped off onto fresh, hewn stone where a delve had been completed and shorings and partitions put into place. With Hylar craftsmen following them, Daewar delvers had dug an open area ten feet high and expanding a hundred feet in all directions from the central shafts. The Hylar had partitioned the space into various cubicles and enclosures, their pillars and masonry walls serving both as partitions and as braces to shore up the ceiling. The great delve, in the living stone of the stalactite, was only just begun, but already there was space enough for twenty Hylar families.

In a cubicle floored by fine carpets and hung with bright Daewar tapestries, Tera Sharn lay in her bed, radiant and determined. Dwarven women were gathered around her, and the new arrivals joined them. When Willen pushed through the crowd, Tera's eyes brightened. "Willen!" she cried. "You've come back! How did it go with the Ergothians?"

"There will be a road," he assured her, leaning over to plant a kiss on her lips. "And you?"

"Splendid," she said. "Everything is well, my love. Our child is—"

"Mercy!" a Daewar woman snapped, tugging on Willen's belt. "Back off, you oaf! Give her room to breathe." Others joined her, and Willen allowed himself to be hauled away. Beyond the crowd he turned and bumped into another dwarf. It was Olim Goldbuckle.

Other boats had landed, and suddenly the little cubicle was packed with people. Slide Tolec was there, and Bole Trune leaning on his cudgel and looking thoroughly out of place, and others, everywhere.

"We heard," the Theiwar said, "so we came. The birth of a child is a—"

"I'll tell the lot of you what it is not!" a Hylar woman hissed, glaring at all the males packed into the room. "It is not a public spectacle! Out! All of you, out!"

Sheepishly, most of the leading citizens of Thorbardin were herded from the room by irate females. One, though, remained. Mistral Thrax refused to budge. He clung to his crutch and to a tapestry, shaking his head. "I won't leave," he insisted. "I am needed here."

"Then stay out of the way," someone said, and turned away to close the doors, shutting out all the other males. For a time the crowded cubicle was alive with bustling, chattering women doing mysterious things, then a silence fell which was broken by a slap and an angry wail. "A boy!" someone said. "A strong, healthy boy!"

The wail had carried through the closed doors, and now they flew open and people thronged in again, deep male voices laughing and chattering, aahing and oohing, hard hands slapping Willen on his armored back as he tried to see past the mob of women. In the bed, a tired and radiant Tera Sharn held her infant close to her and smiled her pleasure.

Mistral Thrax was not watching, though. His hands ached and his heart was pounding, and his gaze was fixed on the open doorway. There was something there—barely visible—something like a whiff of smoke that grew and roiled and formed itself into the tenuous shape of a tall, human man. In dark hollows a pair of spectral eyes opened, and Mistral pushed forward to face the apparition. "No!" he shouted. "No! I forbid you!"

The "eyes" began to glow, a murky red that grew brighter and brighter.

"I killed you once," Mistral Thrax rasped. "I'll do it again!"

The smoke flowed but held its shape, and now all eyes in the room were on it, people backing away in fright. A voice like a whisper of smoke said, "The child. The seed. *In morit deis Calnaris,*" it whispered. "*Refeist ot atium—*"

Roaring a challenge, Willen Ironmaul threw himself at the vision . . . and rebounded as though he had run into a wall. The whispering voice hesitated only an instant, then repeated, "*Refeist ot atium—*"

Raising his crutch, Mistral Thrax flung it at the smoke. It seemed to strike an invisible shield, but it clung there and began to glow. It turned red, then brighter red, and its shape changed. The crutch became a spear—a twin-tined fishing spear in the hand of a tattered, ancient dwarf who seemed only partly visible.

"—*ot atium*," the smoke whispered. "*Dactas ot destis!*"

Fires flew from the glowing "eyes," fires aimed directly at the infant in Tera Sharn's arms. But they did not get there. Like a magnet drawing iron, the spear in Kitlin Fishtaker's hand drew the fires. They raged into its point, along its shaft, and into the spectral dwarf who flamed as bright as sunlight. He flamed, absorbing the curse, then thrust the spear forward into the heart of the smoke, and the flames flowed back from him into the specter. For long seconds the two stood motionless, sharing forces that were beyond imagining. Then the flaming shape of Kitlin Fishtaker raised its free arm over its head and opened its hand. In its palm lay a medallion—a fourteen-point star melded from seven metals. Above the roar of fire-forces, the dwarf-apparition's voice said, "The child's name shall be Damon. He shall be known as Father of Kings."

A moment more the glare raged, then it flared out as though it had never been. The smoke-vision of Grayfen the Magician was gone. The spear was gone. Kitlin Fishtaker was gone, and a stunned silence lay on the packed little room.

There was a tiny thump as something fell to the floor, landing on bright carpet at the foot of Tera's bed. Willen Ironmaul, just getting to his feet, stooped and picked the thing up, looked at it, and then held it up for others to see. It was that same amulet—the one forged by the thanes to bind the agreement among them, the one whose final weld came from the hammer of Colin Stonetooth.

"Father of Kings," Willen muttered, shaken. He turned, gazing at his wife and their infant child, then gently laid the amulet on the pillow beside them. "Damon," he said, touching his son's pink brow with hard, gentle fingers. "Damon. Father of Kings."

In a corner, unnoticed, Mistral Thrax held his hands open before him and gazed at their palms. The marks were gone. As though they had never been there, the scars of magic had disappeared. "I'm free," the old dwarf muttered. "I am clean at last . . . and free."

Without anyone noticing him, he turned and hobbled out of the room, using a guardsman's pike as a crutch. Suddenly he had a real yearning for a mug of cold ale.

DragonLance Saga

THE HISTORICAL SAGA OF THE DWARVEN CLANS

Dwarven Nations Trilogy

Dan Parkinson

The Covenant of the Forge Book One

As the drums of Balladine thunder forth, calling humans to trade with the dwarves of Thorin, Grayfen, a human struck by the magic of the Graystone, infiltrates the dwarven stronghold, determined to annihilate the dwarves and steal their treasure. February 1993.

Hammer and Axe Book Two

Dwarves from many clans unite against the threat of encroaching humans and create the fortress of Thorbardin. But old clan rivalries are not so easily forgotten, and the resulting political intrigue brings about catastrophic change. July 1993.

The Swordsheath Scroll Book Three

Despite the stubborn courage of the dwarves, the bloody Wilderness War ends without a clear victor. The Swordsheath scroll is signed, and the dwarves join the elves of Qualinesti to build a symbol of peace among the races: Pax Tharkas. January 1994.

FORGOTTEN REALMS®

FANTASY ADVENTURE

THE LONG-AWAITED
SEQUEL TO THE
MOONSHAE TRILOGY

Druidhome Trilogy

Douglas Niles

Prophet of Moonshae   Book One

Danger stalks the island of Moonshae, where the people
have forsaken their goddess, the Earthmother. Only the
faith and courage of the daughter of the High King brings
hope to the endangered land.

The Coral Kingdom   Book Two

King Kendrick is held prisoner in the undersea city of the
sahuagin. His daughter must secure help from the elves of
Evermeet to save him during a confrontation in the dark
depths of the Sea of Moonshae.

The Druid Queen   Book Three

Threatened by an evil he cannot see, Tristan Kendrick
rules the Four Kingdoms while a sinister presence lurks
within his own family. At stake is the fate of the
Moonshae Islands and the unity of the Ffolk.